Cathy Williams can remember reading Mills & Boon books as a teenager, and now that she's writing them she remains an avid fan. For her, there is nothing like creating romantic stories and engaging plots, and each and every book is a new adventure. Cathy lives in London. Her three daughters—Charlotte, Olivia and Emma—have always been, and continue to be, the greatest inspirations in her life.

Kim Lawrence lives on a farm in Anglesey with her university lecturer husband, assorted pets who arrived as strays and never left, and sometimes one or both of her boomerang sons. When she's not writing she loves to be outdoors gardening, or walking on one of the beaches for which the island is famous— along with being the place where Prince William and Catherine made their first home!

FORBIDDEN HAWAIIAN NIGHTS

CATHY WILLIAMS

WAKING UP IN HIS ROYAL BED

KIM LAWRENCE

MILLS & BOON

First Published in Great Britain 2021
by Mills & Boon, an imprint of HarperCollins*Publishers*
1 London Bridge Street, London, SE1 9GF

Forbidden Hawaiian Nights © 2021 Cathy Williams

Waking Up in His Royal Bed © 2021 Kim Lawrence

ISBN: 978-0-263-28231-3

MIX
Paper from
responsible sources
FSC
www.fsc.org   FSC™ C007454

This book is produced from independently certified FSC™ paper
to ensure responsible forest management.
For more information visit www.harpercollins.co.uk/green.

Printed and bound in Spain
by CPI, Barcelona

FORBIDDEN HAWAIIAN NIGHTS

CATHY WILLIAMS

To my treasured kids and supportive partner, David.

CHAPTER ONE

Max Stowe listened to his brother's voice down the end of a telephone line thousands of miles away and did his utmost not to cut short the placatory monologue, which was designed to defuse the situation but was having the opposite effect.

James was currently in Dubai, dealing with the final nuts and bolts of the state-of-the-art eco-super-yacht they had commissioned to be hand-built a little over a year ago.

He, on the other hand, was here, staring out from the balcony of his hotel at a long strip of beach, mentally working out the approach he would take to discover the whereabouts of their wayward sister, who had done a midnight flit with only a brief goodbye and 'Don't worry about me' delivered via text message.

Who, Max wondered, had got the better deal?

Jaw clenched, handsome features rigid with the simmering tension that had had ample time to build on the long and exhausting flight to Hawaii, he cut short the conversation and slipped his mobile back into his trouser pocket.

The glorious view was completely lost on him. He had already had a shower but out here, standing on the broad balcony, he was still baking hot and uncomfortable.

And he was in a foul mood.

Under any other circumstances, heads would have rolled for this. He was as fair as the next man, but you didn't get to be at the top of the food chain by accepting incompetence and unreliability.

Unfortunately, these were far from normal circumstances, and with a sigh of frustrated resignation he spun round and headed back into the coldly air-conditioned penthouse suite of the five-star hotel.

Izzy. His sister. Where the hell was she? He knew where she *wasn't* and that was here, in Hawaii, doing what she was being paid handsomely to do.

Max refused to succumb to dark thoughts and alarming hypothetical scenarios. He was a man finely honed when it came to dealing with facts and adept at finding solutions to problems as they arose. Izzy's disappearance was simply a problem and he intended to find a solution to it. He knew exactly what road he was going to take to get where he wanted to go.

He glanced at his watch. It was four-thirty. The sun was beginning to dip outside, even though the heat continued unabated. On that beach, somewhere, lay the answer to this situation in the form of one Mia Kaiwi, age twenty-seven, height five-six, occupation landscape gardener and jack-of-all-trades at the boutique hotel he was currently having built on Oahu.

Two days ago, he had received his sister's text. Two

days ago, he had communicated with Nat, the foreman in charge of the project, to find out what the hell was happening. And two days ago he had found out that, while neither Nat nor his sidekick Kahale seemed to have the foggiest idea where his sister had gone, her close friend, Mia, would.

It had taken him twenty-four hours to close various deals he couldn't possibly leave half finished. During that time, Max had resisted the temptation to get one of his people to track his sister down. It would have been easy enough, but he would wait until he could confront the best friend and get the information he needed from that source himself.

Weighing in with a heavy hand might win the battle but it wasn't going to win the war.

But, hell, this was the last place he wanted to be— waiting for five o'clock to roll round so that he could walk the crowded strip of beach in search of some woman he didn't know. A woman who, according to Nat, would reliably be found teaching surf lessons to kids, which was what she did like clockwork every Saturday afternoon between three and five.

He'd given orders that she was not to be alerted to his arrival. No time to do a runner or to rehearse any non-answers to his questions. No, he intended to surprise the woman into telling him what he wanted to know. Once he'd done that, he would allow himself the grand total of four days to sort out this thorny and inconvenient business so that he could return to London to pick up where he had left off with his fast paced, no-time-to-breathe life.

He would unearth his sister from wherever she was hiding, find out what the hell was going on, remind her of the easy ride she had been given—even if he had to write it down for her in bullet points—and get her back on track.

And he would do it in as non-judgemental a manner as he could possibly muster, even though he was genuinely having a hard time grasping her immaturity at taking off without warning.

Fifteen minutes later, he hit the beach at an easy pace. He'd packed the bare minimum of clothes because he anticipated a speedy return to London. Shorts had not featured. He possessed none. Right now, as he began strolling along the long and extremely crowded arc of sand, he was beginning to regret the lack of them because he was sweltering, even though the sun was beginning to set with dramatic splendour.

He walked slowly, eyes narrowed, missing nothing. The beach was emptying out and it was more beautiful than he had first thought. The ocean was darkening from rich turquoise to deep navy and the buildings behind him, of which his hotel was one, were beginning to twinkle as lights were switched on.

The air was filled with voices, bursts of laughter and the revving of motorbike engines.

And then there she was. Unmissable, as Nat had said. She was stacking surfboards, her movements fast and graceful, and she was so slender that she looked as though a puff of wind might blow her over. Her hair was tied up in a ponytail and she was surrounded by a bunch

of excited kids. *Surf for Kids.* The sign was almost ob-
scured by the upright arrangement of surfboards.

She was laughing and barefoot, wearing a bikini top
and a sarong that dipped just below her belly button.
When the last of the kids was led away she immediately
slipped on a baggy tee shirt, consulted the over-sized
watch on her wrist and began heading away, having
roped the surfboards together and padlocked them.

Max quickened his pace. He was here to do a job
and, the quicker the job got done, the quicker he would
be able to leave.

Mia sensed Max behind her with a sort of sixth sense
she had developed over the years. She had become accustomed to blowing off men who tried to chat her up.
Here on the beach blowing off men was as irritating as
swatting flies and she wasn't in the mood for it. She was
never in the mood for it, and she *particularly* wasn't in
the mood for it this evening.

She spun round without warning and stood back,
arms folded, determined to give whoever it was a piece
of her mind.

Her eyes travelled from the bottom up. From loafers
and long silver-grey chinos, to the white polo shirt with
the tiny black logo on the pocket, and up, up until her
brown eyes collided with eyes very much the colour of
the ocean as it was now—deep, dark and fringed with
the thickest of lashes she had ever seen on a man.

The man was stupidly, sinfully drop-dead gorgeous,
from the perfectly sculpted, lean features to the impos-

ing beauty of his muscled body, which not even his idiotically inappropriate clothing could conceal.

The guy oozed sex appeal and Mia was so taken aback that she could only stare for a few addled, frozen seconds.

She recovered fast from the temporary lapse.

'Forget it.' She turned around and quickly began walking away, head held high, backbone straight, her body language informing whoever the guy was that she wasn't on the market for any kind of casual pick-up.

'Come again?'

His voice was dark, smooth and velvety. Mia didn't stop to look around, but she felt the hairs on the back of her neck stand on end.

'You heard me,' she snapped, spinning round again and then taking a step back, because he was just so damned *tall,* his presence just so damned *overpowering.* 'I'm not interested. I don't want to have a drink with you. I don't want to go to a club with you. I don't want to have dinner with you.'

'I don't believe I asked you to do any of those things.'

Mia heard the coolness in his voice and was taken aback. There was a stillness about him and a feeling of complete self-control that she found a little disconcerting.

Who the heck was he?

The mere fact that the question had the temerity to pop into her head annoyed her.

Mia knew, without a trace of vanity, that she drew looks. She was five-six and slender, with a heart-shaped face and full lips that turned heads. She was olive-skinned by birth, but a lifetime of living and working in the sun had deepened her natural colouring, and she was now a rich bronze with long, dark hair and caramel eyes.

So what if men looked? None of them got to her. After Kai, she had retreated from the dismal, soul-destroying business of looking for love. Her short marriage had been a slow and illuminating process of disillusionment. You go through that, she figured, and you were a fool not to learn from the experience.

She'd learnt.

'I'm not having this conversation,' she said, her coolness a match for his.

'Mia Kaiwi? That *is* your name, isn't it?'

Mia froze on the spot. This time, a thread of apprehension raced through her. She turned slowly to find that he was standing quite still, his head tilted to one side, his expression shuttered.

'Who the hell are you?'

'I'll tell you who I'm *not*,' Max said silkily. 'And that's someone looking for a pick-up.'

'How do you know my name?'

'Is there somewhere we can go to talk?'

'I'm not going anywhere with you.'

How did the guy know her name? Was he a dad to one of the kids in her surfing group?

No, of course he wasn't. You didn't forget a face like that, and Mia had never seen him in her life before.

Even on a beach where most of the guys were in shorts, and many of them young, good-looking and at the very peak of their fitness, this guy attracted attention. She was aware of people walking past, looking once and then looking again. He didn't seem to notice or, if he did, he didn't care.

'Oh, but you are.' Max paused. 'Now…' He looked around. 'Is there somewhere quiet around here? I would suggest my hotel, but as you seem to be under the mistaken impression that I'm about to make a pass at you I don't suppose that would be appropriate.'

'I could call someone to have you arrested,' Mia said, but she was beginning to get the feeling that she was on shaky ground, because there was a self-assurance in the man that was unsettling.

'I wouldn't do that.' Max indicated a café further along the beach. It was a little busy, but they would be able to sit without people jostling them. 'There will do.'

Mia's mouth dropped open as he coolly began walking away, expecting her to follow.

Heart pounding and head beginning to throb with nervous tension, she found herself snapping out of her daze, tripping behind him to the café. At least she knew the owner at this place, so there was no way he could do anything to her.

Although, would he?

She was beginning to think that she had read the situation wrong, even though she couldn't work out what the alternative could be. He glanced over his shoulder to her and then stopped so that she could catch him up.

He must be at least six-three, she thought faintly. He seemed to tower over everyone in the café. Out of the corner of her eye she saw Mack, the owner, and his wife Rae, and she nodded. The café was only just beginning to fill up with another wave of people arriving at the beach. The families had left and all the twenty-and thirty-somethings would be heading down to have dinner at one of the food trucks that lined the strip of road at the back, or else just hang out in groups on the sand.

'Don't worry,' he drawled, looking down at her. 'Your friends will make sure you don't get kidnapped by me.'

'My friends?'

He nodded to the counter. 'I'm guessing you know those two behind. Good. If I can't reassure you that I'm not about to take advantage of you, then the presence of those two should.'

'I would be reassured if you actually told me your name,' Mia returned without batting an eye. 'You know mine, so it's only polite.'

'And I will. What do you want to drink?'

'A glass of water would be fine.'

The man shrugged. There were empty tables to choose from and he opted for one to the side of the café and away from the window.

'Everything okay, Mi?'

Mia forced herself to smile at Rae, an attractive woman with cropped blonde hair and an easy smile who had approached them with a pad and a pen. Right now, there was a question in her eyes, and Mia couldn't blame her. She had spent long enough joking that the next time Mia came to the café she wanted to see her with a nice young man. That hadn't happened yet so her curiosity would be spiked by the sight of Mia with the man semi sprawled in the chair opposite her, their knees practically touching, because the wooden table was tiny.

'Sure!' They ordered their drinks and Rae left them alone.

'Is it always like this?'

'What do you mean?' He had a voice that was lazy, only mildly interested, and yet strangely commanding. She was momentarily distracted by his direct gaze. Something about him was mesmerising and she wasn't quite sure why. Surely it couldn't be just a matter of good looks?

'Recognised wherever you go…'

'I've lived here all my life, and it's not enormous—not when so much of my time is spent on this beach. I teach the kids on a Saturday and a Sunday. I surf whenever I can. It can be a tight-knit community. And you still haven't told me your name.'

'Max Stowe. I'm Izzy's brother.'

Mia went very still.

That was the last thing she'd expected to hear even though she hadn't had a clue what she *had* been expecting.

He looked *nothing* like Izzy. Izzy was small and blonde with big, blue eyes.

This guy was a six-foot-something hunk with black hair and dark blue eyes and *Danger, Keep Away* stamped all over him.

She was still floundering in stunned silence when he pulled out a wallet and extracted a card which he shoved on the table between them.

His driving licence.

'Just in case you still have any doubts,' he drawled.

Mia didn't answer. She pushed the driving licence back towards him. 'I didn't realise you would be coming over,' she stammered.

'No,' Max soothed. 'I made sure to warn Nat and his assistant to keep my arrival under wraps.'

'Why?'

'I didn't want you to get any time to work out how you might avoid my questions.'

'What questions?' Mia asked. It still wasn't sinking in. *Izzy's brother?*

Izzy had mentioned Max in passing. 'Bossy' had been the term most frequently used when it came to a description.

Over five months as they had become firm friends, Mia had gleaned a picture of someone who lived for work and ruled his much younger sister with an iron fist. An autocratic, humourless bore with a God complex.

Sitting here now, she was inclined to believe every aspect of that picture that had been painted in not so many words.

Hackles rising, she linked her fingers on the table and looked at him without flinching. He might be able to bully Izzy but there was no way he was going to bully *her.*

It took a lot of will power to maintain eye contact, and she had to yank herself back from the feeling that she was sinking into the depths of his steady, veiled, darkly mesmerising gaze…that somehow he had the power to scramble her brains.

'Where is she, Mia?' he asked softly.

He leaned towards her and she automatically leaned back to create distance between them.

'I don't know,' she said quickly, too quickly, because instead of thinking about her denial he smiled very slowly.

'Nice try, but I'm not buying it.'

'What makes you think that I know where Izzy is?'

'For a start, you're her close friend, and close friends confide. My sister would never have disappeared without telling someone where she was going. She certainly hasn't said a word to either myself or her brother and Nat is as much in the dark as I am, which really only leaves you.' He had ordered one of the local beers, and after Rae deposited their drinks on the table he tilted the bottle to his mouth, although his eyes never left her face, not for a second. He took his time drinking and then he lowered the bottle and broke the lengthening silence between them.

'Secondly,' he carried on, as though there had been no interruption to what he had been saying, 'your face is giving the game away. You know where she is, and I need to find her.'

'Don't think,' she said coldly, 'that you can bully me into telling you anything I don't want to.'

'And don't forget you work for me.'

Mia gasped. Yes—she worked for him! Of course, the second he had revealed his identity she had subliminally joined the dots, but on some other level she had not consciously registered that she was his employee.

She was registering it now and working out just what that involved.

As a landscape gardener, she had worked for herself for the past five years and had made a good enough living, but this was the first really big job she had ever taken on. And, more than that, she had found herself doing much more than the landscape gardening for the hotel and she enjoyed the additional responsibilities.

She enjoyed liaising with some of the suppliers, sorting out invoices when Izzy had too much on and, after the whole business of Jefferson and the effect he had had on Izzy, she had stepped up to the plate and got involved in most aspects of the business.

And she had been compensated financially for her efforts.

She knew that Max remotely controlled everything, so she knew that he would be well aware of her various responsibilities, and the fact that her pay cheque had been bumped up twice since she had started working for him.

What he wouldn't know was that she had used that money to get a bank loan to cover some vital repair work on her house. It was a loan that would have to be repaid.

She felt the heavy thudding of her heart as she belatedly recognised the consequences of having her pay stopped for whatever reason.

She would survive, but it would be tough, and she would have to go cap in hand to her parents for help, which was something she was loath to do.

Furthermore, she had been planning on this job leading to bigger and better things.

Word of mouth could be a powerful tool when it

came to getting business in these parts. Were she to move on to bigger jobs—landscaping for hotels or offices—then she would be operating in a much bigger ball park and she could really see her earnings multiply.

But for that to happen she would need a damned good reference.

And where was that reference going to come from? The very guy staring at her now with brooding intensity, waiting for her to spill the beans.

'Are you *blackmailing* me?' she asked. She licked her lips and knew that she probably looked as nervous as she felt.

Max shrugged by way of response and sat back, his body language indicating someone utterly at ease with the situation.

No wonder Izzy had launched into a degree she didn't enjoy after her brother Max had proclaimed a business degree to be the best thing she could do, Mia thought. And she had hated it. He had probably used the same intimidating tactics on his sister that he was using on her now!

'I'm suggesting a fair exchange,' he countered. He didn't add to that, instead finishing his beer, giving her time to absorb the situation between them.

Mia thought of the work that had been done on her place, the loan she was repaying, the necessity of the job and the pay cheque she got at the end of the month.

'If Izzy wanted you to know where she was, don't you think she would have told you?' she asked, equivocating.

'Possibly,' Max returned, unruffled, 'but the fact

remains that she didn't, hence why I am here. Tell me what I need to know, I will leave and life carries on un-interrupted for us both.'

'And what would you do if you do chase after her? Drag her back here kicking and screaming?'

He burst out laughing but there was little humour in his laughter. 'You have a vivid imagination, Mia.'

Mia looked down. She could feel his eyes boring into her and she wanted to fidget, restless and hyper-conscious of his presence opposite her.

She sneaked a glance from under her lashes and breathed in sharply, all her senses unfairly assailed by his sheer *beauty*.

His fingers were lightly circling the empty beer bottle. Long fingers, strong forearms, a study in power in repose.

Her breathing slowed, and she was glad she was sitting down, because every part of her body suddenly felt wobbly.

'Has it occurred to you that I might be concerned for my sister's welfare?'

Mia looked at him fully and noted the underlying anxiety in his eyes. She hadn't noticed that before but then, she was ashamed to admit, she had been busy making sure to pigeonhole him and not give him the benefit of the doubt.

'What do you mean?'

'What do you think I mean?' he asked coldly. 'My brother and I got the same text from Izzy, along the lines that things were a bit tough for her at the moment, so she would be taking some time out, but that Nat and

Kahale would be fine to pick up the slack. What do you think went through my head when I read that my sister was going through "a tough time"?'

He leaned forward, his dark features deadly serious. 'I have no intention of playing games with you when Izzy may be in trouble. Whatever you think you're protecting her from, you're not doing her any favours, and if I have to force you into telling me her whereabouts then, believe me, I won't hesitate.'

'There's no need to threaten me!' Mia bristled with righteous indignation, but then sighed, because she could see how easily he might have jumped to all the wrong conclusions.

She knew that this project was his private indulgence. Izzy had let that fact slip after a couple of drinks shortly after they had started socialising, having the occasional meal together when they'd finished work. She'd been on her own, newly arrived, and Mia had enjoyed taking her under her wing. They'd hit it off.

'I know I should be grateful,' Izzy had confided with a hint of shame, 'and I am… I really *am*…but sorting out supplies and invoices and accounts and dealing with bank managers… It's just not *me*.'

Was this intimidating guy sitting opposite her aware of any of that?

And, if he wasn't, then what must be going through his head? He must be frantic with worry about whatever *tough times* he thought his sister might be facing.

'I don't intend to tell you where Izzy is,' she said firmly, but with sympathy in her voice. 'But I can assure you that there's no need for you to worry.'

'Really. What a relief. I'll leave now, shall I?'

'There's no need to be sarcastic.'

Odious, Mia thought. *Odious and rude and arrogant and a million other things I dislike in a man.*

She was mystified by her physical response to this man when her intellectual response to him was so negative. Was it because his looks were so compelling? Surely not? She couldn't be that shallow, could she? Or maybe it was because she had locked herself away behind a wall of ice after her brief, failed marriage to Kai. She and Kai had been kids when they'd married, and neither of them had expected their marriage to last only a mere year and a half because, on paper, the marriage had made complete sense.

Their families had known one another, they'd been childhood sweethearts and they'd both wanted to start their own families as soon as they could, just like their siblings had. Their lives had been mapped out and they had both rather liked the look of the map.

But it was not to be.

Their divorce had been amicable, but lessons had been learnt, and she had sealed herself off from men. But that had been four years ago! In her head, she'd envisaged herself marrying again. Of course she had. But this time she'd compiled a mental checklist of the perfect guy and she had no intention of deviating.

Was this puzzling reaction to Max Stowe simply her body reminding her that she wasn't quite as frozen in ice as she'd thought she was?

There was nothing about the guy she liked, yet his

blue eyes on her made her feel hot and bothered, and *aware* with every pore in her body.

Had her withdrawal from the opposite sex simply not protected her enough from the sort of devastating effect this level of superb good looks could have on her? Was that it? He made her feel wildly out of her comfort zone when it came to men. No one she knew or had ever known was like this guy.

Some of her nerves eased as she rationalised her reactions. She also could not let herself forget that he was also her boss, and in his hands lay the power to make or break her.

She would have to temper her responses, she thought. She was going to have to act like an adult and be as cool, collected and self-assured as he was.

Or, at any rate, she was going to have to try.

Without betraying her friend's confidences.

'You do realise,' Max said, 'that, whilst it would be preferable not to involve a private investigator to handle this situation—which is something I'd hoped to avoid by approaching you directly—that remains an option.'

'She's not in any…trouble.' Mia grudgingly gave way. 'I mean, just in case you're thinking that she might have become involved in anything…dangerous.'

'Define *dangerous*.'

Mia looked at him. He was so…*self-controlled*. She could understand now how Izzy had managed to find herself in a place where she would rather not have been, in a job that did not cater for her creativity. Max Stowe exuded the aura of someone who didn't brook too much disagreement, someone who expected orders to be obeyed.

'She's not into drugs,' Mia said bluntly. 'And she hasn't done anything illegal. Not at all. You should know that. You're her brother.'

She was surprised at the dark flush that appeared on his high cheekbones.

'There is a considerable age difference between us,' he returned stiffly. 'Twelve years. Our relationship is possibly a little more formal than you might expect.'

'Why is that?' Mia heard herself ask.

Max looked at her with thinly veiled incredulity, and she was surprised to realise that she had overstepped the boundaries with that simple, innocuous question.

'None of my business.' She shrugged and he nodded curtly in agreement.

'No. It's not. You refuse to tell me the whereabouts of my sister. You think it's enough for you to say that she is not in a dangerous situation. Why should I believe you?'

'Because I'm telling the truth. I wish I could tell you why your sister needed a bit of space, but it would be breaking a confidence. All I can say is that she doesn't plan on staying away for ever.'

'There are no problems I would not be able to handle,' Max said flatly, his cold, deep voice oozing such supreme self-confidence that Mia's mouth fell open. 'Izzy should know that. When it comes to sorting things out, I have never let either her or my brother down.'

Mia clicked her tongue impatiently and wondered how someone evidently so astute could also be so dense.

She raised her eyebrows but remained silent until he said irritably, 'If you have something to say, then I suggest you just go ahead and say it.'

'I got the impression that you're not that keen on people speaking their minds,' Mia murmured.

'It's strange because, if that's the impression you have about me, then you're obviously undeterred by it,' he returned bluntly, and she blushed.

'Izzy doesn't want you *sorting her out*,' she confessed. 'She hasn't just taken time out—she specifically asked me to make sure you didn't try and locate her. She wants a bit of time and you'd be making a big mistake, in my opinion, if you didn't give it to her...'

CHAPTER TWO

'SHE SPECIFICALLY ASKED YOU…to make sure I didn't follow her…?'

Frustration, bewilderment and something else tore through him, something ill-defined that pressed uncomfortably behind his ribcage.

He had done his utmost for his siblings. When their parents had died twelve years ago, Izzy had been just ten and he had been twenty-two, the same age she was now. Young and fresh out of university, ready to spread his wings. Fate had had other plans in store. His parents had been killed in their light aeroplane, which they had insisted on taking out despite poor weather conditions.

In a heartbeat, Max had found himself catapulted out of his youth and into instant, responsible adulthood. It had fallen to him to become caretaker to both his siblings and he had done so without complaint. He had done his utmost to make sure that their lives remained as steady as possible whilst he had put every thought he had ever vaguely had of taking time out on permanent hold.

Of course it had helped that his parents, both wealthy

in their own right, had left behind a company in reasonably good health, thanks to delegation. Because his father, from memory, had never graced the inside of his office as he'd spent most of his time having fun.

Truthfully, Max had never surfaced from the weight of having to provide for his younger siblings.

And now his sister...didn't want him finding her?

He had made sure to take care of her! He had guided her through her life choices and arranged this job for her here! How many girls fresh out of university were given the golden opportunity to use their business degree to set up a boutique hotel in Hawaii with only a few guidelines and minimal supervision, free to make their own mark and prove their worth?

'That's ridiculous,' he asserted with a dismissive wave of his hand. 'I could do with another drink. And something to eat.' He beckoned someone across without taking his eyes off her.

The café was filling up. In her baggy tee shirt and sarong and flip-flops, she should have stood out, but in fact everyone else seemed to be wearing the same casual uniform. He tugged at the collar of his polo shirt, uncomfortably hot under the sultry overhead fan.

'Why is it ridiculous?'

'Exactly what did my sister tell you? Are you going to stick with water? Refuse the offer of food?'

Mia glanced briefly at the plastic menu Rae had brought over, but actually she knew what was on offer without having to consult any menu, and she ordered a Maui lager and a plate of Korean barbecue wings. She was hungry, and why not?

'Izzy knew that you would want to find her.'

'Hardly a surprise.'

'She…'

'What? She *what*?' Max stifled his impatience. For someone so adept at speaking her mind, she now seemed reluctant to expand on what she had said.

He watched her with brooding eyes, noting the flush in her cheeks and the fact that she couldn't quite look him in the eye. She might be outspoken to the point of annoying—and she might go against the grain, because nearly every woman he met made it their duty to engage his interest—but she was truly exquisite to look at, with her flawless brown skin and expressive eyes.

He shifted uncomfortably and frowned as his libido responded in a way that was utterly inappropriate.

He reminded himself that he was sitting here with this woman for one reason and one reason only. To locate his sister. It was proving more tedious than anticipated but Max had no doubt that he would get the information he wanted sooner rather than later. He had to because he had meetings scheduled and he had no intention of bailing on any of them.

'Look…' Drinks had arrived, beer for both of them, and he cradled his ice-cold bottle for a few seconds before tipping some down. 'I'm not in the mood for playing games. I'm on a tight timetable here. I haven't got time to try and coax answers out of you.'

'Izzy specifically doesn't want you to bring her back. She needs to clear her head. She…she had a bit of a relationship with a guy and it didn't go according to plan.'

Max stilled. He linked his fingers on the table and stared at her. 'Talk to me.'

'I shouldn't have said as much as I did, but honestly, Izzy just needs time to recover.'

'What happened?'

'Nothing happened! That's just it. Nothing at all happened and I think Izzy hoped that something might. That something serious might happen.'

'Who is he?'

Max banked down a surge of anger at whoever the guy was who was responsible for his sister's hasty disappearance. All the protective instincts that had been in place inside him for so many years raced to the surface and he clenched his fists, breathing deeply.

'It doesn't matter who he is,' Mia murmured.

Their eyes met, his dark with rage, hers calm and unruffled, and he felt himself relax a little.

'I'm finding it hard to imagine my sister involved with a scumbag,' he growled.

'Maybe,' Mia said under her breath, 'you're finding it hard to imagine your sister with *anyone*.'

Mia sat back, realising that she hadn't touched her beer, but then every ounce of her attention had been focused on the guy sitting opposite her.

He emanated such simmering power and restless energy that she was oblivious to her surroundings.

Their food was being brought to them now, and she drank some of the beer and hesitantly began picking at the food, trying hard to marshal her thoughts.

Should she have betrayed that confidence? Should

she have mentioned the business between Izzy and Jefferson?

But how else could she have deterred Max from doing what he had threatened to do? Why would he have believed anything else she'd told him? He didn't know her. And if he didn't believe her then what would stop him from hiring a PI to hunt down Izzy? He was rich, so that was something he could easily accomplish with a single phone call.

She knew Izzy well enough to suspect that if her brother hounded her down their relationship would take a battering.

Even so…

She dropped her eyes and tried to enjoy some of the fantastic barbecue on her plate, but her heart was pounding, and her head was beginning to throb with stress.

'What do you mean by that?'

'Sometimes you have to stand back and let the people you care about make whatever mistakes they have to make.'

'I gather from that remark that you and my sister have shared lots of cosy chats together? Izzy has never, *never,* given the slightest hint that she finds me over-protective.'

'Well, you asked me why she disappeared, and I've told you. There's nothing more I'm going to add to that.' She shoved her plate away and wiped her fingers on the damp tissues that had come with the wings.

He had worked his way through a couple of beers and a generous helping of *poke*. He'd managed to get some on his expensive polo shirt and that small detail made him seem much more human, much less forbidding.

He might be tough and ruthless, and downright arrogant in his assumption that getting exactly what he wanted was his right, but he was also human, and she wondered what it must feel like for him to be told that the sister he had spent years caretaking no longer needed to be looked after.

Mia knew about their unusual and unhappy background. Not in any great detail, but enough.

She had felt sorry for Izzy. She had had a very clear idea of what her brother was like. Driven, ambitious, *stifling*. But she had never met him before today, and it was easy to form opinions of people based on what was said about them. Indeed, it was impossible *not* to.

She'd sympathised hugely with her friend. She couldn't envisage a life without the support of parents, or the laughter of a jostling, rowdy household. It was what she had grown up with. Four sisters, nephews and nieces all meeting up as often as they possibly could because they enjoyed their times together. No family was ever without its problems, because such was the nature of life, but she just couldn't imagine the sadness of the sort of silent life her friend seemed to have had.

'I'm sorry.' She interrupted the growing silence and he scowled.

'For what?'

'It can't be easy learning that your sister doesn't want you to…follow her…'

'Thanks for the show of sympathy.' Max looked away, jaw clenched. 'But I'll cope.'

'If you choose to get someone involved to find Izzy, then I can't stop you,' Mia said. 'But I don't think that would be such a great idea.'

'What happened with that man? Was violence involved?'

'Good heavens, *no*!' Mia said, startled. 'You don't have to worry on that score *at all*. Jefferson was an idiot, that's all.' She sensed rather than saw the passing shadow of intense relief lighten his lean, handsome face.

She awkwardly offered to settle half the bill, and for the first time, when he looked at her, it was without the cool remoteness that had sent chills down her spine. When his eyes rested on her this time, they were a little bit startled, a little bit amused.

'I can count on the fingers of one hand,' he murmured, 'the number of women who have ever offered to do that. No—scratch that. I have never been in the company of *any* woman who has ever offered to pick up her share of the bill, so thank you for the offer.'

Mia blushed. Her skin tingled and she was aware of something else that had crept into the conversation, something that didn't threaten and didn't make her hackles rise, and that something sent a shiver racing up and down her spine.

'Well, *I* always make sure to pay my half whenever I go out with a guy,' she countered briskly.

'And I expect those occasions happen frequently?'

Mia's blush deepened. Suddenly, she felt out of her depth. Since Kai, she had been on a handful of dates, all of which had ended up in the 'just good friends' category.

She had not gone on any of those dates because she had really wanted to. All of them, all *five* of them, had been arranged by one of her sisters and Mia had politely gone along because she hadn't wanted to seem ungracious.

She was the odd one out in her family, the only one without a significant other. Two of her sisters were married with kids and the other two were engaged. She was twenty-seven years old and she knew what the unspoken commentary on her life was...

When is she going to settle down?

When will Mia get over her failed marriage, which was four years ago, and find herself a nice, decent guy...?

So when they'd arranged for her to meet one of those 'nice, decent guys', she had known they'd done so because they loved her, and the last thing she'd wanted to do was hurt their feelings.

'It's getting late,' she began, reaching for her backpack.

'I wouldn't dream of asking you to pay for a plate of chicken wings and a bottle of beer, incidentally,' he said with authority.

'In that case, thanks,' Mia returned awkwardly. 'Especially as I didn't give you the answer you wanted to hear. I'll head off now, if you don't mind. I'm going to have to tell Izzy that I've mentioned the business about Jefferson, and of course if she wants you to get in touch then I'll relay the message. Or she'll contact you herself. But if not...' She let the unspoken rider hover between them. If nothing was said, then Izzy didn't want his interference in her life.

'I'll walk out with you.' He stood up and dropped a handful of bills on the table, plenty to cover what they had eaten.

'It's okay.' Mia backed away and licked her lips. She felt ridiculous in her sarong, tee shirt and flip-flops, especially alongside him.

'Well…the truth is,' Max drawled, ignoring her protest and following her outside, where the air was balmy and the beach after a brief lull post families and small kids, was once again busy with young people hanging out in groups, 'we haven't quite finished this conversation.'

'What do you mean?' She looked at him with alarm. 'Like I said, I can't stop you from—'

'Oh, I know what you said, and I agree.'

'Sorry?' She looked up at him, puzzled, and once again was overwhelmed by that weird, disconcerting force-field he seemed to emanate without even realising.

He cupped her elbow, moving her out of the way of a couple of kids jogging past, and that passing physical contact sent a jolt of awareness through her like a bolt of electricity.

He was escorting her away from the beach and towards the road that separated the coast from the metropolis.

Oahu, sometimes nicknamed the Heart of Hawaii, was the most metropolitan of the islands. Honolulu, the capital, boasted bars and restaurants and galleries and museums, and right now all those buildings formed a backlit drop that stretched as far as the eye could see. This was as close as urban could get to coastal, man-made to nature, and at night it seemed even more impressive. The black ocean soothed while the frantic city thrilled. The heat, the noise, the lively thrum of people, traffic and *life* never failed to give her a kick.

Right at the moment, however, it wasn't quite delivering on that front because she was way too conscious of the man walking beside her. He'd dropped his hand from her elbow but the place where he had touched continued to burn and she had to resist the temptation to rub it in the palm of her hand.

'My hotel.' He nodded. Mia knew that he would be staying at one of the most expensive hotels in the city, with views of the sea. She hoped that he didn't have plans to continue their conversation inside his hotel because if he did then she would have to put her foot down—not that she had any idea what more she could contribute anyway.

The thought of being inside a hotel with Max brought her out in a cold sweat because there was something intimate about the confines of a hotel.

'I'm afraid I really must get back home,' she said in a prim, breathless voice, and Max laughed under his breath.

'There you go again,' he drawled as they crossed the busy ribbon of road and began heading into the city at an easy pace. 'Assuming the worst. I wasn't interested in chatting you up on the beach and I'm not trying to coerce you into the hotel with me.'

Mia was relieved he couldn't see the mortified flush that rushed into her cheeks. What must be going through his head? How big must he think her ego?

Her first reaction to him had been to assume that he was chatting her up, presumably because she thought herself *so* irresistible. Then that remark about all those numerous dates she'd gone on! She'd done nothing to dispel that inaccuracy because her private life was none of his business but even so…

And now here she was, assuming, as far as he was concerned, that he was trying to entice her back to his place.

The ironic thing was that Mia was very far removed from having any kind of ego when it came to men.

No matter what she looked like, the bottom line was that her marriage had failed, and she'd realised long ago that, although she had surfaced from that brief and unsuccessful union, she still carried, deep inside her, a sense of personal failure that, because things hadn't worked out, she had misjudged a situation so badly. It had been her own secret shame.

So to have Max, or anyone, somehow thinking that she was full of herself couldn't be further from the truth!

There was no reason for her to defend herself, because his opinion didn't matter, but she still bristled at his misconceptions.

'I'm taking you to the hotel because it'll be easier for you to get a taxi back to your house from there.'

'I'm fine with public transport.'

'Do you *ever* concede anything without a full-blown argument? Are you like that with everyone you meet? I'm going to concede that you might be right about my sister. It's disappointing that Izzy is somehow afraid of

talking to me about what's on her mind, but so be it.'
He'd slowed down as they approached the hotel, with
its dramatic columns and graceful, semi-circular marble frontage and sculpted trees guarded by a stiff and
serious-looking official in uniform. As expected, there
was a bank of taxis waiting outside.

He drew her to a stop and looked down at her. In the
shadowy darkness of the night, his face was all sharp
angles and, staring up at him, Mia felt her mouth go dry.

Was Izzy afraid to talk to him? She suddenly wanted
to tell him that *afraid* wasn't quite the right term.

But, frankly, she was unable to get the words out because he took her breath away. Literally. She was having trouble remembering how to breathe.

'You tell me that she specifically does not want me
to know her whereabouts. That being the case…and I'm
going to take your word for it that a blip in her emotional life is the cause of this drama rather than anything more serious…'

'You shouldn't underestimate how awful heartbreak
can be.'

Staring up at him with the sort of ridiculous fascination that annoyed her intensely but was somehow
impossible to control, she realised that he didn't understand what she was talking about.

Yes, he had accepted that getting a private investigator involved to track Izzy down might not be the best
option, and to all intents and purposes he had trusted
Mia when she'd told him that Izzy hadn't rushed off
because she had become involved in anything shady.
But, judging from the cynical expression on his face,

the notion of anyone tailoring their behaviour because of a broken heart made no sense to him at all.

Against her will, Mia felt a surge of curiosity.

He was so cold, so aloof…

So controlled.

Was he like that in every aspect of his life? Had he never had a broken heart? She vaguely remembered Izzy once telling her that her brother was a workaholic. Did that mean that he had *no* time for relationships? Surely not…?

She imagined that there would be no end of women banging on his door begging to be allowed in, with him looking the way he did.

Her nostrils flared and a sudden heat coursed through her body. She was shocked to the core by the damp pooling of moisture between her legs.

'We'll have to agree to differ on that score,' Max was saying coolly.

Mia, eye level with his chest, was busy trying to ward off intrusive, inappropriate images of what he might look like under that polo shirt.

She heard herself grunt something non-committal by way of response.

'Are you listening to what I'm saying?' Max demanded, and she reluctantly looked up at him and nodded.

'Yes, but I'm beginning to flag. I don't know what else you want me to say about this. I feel terrible about breaking Izzy's confidence, but it was the only way I could think of to stop you from employing someone to find her. But now you know why she vanished, and now you know that she's going to be heading back, and I'm sure she'll be in touch within the next week. So what else is there for us to talk about?'

Max sighed and shot her a kindly and only mildly questioning look.

'Your status as my employee, of course...'

Mia stilled. How could she have let that slip her mind even for a moment? In her head, she had pictured herself heading back to her house never to lay eyes on him again. How naïve of her.

'Well, yes...'

'I hate to get between you and your beauty sleep, but this is going to be slightly more than a five-minute conversation, Mia. Of course, we can conduct it out here, with the passing traffic and beeping of horns interrupting us every two minutes, or we could actually go inside the hotel. To the bar. Where we would be able to sit and converse in relative comfort.' He paused, then added in a tone intended to make her hackles rise, 'Naturally, if you still feel wary about that situation, then we can remain standing out here. I will, of course, choose not to insist that we go inside.'

And there, in a nutshell, was the fist of steel inside the not-so-velvet glove, she thought. She worked for him and, like any boss, he was entitled to give orders. He'd managed to make that clear without actually saying so in so many words.

He'd also managed to remind her of the inaccurate picture of herself she had managed to paint. The implication was that there would be people around them so she could go ahead and feel safe that he wasn't going to do anything inappropriate because she was simply just too irresistible.

Mia ground her teeth together and clenched her fists and thought that she had never wanted to smack someone more.

'Sure.' She did her best to paint a casual smile on her face.

Max tilted his head to one side and was silent for a few seconds, then he nodded and began moving off towards the brightly lit, guarded entrance.

Infuriating man, she thought, following him into the hotel and feeling *really* under-dressed amongst the designer-clad tourists milling in groups.

The lobby was huge and dissected by four impressive marble columns. The white columns and the white walls were a stark contrast to the highly polished dark wood of the floors and the huge rugs, with their pale green leaf motifs that looked too expensive to walk on.

It reeked of opulence and she felt a kick of nerves as she walked alongside him, feeling self-conscious in her beach wear.

It was blessed relief to get to the relative dark sanctuary of the bar, with its bank of arched windows and its long, granite-topped bar behind which several beautiful young people were serving drinks. It was a huge space and very much conducive to conversations not being overheard.

Mia slid into a chair and, once orders had been taken, she leaned forward and linked her fingers on the table.

'You said you wanted to talk to me about my…my status as your employee. I know I didn't give you the answer you wanted to hear, but please tell me whether I still have a job.' Her voice was low and urgent. She was already trying to work out how she might supplement her income should she get the sack.

The landscaping job at the hotel was only in the very first stages but she had been thrilled by the size of the job, and the opportunities it offered to diversify her work, and she had given most of her attention over to it. It was also stupidly well-paid.

She blanched as she did the maths in her head about what would happen should she lose her income.

'Calm down.' He sat back as drinks were placed in front of them along with two heavy glass dishes brimming with hot cashew nuts.

'How can I be calm? You were happy to blackmail me to get what you wanted.'

Max shrugged, unfazed by that accusation. 'All's fair in love and war. If I'd thought you were holding out on information that might have put my sister in jeopardy, then there's no doubt I would have been heavy handed in my dealings.' He paused to sip some of his drink. 'As it happens, I do believe what you've said, and I trust you haven't airbrushed the situation. Personally, I don't see why a disappointing personal relationship is reason enough to dump a dream job and leave the people around you in the lurch but, as I said, we'll have to agree to disagree on that point.'

Mia took heart from the fact that he hadn't yet issued her with her final papers. She still felt the need for some Dutch courage, though, so she sipped the cocktail she had ordered and helped herself to some of the nuts.

It was late, and she was still hungry after her plate of chicken wings, which she had only picked at because her stomach had been too churned up with tension.

'Here's the thing, Mia,' he drawled. 'In Izzy's absence, I'm going to have to hang around here for a bit longer than I had anticipated.'

'Why?'

'Why do you think?' He shot her a quizzical look, as if encouraging her to arrive at what should be a glaringly obvious conclusion.

Mia refused to be cowed. 'Nat is brilliant,' she pointed out. 'So is Kahale. Plus, there's only a minimum of people on board at the moment because the hotel is only really just getting underway.'

She realised that she was propping herself up on her hands, so she breathed deeply and forced herself to relax. 'Workers are on board for the building side of things, and I know that there was a hold-up on some of the supplies, but that's been sorted now. We haven't got any of the actual fitters in at the moment because there's so much basic work still to be done. It's just a twenty-room hotel, though, so it shouldn't take for ever to sort out. Nothing that the boys can't handle. Nat is very experienced when it comes to supervising construction.'

Max remained silent for such a long time that Mia began to fidget.

'You're very knowledgeable on what's going on,' he murmured eventually.

And into that positive remark, Mia jumped feet-first. If her job was at stake, what better way to secure it than to prove to him that she was worth what she was being paid?

'I was taken on to do the landscaping,' she explained with enthusiasm. 'As you know, the grounds are extensive! I should say that, in keeping with an eco-venture, I've made sure to clear as little of the indigenous plant life as possible. I'm a great believer in—'

'I'm getting the message here.' He paused.

Mia had hoped to sell her talents a little more comprehensively but she felt she had possibly done enough at least to sway him if he had been thinking about letting her go simply because she had refused to tell him where his sister was.

She wondered whether she should invite him to have a look at some of the ideas she had detailed in a series of scale drawings, show him how she intended to use some of the land for growing fruit and vegetables. Part of the work had already begun, as it was a big job and would have to be done in stages. She could walk him through it.

Then she thought about showing him around, talking it through with him, being in his presence yet again, and she decided to hold off for the moment.

At any rate, he certainly wasn't making any encouraging noises about her plans for his land. But he did continue to look at her in thoughtful silence until eventually she continued.

'I know it's a bit strange that I've become involved in more aspects of the hotel than you might have expected,' she grudgingly offered. When she tried to read what he was thinking, she drew a blank. It was discon-

certing. 'It's a small team, really. If you exclude the…
er…guys working on the building work, there's really
only myself, Nat, Kahale and of course Izzy.'

'Who is no longer available…'

'But will be back here before you know it!' Mia said
with a level of conviction she was far from feeling.
Reading between the lines, Izzy had fled more than
just a crap relationship and a broken heart. She'd also
fled the confines of a life that had never allowed her to
spread her wings and fly. She had done her utmost to
let her creativity shine when it came to the hotel, to give
herself that grounding, but she had hated the paperwork
and dealing with people down the end of a phone line.
Whenever possible, she had fobbed those jobs off on
Mia, who had picked up the slack without complaint.

Yes, there was no question that Izzy would return
and be better for it, but Mia wasn't going to bet on her
optimistic prediction of 'within a week or so'…

'And in the meantime, you're here,' Max mused.
'And here is where we stand—I'm going to be stuck
here, because I'm giving my sister the time she seems
to need for reasons that are beyond me, but someone is
going to have to step into her shoes and bring me up to
date with what's been going on.' He looked at her, utterly relaxed and yet supremely forceful.

'What do you mean?' Mia knew exactly what he
meant.

'I don't have Izzy, but you're here. Time to step up
to the plate.'

CHAPTER THREE

THIS WAS A situation Max had not catered for. From the other side of the pond, things had seemed straightforward enough when he had boarded the plane to Honolulu. Irritating, but straightforward.

One wayward sister who had to be located and brought back to that little thing called *reality*—namely the job she had abandoned without prior warning. One friend who would spill the beans because she would find out fast enough that she had no choice. Quick debrief with Nat, probably with Izzy in tow so that she could be reminded in no uncertain terms of the very cushy number she was fortunate enough to have. And then he would be able to return to his high-powered life in the fast lane.

That was his comfort zone.

Max Stowe led a life that would have driven many to a nervous breakdown. He never stopped. Everything took second place to the demands of work. He knew that, accepted it and was indifferent when it came to changing his priorities. Why would he? He enjoyed control and he had ultimate control over every aspect of his life.

He worked hard. He liked the pressure. He had enough money to enjoy an expensive life a million times over, but that didn't mean he had any intention of ever slowing down. He worked long hours and, when he rested, he rested with women who knew the score, who knew that he was never going to be in it for the long term. He was a red-blooded male with a libido to match. He enjoyed the women he dated but he was intensely disciplined when it came to knowing just where they featured in his life. He'd never, not once, allowed his head to take second place to any other part of his body.

Buried deep in his formative years were lessons learnt about the havoc emotion caused and the disastrous roads it took people down. As the eldest in the family, he had registered, in ways neither James nor certainly Izzy ever had, the self-indulgence of his parents, who had been so absorbed in one another that parental responsibility was just a game they played at now and again.

He had been conveniently sent to boarding school at the age of seven. By the age of ten, he had given up on his parents showing any real interest in his achievements. By the time he'd hit adolescence, he'd stopped caring.

Bit by bit, he'd sealed the emotional side of himself off. He was naturally gifted academically, and could take his pick when it came to sport, so studying and sport became the two things he'd relied upon. You knew where you stood on a rugby pitch or in a physics exam. Once those values had been cemented, they had hardened over the years, and so here he was now. Pleased to be the controlling hand at the rudder, knowing exactly where his life was going and knowing that it was never going to deviate from the path he had carved out for himself.

Except…things at the moment weren't going quite according to plan, and that got on his nerves. He'd had no hesitation in rousing his PA at six that morning to brief her about various meetings that would have to be put on the back burner or delegated to a couple of his trusted CEOs. He had told her that James would be available should the need arise, but he was stretched dealing with his own arm of the family empire.

Now, sitting in the boardroom he had requisitioned from the hotel, waiting for Mia to show up, he tried to timetable his week going forward. Even dividing it into sound bites did little to paper over the fact that he really had no idea when he would be able to head back to London. The maximum amount of time he would spend here was a fortnight, but it was intensely frustrating not to be able to have a more precise idea of when within that two-week period his departure would take place.

He was sprawled back in the leather chair, computer in front of him on the glossy marble conference table, staring out of the window at another dazzlingly sunny day, when the door opened quietly.

From behind it, Mia paused, heart hammering. He wasn't aware that she had pushed open the heavy boardroom door. He was absorbed in whatever he was thinking, which was probably work-related, given a laptop was open on the massive table in front of him.

She took a few seconds to look at his averted profile and the lazy sprawl of his muscular body as he gazed through the bank of floor-to-ceiling windows that looked out at a stunning vista of buildings and blue sky and, in the distance, the radiant blue-green ocean.

He was wearing a pair of faded jeans and a grey polo shirt and loafers. She wondered whether this was the most casual outfit ever to grace this fabulous space with its long walnut sideboard, on which someone had kindly placed plates filled with various breakfast pastries, its marble twenty-seater table and its elegant drapes.

Mostly, she wondered whether she should have knocked, but then she wasn't his secretary, although she did indeed work for him. She was filling in for Izzy. Bringing him up to date with stuff to do with the hotel. He probably would have this one meeting with her and that would be the end of their communications. He could pick Nat's brain for any additional information.

Couldn't he?

She had spent a restless night, head too full of the day's unexpected events to allow her much sleep.

Surprisingly, top of the agenda for things bothering her hadn't been the fact that he had shown up out of nowhere and tried to demand answers out of her, or the fact that she had released information about Izzy that had been said in confidence—even though at the time Izzy had said nothing about Mia keeping any of the information to herself.

No, what had bothered her, what had kept her awake, had been her own incomprehensible physical reaction to him. In her mind's eye, she had been able to envisage all too clearly for her liking the strong, chiselled lines of his lean, handsome face...the muscularity of his body...the sweep of those long, dark lashes...the brooding intensity of his eyes.

His appearance had impacted her in ways that were vaguely unsettling because they had come from nowhere and caught her unprepared.

She cleared her throat and he turned around. Thankfully, her legs did what she wanted them to do, and she walked towards him, not quite knowing where to sit at the enormous table. If she took the opposite end, she would need a megaphone to be heard.

He spared her the decision by almost imperceptibly nodding at the chair directly adjoining his and sitting up, waiting until she had shuffled into the seat.

He was casually dressed. She, on the other hand, had fished out the most formal outfit she could get her hands on. Her work uniform rarely strayed beyond the parameters of jeans or shorts and tee shirts, with the occasional sarong thrown in for when she was teaching surf to the kids at the weekend. She lived in flip flops, sandals or trainers.

Today she had opted for a sensible knee-length skirt and a blouse, neatly tucked into the waistband. And some proper shoes.

Was it her imagination or did she glimpse a flash of amusement in his eyes when he looked at her?

She pursed her lips and perched on the chair.

'Relax.'

'I've downloaded some facts and figures I thought you might want to have a look at.' Straight down to business. She reached into her backpack and extracted a plastic folder, which she held out to him. He ignored her outstretched hand, so she awkwardly dropped it onto the table.

'No need. I expect there's nothing there I haven't found out for myself.' He sat back, relaxed, and looked at her for a few moments. 'First of all,' he drawled, compounding the image of a male utterly at ease by folding his hands behind his head, 'There's no need for you to change the way you dress because your role has slightly altered.'

Two hot patches of colour appeared on her cheeks. 'I don't think that a sarong, a baggy tee shirt and some flip-flops would be the right dress code for this sort of situation,' she said stiffly.

'Nor do you have to feel obliged to wear clothes you find uncomfortable,' Max returned gently.

Mia didn't say anything. He'd made very clear that she worked for him and she was going to have to curb the desire to snap back at everything he said.

'I spoke to Nat last night,' Max continued briskly. 'He brought me up to date with the supply shortages with the timber. What I'm getting is that Izzy may have been quite out of her depth. I thought I was doing her a favour in handing over more or less complete responsibility for guiding this project through from visual to completion. It seems I was mistaken.'

'She's only twenty-two!' Mia protested.

'You'd be surprised how capable a twenty-two-year-old can be when thrown into a situation,' Max replied coolly, his navy eyes guarded. 'We communicated by email, with the occasional phone call. I was under the impression that this was to be a top-of-the-range, no-expense-spared-when-it-came-to-luxury kind of hotel. From what Nat has said, that was far from what my sister envisaged.'

'I couldn't really comment on that,' Mia muttered.

'I'd planned on going through some of the financial figures with you here,' Max said crisply, shutting his laptop and standing, 'but I think I'd be better served if we leave immediately for the hotel so that I can see for myself exactly what the footprint on the ground looks like.'

He waited for her to get to her feet and then, heading towards the door, continued, 'We're going to be outside. We're going to be tramping through the foundations of the hotel. I don't suppose there will be any convenient air-conditioning so my suggestion would be for you to get out of those stiflingly hot clothes and wear what you would normally wear if you were working outside.'

Every word he said riled Mia. Not only had he managed to hijack her normal life but now, she having made a special effort to turn herself into someone resembling an assistant rather than the gardener she was, he saw nothing wrong in sending her off to get changed.

'Of course.' She stalked towards the door but before she could fling it open his hand was on her arm and she froze.

'I'll come with you to your house and wait for you.'

'Why?' Heart speeding up, she looked at him, banking down a flare of alarm.

'Because it makes sense. I have a driver. You can fill me in on the general design of the hotel on the way to your house and then he can deliver us to the hotel so that you can show me round.'

She nodded curtly and her lips were compressed as they headed down to the lobby and out into the blistering sun.

He was right. If she did anything outside in this weather, wearing these clothes, she would pass out.

But she still felt awkward as she slid into the back seat of the car and told his driver where she lived.

They were travelling in style. The driver was uniformed, with the stony expression of someone highly trained to conceal all emotion and only to speak when addressed. The car was a shiny, black top-of-the-range Mercedes with blacked-out windows and a level of air-conditioning that made her want to sigh with pleasure.

She stroked the soft leather with one finger and, when she glanced across to Max, it was to find that he was looking at her, a smile tugging the corners of his mouth.

'I can't help it,' Mia muttered defensively.

'Can't help what?'

'I don't think I've ever been in a car like this before,' she admitted. 'It's beyond luxurious.'

Max smiled, genuinely amused. He'd started the morning at precisely five a.m. He'd powered through a number of emails and spoken to whoever had been available at that hour, time differences taken into account. He had devoted a considerable amount of time to the situation with his sister, replaying in his head what Mia had told him—that Izzy had specifically requested he not contact her. *Specifically.* He had shrewdly noted

Mia's discomfort when she had told him this and knew that Izzy's insistence on not wanting him to find her was probably even more urgent.

Mia would have tried to soften the harsh reality. That had hurt. He had been assiduous when it came to looking out for his sister and he couldn't deny that it hurt to realise that he had been found wanting.

It was something he had chosen to put out of his mind, however, because the main thing was the business of apprising himself of what had been happening in his absence. He had handed over too much responsibility to his sister, trusting that she would follow through.

At the back of his mind, he knew that he had made inaccurate assumptions and even more badly judged comparisons. Whilst he had taken on board the weight of premature responsibilities when his parents had died, when he himself had been the same age as his sister now, they were different people with different life experiences and different goals. Izzy wasn't him.

He had given her what he saw as a golden opportunity, and maybe it had been, but in all events it had been too soon for her.

She'd wanted to live her life on her terms. She hadn't wanted his interference then and she didn't want it now.

But introspection wasn't something he liked to indulge, and it had kick-started his day on a bad footing.

He'd hit the boardroom an hour and a half before Mia was due to show up, ample time to discover that conversations he had had with Izzy about the hotel and suggestions he had put her way because this was his third foray into the hotel business, albeit on a much, much smaller scale, had been largely ignored.

He'd taken his eye off the ball for the very first time when it came to work and he could have kicked himself.

Yet, when he had turned to see Mia framed in the doorway, all those feelings of edgy frustration had vanished.

He'd never seen anyone look so uncomfortable in his life before. She didn't want to be there, and she'd weirdly decided to wear a strange, starchy suit—which, her expression had managed to convey, was all his fault.

Yet even in the discomforting get-up, and even with her disgruntled, struggling-to-be-polite expression, she was still so stunningly pretty.

Then she'd sat down, he had breathed in the light scent of whatever flowery perfume she was wearing and he'd had to back away from proximity to her. Two hours breathing her in and seeing the tantalising flash of leg so close to his might stretch his powers of concentration a little too much.

At any rate, it made sense to go to the hotel with her so that she could talk him through the finer points. Yet here, in the confines of the car, there was a sizzling awareness of her that he couldn't seem to damp down.

'Rustic mosaic tiles,' he said flatly, angling his big body so that his back was against the car door and he could face her, legs sprawled apart. 'An absurd amount of wooden planks… Four-poster beds…'

'I beg your pardon?'

'I'm giving you a taster of some of the unexpected items I came across, and I've only just begun my search.

Since you seem to know quite a bit about the hotel, care to tell me if any of these items make sense to you?'

His eyes drifted to her full lips. It irritated and bewildered him that he couldn't seem to focus when he was in her presence. Max knew that women behaved in a certain way when they were around him. Even the women he met on a business level. He was very much aware of the fact that they tailored their responses, aimed to please, strove to gain his attention.

He was used to that and he liked it. Life was pressured enough on the work front so, when it came to women, he liked things to be laid back and unchallenging.

Certainly, demanding women were a turn-off, so it was downright puzzling that he found himself so inexplicably drawn to the woman sitting next to him who had done nothing but bicker, argue and overreact from the very second he had announced who he was. Even before that, when he thought about it.

Hadn't her opening words to him been, *'Forget it'*?

She was looking at him narrowly, striving to remember that she was his employee, whilst no doubt wanting to launch into another diatribe.

She'd tied her hair back and he wanted to tell her that, however hard she'd tried to look businesslike, she had failed miserably because she was still as sexy as Hell.

He wondered what she would say, how she would react.

He wondered…what it would feel like to unbutton the prissy blouse she had chosen to wear and slip his hand underneath the bra, which he imagined would be a no-nonsense white affair. What would she look like half-naked? She had small breasts and he had a graphic image of his hand covering one of them, playing with her, watching her scowling, defensive face soften with passion.

A dark flush stained his sharp cheekbones. His imagination was running away and he would have to rein it in. Not simply because he didn't do loss of self-control but also because he didn't do mixing business with pleasure. Delectable she might be, but she worked for him, and as his employee she stood on the opposite side of a very well-defined divide.

Mia met his eyes steadily. He was scowling, his face dark, already prepared to jump the gun and lay into her because he had given Izzy orders—no doubt camouflaged as suggestions—and she had chosen to bypass them. His default position was attack mode, and she would have to be careful to remember that and not be lulled into any false sense of security if he happened to lay on his natural charm now and again.

She inhaled deeply, counted to ten and then said calmly, 'I do know some of the things Izzy had in mind for the hotel, as it happens, and I'm pretty sure you'll get on board once I run through them with you.'

Mia was not at all sure of any such thing. He was so...*rigid*—so very different from his sister. She had never met anyone as tightly controlled as him and she wondered if some of her fascination stemmed from that.

'This isn't my first venture into the hotel business,' Max informed her. He studied her from under the screen of sooty black lashes. 'I know what works.'

'What?' Mia asked a little breathlessly.

'Luxury. Unabashed luxury. People who pay big money want a certain level of indulgence.'

'This is Hawaii...there's more scope to be casual here.'

'No matter if it's Timbuctoo,' Max said smoothly. 'You'd be surprised how much the wealthy tend to follow a certain pattern of behaviour.'

'You could be wrong.'

'When it comes to making money, I'm never wrong,' he said with a level of smooth self-assurance that was frankly mesmerising. 'When our parents died, I was catapulted fresh from university into the family business. I went from dissertations on mergers and productivity in commercial markets to having to work out how to put that into practice. I took the family business from where it was, comfortable but stagnating in the bottom percentile, and hauled it into the millennium. I learned, every step of the way, where to look for opportunities and how to make the most of them. I also learnt fast that it's not enough to have ideas or to put them into practice. It's even more important to know the beast you're dealing with.

'When it comes to hotels, people want to feel that they're being pampered, even if the pampering might be camouflaged. They don't want to pay a fortune, Mia, and find themselves swimming in a real lake, with very real algae and mud at the bottom. What they want is a sanitised pool pretending to be a lake so that they can feel as though they're in the middle of nature but without the tiresome, gritty lack of comfort.'

'That's so cynical.' Mia looked at his tough, hand-some face and then found that she couldn't manage to tear her eyes away.

'If you want to get on in life—' Max shrugged '—you have to be cynical.'

Ten minutes later, Mia realised that they were pulling up outside her house.

She'd had no opportunity to talk about the hotel. She'd been sucked into frantic curiosity about his approach to life, had marvelled that he could be so world-weary when he was still in his mid-thirties. She'd found herself wondering how this all translated into his personal life and had blushed for ever letting her thoughts wander down that route.

If he hadn't taken a call, she was afraid that she might have asked him personal questions that were none of her business. Now it was a relief to hop out of the car and head inside the coolness of her house, with Max safely still on his call and barely seeming to notice that the car had stopped and that she had left it.

Her house was small with a wooden veranda at the back holding old wicker chairs and a bamboo table. It was her favourite spot to relax because her back garden, which was a mixture of earth and patchy grass, overlooked the sea, albeit the view was a distant one. She barely paused to gaze out at that view now, instead heading directly to her bedroom. Now that she was out of the air-conditioned confines of the Mercedes, she couldn't wait to get out of the skirt and blouse, and she rid herself of both in record time.

She'd put a lot of thought into what she had chosen to wear to meet Max and, uncomfortable as it had been, the outfit had conferred some essential distance between them.

She would have to wear comfortable clothes to show him around the hotel, which was currently a building site, so she dressed accordingly in jeans, a tee shirt and her walking boots.

He was still on his call when she slipped back into the car a mere fifteen minutes after it had arrived at her house.

She was still clutching the backpack and now she extracted the sheaf of papers she had taken with her to the boardroom and which he had casually dismissed.

'Ah.' Max ended his phone call and shoved the mobile phone into his trouser pocket. 'You decided to dump the office garb. Good. Feel a little less restricted?'

'I didn't feel *restricted*,' Mia rebutted. 'But this is more appropriate for looking around a building site.'

'Which is going to be a more condensed visit, as it happens. I'll have a quick look round, but I've scheduled a meeting with Nat for this afternoon to discuss various aspects of the costings that will have to be assessed before anything further gets ordered. If I don't like the direction all of this is going, then everything gets halted, and I'll make sure what I want is followed to the last letter.'

'And what about when Izzy returns? She's put her heart and soul into her plans for the hotel. I know they're probably not what you had in mind, but she's spent a lot of time coming up with ideas…'

'That was then and this is now,' Max imparted flatly.

'I can't hang around waiting for my sister to decide that she's got her act together and is ready to return, and even if she does...' He paused for a few seconds, then raked his fingers through his hair. 'Then her role may need to be revisited.'

'What do you mean?'

'If there are aspects of the job she doesn't like, then there's no point to forcing her to do them.' He wearily pressed his fingers over his eyes but, when he looked at her, he was once more in complete control. 'I intend to hire a full-time accountant to deal with the day-to-day financial running of the place and in time, when things start gathering momentum, I will ensure a team is taken on.'

In that moment, Mia felt all her prejudices against him slip and slide uneasily beneath her feet.

When it came to his sister, it was clear that underneath the hard, dictatorial exterior was a real well of love. He might have been too aggressive when it had come to directing her life, but it hadn't been for a lack of strong, fraternal protectiveness.

Life experiences changed people, made them veer off in all sorts of directions that sometimes made no sense to the people around them.

Wasn't she a victim of that herself?

She had married young in a subconscious desire to repeat what her parents had done, what her siblings had done. Marrying young, having a family and replicating what she knew had been a given when she and Kai had married. They had both gone into marriage blithely assuming a happy-ever-after ending, blithely assuming that they would slide seamlessly into the noisy, wonderful chaos of family life.

It had unravelled with speed. The easy familiarity they had always shared had very quickly become the tension of two very young people who had never had to put their relationship to the test. The business of sharing space had revealed flaws they had never noticed before.

But divorce had come at a price. She had retreated from the business of finding love and had made her checklist of required traits so meticulous that the years had gone by. With each passing year, Mia had known that her ability to *feel* was shrinking just a little bit more.

So who was she to point fingers at Max? He was as cold as ice, but having responsibility for two siblings when you were barely out of your teens yourself would have been punishing.

'That's probably a good idea,' she agreed.

'Any interest in applying for the job?'

Mia relaxed and laughed. 'No chance. As it happens, I'm pretty good with the books, but I like the outdoor life.'

'Change of plan.'

'Sorry?'

'You can sit in on my meeting with Nat. He's the supervisor on the job and he will have a pretty good idea of the supply chain, because I know he's been dealing with some of them, but if you're good at accounts then your contribution might be useful.'

'I'm not dressed for a meeting in that boardroom!'

She stared down at the casual clothes and then blushed as their eyes met and held.

Her bra was the thinnest of cotton, just a sliver of stretchy fabric. She felt the push of her nipples as they swelled and tightened under his leisurely appraisal. She was hot all over, her skin tingling. She followed the trajectory of his gaze when she licked her upper lip as it rested for a crazily long time on the innocent gesture.

She'd thought that her divorce had put her into a deep freeze but, if that was the case, she was certainly thawing out now, big time, and had been since she had first clapped eyes on him.

She whipped her gaze away but her breathing was laboured and her fingers were linked so tightly together that when she stared down she could see the pale brown of the stretched skin of her knuckles.

'I wouldn't worry about whether you're over-dressed or under-dressed when you're with me,' Max murmured lazily. 'You could wear a bin bag at a Michelin-starred restaurant and no one would dare raise an eyebrow.'

He paused for so long that eventually she got up the courage to look at him, while her heart thumped like a runaway train inside her.

'At any rate,' he added, dropping his eyes and shifting his big body in the seat next to her, 'you look pretty damn good whatever you decide to wear.'

CHAPTER FOUR

HAVING ONLY EVER worked for herself since she had left college, it was something of a shock to the system to discover that working for Max involved jumping at his command and keeping pace with the speed of his intellect as he went through every detail of the hotel, from the amount of nails ordered, to the teams on standby for when the bulk of the work was to begin.

Their scheduled trip to see the hotel had been put on hold but she knew that he had gone there briefly with Nat the day before. It was the first time in the four days since he had commandeered her life that she had busied herself on a couple of the other small projects she'd had in the mix which required face-to-face meetings and brief land surveys.

Not that she worked with him every minute of the day. He worked in the boardroom, which he seemed to have appropriated for his needs and his alone, and much of the time he was involved in all sorts of conference calls to who knew how many people scattered across the globe. But, when it came to the hotel, he expected her to be at hand, ready to answer any questions he had.

He'd had no problem in telling her that whatever other jobs she had would have to be put on ice, because time was money, and he didn't have a lot of time to sort out the unfinished business his sister had left behind.

'But,' she had told him on day one, 'my job at the hotel has to be taken a step at a time. I've done all the drawings and plans for what I would like to do with the surrounding land, but actual purchasing and planting will have to be done in stages, and can't reasonably begin until work on certain parts of the hotel are underway.'

'And?' Max had quirked a questioning eyebrow. He had been sitting in front of his computer, a commanding presence at the long table in the boardroom, his body language telling her that he wasn't expecting a long-winded conversation with her, because he had things to do, so could she make it brief.

Standing to one side, she was awkwardly conscious of her crisp, clean clothes that were somewhere between the prissy starched outfit she had worn that very first time she had gone to see him, and the outdoor gear she spent most of her days in. Neat shoes, a pair of grey cotton mid-calf trousers and a tee shirt tidily tucked into the waistband of the trousers.

'And in my spare time I focus on a few other jobs. None of them are particularly big but I need all the work I can get.'

'Why?'

'Sorry?'

'You're generously paid by me.'

'Yes, I know that, but in this line of work it's not just about the money. This job will finish in under a year and I need to have other things in the pot that I can turn to. I give one hundred and ten percent when it comes to the hotel and that includes all the extra duties I've taken on over the past few months…'

'Okay, spare me the highlights and lowlights. You're not auditioning for a job. Fact is, I won't be setting aside dedicated time for hotel business. I have a lot of other deals going on, deals that I should be handling back in London, but which I now have to handle here because Izzy's done a runner.'

He had let that settle into the silence between them, a reminder that he was there because he had chosen to give his sister the benefit of the doubt and leave her be until she sorted herself out. A reminder that he had *chosen* to listen to what she, Mia, had advised rather than following his natural instinct to bypass her when he hadn't got what he had come for and hire someone to locate his sister.

'What are these other jobs?' he had demanded.

'I have some tenders I'm looking at…ideas I need to commit to paper. A couple of meetings lined up as well…'

'In which case…' he had gestured magnanimously at the boardroom table '…you can sit anywhere you like at this table and do whatever you have to do right here. That way, you're at hand when I need to ask you a question. As for meetings? You have my word that after five your time is yours.'

He wasn't about to give way on this because he was the sort of man who never gave way on anything.

Mia had thus discovered the joys of the very type of

office job she had often teasingly reminded her sisters was the very depths of boring.

The puzzle for her was that she enjoyed it more than she had thought she would, more than she thought she *should*.

She perched opposite him. She'd brought all her work with her and she had to admit that the surroundings were pretty fabulous. Pastries and coffee were on tap. It was beautifully air-conditioned and, in fairness, he had a capacity to focus that was incredible. When he became involved in conference calls, when he sat frowning in front of his computer, scrolling and making notes, when he spoke to CEOs, voice clipped and every word succinct and to the point, she knew that she ceased to exist.

And when she was in that place where she ceased to exist…her eyes strayed. She couldn't help it. She sneaked glances at him, committing to memory the way he sat with his chair swivelled at an angle…the way he stared off into the distance when he was concentrating…the way he absently tapped his pen on the table when he was working on his computer, a gesture that summed up the restless energy of his personality.

Today, they were going to be meeting with Nat at the hotel, but Mia was already running late.

As luck would have it, and for the first time in weeks, dazzling blue skies had been replaced with driving rain.

It was a little after four and Mia had cycled from one of her clients, a guy with a roof garden and ambitious plans to turn it into a vegetable paradise with wild flowers in tubs. She had had to gently dissuade him from plans to add a couple of bee hives to the mix because he liked honey.

The sun had been shining when she'd left her house but in the space of a couple of hours the skies had gone from cerulean blue to leaden grey and then the heavens had opened.

Instead of the twenty-minute ride to the hotel, she had taken over forty-five minutes, and it was after five by the time she pulled away from the main drag and along the quiet side roads that led to the construction site.

The hotel was located in a brilliant spot, a taxi ride from the city but edging towards the sea, against a backdrop of stunning land dense with trees and threaded with waterfalls.

It was the perfect getaway, a child-free hotel where there would be no limits to the luxury on offer.

The site had been very carefully chosen and it was a brilliant example of the magical juxtaposition on the island of wild nature, urban seaside and captivating metropolis.

The sun was fading by the time she skidded to a stop and wiped the rain from her eyes to look at what had been accomplished over the past few months.

Less than Max had expected. She knew that from a couple of the things he had said after his abbreviated visit there with Nat. In fairness, she couldn't blame him. The schedule had been pushed back several times because first of all Izzy had decided not to go with any of the suggestions her brother had made and then, having charted a different route, she had dithered when it had come to making her mind up on several crucial points.

Tarpaulin protected some of the half-built rooms, and for the rest foundations had been laid and were patiently awaiting stage two. The weeds coiling round the cement and bricks seemed to indicate that several of those foundations had given up all hope of being completed and were happy to wave a white flag and kick back for the duration.

Mia leapt off the bike while shoving it upright all in one smooth motion and sprinted towards the one bit of the hotel that was the least forlorn.

The extensive kitchen was pretty much done, which was to say that there were walls, a roof, concrete ground and various partitions, gaps and openings where appliances would eventually fit. The space was enormous. She arrived in a soaking rush to find Max already there and waiting for her.

The construction workers had kitted out the place as best they could so that they could do some very rudimentary cooking. There was a kettle, some mugs, an electric hot plate and a motley assortment of mismatched chairs.

A working mini-fridge was plugged into a socket and there was an electric fan.

'You're late.'

Still trying to dry herself the best she could in the absence of a towel, Mia screeched to a halt and glared at him.

He was as dry as a bone and had helped himself to a mug of coffee, which he was loosely holding, half-resting it on his lap. He dwarfed the chair, his long legs stretched out in front of him and crossed at the ankles.

He looked dry and comfortable and utterly elegant in an understated way. Faded jeans, tan loafers and a white short-sleeved tee shirt.

'Thank you for pointing that out,' Mia snapped. She gave a final squeeze of her hair and saw that he was holding out a handkerchief for her. Pride made her want to ignore it completely, but pride would have to take second place to practicality, and right now she just wanted some part of her to be dry.

She wiped her face and handed him back the handkerchief. It was late, so a completely wasted trip, because there was no way she would be able to show him anything now.

She'd cycled like a maniac to get here and his opening words were *you're late*?

Mia thought he was lucky she didn't hurl something at him, and she wouldn't have cared whether she was a handsomely paid employee or not.

'I cycled here,' she said through gritted teeth. 'It was fine when I left but, since I'm not a meteorologist, I didn't predict this thunderstorm, so it took a lot longer than I'd banked on.'

Max stood up and continued to look at her while she cast him a glowering, baleful, sullen look.

'You're soaked.'

'Thanks for pointing out the obvious.'

'You should have pulled over and phoned me to cancel. It wouldn't have been the end of the world.'

Mia didn't say anything because that hadn't even occurred to her. She'd been running on adrenaline, not paying as much attention as she should to her client, keen to head off, because the thought of seeing Max had been a hot, driving excitement in her veins.

So hot and so driving that common sense had taken a back seat. Of course she should have called him! As soon as the clouds had started turning an angry black, she should have pulled over, got out her mobile phone and explained the situation. An idiot would have been able to figure out that driving rain would make a nonsense of her timings.

'Come on.' He urged her towards the door, hand cupping her elbow. 'There's a half-dirty tea towel hanging around here somewhere, but no convenient pile of towels, I'm afraid. I'll get you home.'

'Get me home?'

'Nothing to do here. Way too rainy, way too late and way too dark. My driver is waiting.'

She was being shuffled out of the place, barely concentrating on what she was doing or where they were going.

'My bike...'

'Will live to ride another day. Now, run!'

She obeyed instinctively. She was already so wet. The thought of getting any wetter didn't bear thinking about. She was cold too, her teeth chattering and her clothes clinging to her like cling film.

She literally bolted for the dry sanctuary of the car, and she would have made it as well if the wretched, soggy, uneven ground of a building site hadn't conspired to bring her crashing to her knees.

She was racing one minute, and the next she was lying in a heap on the ground, and when she hurriedly began to prop herself back up her foot buckled under her and she gave a yelp of pain.

The rain washed over her, sharply pricking her skin, and overhead there was a crack of thunder that made her start.

All of this took place in a matter of seconds—the running, the falling, the roar of thunder and then the horrifying realisation that he was sweeping her off her feet and sprinting to the car. His driver had opened an umbrella, the passenger door was open, then they were both inside the car and the door was slammed shut behind them.

'Your foot,' Max said as the car purred away from the site and back out towards the city. 'How much does it hurt?'

'It'll be fine,' Mia muttered.

'There's nothing to be gained by being a martyr. Do I need to take you to hospital? Only you can tell me exactly how bad it is, so don't lie.'

'It's fine.' She tentatively tried to circle her ankle and winced.

'Right. We'll go back to your house and I'll have a look but, if I'm in any doubt, I'm getting a doctor out.'

'Don't be ridiculous!'

'I'm not being ridiculous, Mia,' he said coolly. 'All precautions will be taken, because the last thing I need is a lawsuit for negligence. So if I think a doctor needs to come out, then out he comes, whether you agree or not.'

'You think I'd *what*?' Mia gaped, momentarily distracted from the pain in her ankle and the way her clothes were becoming glued to her body. 'Sue you because I was an idiot who fell over?'

Max shrugged. 'As it happens, I don't, but who knows?'

'God, what sort of world do you live in?'

'What do you mean by that?'

'Well, it seems that in *your* world women are either open to a bit of blackmail or else trying to sue you for something that's not your fault! In other words, you're not exactly prepared to give women the benefit of the doubt, are you?'

She looked at him narrowly and was perversely satisfied at the dark flush of colour that delineated his razor-sharp cheekbones. For once, she'd caught him on the back foot, and it felt great.

He looked away, and she wanted to prod at the sore spot she had found, because he *got* to her and it felt good that she could likewise get to him.

'When you get to the top of the ladder,' he said, turning to her, his voice matter-of-fact, borderline indifferent, 'it pays to put *trust* at the back of the queue.'

'You don't trust *anyone*?' Mia asked with disbelief. She might have gone through the misery of a divorce, and she may have built her own ivory tower to protect herself from getting hurt again, but that didn't mean she didn't *trust* people.

Her family...her friends... Her default position wasn't that she had to be on red-hot alert one hundred percent of the time because everyone was capable of hiding a knife behind their back.

She felt a wave of compassion. He might be as hard

as granite, but you didn't get to a position of such cynicism without your past experiences putting you there.

'I feel sorry for you, Max,' she said quietly, and his eyebrows shot up.

'Should I be touched or irritated?'

'I expect you'll be irritated,' she confirmed. 'You said that I'm on the lookout for an argument all the time. Well, I'm no different to you, am I? I'm just being honest. It must be a lonely life if you can't trust anyone at all. You might have all the money in the world but if you're alone in your glass tower then what's the point?'

'I cope.'

Two words signalling the end of the conversation. He didn't look irritated. He looked bored.

A door had been slammed in her face, and she couldn't blame him, because commenting on his private life was way out of order.

He was her boss and her role was to liaise with him about the hotel, end of story. Her role was not to make wise proclamations about his life choices. She wasn't a landscape gardener turned shrink!

Her cheeks stung and she looked away, and with relief realised that they were nearing her house. She'd barely noticed the journey. She'd barely noticed her soaked clothes or her foot!

The driver was out of the car as soon as he'd killed the engine, umbrella at the ready. Max moved with similar alacrity, removing all chance of her taking a stand and trying to hobble to the door unaided.

In fact, her feet weren't allowed to touch the ground at all. Swept off her feet twice in a day, Mia thought with a touch of mild hysteria, and not in the way she'd ever imagined it happening.

'It's in the front pocket,' she muttered, before he could ask her where the house key was, and he duly located it and pushed open the door.

'I'll call you when I'm ready,' he said to the driver, who nodded and returned to the car.

The rain followed them through the open door, but then Max slammed it shut, and it became a steady, noisy beating against the roof and walls.

This was not how he had imagined the day panning out. Of course, it was essential that he had a walk through with her. Not only was she knowledgeable when it came to the accounts system but her main job involved the outside space, the land, and he needed to have an idea of how she intended to utilise the space. When he had discussed the hotel with his sister well over a year ago when it had been in the embryonic stage, he had suggested an infinity pool and all the various outdoor luxuries that came with that, including a state-of-the-art bar nestled among the trees where cocktails and drinks could be served on a more or less non-stop basis.

All those ideas had gone down the drain, so it was necessary to know exactly what was destined to replace it, because the financial projections were all over the place.

Yes, this was a necessary trip, but even so he had been studiously putting it off.

Just having her sit at the other end of that boardroom table had been a challenge.

He'd been *aware* of her in ways that made a joke of

his legendary self-control. He'd had to conduct most of his conversations on the phone, with his chair angled in such a way that she was just on the periphery of his vision, because every time he'd looked at her—her, head downbent, chin propped in the palm of her hand, her brown hair falling to one side —he'd had to fight against getting a hard-on.

It was crazy, and he didn't like himself for it, but he hadn't been able to do a thing about it. If he could have shouted questions across the table, he would have, but she'd had to edge next to him to stare at the same facts and figures on the same computer and her proximity had been great at messing with his head.

He wanted her. That was what it came down to. She was off-limits, but he wanted her, and the more he tried to ignore the tug at his senses the harder the tug was.

So he had deferred the inevitable trip to the hotel, and he certainly hadn't envisaged a sudden torrential downpour bringing him to this place, in her house, with her in his arms.

She was as light as a feather. He could have lifted her with one hand. And was she aware that the way those wet clothes clung…?

He'd fought to stop himself from staring. He knew that he'd reacted somewhat more aggressively than the occasion demanded when she had fallen and done whatever she'd done to her foot.

Had he really said something about getting a doctor because he had to protect himself against a possible lawsuit?

He had opened the door wide to her comments about

the way he lived his life. Not her business, and he could definitely care less, but she had got under his skin and he wasn't sure whether that was because he was just so hyper-aware of her or because she insisted on ignoring all the *Do Not Trespass* signs everyone else managed to read very clearly.

She got to him in every way, and now here he was. In her house.

He looked around him and headed in the direction of the bedroom, while she remained passive in his arms, clearly having given up on fighting him. He could feel her warmth radiating beyond the wet clothes, the softness of her legs and the slightness of her body.

She was so *natural*—so lacking in any artifice. There was no make-up for the rain to wash away.

Never had he been more aware of his body or more alert to the temptation to hold her close, keep holding her, kiss her, touch her...

'You need to change,' he said abruptly.

He looked around him at her small house, with lots of wood and a feeling of homeliness. He'd glanced at the kitchen as he'd walked past and had seen colourful cupboards and an old pine table. The furniture in the living room was squashy and mismatched and the overhead fan was desultory. Here, in the bedroom, the double bed was covered with some kind of old-fashioned patchwork quilt, and there was a rocking chair by the window that overlooked a very pretty, panoramic view of shrubs and flowers and, in the distance, sand leading down to the sea.

The rain continued to pelt against the windows. If it

hadn't been raining, and if night hadn't begun creeping in, casting long, dark shadows, Max was pretty sure he would have been able to hear the roll of the sea through the windows and see a blaze of stars in the sky.

Never one to get swept up in appreciating the scenery, he was momentarily disconcerted. He looked round to see her rising to her feet and he shook his head.

'Tell me where to look and I'll get what you want.'

Judging from her stubborn expression, he was guessing that the last thing she wanted was to direct him to her drawers so that he could fish out dry clothes for her, but she did as she was asked.

'Need help putting these clothes on?' He looked at her. 'It's going to be tricky getting out of those wet things.'

'I can manage.'

'Well, if you find you can't, then I'm within shouting distance. In fact, I'll wait right outside the door. Call me when you're dressed. I'm going to inspect your ankle, and don't even attempt to hobble out to me.'

Mia muttered something under her breath and looked at him with sulky hostility. 'You mean just in case I topple over and sue you for personal injury?'

Max shot her an impatient look and raked his fingers through his hair.

'Okay. I apologise for that.'

Their eyes tangled and her breathing picked up. She nodded and he hesitated fractionally.

'I've learnt that the only person I can trust is myself,' he told her heavily. 'It's just the way I'm built.'

Mia nodded and some of the hostility drained away.

What did he mean by that? No one was *built* to be dis-trustful. She waited until he had left the bedroom and shut the door behind him.

She was as exhausted, as if she'd run a marathon, by the time she had changed into the loose-fitting cotton bottoms, baggy tee shirt and fresh underwear.

The torrential rain had subsided to a steady drum-beat, but she still had to shout to be heard, and she was as tense as a bowstring when he pushed open the door, glass of water in one hand and in the other a couple of painkillers that he held out to her.

'These might take the edge off. Found them in one of your kitchen cupboards.'

Mia silently accepted the proffered tablets and au-tomatically flinched as he levered himself down until he was kneeling at her feet like a supplicant as she sat on the edge of the bed. Or a guy about to propose to the woman of his dreams. A fine film of perspiration beaded her upper lip.

'I'm going to just try and feel my way around your ankle.' He looked up at her.

Mia was finding it very hard to actually hear a word he was saying because she was so conscious of his fin-gers on her skin, gently, very gently, stroking her ten-der, sensitive ankle. She was captivated by his eyes. Her breathing slowed and her mouth went dry. She felt giddy.

'I guess you're wondering why I should know any-thing about ankles and sprains,' he offered, and she nod-ded mutely. 'Well, believe it or not,' he continued, in the same soothing, best bedside manner voice as he began manipulating her foot in tiny, barely discernible circles, 'I did a summer job at a hospital when I was eighteen.'

'You did? Ouch, that *hurts.*'

'I'm sorry. It's going to a bit, I'm afraid. Try not to think about it.' He looked up and smiled crookedly. 'Think about me instead.'

'About you...' She did as he asked and then blinked a little unsteadily. Not a good command to give, because now all she could think about was his hands moving up from her ankle, up along her calf, slipping under the baggy bottoms to slide over her inner thigh...to go further...

Heat rushed through her body.

'Think about me working at a hospital. I was no more than a dogsbody, but you'd be amazed at what a dogsbody can pick up, and I've always been very good when it comes to picking things up.'

His voice was so quiet and so calming that she was aware of the pain in her ankle, whilst almost *not* being aware of it. He was very thorough and strangely tender for someone so big.

He told her about his hospital job. She really wasn't sure whether he was making it all up to distract her or whether he actually *had* worked in a hospital for three months.

He certainly seemed to know what he was doing.

When he asked her to tell him about her family, she sighed and complied. He vanished for a couple of minutes and returned with the first aid box she kept in the bathroom.

He was distracting her. She knew that. He wasn't interested in hearing about her family. Why would he be? She'd spent the past few days sitting opposite him and he'd barely noticed her existence, except on those occasions when he'd looked up and engaged her in something about the hotel. Other than that, she could have been a pot plant on the sideboard next to the platters of breads and pastries.

So did he really want to hear about her sprawling family? Her sisters? Her nieces and nephews? Or about that time when she was eight and they'd all gone on a family picnic by the sea, and she'd wandered off and ended up spending the night in the forest because they hadn't been able to find her for love nor money? Was he really as interested as he appeared to be when she told him about school, and about wanting to be different from her sisters, wanting to avoid university and an office job?

He seemed to be, because he kept asking questions, while busying himself with the bandage, wrapping it around her now swollen ankle with painstaking care.

He was a persuasive listener. The tablets had kicked in and the throbbing in her ankle had eased. The tension had seeped out of her and she'd never felt so relaxed.

Relaxed enough to sigh as she considered all the stuff she'd been through… Relaxed enough to say, as he neatly began finishing the job he had begun with the bandage, 'I guess it's because I come from such a close family that I ended up getting married so young…'

CHAPTER FIVE

'*MARRIED?*'

It wasn't often that Max was shocked, but he was shocked to the core now.

He almost burst out laughing at himself and his erroneous assumptions. Was his version of a divorced woman so one-dimensional? Did he really think that all divorcees were hard, bitter and plastered with war paint?

No. He didn't. But it was a telling assumption, and for the first time he found himself a little unsettled at realising just how pervasive his cynicism had become over the years. It coloured all his opinions and every aspect of his life.

Mia had told him that she felt sorry for him. Naturally, that was a laughable criticism. Anyone sharp enough to have mechanisms in place to deflect the slings and arrows of uncertain fate could never be an object of pity. The thought of it was ridiculous.

And yet, when he thought about it, his life was so intensely controlled...

He was accustomed to obedience on the work front.

He might have groped his way for a while, when he had been thrust into a position of responsibility at the age of twenty-two. He had been surrounded by men and women twice his age. Many of them he had been forced to let go. Many more he had been forced to relocate. He had gritted his teeth and done what he had had to do. Life in a boarding school from the age of seven had toughened him. Sacking people to refine a business that would have to pay for his siblings had toughened him even further.

And now, many years later and with a business that was a thousand times bigger, he had learnt every aspect of control.

Handing over the building and running of this hotel to Izzy was the first time he had ever let go of the reins and look where it had got him.

He should have been the overlord in the equation, and everything would have run to plan. He would have had his hotel with its marble and glass and infinity pool and wouldn't now be wading through a bunch of designs, purchases and supply chains that shouldn't have been required in the first place.

The truth was, though, that his control extended way beyond what happened in his sprawling empire. When it came to women, he allowed no one past a certain point. He had been raised with the consequences of impulse. His parents had specialised in that to the exclusion of everything else. He had been brought up to distrust the so-called power of love and the irrational need to let other people in. His parents had certainly been indulgent when it had come to their all-consuming love, and in the process had ignored everything and everyone else, including their kids. Or at least *him*.

Holding the world at a distance had been one of his strengths. But now he wondered just how insular he had made his fabulous, moneyed world. He let no one in. He knew his parameters at all times.

Coming here had been a step out of his intensely controlled comfort zone. Under normal circumstances, were one of his smaller projects to need a helping hand on the ground, he would dispatch a member of staff. But he had needed to find his sister, so he'd made the trip himself.

And, since then, where was all that control he had always held dear?

He had arrived to find his ideas for the hotel in tatters. His aim to find his sister and leave within a couple of days had been trashed. He seemed to be permanently engaged in a standoff with a woman he couldn't go near without wanting to touch.

There was a battle raging inside him.

Sure, he was attracted to her. She was an incredibly attractive woman.

He'd been out with very many incredibly attractive women. So why was it that this particular one had managed to get under his skin in a way no other woman had?

It made no sense because, beyond the physical appeal, she should have been a turn-off.

She'd kicked off by not telling him where Izzy was. That in itself should have solved the problem of hanging around. He should have just gone ahead and taken the practical route of hiring someone to find her. It would have been easy. Not the most desirable option, but an easy one, given the fact that Mia had dug her heels in and refused to co-operate. Hire someone to do the job, get Izzy back at the hotel within hours—job done, bye-bye Hawaii and hello to the concrete jungle that was the city of London.

But he hadn't.

He'd listened to her—but had that put paid to her mouthiness? Not in the least. She felt utterly free, it seemed, to say exactly what was in her mind. Sometimes, he could tell that she was trying hard to hold back, despite the fact that she worked for him, but the thread that held her back from speaking her mind was gossamer-thin and often broke.

And yet, bewilderingly, he didn't seem to object as much as he knew he should. He was beginning to think that, the more she tried his patience, the more attracted he was to her and the faster his self-discipline got flushed down the pan.

He was her employer! She worked for him. He had always made a point of keeping business very far removed from pleasure. You let someone who worked for you into your life, and you lost control of the reins. That had always been his motto.

And yet, not even her status could detract from her appeal.

And now, finding out that she'd been married…

Been married? Or still was…?

Had she been clear?

'Where is he now?' Max asked abruptly. He stood up and stretched his joints, then cast a satisfied look at the job he had done bandaging her foot. 'And don't try to stand. It looks like a nasty sprain. Bit of swelling but I suspect a day or so of painkillers and keeping it off the ground will do the trick.' He looked at her. She was rain-washed. Her hair was drying in a spiky way but it did nothing to detract from her sexiness.

'So?' Never one to dig deep when it came to women's backstories, he now found that he was burning with curiosity and impatient to continue the conversation.

'So what? I won't stand on the foot. At least not right at the moment. And thank you for…you know…bandaging this up. You didn't have to.'

'The guy you married. Where is he now?'

'Oh. Kai.'

'That his name?' He was still getting his head round the fact that the woman now resting her bandaged foot on the stool he had brought for her, the woman with the sparkling brown eyes and skin as soft as silk, could have been married…could still be, for that matter.

'He lives in Honolulu with his new wife, as it happens.'

'You're incredibly sanguine about that.'

'You think I should be bitter?'

'I think it would be understandable.' He pulled a chair closer to her and dropped down into it. What did the guy look like? More to the point, what had gone wrong? Curiosity dug deep.

'I was very young. We both were. We knew each other from school. You could say that we mixed in the same crowd and then, at some point, we became an item. Both of us came from large families and after we left college it just seemed natural for us to…take things to the next level.'

'You drifted into marriage.'

'Sounds awful, but we had really high hopes. In fact…' She paused and sharply looked away. 'It never occurred to us that it would all fall apart at the seams. That's how cocky and confident we were. But as it turned out we were way too young and, much as we got along, we'd never shared space together. We did everything as part of a group most of the time. We surfed and went to parties and hung out. We liked each other and we translated that into something else.'

'And then…?'

'You don't have to pretend to be interested in my life, Max,' she said gently. 'And you don't have to feel that you need to hang around here for a bit longer because you've been kind enough to bandage my foot.'

'I seldom do anything because I feel pressured,' he returned drily. 'Tell me what happened. I'm interested.'

'Things went wrong.' She shrugged. 'We started arguing. Kai wasn't cut out for staying in. He still wanted to party all the time. We thought we'd be great but in the end we couldn't even play house. It all started unravelling and eventually we called it a day.'

'And yet you seem to have gone past that pretty successfully.'

'I learnt from it.' Mia tilted her chin and firmed her mouth. 'That was years ago, and I made my mind up after that that I would never jump into anything without really testing the waters first. I'd have to be sure that any guy I went out with was the right one.'

Max wanted to laugh. Was there such a thing as 'the right one'? He very much doubted it. There were the loved-up and oblivious, like his parents. That seldom lasted. The magic wore off and in the blink of an eye someone was getting up to something they shouldn't with someone else. Too much fairy dust never augured well for the institution of marriage. Boredom had a nasty way of setting in and *then* where was the fairy dust? On the ground, being swept up by a disillusioned spouse.

Of course, in the case of his parents, the overpowering 'I only have eyes for you' love had lasted, but to the detriment of the kids they'd had.

Whichever way you looked at it, handing your emotions over to someone else and asking them to return the favour was never a good idea.

The 'right one' didn't exist.

A life lived logically was a good life, he mused. And if he ever decided to get married, well, a logical union would be just the ticket. Something that made sense. A business proposition, in a manner of speaking.

His eyes met hers and he held her gaze until she blushed and eventually looked away.

That blush said a lot, he thought with lazy satisfaction. He'd noticed it before—the way she slid her eyes away if he looked at her for too long, and the way she focused on him when she figured he wasn't looking.

A Pandora's box begging to be opened and he clenched his jaw, trying hard to stifle temptation at its source.

'You must be hungry,' he growled. 'I am.' He stood

up and strolled without his usual grace to the window that gave out onto a dark, rainy and windswept night.

'I… There's no need…'

Max, still struggling to hang on to his self-control after too much introspection, and way too much interest in a woman who should be no more than another employee, was more brusque than intended when he replied. 'Repeat—I don't do anything because I feel obliged to. Tell me what you want to eat.'

'I could make something.'

'Italian food? French food? Chinese food? Name it.'

'But Max…'

He'd flipped his phone out and gave her an enquiring, impatient look.

'Okay…anything. Chinese food.'

It took him under five minutes to instruct his dedicated driver to fetch the food as soon as possible. The conversation was brief. He simply told the guy to put a call in to the restaurant with the best Chinese cuisine in the city, give his name and ask them to bring enough to feed two generously.

It never failed to impress Mia just how much money talked. She knew the restaurant the driver would order the food from and they didn't do take away. But he would get one without any trouble because he was obscenely rich. Rich enough to buy the restaurant. Rich enough to have the luxury of never doing anything he didn't want to do because he felt compelled.

The air he breathed and the world he lived in were far removed from hers. He'd arranged that they meet at his partly-built hotel so that she could walk him through some of Izzy's ideas. Instead, here he was in her home, bandaging her ankle, and she wondered if he resented the call on his time.

'I'm sorry...' she began awkwardly.

He had returned to his original position on one of the wide, squashy chairs and now he tilted his head to one side and looked at her questioningly.

'Are you going to apologise for my being here?' he asked drily. 'Because, if you are, then it will turn out to be a replay of the conversation where you tell me that I didn't have to, and I can't be bothered to repeat my response to you.'

'You might have had plans for the evening,' she mumbled.

'My plans were to work.'

'You must miss your...er...life in England.' Somehow he'd ended up knowing a great deal about her and she wanted to find out something about *him.* Was that so unusual? Here they were, and the circumstances had shifted the normal barrier between them. She felt less like his employee and more like just another person.

Besides, they had to talk about *something.* It would be a disaster if they just sat and stared at one another in agonising silence, while her vivid imagination had a laugh at the expense of her common sense.

She hadn't been with a guy on her own for a long time.

The handful of dates she'd been on had been conducted with the buzz of anonymous chaperones all around, people coming and going on the beach, or in a bar or in a busy restaurant.

A sense of intimacy feathered through her, playing with her nerves and unpicking her composure, which had been pretty thin to start with.

'Which bit in particular are you talking about?'

Mia shrugged. 'You must have quite a busy social life. I mean...' she gave a smile that was a mix of re-assuring, mildly interested and screamingly polite '...you've quizzed me about my youthful adventure with Kai but I don't even know whether there's someone back there in England waiting for you!' She shook her head with rueful apology and laughed. 'I guess you must be involved with someone and, if so, then I can only apol-ogise for the fact that you're having to stay here longer than you'd anticipated.'

Outside, the steady pounding of the rain was like a background symphony.

'Why would you assume that I might be involved with someone?' Max eventually asked and this time, when she smiled, it was more genuine.

'Because...you're the kind of guy I guess certain types of women would be attracted to...'

'Certain types of women?' His eyebrows shot up and Mia blushed.

'Sorry. I didn't mean to offend you.' But what she *had* meant to do was deflect him from any suspicion that *she* might be one of those women.

'Firstly, you really need to stop apologising, and sec-ondly, it would take a great deal more than that to offend me. I'm curious, however, to know what these certain types of women might be like.'

Mia bristled because she could tell that he was mocking her. However, she'd started the conversation, and now couldn't see a way of abandoning it. Besides, why not be honest? She was curious. Did he have a type? All men had a type. What was his? It was shameful just how curious she was.

'Sophisticated,' she said, head to one side, frowning in thought while surreptitiously watching him.

There was only one light on in the room and the mellow glow emphasised the harsh beauty of his features. He was so achingly perfect, from the curve of his sensual mouth to the brooding intensity of his deep navy, almost black eyes. He had one hand on his thigh and his legs were spread apart, inviting her to look at the way his jeans were pulled taut across muscular thighs.

'Sophisticated and glamorous,' she added breathlessly.

'Sophisticated...' Max murmured. 'Glamorous... Well, yes, I suppose those women *do* fit the broad spec.'

Of course they would, Mia thought sourly, although still smiling as she looked at him. Sophisticated, glamorous men always went for sophisticated, glamorous women. No big shocks to the system there!

'Although,' he continued, 'there's no one pining for me back in England. It's been a few weeks since I went out with anyone, as it happens.'

'I'm surprised you're not married,' Mia said in a clear breach of the employer-employee relationship she knew she should cling fast to.

He was the most guarded human being she had ever met in her life. He couldn't have been more different from Izzy, from the way he looked to the way he acted, but then she was beginning to flesh out the bigger picture about their family dynamics.

He was the oldest, and he was the one who had been the powerhouse and decision maker of the family. She knew nothing about James, the mysterious middle child, the one Izzy absolutely adored, but she knew that Max had overseen his sister's movements with beady, watchful eyes. Wasn't that why she had ended up in charge of a hotel with a brief to kit it out just the way Max wanted? He had handed her a golden opportunity, just as long as it conformed to what he wanted, and if it didn't then he would not think twice about snatching back that golden opportunity.

He was a workaholic but even workaholics got married, had kids and assumed the mantle of a domestic life. Okay, a high-powered, rich-beyond-words domestic life, but even so...

The sophisticated guy would marry the sophisticated woman because that was always the next step on the ladder.

And Max Stowe was the epitome of drop-dead gorgeous sophistication. He oozed it from every pore. Women followed his movements out of the corner of their eyes and men tiptoed around him, in awe of that aura of powerful invincibility he seemed to radiate.

It had only been a handful of days, but she had seen enough to know that he controlled the world around him and everyone in it with an iron fist.

But she hadn't been kidding when she had let slip that she thought he lived a lonely life. She just couldn't help herself from wondering why he did.

'I don't pay you to be surprised about any aspect of my private life,' he murmured.

His words were like freezing water poured over her yet there was a darkening in his eyes when he spoke that made her skin tingle. He looked relaxed, lazy…and yet strangely alert. There was an undercurrent of sizzling sexuality in the air between them but she wasn't sure whether she was imagining it or not.

Of course you are. He just said that he liked sophisticated women…

'No. You don't…' Her voice hitched in her throat.

'But…' He shrugged and smiled slowly. 'It's no big secret that I don't do long-term relationships, far less marriage.'

'Why not?'

'Life's too short for the complications they bring.' His voice was deadly serious. 'I work hard and I'm only human. I enjoy having fun. But the fun stops when conversations about permanence begin.'

Mia was desperate to probe but the doorbell shattered the bubble they were in. She started and blinked as he vaulted upright and headed to the front door, waving her down, even though she didn't make a move to get to her feet.

He didn't do permanence. He didn't do long-term relationships. He would certainly have no sympathy for a sister who'd cut and run because of a broken affair. Strangely, the fact that he had not hauled Izzy back to make a case for herself was a credit to him. It showed that he had tried to see the bigger picture even though he fundamentally probably couldn't grasp it.

He returned with a selection of delicious looking food.

'I know the whereabouts of your kitchen,' he drawled, dumping the bags on the weathered coffee table he had dragged in front of the sofa where she was sitting. 'I'll bring in everything we need. You stay put. The less weight you put on that ankle, the faster it'll mend. Two days and you should be able to move around.'

The food was amazing. The conversation reverted to normal topics to do with the hotel. They talked about the budget that would be needed to landscape the grounds.

Her head was still buzzing with the taboo subject of his personal life, though...

Watching her as she ate, using the chopsticks like a pro, Max marvelled at a conversation that had veered wildly off course from the straight and narrow to the unpredictable and personal.

Being here, with the rain outside and darkness pressing against the windows, was like being in a cocoon. Being in this country was like being in a cocoon!

Real life with all its boundaries and restrictions was temporarily on hold.

He lowered his eyes, shielding his expression, but every pore and nerve in his body was tuned in to her as she delicately sampled the food straight from the boxes, making little noises of satisfaction that she probably wasn't even aware that she was making.

He'd brought over a couple of books from the bookshelf and stuck a cushion on top for a makeshift footstool. Her bandaged foot was propped on it, the other leg tucked under her. She was supple. She surfed! She was *going* to be supple!

The women he had dated in the past, those sophisticated women at whom he suspected Mia secretly sneered, largely abhorred anything to do with outdoor forms of exercise and swimming would have posed an impossible challenge. Their preferred form of exercise involved designer outfits and working out in a gym where they could see themselves in vast mirrors. Being soaked in open water would have sent them running for the hills. Those women seemed like a species from another planet.

Life on the other side of the pond was, what felt like, a million miles away.

The rigid parameters of his life were a million miles away...

He'd never had a break from being a tycoon. He knew that he was feared and respected in equal measure. From the age of twenty-two, he had made himself impregnable because he'd had no choice. To succeed in the hothouse of big business, you had to be tough, and being tough had come easily because he'd already had a head start in that area.

He'd been emotionally tough from the age of ten and he'd learnt how to use that to his advantage.

Now, over a decade later, he was an iron man.

But suddenly, here...

He questioned whether he had become so isolated in his ivory tower and so focused on maintaining control over every aspect of his life, both emotionally and professionally, that he had managed successfully to eliminate every shred of spontaneous experience that didn't conform to his exacting rules.

Mia surprised and unsettled him. She wasn't afraid to speak her mind. She resented him helping her and was unimpressed with his money. She constantly pushed against the *Keep Out* signs and, instead of slamming the barriers down further, he hesitated. He hesitated because he was oddly invigorated by the novelty of having someone question him.

The fact that he fancied her added to the mix.

All told, a little novelty went a long way and he was jaded. Life in the city was lived in fifth gear. He barely noticed the cool luxury of his house in Holland Park, with its marble and glass and soft silk rugs, and Hockney and Lichtenstein pieces interspersed with more unknown originals. He seldom visited his places in Barbados and the Cotswolds, although he did stay at his penthouse in New York, largely because he went there on business a fair amount. He almost certainly wouldn't spend much time on the family yacht his brother had just bought.

In under a fortnight, he would return to his comfort zone but, for the first time, he wondered if this might not be a chance to step out of the box.

He glanced around him. He'd already half stepped out of the box just by being here. He hadn't been in a place like this for a long time. Never, when he thought about it.

He didn't do hanging out in women's houses but, even if he did, none of the houses would have resembled this one. This was a house filled with its occupant's personality. Every book on the bookshelf told a story. The two hardbacks under her foot were tomes on the virgin rainforests of Borneo and *Gardens that Changed the World,* respectively. Her kitchen was a riot of colour, with reminders stuck on the fridge under magnets. The furniture was old, soft and enveloping. There was not a hint of white, marble, chrome or glass anywhere to be seen.

The house reflected Mia.

It was as much a novelty for him as she was. His resolve never to mix business with pleasure began to fray at the edges.

'Molokai.'

Absorbed in the improbable meandering of his thoughts, Max surfaced to pick up what she had been saying about Izzy's plans for the hotel. 'What did you say?'

'Were you listening to a word I've been saying?'

Max muttered something and nothing. He'd been listening but most of what she had been saying had been sidelined by the more pressing business of watching the movement of her mouth and wondering what it might taste like.

Wondering what it might feel like to rebel against his own self-imposed restraints.

What it might feel like to take a walk on the wild side for a week…ten days, max…

'You were telling me why my ideas for the hotel were flushed down the toilet…'

'I was *telling* you that Izzy went to a lot of trouble to come up with what she felt would really work for tourists wanting to immerse themselves in the real feel of Hawaii and the islands.'

'Carry on. I'm all ears. How is your foot feeling?'

'Much better.' A brief hesitation. 'There's no need for you to stay here any longer. I can make my way to bed and I'll be fine in the morning.'

'Hardly fine enough to trek through the grounds of the hotel so that you can fill me in on all those plans in the making.'

'No. Maybe not.'

'Which is why you need to carry on. Fill me in right now on what Izzy had in mind, ease me in gently to the way my vision for the hotel has been roundly discarded...'

'Well, she did some travelling to the other islands... You know, each island has its own identity. All you've seen is this island and you've only seen a tiny bit of it, the bit that all the tourists see. You see the beach and the surfers and the restaurants and food trucks, but there's so much more to Hawaii than all of that, and that's what your sister was so interested in finding out about.'

'So much more...'

'I *know* you think that when it comes to an expensive hotel cold, soulless luxury is the only thing a rich clientele would be interested in...'

Max burst out laughing, and when he sobered up his eyes were alight with vibrant amusement.

'Not,' he said, grinning, 'that you would ever succumb to gross exaggeration...'

Mia smiled sheepishly and dipped her eyes. 'We worked on it together, really. I think she was impressed by my vision for an eco-friendly outside space, with natural spots between the trees and shady areas bursting with home-grown vegetables and herbs.'

'So she decided to do a bit of adventuring... Did she also decide to stay put on one of the other islands in search of inner peace after her relationship ran aground?' He didn't expect her to answer that one and she didn't. She was staunch in her loyalty and he admired that. Between them, the Chinese food was beginning to congeal. He would see to that later.

'There's no need for sarcasm,' Mia said coldly.

'Absolutely none. Please. Continue. I'm all ears.'

He gazed at her, utterly serious, and she gazed right back at him with narrow-eyed suspicion.

'She got inspiration from all the different islands. Molokai... Maui... Kauai...'

'She...never said. I would never have guessed,' Max said heavily. 'It's inspired. I just wish she'd felt she had the freedom to discuss it with me. No matter.' He began to stand, reaching for the containers and the plates, his voice brisk when he next spoke.

'And don't stand up. I'll clear this and then I'll make sure you're settled with some painkillers to hand before I leave. And tomorrow...?' He paused and their eyes met. 'Well, it's time for me to see first-hand what you're talking about. I have the final say on what gets done on the hotel I'm paying for, but never let it be said that I'm not willing to see things from another angle.'

'And you'll go in with an open mind?'

'I'm taking it from that tone of voice that you're harbouring doubts about my sincerity...'

'Would you blame me?'

'I'm assuming that's a rhetorical question,' he drawled. 'But it's by the by, because the one way you can make absolutely sure that I give it a chance is to persuade me.'

'That's what I've just been trying to do!'

'I need more than persuasion from a sofa in your house, Mia. You tell me about all these inspirational islands…that's fine because you and I are going to travel to all of them and you can talk as much as you want about the vision my sister had for the hotel. And who knows? I might just buy into it…'

In the ensuing brief silence, he watched her face, and in his head, he thought, *What would it feel like to let go for once?*

CHAPTER SIX

THIS DIDN'T FEEL like work. Waiting nervously in her house, unable to relax but likewise unable to walk around because her bandaged foot was still hurting even though the sharp pain of the day before had eased, Mia had no idea how she had ended up agreeing to a four-day tour of the islands.

But, then again, how had she managed to end up confiding all sorts of personal details about her life to him? She rarely confided and she certainly never had heart-to-hearts with anyone about what had happened in her marriage. Had she been so distracted?

One minute, she had been solid in her determination to maintain a businesslike approach to their working relationship and, the next minute, he was carrying her into her house, dealing with a sprained ankle and somehow enticing confidences from her that should not have been revealed.

When she had closed her eyes the night before, she had been overwhelmed with an image of his dark head as he knelt at her feet and again she had felt that powerful urge to lace her fingers through his springy hair to see what it would feel like.

Now, waiting for him to show up at the time he'd said he would, her heart was leaping inside her and she had given up trying to project what this four-day sightseeing hop might look like.

When she started thinking about it, she had to ward off a panic attack, so she'd concluded that her best bet was to cross the bridge when she came to it.

He could have just given her time off work for her foot to heal, because wasn't that what any normal, considerate boss would have done in the circumstances? But, as he had said, time was money, and he didn't have a lot of time to play around with—not with England and his mega-high-powered life impatiently waiting for him. Plus, he was hardly the normal, considerate type, was he?

She just wished she could have felt more resentful, but as she waited for him to show up she couldn't quite subdue a simmering sense of excitement.

She had packed workman-like clothes. If he wanted to explore where Izzy's inspiration had come from, then he was going to be in for a shock, because he wouldn't be on a sightseeing tour of the usual tourist destinations and he wouldn't be taken to the sort of uber-luxurious hotels to which he was accustomed. Accordingly, she had packed a sturdy selection: two pairs of jeans and some cargo pants, tee shirts and hiking boots and thick hiking socks. She wasn't sure whether she would be up to any hiking boots scenario, but just in case…

He hadn't asked her what clothes to bring, so tough if he decided to pack stuff that was inappropriate.

When she thought about that, she couldn't resist smirking, but the tension was back full steam when, at a little after two in the afternoon, she heard the deep roar of his car as his driver pulled up outside her house.

The torrential rain of the day before had disappeared, replaced by the usual bright skies and warm sun. The weather here could be like that. All sound and fury one minute, gently caressing the next.

She opened the door and, even though she was well prepared, she still felt that automatic racing of her heart as she was confronted with him. Groundhog Day. That was what it was beginning to feel like. Whatever bracing talks she gave herself about self-control, one look at him and back she went to square one.

'How's the foot?'

Mia looked down then raised her eyes to his. 'Much better.'

'I've brought you this. Consider it a present.' He held out a fancy crutch. 'I'll obviously try to ensure that you put as little weight on your foot as possible, but that's not going to be possible much of the time.' He watched as she hoicked the crutch under her armpit. 'Unless,' he drawled, 'you want me to carry you…?'

'I'll be fine,' Mia said hurriedly.

He'd taken her rucksack and hoisted it over his shoulder.

He looked sinfully, wickedly sexy. Denim jeans, the usual tan loafers and a fitted, V-necked grey tee shirt that did amazing things for his body.

Mia averted her eyes. Somehow, in the muddle of being talked into this trip, she had failed to pin him down on the details, and as she settled into the back seat of the car she turned to him and said, urgently, 'I don't even know where exactly we'll be going…'

Max angled himself so that he was looking at her. 'To see a bit more of the islands,' he murmured. 'Wasn't that the recommended piece of advice so that I could have an idea of why all my dull and anodyne ideas were jettisoned? You told me that I needed to see the real Hawaii, so I'm just obeying orders.'

'I can't imagine you ever obeying orders,' Mia said under her breath, but not so quietly that he didn't pick it up, because he grinned and raised his eyebrows.

When he grinned like that, she thought distractedly, he was so...*engaging.* She could feel her natural defence mechanisms wobble a little. *Four days!* And she *still* didn't know what those four days were going to look like!

All about work, of course, because this wasn't a holiday, and he was a workaholic who would get his pound of flesh whatever the cost—but what was going to happen during downtime? There was only so much work they could reasonably be expected to do. What happened when the laptops got closed, the briefing was done and the accounts were put to bed? Even with his promise, she would remind him that after five her time would be her own to do with as she saw fit.

'Do you have an itinerary?' she asked briskly and frowned when he grinned a bit more.

'Of sorts.'

'What does that mean?'

'It means that I got someone to run through what I should be expecting on the various islands and I made sure they sorted out our trip accordingly.'

'You got someone...?'

'Nat was very helpful, and his suggestions were reinforced by what the tourist guide at the hotel had to offer. In the absence of knowing anything about the place, I went with the flow and booked various venues accordingly.'

'You should have asked me,' Mia said accusingly and his grin widened.

Dammit, she wished he would stop doing that. It was all she could do not to be seduced into thinking that this was going to be *fun*, when his expression was light and his eyes were amused and the harsh, ruthless, arrogant self-assurance that wound her up so much was not in evidence.

'I would have done,' he said on a rueful, insincere sigh. 'But I thought it best for you to focus on recovering after your little mishap. We can talk about the itinerary when we board the plane to Maui. That's our first port of call.'

'You *do* know that Maui is nicknamed the Beverley Hills Island, don't you? Which is not exactly what I had in mind when it came to showing you the inspiration behind Izzy's reworking of the hotel.'

'But we have to start somewhere,' Max murmured. 'Actually, when it comes to luxury, we'll be starting somewhat sooner...'

He jerked his head and Mia—who had not taken in where they were going, or even how much distance they had been covering in the smoothly purring luxury car—now saw that, yes, they had certainly arrived at the airport. But this was not the section of the airport with which she was familiar.

They were being driven to a shiny black jet and her mouth dropped open in amazement.

'We're getting there in *this*?'

Max nodded, already swinging his long body out of the car while his driver sprang into action and pulled open her door. Hand on the bonnet of the car, he leant in and met her eyes. 'Less stressful than battling with the stampeding hordes at the airport.'

Impressed to death, she hobbled alongside him into the jet. It was ridiculously opulent, big enough to fit up to twelve people, but it was soon obvious that they would be the only occupants.

The seats were a rich, buttery cream leather, the tables were highly polished walnut and the pale tufted carpet made her want to kick off her sandals and riffle her toes through its soft pile. Champagne was offered by a smiling, uniformed young woman. Mia shook her head. Max, barely glancing at either the woman or the tray, grabbed a glass in passing but he was already on the phone as they settled into their seats.

Mia realised that he was completely oblivious to his surroundings. He could have been on a bus for all the attention he paid to the luxurious jet.

The differences between them gaped wide. The differences between him and his sister were even more puzzling, given they both came from the same background.

She settled into the seat and gazed around her. Agenda? Itinerary? She had to drag her mind back to reality as she waited for him to finish his phone call.

Half listening, she realised that he was talking to his brother about a yacht. Had they just bought one? The level of wealth was mind-boggling.

'It's so weird.' She turned to him as soon as he was off the phone and he looked at her quizzically.

'Leading statement,' he said. 'Can't wait to hear where this is going.'

'All of this…' She made a sweeping gesture to encompass the jet, the flute of champagne, the leather, and the walnut and the hush. Because the young woman who had handed them drinks had tactfully faded into the background and the pilot was still on the ground, talking to whomever pilots of private jets needed to talk before they took off. 'You're not impressed, are you?'

He looked absently around him and shrugged. 'I stopped being impressed by the things money can buy a long time ago. When it comes to private jets, I've been on many, and many were bigger, faster and better-looking.'

'You're so different from Izzy.'

'So I'm beginning to conclude.'

'I mean…' Mia frowned and placidly bypassed the unwelcoming expression on his face. 'Of course I knew from the start that she came from a wealthy background, because she told me that she had been hired by you to handle the hotel as a first job experience. How many girls are blessed enough to cut their teeth on such a great job? But, if I hadn't known that, if I'd just met her out and about, there's no way I would ever have thought that she came from money.'

'Because…? And I ask because I don't suppose there's the slightest chance of closing this conversation down until you've said what you intend to.'

Mia was vaguely aware of an impatient edge to his voice, but she was a lot more aware of his forearm resting close to hers on the arm rest of the seat. Her eyes kept straying to its sinewy strength, the length of his fingers, the dark, fine hair.

'Because she never dresses in designer clothes and she honestly doesn't seem impressed by the fact that she can pretty much have whatever she wants. I guess, judging from all of this…'

'I'll have to take your word on that,' Max intoned abruptly. 'I can't say I've ever paid much attention to the clothes my sister wore.'

The pilot was now in the plane and he walked over, shook hands and chatted about the flight. He inspired confidence. It was a relief, because Mia had never been in anything as small as this before. She could surf with the best of them, and the ocean didn't scare her, but on the three occasions when she had flown on a plane she had been sickly nervous of the fact that the ground was nowhere near beneath her. Now, peering out of the circular window, she had disturbing visions of being in a matchbox high up in the air, tossed about by air currents. Her stomach swooped.

She'd been talking about Izzy but now, as the pilot headed towards the cockpit, the conversation was lost in a wave of high-wire tension.

'I've never been on a private jet before.' Her voice was unnaturally high and she cleared her throat.

'I gathered,' Max said wryly.

'No. I mean I've never…' She breathed in deeply as the engines roared into deafening life. She wished she had some vital statistics to hand. How many of these tiny little pieces of metal fell from the sky every year?

Maybe, in this instance, ignorance was bliss. 'I mean…'
She clutched the arms of the chair in a death-defying
grip. 'I've never been up in the air in anything quite as
small as this…'

'Are you okay?'

'Absolutely!'

As the plane began to taxi, she felt her nerves begin
to shred even though she told herself that this was probably safer for getting from A to B than some of the taxis
she occasionally took after she'd been out at night. It
might feel as fragile as a paper plane, but it was as
sturdy as a rock. Surely?

'What's wrong?' Max asked sharply.

'I feel a little sick.'

'Jesus. Are you *scared*?'

'No,' Mia squeaked.

'Look at me!'

She stared straight at him as the jet shot upwards
at what felt like supersonic speed. She felt a rocket
couldn't have gone faster. Her insides were all over the
place and she wanted to whimper even though her head
was telling her to behave.

Two things happened at once. She squeezed her eyes
tightly shut and…he kissed her.

He kissed her!

It was so unexpected that Mia's eyes flew open in
shock. His mouth on hers was a drug, obliterating everything. She felt the warm dart of his tongue against hers
and she sighed, succumbed to the kiss, succumbed to
something she realised she'd been fantasising about practically from the first moment she'd clapped eyes on him.

And nothing could have prepared her for how sweet it would be. How much she would want it to go on and on, for ever. There was no space inside her for fear.

The hand that been clutching the armrest crept up, tangling in that luxurious dark hair, and the other hand somehow managed to find the curve of his cheek.

She felt her breasts tingling, her nipples spiking against her bra, and she was wet, so wet, between her thighs.

He was cupping her face and playing with her ear with one finger. The tiny movements sent electric currents racing through her body, lighting up every part of her, as though she'd suddenly been plugged into a live socket.

Then just like that he pulled away and cold air filled the void.

It took a couple of seconds for Mia to snap out of her daze.

'You should be all fine now,' he murmured, sending her one last look before sitting back and finishing the glass of champagne.

'All fine? What? Oh!' Of course. He'd kissed her and she'd lost herself in it like a teenager in the full throes of adolescent lust. Her lips tingled from where his had been and every pore in her body was buzzing with energy. She wanted to touch her mouth with her hand, and she made sure she didn't give in to any such temptation by firmly clasping them together on her lap.

She'd been terrified as the jet had soared at a vertical angle into the clouds and he'd kissed her to distract her from the terror. He'd seen it writ large on her face and he'd kindly gone for a swift remedy, and it had worked because she had yielded to that kiss and enjoyed every second of it.

Humiliation roared through her. She went hot, then cold, then she shook her head and rolled her eyes and cracked a smile.

'I should thank you.'

Their eyes collided and for a few seconds Max remained silent, his expression veiled.

The last thing he'd considered doing when he'd hit Hawaii in search of his wayward sister was making an impromptu tour of islands he wasn't remotely interested in visiting.

That said, the last thing he'd expected was a woman furiously digging her feet in and denying him the information he had travelled thousands of miles to obtain. And, from there, everything else had been a slow unravelling of life as he knew it.

What he *did* know was that he'd never felt more invested in having this woman.

It was a weakness. He knew that. He loathed the way it undermined his hard-headed logic, but it was an overpowering urge he couldn't seem to fight.

He'd seen her today dressed in her usual 'day at a building site' uniform, and he'd smiled, because no one could accuse her of putting herself out to dress up for him.

Indeed, what she wore was an act of defiance.

He wondered how she would react if she knew just how sexy she was in shapeless cargo pants and a pair of flat sandals, with her hair tied back in a ponytail.

Her beauty was luminescent.

And his body had reacted accordingly. He'd breathed her in as she'd settled into the seat next to him and, of course, predictably, she had entertained him with her forthright, no-holds-barred, uninvited insights into his personal life.

Was it because he'd expected her mouthy, outspoken, full-frontal attack and her sudden panic on the plane had driven him to do what he'd been longing to do for days? Their eyes had met, he'd seen the utterly soft and vulnerable fear there and he'd thought of one thing and one thing only. Kissing her. Kissing that fear out of existence. Kissing her until she forgot everything but *him*.

She'd melted into him and her soft acquiescence had sent his libido shooting into the stratosphere. For the first time in his life, his self-control had been utterly and completely obliterated.

And that had scared the hell out of him.

It was one thing musing thoughtfully about breaking his own self-imposed rules about never mixing business with pleasure. It was one thing contemplating tasting the freedom of straying out of his comfort zone. It was quite another to discover that he just hadn't been able to help himself. His body had taken the decision-making out of his hands, and that had never happened before.

Yet now, even as he sensed her withdrawing at speed, covering up the fact that she had enjoyed that kiss as much as he had, he itched to pull her right back into him and carry on where they had left off.

He could have her. In that moment, he had sensed her want, had known what he had suspected…

But hard on the heels of that pleasing recognition came one that was slightly less welcome.

Lust was one thing but the thought of distancing himself and denial in the aftermath... A moment's pleasure was never worth an hour of post-pleasure angst and guilt, and some inner radar was telling him that post-pleasure angst and guilt might be her natural response.

'Thank me? For the distraction?' He shot her a crooked, amused smile and didn't take his eyes off her flushed face. 'Did you enjoy it?' he murmured, voice low and husky.

'It did the job,' she returned crisply, which made him smile more. Where most women would have offered seconds, she could barely meet his eyes. He felt back in control and that split-second of disturbing unease had been banished. In fact, he felt buoyant.

'In that case, glad to be of service.'

'Tell me about the itinerary.'

'The itinerary...'

'Where *exactly* we're going and where we'll be staying and other such things.'

'I have a printout somewhere.' If she ran any faster from acknowledging that kiss, then she'd be in danger of tripping over her own feet in her haste.

'Perhaps I could see it?'

'We could always wait until we get to the hotel,' he drawled. 'Review it in more relaxed conditions. It's a short flight.'

Flustered, Mia chewed her lip. She was still so unsettled she could barely think clearly. Bringing things back to business should have worked, should have focused her mind, but he wasn't playing ball, and she was at a loss as to how to drag the conversation back to where she wanted it.

Did you enjoy it...?

What kind of question was *that*? she inwardly fumed. He'd been laughing at her. She was sure of it. She'd done her best to act cool and collected but, not to beat about the bush, she'd practically hurled herself into his arms the second his mouth had touched hers. He was a guy with a lot of experience, and he would have had to be blind to miss the shameful enthusiasm of her response. Of course he was laughing at her now! Did he think that she had seriously imagined that he actually fancied her? Yes. Yes, he did.

'I don't even know what hotel you've booked.'

'You'll like it. Trust me.' He grinned and she returned a withering look because she was pretty sure she wasn't going to like what he said next, not judging from the barely contained laughter in his navy eyes. 'Or maybe not... You might find it just more tedious luxury after you've been forced to endure the horror of a private jet.'

'I never said that this was horrible!'

'I know, but somehow you've managed to remind me at every turn that my life choices are too materialistic and therefore leave a lot to be desired.'

Mia sniffed. He didn't sound offended. He sounded amused. The wretched man sounded *relaxed* while she, on the other hand, was in state of churning, inner turmoil.

'I'm very sorry if that was the impression I gave,' she said coolly.

'No, you're not.' He was still grinning. 'If it's one thing you're never sorry about, it's giving me a headache.'

'That's not true!' She bristled.

'I like it,' Max murmured softly.

Wrong-footed for the second time in as many minutes, Mia shot him a nonplussed look from under her lashes.

'I can't believe you're lost for words.'

'I… I…'

'I'm surrounded by people who aim to please. It's refreshing to be in the company of someone who aims to criticise.'

'I don't…aim to criticise…'

He liked it? He found it refreshing?

Mia stifled a sudden rush of pleasure. He found her refreshing? Since when? He certainly hadn't found her refreshing when she'd refused to disclose his sister's whereabouts.

And then…when he'd kissed her…

Had there been more to that kiss than a perfunctory desire to stop her from going into a full-blown meltdown?

Mia had been too long in the game of being careful to let her head be swayed by some good-looking guy with a few well-chosen, softly spoken words. Wasn't she? She was a down-to-earth girl from a down-to-earth family who wanted a down-to-earth guy. When it came to relationships, she was serious. Even though her marriage had crashed and burned, she and Kai had both been on the same page when it had come to wanting the joy of lasting commitment. They just hadn't been able to find that with one another.

All this sizzling excitement that filled her when she was within touching distance of this guy counted for nothing. It was a little reminder that she was flesh and blood with urges just like the next person which, given the fact that she had been in a physical deep freeze for way too long, was fantastic. But, in the end, that was all it was.

If she allowed her imagination to get too carried away, then she would be making a grave mistake, betraying all those principles she had been brought up to hold dear. Not going to happen.

Which brought her back to the importance of grounding the conversation before it developed a momentum of its own.

'This all happened very fast.' She was bolt upright in the leather seat and, although she wasn't looking at him, she could feel his eyes lazily watching her. She fancied that he could detect every shift in her posture, in her voice, in her expression. 'And I didn't have much time to lay down any ground rules.'

Was it possible to feel someone's eyebrows shoot up?

'Ground rules?'

'Yes.' She angled herself so that she was looking at him but immediately regretted that because now all she could focus on was his beautiful mouth. Her eyes flicked up to meet his. 'And, before you tell me that I work for you, I need to remind you that my hours are nine to five.'

'No need to remind me.'

Mia licked her lips. 'We can work out an agenda for during the day, and I'll do that just as soon as I get to the hotel, but at five my working day ends and I… I think it's only fair that I be permitted to do my own thing.'

'I wouldn't dream of handcuffing you to my side and forcing you to work strictly to rule.'

'Good.'

'I expect you know the islands well?'

'I've been to a couple of them,' Mia said, relaxing, because at last here was a conversation she could run with. 'In fact, I spent a few days showing Izzy around when she mentioned that she wanted to see more than just Oahu and Honolulu. She was very much interested in getting off the beaten track. Not that you could ever say that bits of Maui were off the beaten track.' She smiled. 'I guess you'll want to see more than just the touristy side of the islands,' she said. 'We could hire a tour guide.'

'We could do that,' Max murmured, non-committal. 'We'll discuss all of that when we get to the hotel and start going through the nuts and bolts of how this is going to play out. Tell me what I can expect.'

'What you can expect?'

'I've never been to this part of the world before.'

Mia leaned back against the seat and half closed her eyes and watched flashbacks from her past. Growing up with the ocean a stone's throw away… Learning to swim and then, when she'd been barely able to walk, being in-troduced to a baby surf board… The rowdy pleasure of coming from a large family and the numerous picnics and camping weekends they had enjoyed… Her love of the lush greenery and her determination to try her hand at an outdoor life, to explore that side of her that loved nature in defiance of her sisters, who had all entered various professions… When she had started helping Izzy with the 'boring paperwork', as she had called it, it had come as a surprise to discover that she rather enjoyed it.

The jet was landing by the time she had finished talking.

'You should have stopped me.' She blushed and looked at him a little guiltily. 'I've been babbling.'

'Vital information,' Max murmured. 'Right. Hold tight. We're landing. Grab my hand if nerves get the better of you.'

'Taking off is a lot worse,' Mia confided. 'At least there's ground beneath us when we land.' But she didn't shake off his hand when he covered hers with his. In fact, she liked it there, liked the way it made her feel safe.

Four days in the grand scheme of things was not even a blink of an eye.

Stick to work…quit at five…and everything would be fine.

She was barely aware, as the jet shuddered to a stop, of squeezing his hand, or of feeling the infinitesimal pressure as he returned the gesture.

CHAPTER SEVEN

THE HOTEL WAS the last word in opulence. It was perfectly positioned to gaze majestically down at the ocean, interrupted only by meticulously beautiful landscaped gardens, in the middle of which was a huge kidney-shaped swimming pool.

A long, black BMW was waiting for them as they left the jet. From luxury to more luxury, Mia thought.

She was being offered a rare glimpse into how the seriously rich lived and she was guiltily aware that a person could get used to this. It certainly beat tramping through airports, hunting down bags on carousels and then wending your way on public transport in searing heat, dragging a case behind you and apologizing every five steps because you'd accidentally crashed into someone.

Surrounded by birds of paradise as they approached the cool, marble dream of the hotel foyer, Mia tried to forget the dress-down utilitarian outfit she had chosen to wear. She sternly reminded herself that this was work. She wasn't on holiday. She wasn't going to be lounging by the side of a pool, summoning waiters over for cocktails. Indeed, she hadn't even brought a swimsuit with her.

Max was making sure to stick by her side, conscious of the fact that she wasn't quite back on her feet yet, and as soon as they got their respective keys he urged her to go upstairs and relax.

'You can meet me in the bar at six,' he said. 'We can grab a drink, an early dinner and go over the schedule for the next few days.'

Mia hesitated. Wherever she looked, she saw glamour. Designer clothes, designer luggage and so many designer sunglasses that she wondered giddily whether she had stepped into a spy movie.

Max fitted in perfectly without even trying. His clothes were positively shabby in comparison, and yet he looked more sophisticated than everyone around them. It was the way he carried himself and that way he had of implying that he just didn't care what anyone thought. He played by his own rules.

It was his 'leader of the pack' aura that turned heads and she saw very many swivelling surreptitiously in his direction.

She headed up, leaving him in the foyer, to discover that her room adjoined his and was connected by a door that was locked but presumably could be unlocked.

It was a magnificent space, with a sitting area, a small open-plan kitchenette and vast glass doors that led out onto a private balcony with spectacular views of the ocean. The bathroom was as big as a dance floor, with a bowl-shaped, free-standing tub and a walk-in shower with so many various knobs that she wondered whether she would be able to make sense of it without a manual.

The pain in her foot had eased sufficiently to allow

her comfortably to undress and she took her time with a bath.

Her bag had been brought to her room prior to her entering, and unpacking it was a depressing reminder that, while she had been privately smug at the thought of Max not being properly equipped for anything other than luxury, she had failed to consider that she might be poorly equipped for anything other than outdoor casual.

In a short denim skirt and white tee shirt, which had seemed just the ticket for exploring on her own and eating in cheap local eateries, she now felt horrendously under-dressed. And half hobbling with a crutch under one arm didn't help matters when it came to her self-confidence as she later found her way to the bar.

It was a big hotel, with a bewildering amount of rooms on the ground floor and several restaurants dotted in various locations. Mia thought that there should have been an option to download satnav when they'd arrived because you needed it in a place as big as this.

It was a relief when she made it to the bar only ten minutes late, and she spotted him immediately. He was working, frowning in front of his laptop, completely oblivious to his surroundings and with a drink of some kind on the table next to him.

How did he do that? she wondered. How did he manage to look so carelessly elegant without even trying? How was it that, in an expensive bar filled with expensive-looking people, he stood out?

She took a deep breath and threaded her way towards him.

She'd hoped that his attention might remain on whatever was on the screen, but no such luck. He turned to watch as she slowly moved towards him.

Mia had been embarrassed at her outfit before, but she was red-faced and flustered by the time she slowly levered herself into the chair next to his.

'I'm—I'm sorry I'm a bit late,' she stuttered, feeling the hot burn of self-consciousness in her neck and face. 'And apologies,' she continued stiffly, 'but I'm afraid I didn't bring the required wardrobe for a place like this...'

Why on earth had she just said that? Why had she drawn attention to what she was wearing? Of course, she knew why. She felt horribly out of place and the words had shot out of her mouth before she'd had time to think them through.

Max looked around him, as though only now noticing the shameless luxury of their surroundings.

Then his navy eyes rested on her thoughtfully.

Mia bristled defensively, bracing herself for something caustic. Would it be too much to remind him that she was a *gardener* by profession, accustomed to working outdoors? Maybe she could remind him that this was a work situation, so who cared what she wore? Her role wasn't to look like an ornament.

'Does that bother you?' he asked mildly.

'No, of course not,' Mia lied unconvincingly.

'Of course it does. Why wouldn't it? Women look at other women. It would be strange if you didn't find it discomforting to think that you might not be blending in.'

Mia heartily wished that she had kept her mouth shut. But she hadn't, which didn't mean she intended to indulge any long sermons about the stupidity of peer pressure.

She peered down at the drinks menu and made a deal of deciding what she wanted.

'A glass of white wine,' she said when someone materialised to take their order.

He ordered a bottle and rattled off a list of things for them to pick at.

'An early night.' He shrugged. 'Unless you would rather go to the restaurant?'

And just like that Mia knew that he had ordered bar food to spare her having to go to the Michelin-starred restaurant in clothes she'd admitted she felt uncomfortable wearing, and he'd done it without making a fuss.

Something inside her swooped and, when she smiled, it was with genuine warmth and just the merest hint of gratitude.

Nothing was said but their eyes met for a few seconds, and for one moment they were perfectly attuned and on the same page.

It was an effort to remain neutral and professional for the remainder of the evening. The drinks came, the bar food arrived and they talked about the forthcoming agenda.

Maui and Kauai. One stunning and luxurious, the other equally stunning and perfect for nature-lovers. Lack of time dictated that exploring the rest of the islands would have to be put on the back burner.

'I never knew my sister was a nature lover,' he mused as the plates were taken away with a flourish.

After having drunk two glasses of wine, Mia returned honestly, 'It's not that hard to think you know someone only to find that you don't know them nearly as well as you thought you did.'

'By which, I take it, you're referring to your ex-husband?'

Where that would normally have sent her rapidly into reverse, drawing up the bridges to avoid an awkward conversation, the wine had relaxed her, along with that fleeting moment when she had warmed to the streak of empathy and understanding she had glimpsed in him.

There was only the vaguest recognition, somewhere on the periphery of her brain, that he really had an excellent memory. Also…just how much had she been lulled into confiding? And how had he managed to wriggle underneath her barriers, considering they had nothing in common and most of the time she didn't even like him?

She thought of that kiss when he had wanted to distract her…and her skin heated up at speed and she was lost for words for a few seconds.

How had they ended up talking about Kai? Where did her failed marriage fit into a conversation about the islands they intended to visit?

'That's the problem with marriage,' Max murmured into the lengthening silence. 'It ends up throwing up all sorts of problems that you never thought could possibly exist and, before you know it, what started off as the perfect fail-safe relationship degenerates into a train crash.'

'Not always. My parents have been happily married for nearly thirty-five years.'

'Which makes it all the more surprising.'

'Surprising? What's surprising?' When she looked at her glass, it was to find that it was empty. Her brain felt foggy and she was so alert to his presence that the rush of blood in her veins was an unwelcome reminder of the dramatic effect he had on her, against all odds.

'That you haven't sought to move on.'

'Who says I haven't?'

'Have you?'

'I've had other things on my mind.'

'So no one has come along to relieve you of those "other things"?'

'I've been on a couple of dates, but I'm not interested in jumping back into the water.'

'Maybe you just haven't met anyone compelling enough to encourage you to test the temperature.'

Mia looked away. Her pulse was racing, and for the life of her she couldn't work out how this guy could get her to say stuff she would normally never reveal.

To go deeper into this conversation would open up all sorts of confusing avenues. He didn't belong in any of those avenues. He didn't belong anywhere in her life except on a professional basis as her boss.

And yet, the atmosphere sizzled between them, fragmenting her thoughts and turning the ground beneath her feet into quicksand.

'Tomorrow…' she said, and he looked at her for a few seconds in silence before nodding.

'Tomorrow, work begins!'

'So I should head up now, if that's all right with you?'

She began to stand so that he would get the message loud and clear and he waved his hand in easy dismissal.

Max watched her retreat. Her blushing admission about her outfit had not surprised him. Despite the feisty exterior and the almost complete inability to refrain from saying what was on her mind, with or without encouragement from him, she was oddly vulnerable at times, and in her vulnerability so intensely feminine.

And so unbelievably sexy.

He'd followed her progress as she'd made her way towards him and, if he'd wanted her two days ago, he wanted her more now. Released from his own self-imposed restrictions on having any kind of relationship with an employee, was his mind now taking advantage to wander freely?

He had been aware of her in the back of the car as they'd been driven to the hotel, and he'd had to drag his thoughts out of the realm of fantasy.

In this hotel, with its contingent of preening women in designer clothes, she had stood out, her natural beauty marking her out from the crowd, and the fact that she couldn't see that was both bewildering and touching at the same time.

It roused a protective urge in him that was halfway between amusing and unsettling.

Two hours after she had retired, and after a series of calls and emails to CEOs involved in various levels of delicate deal-making in various countries, he retreated to his bedroom.

Her room was next to his, separated by a door. A locked one, admittedly, but the mere fact that a single door separated them played into the fantasies revolving in his head.

The room was icy, thanks to the air-conditioning, but despite that he fancied he could still feel the heat outside, slowing down his reactions and turning his thoughts in directions not taken before.

He had failed to arrange a time to meet the next day and he wasn't shocked when she texted bright and early the following morning to tell him that she would take breakfast in her room.

'Why?' He bypassed the dreary, long-winded business of texting her back and ended up calling her.

'Just washed my hair...couldn't possibly get it dried in time...removing the bandage from my foot...just wanted to hobble without the crutch in private to see how it felt...'

Blah, blah, blah.

'Meet me in the foyer.' He glanced at his watch, cutting through whatever further excuses might have been waiting in the wings. 'In an hour.'

There were a couple of things he needed to do, and both afforded him a great deal of satisfaction.

He was waiting for her when she made it to the foyer bang on time. The travelling outfit had been replaced by one almost identical, bar a slightly different range of colours. Did anyone really need a pair of trousers with enough pockets to hold everything bar the kitchen sink? Surely not?

He rose smoothly from where he was sitting and headed towards her.

Mia paused fractionally. She'd made her excuses with

breakfast, having decided to take time out to remind herself that they were here for business, not pleasure.

Sadly, the very second she clapped eyes on him her heart skipped a beat, her mouth went dry and her eyes became nailed to his face.

Surely she couldn't be falling for this guy? Surely common sense would have prevented that? And yet there was an unescapable awareness that something inside her was being handed over to him... Surely it couldn't be her heart?

She gave a rictus smile and indicated her foot.

Keep it casual. Polite conversation whenever you're not talking about work-related matters...

'So much better,' she said when she was in front of him. 'I still have the crutch, but you were right. It was just an uncomfortable sprain. Probably not even that. Anyway, definitely on the mend! I took a couple of tablets first thing and I can almost walk on it.'

'Excellent news,' he murmured.

'Have you got an itemised plan for how the day is going to play out?'

'I certainly have.'

Mia, waiting for clarification, was disconcerted when he cupped her elbow and began gently ushering her away from the revolving glass door that led outside.

'Where are we going?' She looked behind her with consternation as he continued to guide her back into the hotel.

'You were uncomfortable with what you were wearing in the bar,' he said. 'You're not going to feel any more comfortable in the restaurant tonight.'

'Wh-why would I be in the restaurant?' Mia stuttered on a tide of rising panic.

'Where else do you plan on eating?'

'Out! After work…after five…having a look around…'

'Exploring an island on a crutch isn't the cleverest of ideas, is it?'

'It's on the mend!'

'And that's exactly how we want to keep it! Don't forget, you're here to do a job, and that job is going to be considerably easier if you can walk comfortably on that foot of yours—and hours outside in the baking heat, trying to find places to eat while hobbling from one café to another, just isn't going to do. I need you to be up and moving as fast as possible.'

Mia scowled.

'You still haven't explained…'

'Here we are,' he said with notable satisfaction.

It was a measure of how absorbed she was with him that she only belatedly registered that he was guiding her gently but firmly towards the bank of expensive shops nestled in the heart of the hotel.

Mia had no idea what was going on and she certainly wasn't about to be led anywhere like a sheep. 'Here where?' she questioned politely. 'I'm seeing a shop.'

'You didn't feel comfortable in the clothes you brought with you—' he shrugged expansively '—so we're going to change that.'

'Please don't tell me what I will and won't be doing!'

'A handful of outfits.' He shrugged. 'Pick what you like.'

'I don't need a handful of outfits!'

'And I don't need to be the object of avid curiosity because you're making a scene.'

Mia's eyes slid to where two elegant saleswomen were watching their antics, although they immediately averted their eyes when spotted.

Where Max could brush off that sort of thing, because he honestly didn't give a damn, *she* couldn't. She hadn't been raised that way. Other people's opinions *mattered* to her.

'This is ridiculous.' She tried to make her protest as cool and collected as possible. 'Furthermore, I can't afford anything from a place like this.'

'Do you imagine for a single second that I would allow you to pay for anything from this place? You're here because of me and I intend to cover all the costs.'

Their eyes met and held for a few seconds. There was no way she could express what she felt. How could she articulate that? That choosing clothes to have dinner with him felt dangerously intimate?

'Don't fight me on this, Mia.'

Mia glanced towards the elegant boutique and made a decision. 'Fine.' She shrugged and looked at him squarely. 'If you think it's necessary for me to have a new wardrobe, then I'll get a new wardrobe, but I'm a big girl and perfectly capable of choosing my own clothes. So, if you want to arrange a time and a place to meet, I can join you later.'

She pulled out her phone to check the time, crisply arranged when to meet and watched as he raked his fingers through his hair before nodding wryly.

It was an experience, what could be done with a bottomless bank account in a very expensive boutique. Mia was hardly aware of what was being chosen because the eager shop owner, having marvelled at her figure, proceeded to turn her into a mannequin for the next hour. At last, dazed, Mia was standing in front of an array of black and gold bags, that conveniently would be sent to her room so she didn't have the bother of carrying anything, and wondering what, exactly, she had purchased in the flurry of things being tried on.

'How was the torture chamber?' were Max's first words when she met him at the designated place.

'It was fine!' Mia said. She knew that she had been dragged way out of her comfort zone. In her world of surfing, landscaping and working in the open air, she had been able to shun fancy, girly-girl clothes, faintly scorning the preoccupation of the prom queen types who only cared about how they looked.

She was forced to concede that she had actually enjoyed the experience, and even more so when she guiltily thought of him looking at her in her new-fangled get-ups. Surely she couldn't be that shallow?

They settled into the back of the car he had commissioned for his personal use as and when. The scenery they looked at as they drove along the uncrowded roads was scenery that was in her blood. Overhanging trees, lush and in colours of every shade of green, over-sized bushes awash with purple and red flowers, fringing the road in bursts of vibrant colour. It rained a lot on this island, she explained, hence the lushness of the foliage.

The driver was an expert tour guide, who could name

every tree and flower, and Mia found herself competing with him about who knew more, even though she was still so aware of Max sprawled beside her.

They crossed one-way bridges and they opened the windows, breathing in the warm breeze. He asked a lot of questions, and it was just as well, because it established a bit of normality between them after his earlier provocative remarks.

If only she could truly relax! She had been to the island many times and she directed them to the Halfway to Hana café, where they indulged in banana bread and shave ice. It was on a busy beach, with lots of noise and music. She vaguely remembered feeling smug at the thought of him in surroundings just like this— sitting in a hot café and being jostled on all sides, informal and brash, with loud music and lots of people and food to be eaten without knives and forks. Yet, when she looked at him, he couldn't have appeared more at ease in his surroundings.

She heard herself jabbering away about all manner of things throughout the course of the day, and it was blessed relief when at last they were back at the hotel at a little after four.

'Meet me at seven,' he told her, naming one of the fancy restaurants in the hotel as she was about to head to the lift, leaving him behind. There were few minutes in the day when he wasn't working and the day's outing had taken up quite a few of those precious minutes.

Back in her hotel room, she forgot what she'd hastily picked in the boutique. She pulled out the assortment of clothes and it was almost as though she was seeing most of them for the first time.

Her hand hovered over a dark blue shift…and then veered away to something smaller and more figure-hugging in just the sort of bold pattern she wouldn't usually wear…but loved the look of.

She used to wear dresses like that…

Back in the day. Before, she suddenly realised, a broken marriage had instilled a level of reserve she never really used to have.

Once upon a time, she used to laugh a lot more, wear brightly coloured clothes and let her hair lie long and loose over her shoulders and down her back.

Suddenly pierced with nostalgia, she stuck on the dress and looked at herself in the mirror, and was startled when someone much younger looked back at her.

Where had that girl gone and how had she not noticed her absence?

Mia made her way down to the restaurant. She carried the crutch, but she didn't really need it, and she almost regretted having brought it along because it felt like a prop.

The restaurant was small and intimate, and yet busy. Waiters buzzed around with huge circular trays. The atmosphere was casual, but nothing could quite disguise the fact that it was a mega-expensive venue. There was something about the tasteful pale green of the walls, the soft, faded silk rugs underfoot, the crisp white linen of the table cloths and the mellow lighting…

She saw him as instantly as she'd seen him in the bar the evening before. This time, he was dressed more formally in a white, short-sleeved shirt and a pair of charcoal-grey trousers. He looked so heart-stoppingly masculine that she faltered for a few seconds and then powered on.

Max had managed to secure the perfect table in a corner of the room, and he watched her progress with a veiled expression. He'd been waiting for fifteen minutes in a state of keen anticipation that was uncool, to say the least.

Why the hell was he playing with fire? Since when had that been a recommended game for a guy who exerted such control over every aspect of his life?

But today it had been torture, being with her for hours, breathing in her fresh, floral scent, his eyes stubbornly lingering on her startlingly pretty face.

He had given up trying to rein in his imagination.

He wanted her. It was something he couldn't quite explain to himself.

Maybe if he hadn't sensed that chemistry between them, hadn't tasted the softness of her mouth or watched the hungry flick of her eyes when she thought she was unnoticed… But he had and it fired him in ways that were shocking.

Now, watching, he felt the hot rush of blood heavy in his veins.

She was wearing a dress and it was the first time he'd seen her in one.

She looked so…*delectable*. He breathed in slowly, taming his body. He didn't play games when it came to women but now…this…felt like a game, a dangerous game, and he couldn't wait for the starting gun to be fired.

CHAPTER EIGHT

AFTERWARDS, MIA WAS hard-pressed to figure out just when the atmosphere between them had shifted.

The dress had done something for sure, flicked a switch in her head, because as she walked towards him, barely using the crutch at all, she felt like a million dollars. The brush of cool silk against her skin was seductive. And then his eyes…veiled and hooded…as he watched her get closer.

The food was amazing and there was champagne.

And the conversation was so work-orientated as he plied her with questions about bits of the island they hadn't got round to seeing. They discussed the various financing avenues for some of the plans his sister had begun to put in place. They worked out what would make sense and what wouldn't. More champagne was poured. He all but brought out his laptop so that they could study costs and projected revenues.

It was a conversation that should have relaxed her, because it reinforced the status quo between them without her having to remind herself of it every five seconds.

But behind the affable exchange of ideas, and discussion of timetables and supply chains, there was the steady pulse of something else, something she glimpsed just like a shadow, when she felt the brush of his knee against hers under the table or caught the glitter of guarded amusement in his eyes and in the curve of his mouth.

Another conversation was being had under the surface and it was *exciting.*

She liked it. She liked the fizz of the champagne, the fizz of excitement running through her veins, the quiet, casual elegance of their surroundings and the shiver of not quite knowing what was going to happen when the evening drew to an end.

As it was doing now. They floated from the restaurant to the bank of lifts, purring up to their floor.

'So...' Max drawled, staring at the brushed steel of the lift door. 'What do you think of the accommodation?'

'My room?'

'Like it?' He shifted to glance over at her.

'It's the nicest hotel room I've ever stayed in—not that there have been very many. Of course, when it comes to delivering on the sort of atmosphere Izzy had in mind for—'

'I'm not interested in talking about my sister or what she happened to have in mind.'

'I just thought...' The doors pinged open and here they were, in the wide marble and walnut corridor leading to their adjoining rooms.

'We've spent the past two hours talking about work,' Max murmured. 'We now have two minutes before we reach our rooms to talk about what we both really wanted to talk about over that dinner.'

Mia's heart sped up. She wasn't looking at him, but she could feel him with every pore in her body. Then their eyes met and held. She had a choice to make. A fierce longing tore into her, and as it did common sense and prudence, two of her loyal companions when it came to her emotions, began to shrivel under the hot glare of her simmering excitement.

She was young! Didn't she *deserve* to have a bit of reckless fun for once in her life?

She had never anticipated this sledgehammer kind of lust, but here she was, and what was she going to gain by denying it?

Mr Right had yet to come along but why not enjoy Mr Wrong? Mr Wrong would be *fun*!

'Maybe we could have a nightcap…or something…' she murmured and just like that she jumped off the side of the precipice.

Max gazed down at her averted face and clenched his hands as every dream and longing he'd ever had seemed to coalesce in this single moment.

Jesus, how could he ever have underestimated the power of desire?

He wanted to take her right here and right now, push her against the door and do what both their bodies wanted them to do.

He might have done if there'd been the slightest chance of privacy. Instead, he curled his fingers into her hair and lowered his head and stifled a groan of absolute pleasure as his mouth covered hers. He shifted his big body against her, felt her slenderness curve into him, and a syringeful of adrenaline couldn't have had a more dramatic effect on his already soaring libido.

'We have to get out of here,' he groaned thickly, pausing only to step back an inch.

He didn't give her time to answer, instead simultaneously flipping out the key card and lifting her off her feet.

The crutch fell to the ground, but he ignored it as he carried her caveman-style into his bedroom, which was shrouded in silvery light.

He liked that, liked seeing her—liked even more the thought of seeing her with nothing on, of satisfying the curiosity that had been burning in his blood since he had first laid eyes on her.

He hadn't known how the evening was going to end. He'd *hoped*, but she was an unpredictable entity, quite unlike the women he was accustomed to. He had made sure to contain the conversation, to keep it in safe territory. Pride had dictated that he not make a blatant pass at her, but that had all gone down the drain as they'd headed to their bedrooms.

He'd been able to keep his desire at bay so far. He'd wanted to play it cool—hadn't happened.

She was on his bed, just where he'd dreamed of her being. The dress was still on, but the shoes were off, and the way she was watching him, half-shy, half-bold and plenty hungry, made him cup his hardness, controlling it through his trousers.

He breathed in deeply and half closed his eyes, hunting around for his self-control which had gone AWOL.

Then he began to undress.

Mia watched in downright fascination, mouth parted, nostrils flared. She was so wet between her legs that she had to control an irresistible urge to touch herself, to satisfy the tickling there.

He was wearing navy boxers and her eyes were riveted to the impressive bulge distorting them.

Her breath hitched as those boxers dropped to the ground, and she shuddered and closed her eyes, parted her legs as the mattress depressed under the weight of him.

'I want you so badly,' he groaned, straddling her.

Mia could only stumble out a thick, 'Same…' and then he was reaching under the dress and tugging down her panties, and she couldn't get them off fast enough.

His mouth ravaged hers and she writhed under him, trembling, hot and aflame. He'd taken protection from his wallet, and he was fumbling to rip the foil pack open, but then he was over her once again.

Her blunt nails dug into his back as he pushed apart her legs and drove into her, fierce and deep, filling her and… *God, it felt so wonderful.*

Nothing in her life had ever warned her that her body could feel like this. Her brain shut down and she could hear herself cry out, a high, rasping sob as she came, soaring, soaring and splintering into molten hot orgasm.

Afterwards she lay still, breathing hard, utterly spent.

Her body was cool as he rolled off her, but then he manoeuvred her onto her side so that they were facing one another, belly to belly, her leg draped over his, her arm resting lightly on his waist.

It felt so natural.

'I'm sorry,' he said, and she frowned. 'You still have your dress on. I... It's not like me at all...'

He cupped her face and looked at her gravely, rue-fully.

'This isn't how it was supposed to happen. You shouldn't still be wearing your dress. I just couldn't stop myself, couldn't slow down. It was all too fast, and I am truly sorry.'

'Don't be,' Mia whispered. 'It was the most won-derful thing...'

'For me too. Incredible. But next time it will be even more incredible.'

Next time... Mia loved the sound of that. Fast sex in a hotel room with a guy she wasn't in a relation-ship with...

All of that went against the grain. It just wasn't her, and she didn't know how cool and casual she would have been if this had turned out to be a one-night stand.

She hadn't given that a moment's thought when she had entered the bedroom with him, but now something inside her leapt at his words.

'Next time,' he delivered huskily, unsteadily, 'I'm going to go slowly...'

Mia's eyes fluttered. She had just come, her body was still warm with the afterglow of her orgasm, and yet she could feel a rising tide of desire overtaking her.

Was this how a person emerged after years of celi-bacy? From deep freeze to fire in the space of ten sec-onds?

She curled against him and he smiled, stroked her

dampened hair away from her face and kissed the corner of her mouth.

In return, she trailed her hand over his chest and smiled back.

She began to prop herself up so that she could get rid of the dress but he stayed her.

'This time,' he said, sitting up, 'I'm going to pleasure you the way I should have done before. Slowly. I was selfish and it's not going to happen again. Trust me.'

He removed the dress. She leant back against the pillows and saw the flare of hunger darken his eyes as he looked at her. Never had she felt more desired. A girl could get used to this kind of thing.

She reached to unclasp her bra from behind, freeing her small breasts.

'You are beautiful,' he said in a roughened undertone. 'It's going to take every ounce of willpower to do what I'm about to do...'

'Which is?'

'I'm going to run a bath.' His voice was shaky. 'And I'm going to fill it with bubbles, and I'm going to soap you very, very gently, and then I'm going to dry you and carry you right back to this bed so that I can make love to you, taking my time.'

Every single word made her blush like a teenager transported for the first time to cloud nine by the boy of her dreams.

She let herself be pampered by him. Being naked with him like this was crazy and great at the same time and, whereas she might have quailed at the thought of walking around without her clothes on with anyone else, she found that she positively relished it.

He did as he had promised and Mia luxuriated. The bath was big enough for both of them, and sliding into the warm water with all the fragrant bubbles was heavenly.

This—all of it—felt heavenly.

Her voice was soft and relaxed as she chatted, leaning back against the white porcelain, eyes half-closed, feeling his thighs on either side of hers. The bubbles concealed their bodies, but she knew his now, and her body tingled in eager anticipation at touching him again, being touched by him.

What was going to happen in this evolving scenario? She didn't know and she didn't care.

He got out first, dried fast and roughly and told her to stay where she was. Then he ran more hot water and began to soap her at the back of her neck, massaging her shoulders, curving his big hands over her breasts.

He had wrapped a towel around his waist and he looked like a beautiful Roman emperor with his dark hair slicked back, emphasising the strong, angular lines of his remarkable face.

He beckoned for her to stand and she did, feeling exposed as the water ran off her in rivulets.

She tilted her head back, her hair damp against her back, and closed her eyes. Her skin cooled and then his soapy hands were on her, slowly working their way from her breasts, along her stomach and then parting her thighs so that he could take his time, gently soaping between her legs.

'I can't keep standing!' She gasped. 'It's too much.' Her legs had turned to jelly and she subsided back into the water...but not for long...just until he lifted her out, dried her then lifted her again and carried her over to the bed.

She was still draped in the white towel. His had slipped lower down his lean hips. He stood back and looked at her, and she smiled at him and squirmed under his scrutiny.

'Slowly this time,' he murmured, unhooking his towel and dropping it to the floor to move closer to the bed. 'This time, I'm going to explore every inch of your beautiful body.'

Max wasn't quite sure how he was going to achieve that. There she was, with that towel loosely covering her body, and he was raring to go, as horny as though he hadn't just had her. She was exquisite—so slender, so smooth—every bit of her in stunning proportion, from her small breasts to her narrow waist to the length of her legs.

He slowly removed her towel and a rush of blood fired up inside him with the immediacy of a conflagration. She was incredibly delicate, but so well-toned from the amount of physical exercise she got from just her daily activities.

He joined her on the bed, trailed his finger across her cheek and then along her collarbone and enjoyed the way she trembled, sighed and quivered. He found the tip of her brown nipple and teased it in ever-decreasing circles until it was stiff and throbbing. In response, she covered her face with her arm, but he could see her mouth half open with pleasure.

It took willpower he'd never known he had to resist the urge to go hot, hard and fast. Instead, he lowered to take one throbbing nipple in his mouth, and she moaned as his questing mouth suckled and teased.

His big body tensed and then relaxed when she stroked his shoulder lightly, curling up to caress his ear and the side of his jawline.

Her legs were open for him. He could feel her knees pressed against his thighs, inviting him, and he couldn't resist. But still he took his time, inching down her stomach with his tongue to circle her belly button and jab delicately into the small indent, while the rhythm of her body told him just how much she was enjoying this.

He planned on her enjoying it even more. He was going to take her to paradise and back, and it felt very, very important that he do that…that he show her just how much he could pleasure her, how much they could enjoy one another. Nothing had ever seemed more vital.

She weakly tried to clamp her legs together as he nudged his way there, but he gently, firmly parted her thighs, a hand on the soft inner flesh of either one, and darted his tongue along the slippery groove of her womanhood, sheathed in soft, downy pubic hair.

He probed the delicate folds with his tongue to find the pulsing nub of her clitoris and he settled down between her legs, teasing that sensitive place while she squirmed against him, pushing towards his mouth and pulling away, coming so close to the edge and then backing off.

He wasn't going to let her come against his mouth, but he couldn't hold off much longer.

He raised himself, breathing hard, and for a few moments just rubbed his aroused hardness against her silky wetness, only breaking off to protect himself and relishing the few seconds it gave him to try and contain his wild response.

This time round, he came into her slowly, easing himself in and feeling her tightness around him with a groan of pure pleasure. When he kissed her, it was with great tenderness. He kissed her mouth, her eyes, the soft flesh of her cheek. He waited for her to be just ready for him to take her to that place and, when she was…when she urged him on, face flushed and her body burning up with wanting…then and only then did he thrust deep and hard, taking them both to a shuddering orgasm.

He'd never felt anything like it.

Utterly spent, he lay on her for a while.

'I'm too heavy for you.'

You're perfect for me… Mia thought.

He rolled off onto his side and then pulled her in against him.

'Was that as amazing for you as it was for me?' he asked softly, and she smiled.

'Better. Better than amazing. After my marriage broke up, I guess I hid away from relationships. At first, I was just grieving the loss of my marriage, but then after a while… I suppose I just found that I wasn't interested.'

'You must have had guys asking you out?'

'When I thought about dating again, my mind went blank. It became a habit to be on my own. I enjoyed it.'

'Everything becomes a habit after a while.' He stroked her hair from her face.

'What's become a habit for you?'

Max hesitated. Out here, being with this woman, was like being in a temporary bubble and, from within it, his life back in London seemed gilded but jaded. Was that because work had become a habit? He shifted uncomfortably at the thought of that because he was defined by work. Where would he be if it became no more than something that filled the days? Something he had grown accustomed to, without any merit of its own?

Of course, he had women, but if *her* habit had become avoiding the business of dating, then surely his was avoiding the business of dating for longer than two months?

'There's a certain tedium attached to the business of making money,' he eventually murmured.

'But you don't have to do it, do you? Surely you have enough?'

He grinned at her. 'You'd think.' He frowned. 'It's not so much the business of having cash in a bank account. If it were simply a matter of money per se, then you're right. I have enough. It's the enjoyment of how that cash gets made that's addictive.' He grinned again at her silent scepticism. 'And maybe...' he added thoughtfully.

'Maybe what?'

'And maybe...' His voice lightened. 'We should grab some sleep. I have a packed itinerary for tomorrow and the crutch will have to be left behind. I'll carry you if needs be.'

Maybe the habit of having to make money because his siblings depended on it had become too ingrained to break, but really, was there any need to drive himself for the sake of James and Izzy? He'd done his bit. James, certainly, was incredibly successful in his own right, contributing to the family empire while also running his own highly profitable computer software businesses, and Izzy was clearly a big girl now, even if he hadn't seen it coming.

So what was with the pressure to keep earning?

And what did he think would happen if he kicked back?

Would he have to re-evaluate his priorities? He dismissed any such thought with consummate ease.

Mia kissed his chin. There were times, few and far between when something happened between them, when she glimpsed a vulnerability inside him that roused feelings in her, far removed from sexual feelings, that were oddly tender.

He'd confided in her, but then he'd stopped, and she wasn't going to press him to tell her anything he didn't want to.

He was proud and he was arrogant but not because he set out to be that way. That was simply the way he *was*, nothing to do with trying to impress or instil fear. She loathed all forms of arrogance but she'd come to see that, with Max, it was a trait that was intensely appealing, and very, very sexy, because it was so utterly unconscious.

She began to sit up, scouting around for the dress and her underwear.

'Where do you think you're off to?' he drawled lazily, running his finger along her spine and then tugging her back so that she fell against him, laughing.

'Off to my room,' Mia told him, wriggling so that she could look at him.

'No way.'

'What do you mean?'

'I might want you in the middle of the night, and then what am I supposed to do if you're not in my bed?'

Mia laughed. Inside, she was thrilled—*too* thrilled. She wanted to keep reminding herself that this was a fling and nothing more, no castles in the air waiting to be built.

She opened her mouth to remind him that he was her boss, and if they had temporarily suspended common sense then that didn't change the reality of the situation, but she didn't go there. She knew, almost immediately, that she didn't want that untimely reminder to spoil anything.

She'd just had the most incredible experience of her life. Why would she want to give him the wherewithal to end it? Like a thief in the night, she wanted to grab whatever more there was to come, steal those experiences so that she could hoard them inside her for the rest of her life.

On the other hand, there was such a thing as pride.

'Who says I would want to be awakened at some ungodly hour in the morning to…to…?'

'To make sweet, passionate and unforgettable love

with me?' He kissed her, a long, slow-burning kiss that had her weak with wanting more.

'I'm not used to sharing a bed with anyone,' she said truthfully, and he drew back to look at her seriously.

'Nor am I.' He kissed her eyes and the side of her mouth, tugging her hair so that he could feather more kisses along the slender column of her neck. 'But there are such things as exceptions to rules…'

'There are, I guess.' She tried but how was she supposed to resist what he was doing to her? His words were as seductive as melting honey. Wading through them to get to the cautious, sensible person she was at the other side seemed an impossible mission.

She sank back in his arms and allowed herself to be thoroughly kissed.

And sleep that night?

Very broken. She was so conscious of the weight of him next to her. In the darkness, she could make out his outline, one leg splayed across the cool cotton sheets and his arm across her nakedness even when he'd fallen asleep.

At some point she too must have fallen asleep, because she was roused, slowly and sensuously, by the nudge of his swollen girth against her, finding her building wetness.

'You said,' he murmured with laughter in his voice, 'that you might object to being awakened at an ungodly hour in the morning by me…'

'Did I?' She curved against him and reached down to feather her finger along his throbbing penis. He was rock-solid. She could feel the veins of his shaft and he inhaled sharply when she teased the tip of it with her thumb in small, circular movements. 'I can't remember that at all.'

She felt his rumble of laughter. If he could tease her beyond sanity, then she could tease him as well, and the silent darkness was a comforting blanket, squashing any vague notions of shyness she might have felt.

She manoeuvred herself with dexterity until she could administer to him with her tongue and her mouth. She had never been this intimate with a man before and it was a slow, sweet process of discovery.

As she licked and teased with her tongue, as she folded her lips over him and gently sucked, she was finding out that he was as weak as she was when it came to resisting the build-up of desire.

She had absolute control here, in this bed, in the darkness of the night, over this big, invincible, self-assured male, and she loved the feeling.

She gasped when he hoisted her gently so that he could do to her exactly what she was doing to him.

His face buried between her thighs and the dart of his tongue sent her pulses racing, deprived her of breath, and they pleasured one another for as long as they could before it wasn't enough.

Their lovemaking was fast and hard and she came on a sob of wrenching abandon, shuddering as her orgasm brought tears to her eyes.

How could she ever have thought that sleeping on her own in a cold bed could be better than this? And how had she never been curious about the joy of sex when you were still warm from the languor of sleep?

'Time for sleep,' he mock-ordered in a soft, amused voice when their breathing had finally returned to normal. 'We have a packed agenda tomorrow. I can't have you waking me up all the time to satisfy your needs.'

Mia giggled and mentally added 'funny' to the list she was compiling in her head. Where had that one-dimensional guy gone? The one she had written off as a workaholic with not much else going for him? Every second she was in his company revealed more and more complex and fascinating sides to him.

She certainly didn't wake him, at least not for the remainder of the night, although she couldn't resist reaching out when, at a little after six the following morning, she woke to his warmth next to her on the bed, so close, breathing deep and even, begging to be touched.

She greedily stole a long, satisfied look at his beautiful face, drinking in the strong lines, so much less forbidding in repose. He had the most amazing lashes. Long and thick and dark.

Then she touched him, touched and settled her hand around his shaft, keeping it there as he opened his eyes and looked at her.

No words were spoken. Some time during the night—or maybe in the early hours of the morning... she didn't know when—he had obviously switched off the air-conditioning and chosen to use the overhead fan instead. Now, the faint whirr of the blades was the only sound in the bedroom.

That and their breathing.

Eyes locked, she pushed clear the sheets and continued slowly to massage him, ever so gently, but firmly building a rhythm, watching with mounting desire as she began taking him to the edge. His groans were deep and unsteady and his fingers curled into the sheet.

He erupted in her hand with a long moan of satisfaction. She felt his hot liquid running over her flesh and nothing, she swore, had ever felt better.

'Wicked.' His navy eyes glinted and he pulled her down to him. 'But very, *very* nice.'

'Happy to be of service,' Mia said, kissing him and sliding one leg over his so that she could ease the urgent ache between her thighs.

And lovemaking, as she soon found out, was not one-sided with him.

He took her to the same heights she had taken him, and afterwards she was so pleasantly content that she could have fallen asleep again.

'Shame we have to work,' she said, drowsy and flushed in the aftermath of their morning lovemaking, and he smiled a long, slow smile.

'Work? I don't think so. For once in my life...' His tone was oddly quizzical. 'I think I'm going to take some well-deserved time out...'

CHAPTER NINE

TIME OUT WAS...a holiday.

Max hadn't been kidding when he'd told Mia that time out was a once-in-a-lifetime experience for him. When was the last time he'd jettisoned work in favour of relaxation?

They spent three nights in Maui. They were driven to local beauty spots as Mia's foot healed. There was over one hundred and twenty miles of coastline and over thirty miles of beach. They went to South Maui and sat with an elaborate picnic at one of the tables at Makena Beach, watching the people and the activity, and the deep turquoise sea and the billowing clouds, blowing fast in a blue sky.

She was discovering just how the world of the truly rich worked and it was nothing like anything she'd seen in her life before. People jumped at his command. After their first night together, the following day he had announced that he wouldn't countenance her sleeping separately from him.

'We could...er...get the hotel to unlock the adjoining door,' Mia had suggested.

He was used to obedience. He spoke, people listened and then they duly did as they were told.

She could understand how Izzy had fallen into line with all the laws and regulations he had laid down over the years.

She wasn't his sister, however, and, although she was his employee, they were now on a different standing, in a different place, and she was not going to succumb to the overwhelming power of his personality.

At least, she certainly wasn't going to join the troupe of *yes, sir* people who surrounded him.

She fought to stick to sleeping apart but an open door between their suites had been a recipe for a very disrupted second night.

He'd come to her bed and scooped her up, had carried her to his, and then had duly delivered her right back to her own bed. But she missed him. If he wanted to have her right there at hand, then it was a two-way street, because she wanted the same thing.

By night three, all notion of sleeping apart had duly been abandoned.

'You're very bossy,' she'd told him at one point, and he'd burst out laughing.

'I have no idea what you're talking about. No one's ever called me *bossy* before.'

'That's because they're all scared of you,' Mia had retorted without blinking an eye, which had resulted in yet more mirth.

'Everyone but you,' he had said softly.

'When you come from a large, noisy family, it doesn't pay to be shy and retiring.'

But she was uneasily aware that the power of his personality and his assumption that he called the shots was an almost irresistible force and, quite often, she just relished basking in his alpha male strength.

They left Maui on the very same private jet that had delivered them there, flying in to Kauai.

He'd booked yet another luxury five-star hotel.

Now, as the jet disgorged them into brilliant sun, and humidity that made her clothes instantly stick to her back like glue, Mia tilted her head up to look at him.

He took her breath away. Especially now that her thoughts were no longer forbidden. She was *allowed* to admire him; she was *allowed* to appreciate his superb masculine beauty. The very slight breeze ruffled his dark hair, which was longer now, and her breath caught in her throat. He was in a white polo shirt and a pair of light grey shorts that just about hit his knees and loafers, and he looked every inch pure sex on legs. His fingers linked through hers was a vibrant reminder of the bond they now shared.

Over the past few days, he had expanded his wardrobe. The prospect of actually going to one of the many designer outlets and trying anything on had clearly bored him to death so he had simply snapped his fingers and got someone to do the leg work, returning with everything he'd asked for. He'd simply glanced at what had been bought, nodded and got someone else carefully to put them away.

'You're so spoiled,' Mia had said, although his complete expectation that he could be spared all manner of what he called 'dreary, non-profitable nonsense I can't be bothered with' was somehow incredibly appealing and very amusing.

'Why do what other people can do better?' he had countered. 'I'm a lousy cook, so I have a personal chef, and I dislike shopping so I get someone else to do it for me. Seems to make perfect sense, as far as I'm concerned.'

'This hotel we're booked in,' Mia said now, as they were escorted from the opulent confines of the jet to a similar level of opulence in a shiny black Range Rover.

'Yes?' Once inside the car, he turned to her and raised his eyebrows. 'I'm beginning to recognise a certain tone of voice. It usually warns me that your school mistress hat is about to be donned...'

'No idea what you're talking about,' Mia sniffed, and he grinned.

'Have I ever told you you're very sexy when you're wearing that particular hat?'

'I admit I *am* about to offer a suggestion which you may or may not like...'

'Would I need a stiff drink to deal with what's coming?'

Mia looked at him but trying to maintain any hauteur was out of the question when she saw the warm, teasing glint in his eyes.

Had she ever felt this comfortable with any guy in her life before? Even Kai?

'It's fine staying in posh hotels, but you know Izzy had something else in mind for your hotel. In fact, there's a hotel she specifically visited this island to stay on. She was so enthusiastic about it afterwards. Showed me photos. Well, I think it would be a nice idea for us to go stay there. I know it might be a bit inconvenient, because you've booked this place we're heading to for a couple of nights, but…'

'I could go with that,' Max said thoughtfully.

'Really?'

'Really,' he said, voice wry. 'Why the doubts in the first place?'

'You like your comforts.'

'Who doesn't? Mia, answer me truthfully. Would you rather be in this car or standing in a queue waiting for a bus to trundle along, in soaring heat and insane humidity.'

'I never minded before,' she said stoutly. 'I happen to be very accustomed to taking public transport to get everywhere. Or cycling. In soaring heat and insane humidity.'

'But, my darling, that was before you met me.' His voice was low and lazy and teasing.

Mia shivered.

Had she changed? Had she grown used to his world? No, she was still the same girl she'd always been, even if this girl was now moving in a different world. What had changed was that this girl now had fun. He could make her laugh the way no one else could and every second in his company thrilled, challenged and excited her. But what was going to happen when she packed her bags and left that world behind?

He had said that this was time out for him, and he hadn't been lying. Work had been left behind in Oahu. He touched base with his sprawling empire for a couple of hours, often in the early hours of the morning. They didn't talk about the hotel or any of the myriad things that needed doing.

What had started as a four-day trip had very quickly blossomed into a ten-day plan.

'I can do whatever I want.' He had shrugged when she had asked him about that. 'Working all the hours God made does confer certain advantages. Freedom of movement is one of them.'

She'd been guiltily thrilled at that, but time was moving on and was she digging a hole for herself by settling into this uber-lavish life he had handed her on a plate? Shouldn't she be remembering that there was no such thing as a free lunch and that, when the time came to say goodbye to all of this, she might just find it harder than she could ever have imagined?

Shouldn't she be remembering that when the time came to say goodbye to him she might just find it impossible?

They had fun. The lovemaking was intense and extraordinary. They seemed to physically fit one another like a hand in a glove. They talked and laughed but no mention was ever made of anything beyond the moment. He had no expectations that what they had was going to last. When he spoke about returning to London, she was noticeably absent from any of the scenarios.

She had talked herself into taking what was on offer, because she deserved to have a bit of fun in her life for once, but had she bitten off more than she could chew?

He was a man of the world, experienced when it

came to picking up women, enjoying them and then moving on without a backward glance.

She was wet behind the ears in comparison.

'I'm the same person I always was,' she said now. 'I haven't changed.'

'No?'

'Have you?' She turned the question to him. Suddenly, it felt very constricted in the back of the car. He looked at her through narrowed eyes and she flushed, wondering whether he could read what was going through her head.

'Not getting where you're going with that question,' he drawled, and the teasing warmth she had grown accustomed to was absent.

Suddenly, she wanted nothing more than for this sudden tense atmosphere to go away. What was the point in trying to find out whether there was more to what they had than this? Gut feeling told her what would happen if she pressed the point. He would walk away. She knew it.

With sudden clarity, she recognised what she had wilfully been hiding from herself. She had developed feelings for him. Strong feelings. Feelings that went way beyond lust, desire and all those other convenient descriptions she'd been using.

Lust and desire were passing viruses. Once she'd established that with herself, she'd had no trouble reasoning with herself that she was in no danger of being hurt. But now…

His fabulous eyes were on her face, incisive, penetrating and looking for…something she had no intention of revealing.

'You don't work as much as you used to,' she said, deflecting his question. 'Do you think you'll slow down when you get back to London?'

'Not a chance of it,' he murmured, dropping his eyes, his long, lush lashes shielding his expression for a few seconds before he looked at her once again. 'This is a holiday, but holidays don't last for ever…'

'You're so right.' She smiled while something inside twisted painfully, because if this wasn't telling her like it was, just in case she started getting ideas, then what was? 'The reason I asked is… I'll be very happy indeed to go back to my usual life. I miss my surfing and, believe it or not, all this luxury travel is terrible for a girl's figure!'

'How so?'

'Not enough exercise and too much fine dining. I shall end up the size of one of those humpbacked whales in Maui if I'm not careful! Also, I just thought about my backlog of work. Neither of us has been up to speed with work-related issues.' *Work-related issues?* She sounded like a business manual!

'I'm assuming there won't be a lot of fine dining when we shift location to whatever resort you have in mind?'

Mia began to relax. Somehow, they'd skirted around what had suddenly felt like a contentious issue, and she was pleased to be back in known territory.

Except…something had been added to the mix and she would be an idiot not to pay heed. He'd reminded her that all good things would have to come to an end.

'And as for your other work,' he said, 'I don't think

taking a breather for a few days is going to cause any insoluble problems with whatever work you might have on at the moment, will it?'

Mia frowned and thought about a couple of her outstanding projects. She had been in touch with the clients, explained the situation, and had emailed them various landscaping ideas. It would take time to order in just the right plants anyway, and they had been happy to wait until her return.

That said, pride clamped firmly round her fragile heart, stiffening her backbone. If he could issue his opportune reminders, then surely she could respond in kind?

'I'll set aside some time later to deal with any outstanding issues,' she murmured.

'And let me know if you run into any roadblocks...'

'Why would I do that?' she asked, surprised.

'I'm extremely good at sorting out road blocks, my darling.' He sent her a slow, curling smile that made her shiver and sent a shot of hot adrenaline racing through her bloodstream.

From tension to blistering excitement in the space of five minutes. Was it any wonder she had landed herself in more hot water than she could ever have imagined? She wasn't adapted for an emotional life lived in the fast lane.

'Really?' she murmured, keeping her cool and giving no inkling to her tumultuous emotions. 'And how would you solve those sorts of roadblocks?'

'I'd get whoever was kicking up a fuss to get in touch with me.'

'Now you sound like someone from the Mafia.' But her eyes were glinting with helpless amusement.

Max laughed, his gaze resting on her face, looking at her as though she were the only person on the planet. 'Nothing so dramatic,' he drawled, feathering his finger on the inside of her wrist and setting up a ferocious fire trail of response inside her. 'Or dangerous. I would merely give them enough money to persuade them that I need my woman by me for a few uninterrupted days.'

His woman. Giddy thought. Also foolish, because she wasn't his woman...she was his passing interest. 'A few uninterrupted days' said it all.

'Well,' she said crisply, 'I'm sure it won't come to that. I have very understanding clients, and in Honolulu people are patient when it comes to getting work done.' She paused and looked at him seriously. 'But if I *do* encounter any problems—' she grinned, lightening her tone '—I'll make sure *not* to tell you! The last thing I'd want is for any of them to be scared away by a Big Bad Wolf!'

She looked ahead as the car slowed and realised that they were here. Destination reached before the conversation could go down any more tricky roads. 'Looks amazing.' She directed her dancing eyes at him. 'Make sure you lap up the luxury. You never know where I'm going to take you tomorrow!'

Max gazed at the ocean in front of them. It was after six. Behind them, nestled in swaying trees, was a beast of a motorbike that he had rented a couple of days ago so that they could tour the island and get to all the places that Mia had told him in no uncertain terms he needed to see if he were to fully understand his sister's vision for the hotel.

He hadn't ridden a motorbike since his university days. Along with his vague plans to see something of the world before settling down and joining the rat race, motorbikes had been ditched when his parents had died and he'd had his wake-up call.

Along from the trees, via a network of winding paths through coconut palm trees and giant firs, was the eco-hotel where they were now staying.

When he'd first seen it, he'd thought they'd made a mistake and landed up at someone's house. A triangular children's drawing of what a house should look like, with a red roof and weathered turquoise walls and wide shallow steps leading up to a heavy wooden door. Around them, there must be a million different types of tree and bush and flower and fern, all pressing against the open clearing around the hotel, for hotel it was, as he soon discovered once they were inside.

There was an air of casual professionalism about the place. The floorboards shone and there were plants everywhere. There was no air-conditioning, which they considered a threat to the planet, but instead overhead fans. It was tiny in comparison to the places he was accustomed to, and although clearly busy it felt uncrowded, with everyone having their own space, and most people out exploring the great outdoors.

A constant breeze blew through all the many open windows and the dining was informal, with a choice of individual square white tables or else a long, gleaming communal table for anyone wanting to socialise with other guests and listen in to the various speakers they had on a twice-weekly basis.

It was out of his comfort zone, but then what wasn't ever since he had landed in Hawaii?

He gazed down at the woman lying curled into him. The silence between them was comfortable, peaceful. They'd biked straight here from the lush waterfalls they had visited earlier. They were tired but still too wired to head into the hotel.

'Fancy a dip?' She turned to him and he frowned.

'What, now?' He looked out to the ocean which was black, streaked with silver from the full moon.

'Sure.' She sprang to her feet, lithe and supple and sandy and utterly bewitching.

'No chance.'

'You're not scared, are you?' she teased. 'You don't have to worry. I'm an expert swimmer. I'm used to the sea, in the daytime and at night.'

'You've done this before?' Max asked gruffly.

'Of course, I have! Lots of times. Don't forget, this is my home. I grew up with the ocean all around me. I don't scare easily when it comes to the sea.'

She was already stepping out of the small denim shorts she was wearing, reaching to strip off the cropped white tee shirt. Her hair was all over the place, half over her eyes as she looked down at him, laughing.

And he looked right back at her, and all he could see was a vision of her being consumed by the deep, black ocean. The rush of protectiveness that attacked him was so fierce that for a few seconds he couldn't breathe.

His heart was hammering and he had all the symptoms of a man in full panic attack mode.

He wanted to leap to his feet, hold her tight and keep holding her. He wanted to keep holding her until she was persuaded never to enter the water again at night, never even to contemplate the idea, never, indeed, to stray far from his possessive gaze.

What the hell was going on?

This was what his parents had all been about, he thought, as the reality he had kept at bay now slammed into him with the force of a freight train.

Hadn't he seen the havoc emotion could cause? Hadn't he been a casualty of their all-consuming love? They had abandoned restraint in the name of love and he—all of them—had paid the price.

He had sworn from an early age to exercise control over his life, but here he was now, worrying over a woman who hadn't even done anything yet. Worrying at the thought of her swimming in that dark ocean, prey to currents, eddies and whatever dodgy sea creatures might be lurking just below the surface.

It was an alien experience and he didn't like it. It made him edgy and unsettled.

His original plan for a flying visit to a country he'd had no interest in seeing had been scuppered at the starting block. Instead of reining in the situation, he had found himself going along for the ride, curious to see where it would lead.

What did they say about curiosity killing cats?

He had allowed lust to dictate the pace of a relationship with a woman who worked for him. Yes, the situation was an unusual one, but she was still his employee, and he had always had very clear ideas about having any sort of physical relationship with someone who worked for him.

And yet, he had fallen into bed with Mia with only the merest of reservations.

He'd managed to persuade himself that this was a different life. Somehow. He'd successfully managed to convince himself that this was a much-deserved holiday, under which banner it had been okay to push aside all dissenting inner voices.

He'd slept with her and she'd stayed in his bed and he'd wanted her there. Sleeping next to him, warm and responsive to his touch, always there when he wanted her.

And this four-day trek across the islands? He'd sensibly written that off as an important way of getting to grips with what his sister had been after when it came to the hotel. Sure, by then, he'd also seen it as a good way of having Mia to himself, of indulging a need that had tailgated him from behind and thrown him off course when he had least been expecting it.

Everything neatly wrapped up as acceptable because he deserved a holiday...deserved some time out...

Roll the clock on, and here he was, worrying about her, looking at her and imagining all sorts of nonsense, his stomach clenched into a tight knot.

He felt as though he had hit some kind of crossroads.

Where did he think this was going to go? he asked himself. They lived in different countries. He had to return to London. He couldn't put his life on hold indefinitely and there was no way he was going to contemplate the unthinkable—there was *no way* he would contemplate asking her to return with him. He didn't want a woman in his life on any sort of semi-permanent basis. Never had, never would. They'd shared a handful of days together…but he would never allow himself to get so wrapped up with any woman that he couldn't consider a life without her.

Mia couldn't quite make out the expression on his face but, with a sort of sixth sense she seemed to have developed when it came to him, she *knew* that something was wrong.

What?

'It…it was just a thought,' she stammered. 'I mean, the business of going for a swim…'

Scrambling to try and work out what was going on, she chanced a smile and held out her hand to him, desperately wanting to feel the warmth on which she had become dependent.

He stood up and when he didn't take her hand she let hers drop to her side. A coldness was spreading through her.

'I didn't tell you,' he drawled. 'I heard from Izzy.'

'What? When?' She was swamped with relief because it must be whatever conversation he'd had with Izzy that had thrown him off-balance. Had he been waiting to talk to her about it once their hectic day came to a close?

'Pretty much as soon as we got back here.' He began walking towards the hotel, leaving the motorbike where it was, only glancing at it in passing. He would ask someone to ride it to the courtyard and secure it. His hands were shoved into his pockets and she hesitated to take one because something didn't feel right.

The hotel was brightly lit, the trees rustling in the breeze and shadows cast by the moonlight. The air was cooler but still balmy, still humid.

'Are you going to tell me what she said? Is she okay?'

'She won't be returning just yet.' He carried on walking straight through the foyer, where several guests turned to them and smiled. In a small hotel, you quickly got to know who your fellow travellers were.

They were heading straight up to their bedroom suite. It was an expansive space with billowing voile curtains, a mosquito net draped over a super-king-sized bed, an overhead fan and lots of bamboo furniture that complemented the rich patina of wood everywhere.

'It's time we had a talk,' he said, as soon as the door was shut behind them, and the coldness she had felt earlier returned with force. But she held on to her composure, because surely she'd known that this moment would come, sooner or later?

'Has she said why?' Mia sat on a rocking chair by the window, but then leaned forward, tense with nerves.

'She's…somehow got herself involved with trying to save my mother's nanny from being evicted from her house. Long story short, she decamped to my mother's house in California. Should have put two and two together and worked that out for myself but…' He shrugged. 'She'll be back, and I'm willing for her to have a revised role when it comes to the hotel.'

Mia hadn't heard from her friend for a while and she

breathed a sigh of relief that everything was okay. She wasn't surprised that Izzy had adopted a noble cause. She had a tender heart and a hugely caring disposition.

'That's all good, then, isn't it? It must have been awesome talking to her, having her call you.'

'At any rate, if you recall I had begun the process of auditioning for someone to take over the financial side of the operation…'

'I know you said that Nat's interviewed a few candidates.'

'He has but I was holding off for my sister's decision one way or another. That decision has been made and an offer has been tendered to a highly respected chartered accountant with a background in the leisure industry. He should find the process of dealing with all the various supply chains easy to manoeuvre.'

Mia nodded but she was wondering where this was going and why she had such a bad feeling about the direction of the conversation. Was it the flat coolness in his eyes? Or was she imagining that?

'So,' he went on, 'you could say that my time here is officially at an end.' He lowered his eyes and then looked at her without expression.

Mia's heart slowed down. This was how it had always been going to end. Not with a bang, but a whimper. No great fireworks, no storming off after a heated argument, no revelations and tears. Just a quiet ending to something that always had a timeline attached to it. It was up to her to deal with it because she had gone into this with her eyes wide open.

'Well…' She floundered, trying hard to contain the

burst dam through which her emotions were pouring. 'It's great that everything's been settled.' She smiled ruefully. 'And you're right. All good things come to an end.'

'And this has been good. Really good.' Rueful smile for rueful smile.

There was a heartbeat of a pause, then Mia resumed the conversation. She was frozen to the spot, and breaking up inside, but thankfully her voice was steady.

'Yes, it has been,' she said politely. 'And I should thank you.'

'For what?'

'For…' She sighed and meant every word when she said, 'For getting me out of my hibernation. I've said this before to you—the failure of my marriage affected me a whole lot more than I could ever have anticipated. I went into hiding, and then you came along and you led me out, and I will always be grateful to you for that.'

'Grateful…' Max murmured.

'You've done me a huge favour,' she said brightly.

'And you could do me a huge favour now,' he growled with an edge of harshness to his voice that she just didn't get. Because what the heck did he have to be annoyed about? Wasn't he about to head back to his high-powered life with its sophisticated women? Back to what he knew? He probably couldn't wait. She'd done her bit and now he'd probably had his fill of down time for the next five years. Leopards never changed their spots.

'How so?'

'By coming here.' He didn't give her time to answer. He moved towards her and cupped the nape of her neck

and drew her towards him. Their bodies were still sticky
from the heat and the humidity. He kissed her. Long
and hard and with a hunger that was like nothing she'd
felt with him before.

He propelled her back towards the bed, holding her
so tightly that it was very nearly painful.

And then everything in a rush. Clothes shed… His
hand on her breasts, her thighs, between them… Just
time to fumble for protection but barely breaking away
from his devouring embrace…

He lifted her off her feet and she wrapped her legs
around him, felt the powerful thrust of his erection hard
inside her as he backed them towards the wall.

She heard herself cry out on a guttural sob of release,
a long shudder tearing through her, and afterwards she
clung on. Just for a while. Just for her time to say goodbye in that embrace. Tears would come later.

CHAPTER TEN

M<small>AX STARED OUT</small> into an impenetrable night. Two weeks. Two weeks, three days and he could probably count the hours if he put his mind to it.

In short, a lifetime since he had boarded that plane back to London, and back to his precious comfort zone, without which he had been convinced he could not live. Life was work. Work allowed him the control he craved. He knew where he was in the complex, cut-throat world of making money and he liked knowing where he was.

That was what he had told himself when he had left Hawaii, and he had kept feeding himself the same lines, over and over and over.

Izzy was still away, playing Good Samaritan to their mother's elderly nanny and friend. They had now spoken several times and a cool layer of ice he had not really known existed was rapidly thawing. He had gone to Hawaii to drag his sister out from wherever she was hiding, to find out what the hell she thought she was playing at and to return to London, mission accomplished, within the week.

Instead, his life had been turned on its head.

He now had more insight into his sister than he had ever had before. She would be returning, but with a new, creative role and his absolute trust that she would do a fantastic job taking the hotel down a completely different direction from the one he had originally had in mind.

The new accountant was settling in with flying colours. He'd had frequent communications from Nat, in which details were given of each and every aspect of the hotel in laborious detail.

And Mia...?

Nothing. Not a word. Zilch.

He had walked away and she had cheerfully waved him off. That last night on the island, in that special bubble that had been about to burst, had been incredible. If something inside him had been strangely painful, he had successfully managed to sweep the feeling under the carpet, because he had already begun his mantra on the importance of returning to real life.

Besides, he could remember thinking, it wasn't as if *she* had kicked up a fuss that what they had shared was coming to an end. She had shrugged and smiled and been philosophical, and had behaved in exactly the way he should have been cheering about. Instead, he had been inexplicably disgruntled by her nonchalance.

But that too he had swept under the carpet, consigned, he'd thought, to oblivion, with his comfort zone back in London already within striking distance.

Of course, he would miss her. She had occupied a unique place in his life. For the first time, he had dared to stop being the man the rest of the world feared. He had dropped the shutters safe in the knowledge that it was a temporary situation, no harm done.

But now, here he was, staring through the windows of his multi-million-pound penthouse. Finally, he had to admit in the still of the night what he had known all along.

He missed her.

He thought about her all the time. He could barely focus on his work.

He remembered everything about her, from her smile and her laughter to the way she could prise information out of him so that it had always felt good to confide.

He remembered the way she felt and moved and curved against him, and the feeling that they had somehow *belonged* together.

But for all that, when the crunch had come, the barriers had been raised and he had pushed her away. Why? Because he had been scared. He had remembered his parents and the way their love had been so all-consuming that everything and everyone had been filtered out. Poor decisions had been made, responsibilities abandoned.

The second he had felt the shift of quicksand underneath his feet, he had responded with knee-jerk speed. No way had he been going to let someone get under his skin. That could only spell disaster.

He'd been a coward. He hadn't been man enough to admit to himself that he'd fallen in love with her, but subconsciously he had recognised those feelings, and had reacted by running away because to love was to love control of your life.

It had been safer to escape.

Fact was, he had fallen in love with Mia almost from the start. He'd told her that she was refreshing, but not once had he stopped to consider how much he adored that, how little he'd minded her consistently trampling over the barriers.

At every turn he had made excuses for feelings that had grown and grown until he had been forced to confront them on that last day together.

Izzy's decision to stay on in California was the catalyst he had used to propel him back to London. His time in Hawaii was at an end and he had to return to his wonderful life in London—which, he'd discovered, wasn't worth living because the one person he wanted in it was thousands of miles away.

Thing was…did she love *him?*

She did. Didn't she? So much tenderness… And when she'd looked at him…

He'd never asked, never implied that he felt anything for her at all except lust. He'd promised nothing and had reminded her on more than one occasion that what they were having was a holiday fling. He'd encouraged her at every turn to look forward to walking away, even if he hadn't always come right out and said so, because he would return to London and that would be the end of them.

He'd been a fool, but even fools deserved second chances. They at least had to try and get them.

He finished his drink and it took less than an hour for arrangements to be made to take him back to Hawaii.

He'd surprised her once. He would surprise her again.

* * *

The sun was fading but it was still very hot. Mia could feel the stirrings of a headache. Nothing new there. For the past two and a half weeks, she had felt under the weather, as though somehow all the energy had been sucked out of her and, just like that, she'd deflated. A slowly leaking balloon, lifeless and drifting on the wind.

Out here, the beach was packed with people. Tourists, locals, old, young, fat, thin—all out enjoying the sun and the sea and the surf. She could smell all different kinds of food in the air, their aromas blending and mixing and vibrant. Music was playing. The kids she had just finished teaching were babbling and laughing, and she knew that she was going through all the right motions but her heart wasn't in it.

Her heart had been left behind on another island, broken up into pieces when Max had calmly told her that what they had was over. Things had been settled with the hotel in Hawaii and there was no longer a reason for him to remain.

She'd smiled and smiled and smiled, and told herself that she should have been braced for this, because it was always going to end, and it wasn't as though she hadn't had ample warnings. They'd made love, had breakfast together and carried on talking, both adults, cool and composed—but for her every minute spent in his company had been a shard of glass piercing her heart.

Somewhere deep inside she wished she'd had the courage to say what she was thinking, to tell him how she felt, but in the end what would have been the point?

She would have to carry on with her life, just as she'd

carried on with her life after her marriage had crashed and burned. Only with Max…

She could never have foreseen how deeply she would fall in love with him. Nothing had prepared her for that because he was so unlike the kind of guy she had ever imagined herself falling for.

Just went to show—life had a nasty habit of throwing curve balls.

She was a million miles away when she knew, *sensed,* that someone was behind her.

The hairs on the back of her neck stood on end but she kept on walking away from the beach and back towards her bicycle, a good ten-minute walk away.

She only felt a tug of apprehension when she realised that whoever was following her was speeding up, moving alongside her, ignoring the fact that she was walking fast, eyes down, body language rejecting any attempts at conversation.

Her fists were clenched, and she wasn't expecting it when suddenly someone's hand was on her arm.

She swung round, absolutely enraged that anyone would *dare* lay a hand on her, try to stop her. Basically, that was called assault, and in her frame of mind, with all the unhappiness and misery pent up inside her, she was ready to punch.

She raised her eyes and stopped dead in her tracks and her mouth dropped open and she stared at the last person she had ever expected to see.

He'd accosted her once before on this very beach and she had to blink to make sure her eyes weren't deceiving her.

They weren't. He was standing right there in front of her, his back to the sun and as tall, dark and gloriously, sinfully handsome as she remembered.

She recognised the grey-and-white-striped polo shirt. She recognised the slim, grey Bermuda shorts that accentuated the muscular length of his legs. She recognised the loafers. He'd worn them on the last day they'd spent together, when his bags had been packed and he'd been ready to go.

Most of all…oh…how she recognised the depth of those navy eyes, the curve of his sensual mouth, the proud symmetry of his beautiful face.

'Max!' Something must have happened with the hotel. She'd limited her time there to working furiously on the acreage, having sections cleared for the plants on order so that everything would be ready and waiting when the time came. She hadn't been near the hotel at all, although she knew that it was coming along in leaps and bounds now that Izzy's original designs had been approved.

Had he been unable to locate Nat? She assumed he needed to know something about her end of things.

All of this raced through her head in seconds, over-riding the simple question: couldn't he just have emailed her if he had something to ask?

In her head, she frantically joined the dots… *Max, here, work.* She should smile. She shouldn't let him see that the memories were just so intense that she was on the edge of breaking up. She hadn't cried since they'd parted company. It was as if all her tears had collected in a pool somewhere deep inside her and had refused to come out.

She cracked a smile. He still had his hand on her arm, but now he released her, raking his fingers through his hair, edgy and awkward.

'What a surprise!' she chirped. 'What brings you back across the ocean?' Before he could see the glimmer of dampness in her eyes, she spun round and began heading to her bike. If he wanted to ask about the landscaping, then he could jolly well do so while they walked.

The silence that greeted her question forced Mia into speech, but her voice was simmering with hostility, even though she was trying so hard to keep a grip on her emotions.

'Has Nat contacted you about my designs for the outside space? You could have emailed me if you had any questions.' They were at her bike now and she circled round it so that they were standing on either side, staring at one another, while she pointedly clutched the handlebars. Let him be in no doubt that she was tired and on her way home, and if he had something to say then he'd better just come right out and say it.

'I haven't come here to ask you about the landscaping.'

'Then what are you doing here?' The smile dropped from her face.

'I came to…talk to you…'

'What about?'

'About us.'

Mia laughed shortly. 'Really? What about us? It's

an awfully long way to come to have a conversation about nothing.'

'Is that what you think we are?'

'Yes.' She tilted her chin at a defiant angle. Her eyes stung. 'We said goodbye, Max. What else is there to say?' She began unlocking her bicycle.

'I've had two weeks to think…to miss you…to realise that saying goodbye was the wrong thing for me to do.'

Mia's head shot up and she glared at him with sudden fury. All those little hints and warnings he had dished out rushed at her and she saw red. Talk? He wanted to *talk* about them? Because he'd had a couple of weeks to think, and to miss her, and to realise that saying goodbye had been the wrong thing for him to do…?

Could he be any more arrogant? To assume that he could remind her that he wasn't in it for the long haul because holidays always came to an end, but then, having decided that he might want a bit more of a holiday, maybe a mini-break, assume he was entitled to hop back on a plane, chat her up and…what? She'd fall into his arms and take whatever was on offer?

All the pain and heartbreak she had felt when things had ended between them now surfaced with crippling speed.

'Tough.' She gritted her teeth.

She began cycling off and he began jogging alongside her. She wasn't looking at him, but she was aware of heads turning in their direction. A blistering argument in full throttle was always a captivating sight for curious bystanders.

Annoyingly, he wouldn't give a damn, while she could only wonder if anyone looking at them might know her.

'Go away,' she puffed, gathering pace, while he did likewise.

'Not until we talk.'

He'd dictated the pace and the direction of their intense, short-lived relationship. She'd been so determined not to let that happen, but happen it had, because she'd fallen madly in love with him until bit by bit she'd become the puppet manoeuvred by his all-empowering hand. The only blessing was that she hadn't been idiot enough to show him how she felt. She was sure that, if she had, he wouldn't be running alongside her now telling her that he wanted to pick up where they'd left off.

She'd had plenty of time to make sense of this guy. He was a sensualist who enjoyed a casual acceptance that whatever woman he wanted would dance to his tune. She was sure that, when it came to the relationships he had had in the past, *he* would always have been the one to end them because he would have become bored. Circumstances had dictated that he make a decision about them. He couldn't have remained in Hawaii for ever, so he had walked away. But she thought now, pedalling furiously, he hadn't quite had time to become bored, so he had returned to continue what they had until he *did* become bored. At which point, she would see the dust kicked up by his rapidly departing feet.

Thanks, she thought, but no thanks.

'Okay!' She braked so suddenly that he was still running but he swivelled round, slowed his pace and stood looking at her. He didn't even have the decency to be out of breath. 'Talk! No, let *me* say what you're about to say! All this stuff about your two-week thinking period? I know where you're going, Max.'

'Please let's not have this conversation here, Mia,' was all he said, but there was something about the tone of his voice, the way he was looking at her...

She hesitated, annoyed with herself. There was a café several paces along which looked reasonably quiet, probably because it looked reasonably pricey. She gave a curt nod towards it and headed there.

It was mellow inside. Some of the tables were full, and the area around the bar was busy, but they were still able to grab an empty table to the side where they sat in silence until orders for drinks were given.

Tempted to go for a bracing Maui lager, instead she had a soft drink.

The silence was making her even more edgy. She didn't want to look at him, because she didn't want to be reminded of just how much he had come to mean to her, but it was an effort to sit in stony silence with her eyes averted.

'You were going to tell me that you were a mind reader,' he finally said, quietly. 'I'm willing to bet that you aren't.'

'You came over here because you're not quite through with what we had,' Mia scorned. He had knocked back drink number one, a whisky, in record time, which was alarming. He also couldn't quite meet her eyes. 'Am I heading in the right direction?'

'It's no good trying to pre-empt what you think I'm going to say,' he told her, but in such a low, driven voice that she had to lean forward to catch what he was saying. He ordered another whisky and she couldn't help herself when she said anxiously, 'Why are you drinking so quickly?'

'Dutch courage,' he said with a wry smile.

'Dutch courage? Why would you need Dutch courage? When have you ever been scared of anything? If this is some kind of tactic to get under my skin, it's not going to work!'

'I need Dutch courage because I've never had this kind of conversation before. I've never…felt this need before.'

'I think you're confusing *need* with *lust*.'

'I don't think the two are connected at all, and that's why I'm finding this difficult. I've never felt this way about anyone before. Never thought I could. Just hear me out and, if after you want to walk away, you have my word that I won't follow you. Thing is, Mia, you came at me like a bolt from the blue. One minute I had a plan for my life, and the next minute you'd managed to blow a hole right in the middle of it and I didn't know what the hell had happened.'

Mia shifted uneasily. Something was blooming inside her and she couldn't shove it down where it belonged.

She wanted to hear more. She didn't want to hear more. So she waited in silence.

'I just know that what started off as something simple became more and more complicated with each passing second. You got under my skin and you stayed there.

I should have known my life was changing when I realised I didn't want you to leave my bed. I wanted you to fall asleep next to me and wanted you to be the first person I saw in the morning when I woke up.'

'Really?' But there was doubt in her voice.

'Really.' He smiled tentatively, and that was so novel for a man as self-assured as he was that she softened and began to open up, began to let those shoots of hope grow. When he absently took her hand and fiddled with her fingers, she didn't pull back.

'For as long as I can remember,' he confided huskily, 'I've been distrustful of relationships. My parents, as far as I was concerned, sacrificed everything in the name of love. Work…responsibilities… Me. When they were killed in that plane crash, it seemed just another example of their reckless adventuring which always took precedence over everything else. They should never have gone up. The weather was terrible, but there they were, like a couple of love-struck teenagers, acting with the folly of youth instead of a couple of middle-aged parents with three kids to think about.'

He sighed and pressed his thumbs to his eyes, then he looked at her. 'I vowed to always, always be in control of my life. There was no way I would let anyone get me to a place where I forgot what my priorities were. Security. Stability. Relationships were enjoyable breaks in between the more important things in life, and that worked until I met you.'

'And then what happened?' Mia asked breathlessly.

'Then I met you and I fell in love.'

'You…you what?'

'I fell in love with you, my darling. I had all the symptoms but I failed to recognise the illness. Bad metaphor.' He grinned. 'I was so used to the humdrum monotony of having my feet planted on the ground that I failed to appreciate the joy of being able to fly, which is how you make me feel.'

'Me too,' Mia admitted. She felt tears gathering in the corners of her eyes. 'It was so hard not being able to tell you, knowing that you would run a mile if you had any inkling that I was falling madly in love with you. When we were island-hopping, there was always this tightness inside me because I knew it was going to end and when it did...' She shivered and closed her eyes briefly.

'You didn't say anything.'

'How could I? I was proud. Proud enough to think that I had to walk away with my dignity intact.'

'I didn't realise how much that would hurt.'

'Why...? Why didn't you say something sooner?' Mia couldn't help but ask and he shot her a rueful smile.

'You talked about pride,' he said drily. 'You don't have a monopoly on that particular emotion. It was more than that, though.'

His voice was thoughtful now. 'I just kept telling myself that I would adjust back to the life I'd always known, kept telling myself that I should be pleased that you'd accepted the inevitable with such...indifference. I shut down all the pain and bewilderment and hurt because, for the first time, I wanted a woman to stop me from walking away and you didn't. I told myself that it was only a matter of time until things returned to normal. On all counts, I was wrong. It just took me a while to figure that out. I've been a fool, my darling, but I came here to set the record straight.'

'I love you,' she said simply.

'I want to do everything right,' he told her solemnly. 'No half-measures. No being scared about what might lie in front of me. There's no room when you love someone for playing games or trying to hang on to control. It's about letting go. I love you, need you and want you to be the one I let go to. For ever. So, my darling Mia, will you marry me and be patient with me while I learn how to be less driven?'

'I think I can handle that.' She laughed and touched the side of his face. Such a dear face.

From cloud nine, the whole world looked like the most wonderful place to be.

'I warn you, you're in for quite a riotous ride with my family,' she said.

'Four sisters… I'm guessing I'm not going to get much of a word in edgeways, especially if they're as wonderfully opinionated as you.'

'Just as opinionated and very noisy. But they're going to be so happy to welcome you into the family, and I guarantee my two brothers-in-law will be whooping at the thought of having another guy in their corner for back-up.'

'I can't wait,' he told her, drawing her towards him and kissing her, well aware of the indulgent, amused looks they were attracting.

'Nor, my wonderful husband-to-be, can I…'

* * * * *

WAKING UP IN
HIS ROYAL BED

KIM LAWRENCE

To Jane and the 'Artists Unlocked'.

CHAPTER ONE

BEATRICE RESISTED THE instinct to fight her way through
the layers of sleep, instead easing her body closer to
the warmth of the hard male contours she was lying…
Male… The shocked acknowledgement hit at the same
moment a distant clatter was joined by the melodic voice
of her sister, who had clearly recovered from her migraine of the previous night and was singing something
catchy and irritating downstairs.

One of the major differences between them, beyond
the fact her sibling was not blonde, did not have blue
eyes and was frequently referred to as petite and delicate, was that Maya was a morning person who woke
with a smile on her face and a spring in her step. She
could also hold a tune, and finally Maya would never
have woken up beside a man who had walked into a bar
alone and walked out minutes later *not* alone!

A protective hand went to Beatrice's face before she
conquered her sense of dread and opened her eyes, wid-
ening her fingers fanlike to peer through them.

Maybe it was all a bad dream—with some very good
parts.

It wasn't a dream!

Connecting with the pair of dark polished ebony eyes
framed by lashes too thick and curling for any man,

containing a sardonic gleam that stared right back at her, she loosed a low moan, scrunched her own eyes tight and twisted away.

The reaction of the owner of the eyes and the body, which even fully clothed had had every woman in the bar regarding her with envy as she had left with him, prevented her rolling into a foetal bundle of denial.

In her head she had stiffened in reaction to the heavy arm thrown casually across her ribcage; in reality her body softened and the determination to put some distance between them was overwhelmed by a fresh surge of toe-tingling heat, as a voice as deep and sinfully seductive as the warm breath against her earlobe sent sharp tingles outwards from the core of liquid warmth low in her belly.

'What's the hurry?'

Eyes closed, she loosed a quivering sigh and then moaned as he brought his hard body suggestively up against the curve of hers, providing enough reasons not to go anywhere as her resistance to the heavy throb of desire that robbed her limbs of strength dissolved utterly.

For several long languid moments she allowed herself to enjoy the feel of strong, sensitive hands and clever fingers moving up her ribcage, tracing a line down her belly, causing her to suck in a shocked, excited breath, before lifting to cup the weight of one breast, his thumb rubbing across the tight, aroused peak.

'Stop it?'

Now where did that question mark come from? she wondered, feeling a stab of frustration when he did just that, pulling his hand away. An action that caused her to squirm backwards a little and catch the thumb

of the hand that came to rest on the curve of her jaw
between her teeth.

'Play nice, Bea.'

Before she could react to the husky remonstrance,
she found herself flat on her back. It wasn't his superior
strength that kept her breathless there—she could have
easily slid from underneath him. There was air between
their bodies as, hands braced flat on the pillow either
side of her face, knees either side of her hips, his body
curved above her.

She was pinned there as much by the hungry ache
inside her as his predatory bold dark stare fastened onto
her face, lingering on her lips that still felt swollen from
the kisses that had continued last night, even as they
had torn each other's clothes off as they had stumbled
across the room to the bed.

Her eyes darkened at the memories of the passionate coupling. The stress of discovering him beside her
was pushed to the fringes of her mind as she stared
back. His face was really a total miracle. Perfect was
too mild a word to describe the sculpted arrangement
of his perfect bone structure, the deep golden tone of
his skin, dusted on his hollow cheeks and square lower
jaw by a shadow of dark sexy stubble, the sensuality of
his mouth, the firm upper lip counteracted by the full
sensual lower.

She blinked and cleared her throat. 'I don't want to
play.' She husked the words out past the ache in her
throat. It was true there was nothing light or playful
about the ache. It was on a par with the need, the *craving* for oxygen as she opened her eyes and managed to
disconnect from his stare, but only escaped as far as
his mouth, which did an equal amount of damage to
her nervous system.

The sharply etched angle of his carved cheekbones, the hawkish dominance of his nose blurred as his head lowered. The first kiss was a warm, tormenting whisper across her parted lips, drawing a fractured moan from her throat. The second, still soft on the side of her mouth, drew her body up into an arch as she tried to deepen the pressure. The ones that followed increased the torment until, unable to bear it any longer, she reached up, her fingers sinking deep into the thick dark hair, her hands locking on the back of his head as she dragged his face downwards, glimpsing the glitter in his dark eyes, before she pressed her mouth to his and closed her eyes.

Restraint gone, they kissed with a wild hunger, and they fell back. Warm bodies sinuously twisting to deepen the contact, driven by a passion that drove every other thought from Beatrice's head.

'Bea, are you coming down or shall I bring your coffee up?'

Beatrice stiffened as she was jarringly jolted back to reality. Eyes scrunched, a moan of self-recrimination locked in her throat, as without a word she rolled away from the warm body she was pressed against.

'Weak…stupid…weak…stupid!' she mumbled, beating herself up verbally as she swung her long legs over the side of the bed and, with a sinuous, graceful swoop, grabbed a sheet that had at some point fallen on the floor. She didn't stop until she reached the far corner of the room, where she stood, shoulder blades pressed to the wall, holding the sheet against her body. It was an inadequate shield but better than nothing.

She glanced nervously at the door; a nightmare scenario played in her head of the door opening and Maya appearing.

'I'll be down just now!' she yelled. 'You need to go!' she whispered, transferring her agonised glance to the man lying in her bed.

He looked in no hurry to go anywhere any time soon as he rolled onto his back, tucking one hand behind his head, causing the light sheet that lay across his narrow hips to slide another inch lower. He was totally at ease with his naked state but she was not. He was a living, breathing sculpture of perfectly formed muscles and warm olive-toned skin—just looking at him made things shift deep inside her.

The mockery in his expression was not quite in tune with the dark frustration in his heavy-lidded eyes as his glance came to rest on the swell of her full breasts above the sheet she held clutched against herself.

As he watched her struggles to control the white swathe, he visualised the slim curves beneath the tented fabric. The smooth, warm scented skin, the silk touch of her long legs as they wrapped around him. The thousand razor cuts of desire that came with the memory darkened his eyes to midnight.

'That is not what I need, *cara*.'

Before she was fatally distracted by the bold challenge of the seductive gleam in his heavy-lidded eyes, the timely interruption of her sister's voice drifting up the stairs again saved her from getting sucked back into the dangerous sexual vortex.

She clenched her even white teeth so hard she could hear the grind of enamel. She didn't feel saved at all, or maybe she didn't want to be saved?

'Oh, my God!'

He grinned a slow devilish smile of invitation.

'Oh, my God!' she whispered again with even more feeling as she realised how close she had come to ac-

cepting the invitation in his sinful eyes. She took a deep breath and thought, *Do not go there*. Her eyes flickered towards the figure in the bed—*again*!

Once was enough—actually it was too much!

She cleared her throat. 'I'll be right down!' she belted out, then directed an accusing glare at the figure occupying the bed, even though she knew the guilt was as much hers. When it came to Dante, why was she such a weak idiot? 'Do not make this any more difficult. You need to get out of here.'

His brows, dark, straight and thick, lifted above polished ebony mocking eyes. 'Why?'

'You can ask that?'

He casually levered himself into a sitting position with a distracting display of contracting muscle in his washboard belly. 'I really don't see what your problem is.'

Eyes indignantly wide, she managed to drag her gaze upwards, not that the breadth of his muscled shoulders and chest offered much respite for her wildly surging hormones.

'What?' he responded with an innocent look and a seemingly mystified shrug that intensified her murderous glare. 'Unless you have forgotten, we *are* married.'

CHAPTER TWO

HUFFING OUT A defiant gust of breath through clenched teeth, Beatrice refused to drop her gaze from the challenge she saw in the dark eyes of Dante Aristide Severin Velazquez, Crown Prince of San Macizo.

Her husband.

'If only I *could* forget.' Her mumble came with a resentful glare, at odds with the mood of their civilised divorce.

She never had really understood what a civilised divorce entailed, but she was pretty sure it did not entail having a night of passionate sex with your soon-to-be ex. But on the plus side, her peevish attitude did provide some sort of cover for her deep inner despair.

Everyone made bad choices, and she was no exception, but it sometimes felt that from the moment Dante had walked into her life the only sort of choices she'd made were of the bad variety—actually, *disastrous*!

She had always operated on the principle that your actions had consequences, and you lived with them. Or, in her case, you neatly plotted a course around them, or at least the more dangerous ones.

Then Dante happened and she forgot her philosophy; her navigation skills took a vacation. She didn't so much forget as didn't give a damn about the consequences.

The primitive instincts that he had awoken in her were totally in charge. Instincts that had drowned out the warning bells that she had remained determinedly tone deaf to. Actually, last night there had been no bells, just a fierce *need*.

She had lifted her head and seen the reason why the crowded bar had fallen silent, and had felt a bone-deep desperation, much like any addict who found their drug of choice was close enough to smell. Dante was her addiction, the virus in her blood she had no antibody to.

Which made it seem as though she'd had no choice, but she had. She hadn't sleepwalked into the situation. She had known what she was doing every step of the way. Admittedly she had not typed his name into a search engine when she'd accepted the offer of dinner, knowing that he wasn't actually talking about a dinner. But you didn't need a bio to see at one glance that he represented the sort of danger she had spent her adult life avoiding.

The idea of experiencing an attraction strong enough to make her share intimacy with a man she didn't know had been a concept she had considered with a disbelieving smile, tinged, if she was honest, with smugness. But she'd had total confidence in her belief that any relationship she had would come from friendship and respect.

She'd slept with Dante that first night. She had been so determined to have that first night end the way she had imagined from the moment she had set eyes on him that she hadn't told him that this…that *he*…was her first, in case it made him back away.

Her instincts there had been bang on because Dante had not been pleased by the discovery she was inexperienced, sternly telling her that virgins were *not his thing* and demanding an explanation.

It could have ended there—it should have—but it hadn't, because she hadn't wanted it to.

When she had retorted that she wasn't a virgin any more so that was one obstacle gone she'd made him laugh, and he'd laughed again when she had explained that it hadn't been a conscious choice. She hadn't been waiting for the right man or anything, she simply wasn't a particularly *physical* person.

They had spent the next three days and nights in bed disproving this theory. Nothing and no one had disturbed them in the penthouse with million-dollar views that she'd never even looked at, and Beatrice had savoured every hot, skin-peelingly perfect moment of the intimacy because she'd known this heaven wasn't going to last. Dante had made that painfully clear.

He had left no room for misinterpretation when he'd explained that he was not into long-term relationships, or actually any sort of relationship at this point in his life.

Facts she'd already known, having finally typed his name into her phone's search engine—even if a tenth of the women he was alleged to have slept with were actually real, it would be amazing that he found time to be so hands-on with the charitable foundation that he had founded.

It made a person wonder if he ever actually slept, except she knew he did. She had watched him and been utterly fascinated by the way the strong lines on his face relaxed in sleep, made him look younger and *almost* vulnerable in a way that made her conscious of an empty ache inside her.

There had been more than one occasion over that weekend when he had felt the need to drag her feet back to earth by reminding her.

'This is just sex—you know that, right?'

The fantasy bubble she had spent the weekend in had ended when she'd opened her eyes and found him standing there, suited, booted and looking every inch the exclusive playboy prince who was always good for a headline.

She remembered fighting the self-respect-killing urge to run after him when he had stopped of his own volition, his long brown finger curled around the door-knob. She had managed a response as cool and offhand as his suggestion that they meet up in three weeks when commitments would be bringing him back to London.

By the time three weeks had come around things had changed, and the consequences of her actions had been impossible to ignore. Even without the multiple tests she'd *known* why she felt different; she'd known even without the blue line that she was pregnant.

She'd also known exactly how this next step was going to go, with a few gaps she'd left for his shocked, angry reaction. She had played the scene out in her head and, allowing for a few variations, she'd known exactly what she was going to say.

When she'd been buzzed into the building she'd *still* known *what she* was going to say, as she'd been escorted in the glass-fronted lift by a silent suited man.

She'd walked in, and she'd known not just what she was going to say but when she was going to say it. She'd allow herself their *last* night and then she would tell him.

In the event, the door had barely closed before she had blurted it out.

'I'm pregnant and, yes, I know we…*you* were careful.'

She had a vague recollection of dodging his eyes,

allowing her hair to act as a screen to hide her guilty blushes. The memory even now had the power to make her insides squirm.

'I've done three tests and…no, that's a lie, I did six. I am not…do *not* suggest *that*… Just know that I want nothing from you. I'm going home tomorrow to tell my mum and sister and we'll be totally fine. I'm not alone.'

He had stood there totally motionless during her machine-gun delivery of the facts. Strangely, saying it out loud had made the secret she had nursed to herself seem slightly less surreal.

She'd thought she'd been prepared for his every reaction, most had involved noise, but him turning on his heel and walking out of the door before she could even draw breath was not one she had been prepared for.

It might have been minutes or an hour, she didn't have a clue, but when the door had opened again she hadn't moved from the spot where she'd been before his abrupt departure. He had re-entered, still pale but not with shock now; determination as steely as his stare had been etched into the lines of his face.

'Well, obviously we need to get married. I don't need to involve my family in this—it's one of the advantages of being the spare. Carl is getting married and they probably won't even notice. How about you?'

Carl? What did his older brother have to do with this? *'Family…?'* Her thought processes had been lagging a confusing few steps behind his words.

'A big wedding, given the circumstances, is not an option, but if you want your immediate family to be there I can accommodate that. I have business in the area, so how does Vegas next week sound to you?'

He had paused, presumably for breath. She had definitely needed to breathe!

'You're not joking…? Dante, people don't get married because of a baby… Let's forget you ever said that. You're in shock.'

He didn't appear to appreciate her consideration. 'I may only be the spare but I am still second in line to the throne…*my* child will not carry the stigma of being a bastard. Believe you me, I've seen it and it's not pretty.'

'You're insane.'

Every argument she'd made against his plan he'd had a counterargument to. The most compelling one having been it was the right thing to do for the baby's sake, the new life that they had made.

She had ended up agreeing, of course. Saying yes to Dante was a habit she had to break if her life was going to get back on track.

As for last night! How could she have been that stupid *yet again*? And she had nobody to blame for it but herself! Dante didn't have to do anything to make her act like a lemming with her sights on a cliff edge, he just had to *exist*.

And nobody had ever *existed* as much as Dante—she had never met anyone who was *so* alive. He had a presence that was electrifying, and there was an earthy, raw quality to the megawatt vitality he exuded that made the idea of forgetting anything connected with him laughable.

But she had to. She had to put last night behind her and start again—it would get easier. It had to! First, she couldn't run and hide or pretend that last night didn't happen. She just had to accept she had messed up and move on.

Again…!

'What are you doing here, Dante?' Falling in love was not at all as she had imagined it—in fact it re-

ally should come with a health warning, or at least a
misery warning!

'You invited me. It seemed rude—'

'How did you know where I was? How did you know
we had gone away?' For the first few weeks after she
had left Dante she had moved in with her mother, then
she had taken residence on Maya's couch until a flat
they could afford together had come up.

He arched a sardonic brow and she sighed.

'All right, stupid question.' She had considered fighting the insistence that she needed any sort of security,
even the ultradiscreet team of men who in pairs watched
her around the clock, but she had learnt that it was better
to fight the battles you had a chance of winning. 'You
know, there was a time when my life was my own.'

'It will be again.' Unlike Dante's. The moment his
brother had stepped away from the line of succession
had been the moment that Dante had known his life
had changed forever. He was no longer the playboy
prince and unexpected father-to-be. He was the future
of the monarchy.

His flat delivery brought a furrow to her smooth
wide brow, but his expression told her nothing. 'A friend
of Mum's owns the place. We used to come here when
we were kids.'

His glance lifted from his grim contemplation of his
clenched hands and his future, as she glanced around
the wood-lined walls of the modest ski lodge.

'Ruth, that's Mum's friend, had a last-minute cancel-
lation and offered it to us for the fortnight for a song.
Maya is working on ideas for a sports line and we
thought the snow might inspire her.'

'So the business is going ahead? The fashion industry is notoriously tough.'

'Slowly,' she said, bringing her lashes down in a glossy protective sweep as he adjusted his position, causing a rippling of the taut muscles of his lean torso. He didn't carry an ounce of surplus flesh; his broad-shouldered frame would have made many a professional athlete sigh with envy.

She would have retreated if there had been any place to retreat to. Instead she ignored the pelvic quivering, and pretended her skin wasn't prickling, and tossed her hair as she adjusted her sheet once more.

'It would go a lot quicker and easier if you made the bank that is playing hardball aware of the settlement that will be yours. Do they even know you're going to be a very wealthy woman soon?'

Wealthy and single. She refused to acknowledge the sinking feeling in her stomach.

'And I'm more than happy to make the funds you need available to you now.'

Her lips tightened. If people called her a gold-digger that was fine, so long as she knew she wasn't. 'I don't want your money. I don't want anything—'

I want to go back to the person I was, she thought forlornly, aware that it was not going to happen. She might only have been married for ten months, and been separated for six more, but she could never be the person she was before, she knew that.

'Well, then, *cara*, you chose the right lawyer. Yours seemed more interested in golf than your interests.'

'Could you pretend, even for one minute, that you don't know every detail of what's going on in my life? I repeat, why are you here?'

Good question, Dante thought as he dragged a hand through his hair, leaving it standing in sexy tufts across his head.

He'd told himself when Beatrice left that it would be easier if he could focus on his new role, without the distraction of worrying how she was coping, of knowing that behind her smile she was unhappy, resentful or usually both. That no matter how tough his day had been, hers had probably been worse.

Dante had never been responsible for another person in his life. He'd lived for himself, and now he had an entire country relying on him and Beatrice—that really was irony, of the blackest variety.

Except now she wasn't relying on him. The reports that landed on his desk all said as much. She was doing well…he had just wanted to see for himself. It was an option that would soon not be open to him. The list of potential successors to fill the space in his life Beatrice had left, candidates who would know how to deal with life inside the palace walls without his guidance, was already awaiting his attention. His stomach tightened in distaste at the thought of the breeding stock with good bloodlines.

'There are a few papers for you to sign,' he said, inviting her scorn with his lame response and receiving it as he skated around the truth in his head.

'And now you're a delivery service?'

He sighed out his frustration as his dark, intense gaze scanned her face hungrily. She was still the most beautiful thing he had ever seen in his life and for a while their lives had meshed. But things had changed. He had another life, responsibilities, duty. At some level had he thought coming here would offer him some sort of closure?

'We never actually said…goodbye.'

She blinked, refusing to surrender to the surge of resentment that made her heart beat louder. 'Didn't we?

You probably had a meeting, or maybe you left me a memo?' She bit her lip hard enough to raise crimson pinpricks of blood. Could she sound any *less* like someone who had moved on?

'You felt neglected?'

'I felt…' She fought to reel in her feelings. 'It doesn't really matter. This was a conversation we never had, let's leave it at that. Let's call last night closure.'

He shook his head, the antagonism leaving his face as he registered the glisten of unshed tears in her eyes. His shoulders dropped. 'No, it wasn't planned. I just… I'm sick of receiving any news about you through third parties.'

'I miss…' She stopped, biting back the words she couldn't allow herself to admit to herself, let alone him. 'I think it's safer that way,' she said quietly.

'Who wants safe?'

The reckless gleam in his eyes reminded her of the man she had fallen in love with. There was an irony that she had to remind him he wasn't that man any more. 'Your future subjects and, frankly, Dante, I have all the excitement we can handle without…'

She closed her eyes and pushed back into the wall until the pressure hurt her shoulder blades. It was true—after she had walked away from the royal role she had never been equipped to fulfil, she had thrown herself into her life, and there were new, exciting and sometimes scary challenges to fill her days. She had recovered some of her natural enthusiasm, though these days it was mingled with caution. A caution that had been sadly missing last night. Dante walked into a room and all those instincts and hungers he woke in her roared into sense-killing life.

Sense*less*, she thought, underlining the second syllable in red in her head. Last night had had nothing to do with sense. Her insides tightened as the warm memories flooded her head. It'd had everything to do with passion, craving and hunger!

So she had a passion for chocolate, but if she gave into that indulgence Beatrice knew she'd need a new wardrobe. Exercise and a bit of self-control meant she could still fit into last year's clothes.

The trouble was Dante was a perfect fit, in every sense of the word, and he always had been.

When in one of her more philosophical moments she had told herself that she would take away the good bits from her marriage, she had not intended it this literally. Though even when everything else was not working in their marriage the sex had still been incredible. The bedroom was one place they always managed to be on the same page. Unfortunately, you needed more than sexual chemistry and compatibility for a marriage to work, especially when it had hit the sort of life-changing roadblocks theirs had.

With a self-conscious start she realised that during her mental meanderings her glance had begun to drift across the strong sculpted breadth of his chest, and lower, to the ridged muscular definition of his belly, before she realised what she was doing, and brought her lashes down in a protective sweep. Not that they provided much protection from the raw sexual pulse he exuded, or his unnerving ability to read her mind.

'Do you regret it?'

Her response to the question should have been immediate, a reflex, and of course she did regret what had happened, on one level. But on another, shameful level she would not have changed a thing, because Dante bypassed her common sense. She only had to breathe in the scent of his skin to send her instincts of self-preservation into hibernation.

I really have to break this cycle!

Easy to say, easy to think, but less *easy* when every time he touched her something inside her said it was *right*.

Then don't let him touch you!

Cutting off her increasingly desperate internal dialogue, Beatrice cleared her throat to give herself time to think of a next move that would manage to convey that last night didn't mean she wasn't totally over him. An action that wouldn't draw attention to the skin-prickling awareness and the warm pelvic heaviness.

A next move that established that she could walk away just as easily as he could after satisfying a primal itch. That he wasn't the only one who could compartmentalise his life.

'Last night was—'

His deep voice, the edges iced with impatience, cut across her before she could establish anything. 'Considering you are standing there huddled in a sheet, acting like some outraged virgin, I'm taking that you regret last night as a given.'

The accusing note in his voice brought a tinge of angry colour to her cheeks.

'That's really astute of you,' she drawled sarcastically. Where Dante was concerned her virginal outrage had always been zero, even when she'd had a right to the title. She had had no qualms about giving him her virginity, though he had been a lot less *relaxed* about receiving the unexpected gift.

'Do you regret marrying me?' Asking the second time did not make it any clearer to him why her answer mattered to him…except to lessen his guilt, maybe?

The irony was not lost on him. There could be few people who had spent a life where guilt featured less heavily… His upper lip curled in a bleak smile.

If he'd been a man who believed in karma he might think that his present situation was Fate's way of making him pay for an empty life of utter hedonism. Where the only way was the easy way. Having once rejected the concept of duty, now he was ruled by it.

He'd imagined that he was doing the *right thing* when he had proposed, never for one moment asking himself what the right thing was for Beatrice. He'd been the one making the ultimate sacrifice. Unwilling to own his thoughts, jaw clenched, he pushed out a breath through flared nostrils.

She blinked, her long lashes brushing the smooth curve of her cheeks like butterfly wings. 'There's no point regretting, is there?'

'Which means you do.' Did she ever ask herself if things might have ended differently if their baby had clung to life and not simply been a heartbeat that had vanished from the screen?

His guts tightened like an icy fist as the memory surfaced of the doctor relaying the news alongside the information that the baby had just faded away.

He had been consumed by a devastation that had felt as if he were being swallowed up. It had made no sense. He'd never wanted children—hadn't wanted a child.

'I'm looking forwards.'

His glance lifted as his thoughts shifted back to the present moment.

The intensity of his stare made Bea lose her thread, but after a momentary pause she managed to regain control and her defiance.

'The past is done and gone. I'm not interested in

revisiting—' She felt the sheet slip and yanked it up. As she did the colour seeping under her skin deepened the golden-toned glow as the irony of what she was about to claim hit her. Sometimes honesty, wise or not, was the best, or only, policy.

Her shoulders lowered as the defensive antagonism drained away, exposing the vulnerability that lay beneath. Dante looked away but not before he felt something twist hard in his chest.

'I have a lot of lovely memories that I will always treasure. I'm just not as realistic as you are sometimes.' She bit down on her quivering lower lip before the emotion took her over.

A spasm played across the surface of his symmetrical features that had more than once been called *too* perfect. 'Maybe I have lower expectations... You should try it, Beatrice. Less disappointment in life,' he suggested harshly.

'You want me to be as cynical as you are? That's a *big* ask, Dante.'

Heavy eyelids at half mast, his eyes gleaming, he quirked his mobile lips into a mocking smile that invited her to share his joke as their eyes connected. 'You call it cynicism. I call it realism, and it's all about baby steps, *cara.*'

It wasn't just her expression that froze, time did too. He could almost hear the seconds count down before her lashes came down in a protective sweep, but not before he had seen the hurt shimmer in her eyes.

Jaw clenched, he silently cursed himself. Of course he knew the self-recrimination might have been of more use if it had come sooner. Like when the loss of their baby had become not a personal tragedy, but one debated by palace mandarins and *sources* close to the throne.

It had come as no surprise to him—he'd known the moment his brother stepped away from the throne what lay ahead for him. But to Beatrice it must have felt like an alternative universe.

She waited for the toddler in her head with Dante's eyes to take his first faltering steps before she let the image go and looked up, ignoring the ache inside her. Dante didn't meet her eyes—maybe he was thinking about the *practical princess* he would replace her with...the one that could give him babies.

The babies she had tried so hard to give him; ten months of married life within the palace walls and ten months of waiting and hoping, then the awful inevitable sense of failure.

He swung his legs over the side of the bed, causing the rumpled sheet across his middle to slide a few treacherous inches lower.

Fighting the dormant protective instincts that Beatrice woke in him, Dante shrugged, but the truth was the thing she actually needed protecting from was him.

'I'm sorry.'

Cheeks hot, eyes wary, she dragged her wandering gaze up from his muscled thighs, but his expression was frustratingly hard to read.

'For what?' If he said he was sorry for last night she would hit him, she vowed grimly. 'Marrying me? I knew what I was doing,' she retorted, not happy at being cast in the role of victim.

'And now you're getting on with your life.' *Without him.*

'That might be easier if you weren't sitting in my bed.'

'I need to be in Paris tomorrow. The meeting was delayed and—'

'You wanted to mess my life up some more?' There was more weariness than reproach in her voice.

'I didn't invite myself into your bed, Beatrice.'

Colour scored her cheeks. Did he really think she needed that spelt out? 'Sorry. I'm not blaming you. You've been very good about making it easy for me to leave.

'So are there any papers?'

'There are papers, but…'

'But?'

'The tabloids love to—'

She tensed, suddenly seeing where this was going, and why he wasn't quite meeting her eyes. Pale but composed, she cut him off. 'Congratulations.'

His brows knitted into a perplexed frown. 'For what?'

'You're *engaged*…?' Her racing thoughts quickly joined the dots, swiftly turning the theory in her head to fact in seconds. It would be something official. He wouldn't have come all this way to tell her in person that he had a lover. She had kind of taken that for granted. A sensual man like Dante was not built for celibacy.

His steady stare told her nothing, but she knew and she was totally fine with it, or she would be if she didn't throw up.

'Aren't you?'

Finally, a low hissing sound of amazement escaped his clenched teeth. 'Engaged would be a little premature. I'm not divorced yet.'

Her eyelashes flickered like butterflies against her cheeks. 'Oh, I just…'

'Made one of your leaps based on the well-known

scientific theory that if something is totally crazy it is true.'

'It was a perfectly reasonable assumption,' she retorted huffily, hating that she felt almost sick with relief, but adding for her own benefit as much as his, 'You will get remarried one day—you'll have to.'

His gut twisted in recognition of the accuracy of her words *have to*. She said *have to*—the people around him, his family, the courtiers, called it duty. Every word he spoke, his every action would be observed and judged. *He* would be judged.

The bottom line was his life was no longer his own. Even as he opened his mouth to respond Dante recognised the hypocrisy of his occupation of the moral high ground. 'So, you think that I'd be engaged and sleep with you?'

'Yes,' she said without hesitation, the damning shame curdling inside her reserved for herself, not him, because she knew that nothing would have stopped her sleeping with Dante last night. 'You'd only be keeping up the family tradition,' she sniped.

One corner of his mobile lips quirked upwards as he remembered how shocked she'd been when she'd realised that his parents both had lovers who upon occasion slept over. His normality was her shocking.

'Will you sit down? I'm not about to leap on you.'

'No.' She backed a little further into the corner. It wasn't *him* she was worried about; they were both naked, and sitting was just one touch away from lying down. Her eyes widened as another equally and actually more probable explanation for his presence occurred to her. 'Is this about the divorce?' Her voice rose a shrill octave as she gulped and tacked on, 'Is there a problem?'

'No, it is not about the divorce. It is about Grand-father.'

'Reynard?' She stopped nervously pleating the fabric she held tight across her breasts and smiled. The old King, who had stepped back from the throne in favour of his son, Dante's father, after he suffered a stroke. Reynard had been one of the very few people she had been able to relax around in the palace.

Known for his acerbic tongue and a wit that took no prisoners, he'd made Beatrice laugh, though she had not realised until after the fact that being taught chess by him was considered a rare privilege.

They still played chess online. 'One of these days I'm going to beat him.'

One corner of Dante's mouth lifted in a half-smile. 'If you ever do it'll be for real. He won't let you win.'

'I hope not… So how is he?' She read enough in his face to make her panic; it wasn't so much his expression that made her heart lurch, more the careful lack of it. 'Oh, my God, he's not…not…?'

'No…no…he's all right,' Dante soothed.

She had barely released a sigh of relief when he added, 'He has had another stroke.'

'Oh, God, no!'

'Don't panic, the doctors gave him the clot-busting stuff in time, so they say there's no permanent damage, no further damage at least.'

She huffed out a sigh of relief but still felt shaky and sad because one day her worst-case scenario would be true, and a world without that irascible character would be a lesser place.

'We've kept everything in-house but it's inevitable that the news is bound to leak soon, and you know how they play up the drama disaster angle. I wanted you to know the facts, not the exaggerated fiction.'

'Why didn't you just say this was why you came?' His eyes captured her own and Beatrice felt the blush run over her skin. 'All right,' she cut in quickly before he could point out that last night had not involved much talking. 'You could have messaged me…rung…?'

'Yes, I could.' He released her eyes suddenly.

'It wasn't kind coming here. This hasn't been easy for me…'

His jaw clenched. 'You think it has for me?' he pushed out in a driven tone.

'Right, so let's just call last night goodbye.' It had to be because she couldn't do this more than once. 'Give my love to Reynard. I really wish I could see him. He *really* is all right?'

'He really is. You *could* see him.'

Beatrice gave a bitter laugh. 'Come back to San Macizo? I presume you're joking.'

'Were you so unhappy there?'

She kept her expression flat. 'I was irrelevant there.' The only function that would have made her acceptable was producing babies and she hadn't done that. The month after month of raised expectations and then… Dante must have been relieved when she had announced that she'd had enough. The recognition made her throat tighten; she ignored it.

She was ignoring so hard she nearly tripped over the draped sheet. Enough was enough!

Head high, not glancing in his direction, she stalked across to the wardrobe and, presenting him with her back, pulled the turquoise silk robe from its hanger on the door.

There was a sheer ridiculousness to her display of

false modesty around Dante, who knew every inch of her body—intimately. She let the sheet fall.

'I tried for ten months,' she said, throwing the words lightly over her shoulder, glad that he couldn't see her face. 'I tried to do the *right* thing, say the right thing. I tried to fit in. I tried…' She didn't finish the sentence, but the unspoken words hung between them like a veil. They both knew what she had tried and failed to do, the only thing that would have made her acceptable to his family: provide an heir.

CHAPTER THREE

BACK TURNED TO HIM, Beatrice tightened the sash before she turned, doing her best to not notice the molten gleam in his eyes as he watched her cinch the belt a little tighter.

She tilted her chin to a defiant angle and tossed her hair back from her face before tucking it behind her ears as she stomped over the sheet, her pearly painted toenails looking bright against the pale painted boards scattered with rustic rugs.

Despite the snow that had begun to fall again outside, the temperature was if anything too warm, thanks no doubt to the massive cast-iron radiator that didn't seem to respond to the thermostat.

Pretty much the way her internal thermostat ignored instructions when Dante was in the vicinity.

'You were the one who was hung up on that.'

The claim made her want to throw something at him.

'You were never irrelevant. A pain in the…but never irrelevant,' he drawled, unable to stop his eyes drifting over the long sensual flow of her body outlined under the silk. 'Have I seen that before? It brings out the colour of your eyes.' Which were so blue he'd initially assumed that she wore contact lenses.

She sketched a tight smile. 'It's been six months. I've

added a few things to my wardrobe. You probably have a list somewhere.'

'Six months since *you* left, Beatrice. I didn't ask you to go.'

She'd left. It was not an option for him; he could never walk. He was trapped, playing a part. He would be for the rest of his life. Typecast for perpetuity as a person he would never be.

Beatrice felt her anger spark, the old resentments stir. He made it sound so simple, and leaving had been the hardest thing she had ever done. How much simpler it would have been if she had stopped loving him, how much simpler it was for him because he never had loved her, not really.

It was a truth she had always known, a truth she had buried deep.

'You didn't try and stop me.'

'Did you want me to?'

'Even if I had got pregnant, a baby shouldn't be used to paper over the cracks in a relationship, which is why this can't happen again.'

'*This...?*'

'This, as in you turning up and...' She caught her eyes drifting to his mouth and despaired as she felt the flush of desire whoosh through her body. This *need* inside her frightened her; she didn't want to feel this way. 'I think in the future any communications should be through our solicitors,' she concluded, struggling to keep her voice clear of her inner desperation, making it as cold as she could.

Dante felt something tighten in his chest that he refused to recognise as loneliness, as he pushed back fragments of memories that flashed in quick succession through his head. The tears in his brother's eyes as he said sorry, the coldness in his parents' eyes as they informed him that the future of the royal family rested on his shoulders.

'So, you don't think that exes can be friends.'

Her hard little laugh sounded unlike the full, throatier, uninhibited laugh he remembered. A few weeks into their marriage and she hadn't laughed at all.

'This isn't friendship, Dante. Friends *share*.'

Share, she said. He almost laughed. The last thing he had wanted to do was share when he was with Beatrice. He had wanted to forget. He didn't want to prove himself to his wife; he was proving himself to everyone else.

For the first time in his life Dante had been experiencing fear of failure, something so alien to him that it had taken him some time to identify it. Worse than the weakness was the idea of Beatrice seeing those fears, looking at him differently... He knew the look. He had seen it every day and he couldn't have borne it.

He had seen that look in the eyes of the team who had been put in place to coordinate his own repackaging, even while they *told* him they had total confidence in him, before asking him to embrace values that he had long ago rejected. They appealed to his sense of duty.

The real shock, at least to him, was that he possessed one. He'd spent his life trying to forget the early lessons on duty and service, but it seemed that they had made a lasting impression.

He didn't share this insight, unwilling to give anyone the leverage this weakness would have afforded them. Instead he listened and then worked towards cutting the team down to three people he could work with.

He would have liked to get rid of the lot, but he was

a realist. It had taken his brother a lifetime to recognise what he had grasped in weeks wearing the mantle of Crown Prince. You really couldn't have it all, you had to make sacrifices.

His glance narrowed in on Beatrice's lovely face. *What* you were prepared to sacrifice was the question.

'I can't be half in, half out, Dante, it's not…fair. It's cruel…' she quivered out.

His glance flickered across the lovely, anguished features of the woman he had married. Finally *seeing sense* was how his father had reacted when he had broken the news that they were splitting up.

'She has come to her senses. Beatrice is leaving me.'

Dante had pushed the fact home that this was her choice, though not adding that fighting the decision was about the only noble thing he had done in his life. Lucky for him *nobility* was not a prerequisite for the job of King-in-waiting, unlike hypocrisy.

He knew that he ought not to be feeling this rage, this sense of betrayal. Their marriage had been about a child, then there was no child. Beatrice's decision had been the logical one. He could not see why it had shocked him so much.

Most successful marriages owed their longevity to mutual convenience and laziness, or, as in his parents' case, they were business arrangements, two people living parallel lives that occasionally touched. This was not something that Beatrice could ever understand.

In the end, the official line had been trial separation, while behind-the-scenes lists of replacements were drawn up for when the *trial* was officially made permanent.

He wasn't much interested in the lists, or the names

of those that were added, or deleted after a skeleton emerged from their blue-blooded closet.

One *suitable* bride was much the same as another to him, though he wondered if the woman who had been chosen to share the throne with his brother, and had unwittingly been his brother's tipping point, had been included. He could not remember her face or name, just that she belonged to one of the few minor European royal families he and Carl were not related to.

Carl had choked before it was made official, choosing to step away from the lie and his life...because though San Macizo was considered progressive, the idea of an openly gay ruler unable to provide an heir was not something that could be negotiated.

His option had been walk away, or live a lie.

Dante had wondered whether, if the situations had been reversed, he would have shown as much strength as his brother.

One of the things that had struck him, after his initial shock at the revelations, was that he *was* shocked that he really hadn't seen it coming. When his brother had revealed his sexual orientation and his deep unhappiness, Dante hadn't had a clue. But then he never had been much interested in anyone's life but his own, he acknowledged with a spasm of self-disgust.

There was an equal likelihood that he hadn't recognised his brother's struggles because it really wouldn't have suited him to see them.

His glance zeroed in on Beatrice's face, the soft angles, the purity of profile, the glow that was there despite the unhappiness in her eyes. Just as he had tried not to see Beatrice was unhappy.

'And you're out.' His shoulders lifted in a seemingly negligent shrug. 'Fair enough.'

She blinked, hard thrown by his response, a small irrational part of her irked that he wasn't fighting. 'You agree?'

'I already did. We are getting divorced, so relax, things are in hand,' he drawled.

'Are they?' Yesterday she'd have agreed but yesterday she hadn't been breathing the same air as Dante. Since then she had been tested and had come face to face with her total vulnerability, her genetic weakness where he was concerned.

'It's in everyone's best interests for this to happen. We're all on the same page here.'

'Pity the same couldn't be said for our marriage.'

It shouldn't have hurt that he didn't deny it, but it did.

Her decision to leave had been greeted with thinly disguised universal relief, which gave a lie to the myth that divorce didn't happen in the Velazquez family. It made her wonder if there had been others before her who had been airbrushed from royal history.

'I don't think anyone expected it to last, not even you…?'

Dante shrugged and deflected smoothly. 'I never expected to get married. I think it has a very different meaning for us both.'

In his family marriage was discussed in the same breath as airport expansion, or hushing the scandal of a minister who had pushed family values being caught in a compromising position, and the latest opinion poll on the current popularity of the royal family—it was business.

His heart had always been shielded by cynicism, which he embraced, but maybe it was the same cynicism that had left him with no defence against the emotional gut punch that Beatrice and her pregnancy had been.

'You're right.' He unfolded his long lean length and stood there oblivious to his naked state before casually bending to retrieve items of clothing, throwing them on the bed before he began to dress.

She couldn't not look; his body was so perfect, his most mundane action coordinated grace. She just wished her appreciation could be purely aesthetic; just looking made her feel hungry and ashamed in equal measure.

'I am?' she said, the practical, sane portion of her mind recognising this was a good thing, the irrational, emotional section wanting him to argue.

He turned as he pulled up his trousers over his narrow hips, his eyes on her face as his long fingers slid his belt home.

'Our lives touched but now—' Touched but nearly not connected—maybe it had been the sheer *depth* of his reaction that had made him show restraint, and it had required every ounce of self-control he possessed not to seek the glorious woman with endless legs and golden skin he had seen across the crowded theatre foyer, or at least find out her name…but he had walked away.

When, days later, he had found himself in the front row of the catwalk show of the hottest designer of the season with…he really couldn't remember who he had arrived with, but he could remember every detail of the tall blonde under the spotlight drifting past, hands on her hips, oozing sex in a way that had sent a collective shiver of appreciation around the audience. She had been wearing an outfit that was intended to be androgynous but on her it really hadn't been—it had felt like Fate.

He had allowed his companion to drag him to the sort of back-slapping, self-congratulatory, booze-fuelled backstage party that he would normally have avoided, where he got to know her name, Beatrice, and the fact she had already left.

His companion, already disgruntled by the lack of attention, had stayed as he'd run out of the place…in the grip of an urgency that he hadn't paused to analyse.

An image of her face as he'd seen it that day supplanted itself across her features. She'd stood too far away then for him to see the sprinkling of freckles across her nose. But they'd been visible later, when he had literally almost knocked her down on the steps of the gallery where the fashion show had been held. She'd looked younger minus the sleeked hair and the crazy, exaggerated eye make-up and he had decided in that second that there was such a thing as Fate—he had stopped fighting it. Never before had he felt so utterly transfixed by a woman.

She didn't fit into any stereotype he had known. She was fresh and funny and even the fact she'd turned out to be virgin territory, which ought to have made him run for the hills, hadn't.

A clattering noise from downstairs cut into his reminisces and made Beatrice jump guiltily.

'How is Maya?' he asked.

'People are finally recognising her artistic talent.'

Her sister might think that talent spoke for itself but Beatrice knew that wasn't the case. That was where she came in. She had done night classes in marketing during her time modelling, while everything she'd earned during that period had gone into their start-up nest egg for their own eco-fashion range.

Dante grunted, in the act of fighting his way into his shirt. Beatrice willed her expression calm as his probing gaze moved across her face.

'Will you be all right?'

'I'll be fine.' She would be; she wasn't going to let her Dante addiction of a few months define her or the rest of her life. She had accepted that it would be painful for a while, but she was a resilient person by nature, strong. Everyone said so.

So it must be true.

When her dad had died people had said how strong she was, what a rock she was. Then when Mum had married Edward she had been there for Maya, who had been the target of their stepfather's abuse. For a time, she had been the only one who had seen what the man was doing, because there had been nothing physical involved as he had begun to systematically destroy her sister's self-esteem and confidence.

For a while their mother had chosen the man she had married over her daughters, believing his lies, letting him manipulate her, controlling every aspect of her life. It had been a bad time and for a long time Beatrice, more judgemental than her sister, had struggled to forgive her mother her weakness.

The irony was that marriage to Dante had shown her that the same weakness was in her, the same flaw. Dante hadn't lied, which perhaps made her self-deception worse. She had wanted to believe he was something he wasn't, that they had something that didn't exist.

She pushed away the memories, focusing on the fact that she and Maya had forgiven their mother; their bond had survived and so had they. Now all they both wanted was their happily divorced mum to stop feeling so guilty.

'And how are your parents?' She felt obliged to enquire but could not inject any warmth into the cool of her voice.

'Pretty much the same.'

She lifted her brows in an acknowledgement as the memory of that first-night dinner in the palace with his parents flashed into her head. The shoulder-blade-aching tension in the room had taken her appetite away, and, if it hadn't, the unspoken criticisms behind the comments directed her way by the King and Queen would have guaranteed she was going to bed hungry.

And alone.

It had been two in the morning before she'd sat up at the sound of Dante's tread. She remembered that waiting, checking the time every few minutes. In the strange room, strange bed, in a strange country it had felt longer.

She had switched on the bedside light.

'Sorry, I didn't mean to wake you.'

She remembered so clearly the empathy that had surged through her body when she saw the grey hue of exhaustion on his normally vibrantly toned skin. Her throat tightened now as she remembered just wanting to hold him. If that day had been tough for her, she had told herself, it must have been a hundred times worse for Dante.

'I wasn't asleep,' she'd said as he'd come to sit on the side of the bed.

'You were waiting up.'

She'd shaken her head at the accusation. 'You look so tired.' She'd run a hand over the stubble on his square jaw—he even made haggard look sexy as hell.

'Not too tired.' She remembered the cool of his fingers as he'd caught the hand she had raised to his cheek and pulled her into him, his whisky-tinged breath warm and on his mouth as he'd husked against her lips, 'I just want to...bury myself in you.'

She pushed away the memories that were too painful now. They reminded her of her own wilful stupidity—for her that night it had gone beyond physical release. Dante had always taken her to a sensual heaven, but this connection had gone deeper, she had told herself as she'd lain later, her damp, cooling body entwined in his, tears of emotion too intense to name leaking from the corners of her eyes. She had felt so…complete.

But it had been a lie, her lie, and the cracks had started to appear almost immediately—before their heated, damp bodies had finished cooling in the velvet darkness.

CHAPTER FOUR

BEA WAITED UNTIL he had finished dressing before voicing the question that had inserted itself in her head and wouldn't go away. If she didn't ask she knew from experience the anxiety would start to eat away at her.

'I was wondering…' She paused, wishing she possessed Dante's enviable ability to distance himself from negative emotions. The world could be falling apart, panic endemic, but Dante, all calm, reasoned logic, would stand apart.

'Wondering?'

'Will last night affect the divorce?' What was the legal take on sleeping with your *almost* ex-husband?

'That's what you're worried about?'

'Well, aren't you?'

He gave a twisted smile. 'Are you going to tell anyone about it?'

The colour flew to her cheeks. 'Of course not, though of course Maya will—'

'Will be waiting for our walk of shame.'

'Maya doesn't judge.' Or blab, which was just as well when you considered the things she had told her sister.

'Of course she doesn't.'

She ignored the sarcasm and pushed him for an answer. 'Well, will it?'

'I see no reason it should.'

'Right, so we can forget last night happened and get on with our lives.'

'You seem to be already doing that...'

Underneath the smooth delivery she picked up *something* in his voice, an unspoken *suggestion* that she shouldn't be. It brought a flare of anger and she embraced it, embraced anything that wasn't the emotions of this slow, never-ending, nerve-wracking goodbye.

'Well, I *thought* about sitting in a room and fading away, but then I thought there might be life after Dante and you know what—' she widened her eyes in bright blue mockery '—there is.'

Jaw clenched, Dante viciously shoved a section of shirt in the waistband of his trousers and dragged a hand across his hair. 'So, who is he?'

'Who...what...?' She expelled a little sigh of comprehension as enlightenment dawned. This time she didn't need to jab her anger into life. 'Oh!'

For a split second she was tempted to invent an active love life—after all, she seriously doubted a man with Dante's appetites would have been celibate. His morals were certainly flexible enough for him to not allow something like a *nearly* ex-wife to keep him faithful.

Would he be jealous?

It was a sign that she had a long way to go in her journey to not caring to know that she wanted him to be.

'Does there always have to be a man?' she countered, viewing him with arch-browed disdain. 'I don't need a man to complete me! *Any* man! I am not my m—' She stopped before she voiced the comparison that was in her head.

It took a moment for his muscles to unclench and banish the image in his head of a faceless male exploring the delights of Beatrice's body. He'd get used to the idea, but it was too soon yet, which sounded like a rationalisation and was, which was new territory for a man who had never understood the concept of jealousy in relationships.

But now the idea of another man appreciating Beatrice's long lush curves, beautiful face, the shape and intensity of colour of her wide-spaced sapphire eyes, the wide, generous curve of her lips and the smooth pallor of her flawless creamy skin filled him with an impotent rage.

The idea of the laughter in her eyes and her deep, full-throttle, throaty laugh being aimed at someone who was not him made his grip on his self-control grow slippery.

'We should have had a wild passionate affair.' Wild passionate affairs had a beautiful simplicity. They burned bright, they hit a peak and they faded. Controlled madness that was temporary, that left no regrets, no sense of unfinished business.

His words made her flinch. 'Instead I got pregnant… The irony is, of course, that if we'd just waited there wouldn't have been a baby to get married for.'

His expression darkened. 'That wasn't what I meant, and you know it. I know you blame me for the miscarriage but—'

'I blame you?'

His lips twisted in a cynical half-smile that left his dark eyes bleak as he challenged, 'So you have *never* thought that if you hadn't been forced to transplant yourself to another country, an alien environment, being isolated from everything you knew, your entire support system, you might not have lost the baby?'

'I thought none of those things.' But it was clear

from his expression that he did. Why had she never suspected that Dante felt guilt for the loss of the baby? 'The doctors told us that a high portion of pregnancies end early on—a lot of women don't even know there ever was a baby.'

'Stress plays a part in these things. And an affair would inevitably have burnt itself out and we could have parted friends.'

'I think we have already established that isn't going to happen. You do realise that that was spoken like a true commitment-phobe.'

Dante shrugged. He had no problems with the description, though it implied that he had been running or avoiding something, which he hadn't.

Dante had never felt anything that inclined him to believe that he was marriage material. He would, he had always suspected, make a terrible husband. Well, on that at least he had been proved right—he had been, and he was.

'You need to leave.' She caught her lower lip between her teeth, her eyes swivelling from him towards the door, recognising the danger, the anger between them often found release in a *physical* way.

'Yes, I do.'

It had all gone quiet downstairs but the main thing was making Dante vanish and failing that…there was no way she could smuggle Dante out without Maya seeing him. She paused mid thought, almost wanting to laugh that she had been considering the smuggling option!

About time you took responsibility for your own actions, she told herself sternly, knowing full well it wasn't Maya's judgement she was trying to dodge but her own. She tightened the belt on her robe, causing the neckline to gape and drawing his eyes like magnets to the smooth swell of her cleavage.

Beatrice swallowed. His eyelids had dropped to half mast; the gleam below made her throat dry.

'That's the exact same colour as the top you were wearing when we first met. You had something in your eye.'

'Did I? I don't remember,' she lied.

'You were making it worse, stabbing your eyes with that tissue. And swearing like a sailor. You bumped into me.'

'You bumped into me,' she contradicted, her breath coming fast as she remembered him taking the tissue from her fingers, ignoring her protests. *'Let me,'* he'd said and she had—soon she had let him do a lot more.

She'd *begged* him to do a lot more!

'You looked so—' Young, fresh and a million miles away from the sleek creature on the catwalk, but even more sexy without the dramatic make-up, her pale hair no longer sleeked back but loose. It had spilled like silk down her back. He should have realised then that she was an innocent but he hadn't, and when he had, it had been too late.

You think it would have made a difference? his inner voice mocked as he dragged himself back to the moment and watched as Beatrice shook her head.

The effort to escape the memories in her head hurt but it was worth it. She had moved on and, more importantly, *she would never become her mother.*

'So, we have an understanding. From now on any communication will be through our legal teams,' she said, making her voice cold.

'You don't have a team. You have a solicitor who

spends more time watering his roses than looking after his clients' interests.'

Left to that guy Beatrice would be walking away from their marriage just as poor financially as she'd walked into it, if he had not issued some instructions that made his own legal team look slightly sick. There were some lawyers who recognised a moral scruple when they saw one, but none of them worked for the Velazquez family.

'Bea, shall I bring the coffee up?'

Dante watched as Beatrice responded to the voice that drifted up the stairs with an 'over my dead body' expression on her face, which she backed up with a dagger look.

Not analysing his motivation, he walked past her and pulled the door open.

'We'll be right down, Maya!' He let the door close with a snap.

Feet apart, hands on her hips, she fixed him with a glare of seething dislike. 'Well, thank you for that.'

'Call it a parting gift.'

'I'd call it a cheap shot.'

He sighed out his irritation. 'Would it be preferable for me to just appear? At least she's had some fore-warning. Unless you were going to smuggle me out?'

Beatrice felt the guilty wash of colour stain her cheeks. 'Let's just get this over with. Don't say *any-thing*,' she hissed.

'Is there anything left to say?'

'I suppose not.'

Her expression was as blank as her voice. Once, he had been able to read everything she felt because she had worn her emotions so close to the surface. Was this what palace life had done to her?

What you did to her.

He'd set her free, which ought to make him feel good. It didn't, but then he'd always thought doing the right thing was overhyped.

Her sister, dressed in dark ski pants and a chunky cable sweater she wore with the sleeves rolled up, didn't turn as she continued to stir the scrambled eggs on the stove.

There was an unmistakable chill in the air.

'Good morning, Dante.'

'Dante was just—'

'Let's not go there, shall we?' Maya stopped stirring and turned, spoon in hand. She blanked Dante, which was something not many people could manage, and slanted a wry look across at her sister.

Beatrice bit her tongue, though not sure of the words she was biting back. Would the jumble in her head have emerged as a defence or apology?

Maya turned back to her stirring. 'Want some breakfast, Dante?' she asked, still not looking at him.

'No, he doesn't,' Beatrice said before Dante could respond. 'He was just going.' To emphasise the point she went to the door and opened it. The waft of cold, fresh, snowy air made her gasp but she stood her ground, appeal mingled with the determination in the glance she sent to Dante.

'Nice to see you, Maya.' The petite figure continued to stir, presenting her back to him, but he could feel the disapproval radiating off her in waves.

The door closed; the tension left Beatrice's body. She grabbed the back of one of the dining chairs and lowered herself into the modern plastic bucket seat. 'How's your head? The migraine gone?'

'Fine. All I needed was an early night, but it seems

that things got interesting after I left.' Maya took her pan off the stove and poured a coffee from the full pot. She placed it on the table in front of Beatrice, a worried frown puckering her brow as she scanned her sister's face.

Beatrice cleared her throat. 'You must be wondering.' Now there was an understatement.

Maya shook her head. 'Just tell me you're not getting back together, you're not going back to San Macizo…'

'I'm never seeing him again,' Beatrice said and burst into tears.

As for San Macizo, the last time she had left she had left behind part of herself. If she went back she knew she'd lose what she had left.

'Thank God!' Maya hefted out a deep sigh of relief.

Beatrice sniffed and dashed the moisture from her face with the back of her hand.

'Oh, I know it's not my…and I'm *trying* to be objective, but honestly, when you came back last time looking like a…a…'

Shocked by the expression on her sister's face, Beatrice covered her small hand with her own. 'I'm not going back,' she cut in, holding her sister's teary, scared gaze.

'So what was he…?'

'Reynard has had a stroke.'

Dismay spread across Maya's heart-shaped face, melting away the last wisps of disapproval. 'Oh, I'm so sorry. Reynard was such a lovely man, with such a wicked sense of humour. When is the funeral? I'd like to come if I may?'

'It wasn't fatal,' Beatrice said quickly. She got up, picked up a piece of toast and started to butter it, not because she could have eaten a bite, just for something to do. 'So those buyers lined up to view the samples…'

'Changing the subject, Bea?'

'I know you don't like Dante.'

'I think Dante is perfectly charming,' Maya inserted, her lips curving into a wry smile, before adding, 'But I don't, I can't, *like* anyone who makes you unhappy.'

'I'm not unhappy.'

It was an obvious struggle for Maya not to challenge this statement, but lip-biting won out.

'And Dante is gone. He's never coming back.'

This time the crying went on a long time.

CHAPTER FIVE

'*DATES!*'

Beatrice blinked, caught between confusion and panic. She dragged her wandering blue gaze back to the young GP's face and allowed the professional encouraging smile to drag her back from the brink of panic. Though kick-starting her brain remained a non-starter—she felt utterly incapable of forming coherent thoughts.

'Dates...?' she echoed, as though she were thinking about it, which she wasn't. Thinking was simply not an option.

The reality was she could barely remember her name, let alone the information the locum GP, a young woman her own age, was asking for. Her regular doctor was, ironically, given the circumstances, on paternity leave.

'I know... I think...' She clenched her hands as she struggled to push past the loud static buzz in her head, which she explained by telling herself she needed a sugar hit. She hadn't managed to keep her breakfast down or, for that matter, last night's supper...*again*!

'Take your time,' the woman said, even though Beatrice was sure she had overrun her allowed time slot by a long way. An image of the foot-tapping disapproval as fellow patients glanced at the clock on the waiting-room wall flashed into her head—she'd been there, done that herself.

This doctor, with the relaxed attitude to time, seemed nice and sympathetic, which might not be a good thing. She had reached the point where it would only take a kind word to release the tears she could feel pressing against her eyelids.

So Beatrice avoided the sympathy and focused on the hole in the woman's tights as she wrapped her arms around herself in a self-protective hug to combat the cold inside her that was making her teeth chatter and sending intermittent tremors through her body.

'So, I'm assuming that this wasn't planned?' the medic, who had scooted her chair around to Beatrice's side of the desk, suggested.

Beatrice shook her head and wished the medic's calm were contagious, but then the professional had seen this a hundred times before and this wasn't professional for Beatrice.

'Statistically pregnancies rarely are planned.'

Tell me about it, she thought, swallowing the ironic laugh locked in her aching throat. 'Really?' If that was meant to make her feel better, it didn't.

'Did someone come with you?'

Beatrice reeled in her wandering thoughts, back from the unknown and scary future they had drifted towards, and tried very hard to focus on the here and now and not fainting—she *never* fainted.

'Someone…?' She moved her head, a tiny jerky, shaking motion, before clearing her throat, relieved when she responded with a close approximation of someone who had not totally lost it. 'Yes…yes, my sister.'

Who had refused to take no for an answer and had tagged along to the appointment that Beatrice had made after the stomach bug had not cleared up. Had Maya sussed the truth…had she?

Of course she had, but she'd buried the knowledge so deep…constructed so many perfectly reasonable, safe alternatives that it had not lessened the mind-deadening shock when confronted with the inevitable reality.

Despite the shock, her body continued to perform all its automated responses: she was breathing and moving, putting one foot… Actually she wasn't—she was sitting down and her knees were shaking. She was thinking, *Well, maybe not.* Her thoughts continued to refuse to move beyond the big mental brick wall. *I am pregnant.*

In her head she tacked several large exclamation marks on the acknowledgement, which did not make it feel any more real.

'I'm six weeks,' she said suddenly, her tone making it clear there were no ifs and buts or maybes about this. A warmth heated her pale cheeks as her thoughts drifted back to the night she'd spent under the duvet in the ski lodge with Dante. Sometimes on top of the duvet and sometimes… She felt a shameful flash of heat and closed down the thought of the night they had made a baby. 'It's our eighteen-month anniversary today…'

'Congratulations. Your husband isn't here today?'

Beatrice watched the doctor tap some keys on the computer and grimace as she noticed the hole in her tights.

'He's out of the country,' she said carefully.

'Would you like me to…? Shall I ask your sister to come in?'

Beatrice gave a pale smile of gratitude. 'Yes, please.'

A short while later she and Maya were out of the surgery and back in the fresh air. Beatrice expelled a long shuddering sigh and squeezed her eyes closed, opening them as she felt Maya's arm link with her own.

'Fancy walking back through the park?'

'Didn't we drive here?' If she had imagined that she was in even worse shape than she thought, Beatrice decided.

'Yes, but the fresh air might do us good... I'll pick up the car later.' She glanced at the little vintage car they had jointly bought when they first set up home together. It had seen better days.

Beatrice shrugged. 'Why not?'

The watery spring sun had come out from behind the clouds as they trudged beneath the skeletal branches of a row of poplars and past the snowdrops that were pushing up through the cold ground.

It was Maya who broke the silence.

'I love the smell of spring, all that promise of new life...' She pulled her wandering gaze, which had drifted to her sister's flat stomach, upwards. 'Sorry, I didn't mean to be profound or anything.'

Beatrice turned her head, then, as her eyes connected with the concern clouding Maya's eyes that her sister was unable to hide, she quickly looked away. 'You knew?' she asked, digging her hands into the deep pockets of her coat.

'It seemed...a...possibility...'

'You must think I'm a total idiot!' So must the doctor, not that she could remember the things she had said or any details of her own responses.

'I will think you're an idiot if you carry on saying daft things like that.'

Beatrice produced a pale, lacklustre smile in response. 'I suppose I must have known,' she admitted, thinking of all the signs that had been there. 'But I didn't think it would happen again...after...' Her voice trailed away, a faint ironic smile tugging at the corners of her lips as her thoughts drifted to the words of unbidden advice Dante's grandfather, still autocratically regal despite the fact he had passed on his official title to his son after a stroke, had offered. *'Relax, woman.'*

His words had stuck in her mind, mainly because at the time everyone else had been telling her to panic, if not in so many words—it had not been hard to read between the lines or the glances and conversations that halted abruptly when she appeared.

Well, it turned out that old Reynard was right all along. All she had needed to do was relax...

Oh, God, no one had ever accused her of having good timing.

Beatrice turned her head. The worried expression on her sister's face pushed her into speech. 'It's just everyone was waiting, every month...and letting myself hope, and then having to tell Dante when it didn't happen.' He had acted as though it didn't matter, but she knew it did; she knew that as far as the palace was concerned her fertility had stopped being a private matter the moment Dante became Crown Prince.

She looked down at her flat belly and tried to separate the confusing mess of conflicting emotions fighting for supremacy in her head. 'A year ago, this would have made him so happy.' Frowning, she worried her full lower lip and wondered about his reaction now. Who was she kidding? She knew *exactly* what his reaction would be when she discovered that she was carrying the heir to the throne.

This was the end of her new life; there was no way he would allow her to bring up his child outside San Macizo.

'Is that why you left…?'

'Left?' Beatrice gave a vague shake of her head.

Maya studied her sister's face and glanced around for a convenient park bench, hoping they would make it there before Beatrice folded.

'You never said *why*, just that it was over, when you got home.'

Beatrice gave a sad smile. 'I'm pretty sure that it was why Dante made it easy for me to go.'

Maya caught her hand as Beatrice's voice became suspended by tears.

'You never asked me before,' Beatrice said.

'I thought you'd tell me when you were ready.'

'It's hard to explain my life. I felt like I'd stepped into a trickling stream and ended up trying to keep my head above raging white water. Things happened so fast—one minute I was me and the next I was pregnant and married.'

'Then you were a princess.'

Beatrice forced a laugh. 'A very bad one…then I lost the baby and there was no time to grieve.' She compressed her quivering lips. 'I was expected to do my duty and provide an heir. People acted as though our first baby had never existed. I hate now that I kept apologising, when I wanted—' She had wanted to hear Dante say that she didn't have anything to apologise for, that a baby shouldn't be about duty, it should be about *love*.

But he hadn't.

But then love had not been a word her husband had ever used. *Did he even believe it existed?*

He had been happy to tell her how much he *wanted* her, his throaty voice making her insides dissolve. But even then, sometimes she'd got the impression that he'd given in to the desire she awoke in him reluctantly.

She had told herself that discussing feelings was hard for some men, but beneath the rationalising she had known it was more than that.

She couldn't acknowledge her secret fear that the issue wasn't his inability to acknowledge his deep feelings; no, she worried that he just didn't have them. After the baby was gone, there was nothing deep connecting them, just passion... And now there was another life.

She gave a bleak little laugh and turned to Maya. 'I wonder if there are any statistics about the rate of divorce for Vegas marriages?'

'You sure there is going to be a divorce now?'

Beatrice decided not to acknowledge the doubt she could see in her sister's eyes. It was a doubt she shared, a doubt she was trying very hard not to confront.

'I think you need to sit down,' Maya added, stepping off the pathway and approaching a bench.

It took Beatrice a few moments before she roused herself enough to react to the prompt of her sister patting the seat beside her.

Hunched forward, Beatrice planted her hands on juddering knees.

Maya put one small hand onto one of hers. 'Tell me to shut up, it's none of my business, but what happened, Bea?'

'I found it pencilled into my diary.'

'What?'

'An appointment with an IVF specialist,' she said. Maya was the only one who would know the full significance of that.

Her sister did. 'Oh, my God, what did you do?'

'Other than not be like Mum, you mean? Oh, you

know me, very subtle and royal to my fingertips. I charged into Dante's meeting with a room full of the island's captains of industry and told him that enough was enough. That I didn't want staff, I didn't want a diary and that my childbearing hips were not a subject for staff meetings!'

She remembered the white line of fury outlining his sensual lips as he had escorted her from the room.

Beatrice shrugged, her eyes following the antics of a squirrel that was running through the branches of a nearby tree.

'He called me naive and said I was overreacting.' The lingering bitterness hardened her voice. 'I probably was, and, oh…it's hard to describe what it's like in the palace.' She lifted her hands, her long fingers sliding through her silky blonde hair, lifting the tangled strands off her neck before she let it fall in silky waves down her back.

'I wanted to wait. I didn't want a baby then. I was still grieving for the one I'd lost… Oh, I know they were only a bundle of cells, but—'

'Of course you needed time. Didn't Dante understand how you felt?'

'I never told him. We didn't discuss it…or actually anything much. With Carl gone, he was under a lot of pressure. Maybe I'm more like Mum than I thought,' she mused, remembering her words of moments ago— it would have made *him* happy.

When did she stop asking herself what would make her happy?

Like her own mother, she had seen what she wanted to; she had put her own needs to one side to please a man.

'Oh, Bea, you know that's not true!'

Beatrice's glance fluttered from her sister's face

across the flash of cheery yellow where winter jasmine was in bloom.

'I'm going to have a baby.' She said it like a practice run, imaging herself throwing the line into the conversation, but no, her imagination fell short. It still didn't feel real. 'I really do have great timing, don't I?'

'I wouldn't say the timing is just down to you,' her sister responded drily.

'I will have to tell Dante.'

Maya's expression softened into sympathy as she saw the realisation hit home for Beatrice, who began to scrabble for her phone in the bag that was looped across her shoulder.

'Give yourself time first, to get your own head around it,' Maya advised, trying to hide the worry she felt behind an encouraging smile.

Beatrice, her teeth worrying at her full lower lip, shook her head. The way she felt right now, that moment might never come and the longer she left it—well, it was never going to get any easier.

'Do I have to tell him?' she said with a surge of wild hope that vanished into guilt as she connected with the sympathy in her sister's eyes. 'I didn't mean that. It's just that everything will change. This baby is second in line to the throne.' It seemed like a terrible responsibility to give a child before they were even born. 'Dante had a bad childhood, you know, and now this baby will be brought up in that world…'

'Dante had a bad childhood because his parents are vile self-centred narcissists. This baby will have you.'

'If I go back.' In her heart she knew there was no *if* about it. The baby made it a forgone conclusion. 'It won't be like the last time. I won't be brought out like some sort of—'

'Don't tell me, Bea,' Maya cut in. 'Tell him. Did he know about Mum and the IVF thing?'

Beatrice shook her head. 'It seems like yesterday sometimes.'

The sisters' eyes met, their glances holding as they both remembered the period in their teens when, in an attempt to satisfy her husband's demands for a child of their own, their mother had turned to IVF to give him the *real* child he had wanted, which he had said would make them a *real* family.

Witnessing the physical and mental toll that cycle after cycle of treatment had wrought on their mother's health had been bad, but what had been worse was the blame game that had come after each failure from the man who held his wife responsible for not providing him with his *own* child.

'Do you have any idea what this is doing to me?'

The familiar petulant response had soon set the tone of their stepfather's reaction to having *his* plans disappointed. It had always been *her* fault: if she had *rested* more, if she had been more motivated, healthier, thinner, fatter…*if*…*if*… The list of accusations had been endless.

When one specialist had refused to treat them any more because of the impact on their mother's health, they had moved on to the next clinic.

'I used to think that I'd never go down that road…' Maya said suddenly. 'But, do you remember Prue?'

'The Prue who married the cricket player, but is much more famous for doing your maths homework?'

'She and Jake had twins through IVF. I've never seen two people happier.'

'That's not the same. Prue and her cricketer wanted a baby because they loved…' Beatrice felt her eyes fill.

'It wasn't duty. I left of my own volition, but it was only a matter of time before Dante would have been forced to put me aside for someone with a more reliable reproductive system.'

'He is a total bastard,' Maya said conversationally.

'He's the father of my child.'

Maya grimaced. 'I'm sorry…'

'I'm not.' Beatrice pressed her hands to her still-flat stomach. The panic was still there but it was pushed into the background by a certainty. 'You probably think I'm mad, but I *want* this baby.'

Maya smiled. 'I don't think you're mad, I think you're… I think you'll make a marvellous mum and I intend to be a pretty great auntie too.' Her eyes widened with awed realisation. 'God, with you as a mum and Dante as a dad, this baby really has hit the gene jackpot.'

CHAPTER SIX

'I'M AFRAID HIS Highness is—'

'Unavailable at the moment?' Beatrice inserted, her words dripping with saccharine-coated sarcastic venom, not caring by this point that she was killing the messenger.

This messenger at least.

It had taken all her courage to make that first call and she had felt physically sick as she had punched in Dante's personal number, only to have her call diverted to someone who had identified herself as 'His *Royal* Highness the Crown Prince's office'—not actually an office but a snooty-sounding female, whom Beatrice took an instant dislike to.

Over the last few hours her instincts had proved to be bang on. She also knew that her husband was ghosting her—every single number or email address she had for him came up as unrecognised or no longer available.

The only number that was taking her calls was this one.

'His *Royal* Highness is not taking calls but I can pass on a message.'

'Yes, you mentioned that,' Beatrice cut her off before she went deep into auto message mode.

This was the fifth time now that she had tried to

contact Dante and the fifth time she had been given the same runaround by this faceless underling with the nice line in patronising.

'But if you would prefer to address your questions to His Highness's legal representatives... Do you have the number of the law firm? I can—'

Eyes squeezed tight, Beatrice told her exactly what she could do, and heard the shocked, offended gasp on the other end. She wasn't proud of it, but there were limits, and she had reached hers and then some.

In the periphery of her vision she was aware of Maya's frantic hand signals as she mimed zipping motions across her lips.

She ignored them and smiled. She wasn't enjoying herself, but it was a relief to stick her head over the parapet and stick it to Dante's messenger.

'I don't actually have any *questions*, I just want to deliver some information.'

'I will pass on any important information.'

'It is personal information. Sensitive information.'

'I am a *personal* assistant.'

'In that case...why not?' Beatrice came back smoothly. 'Do you have a pen? Fine, yes, well, take this down, will you? Tell my *husband*...' She ground the title home as she jabbed the pencil she had picked up into the stack of unopened post on the table. 'Tell him that I thought he might like to know that he is going to be a father. Got that?' she asked pleasantly, and decided to take the choked sound at the other end of the line as an affirmative. 'Well, thank you so much for your help. I'll be sure to mention your name when I speak to my husband!' Her breath gusting fast and frantic, she ended the call, her glance moving from the phone, still grasped in her white-knuckled hand, to her sister.

She pressed her hand to her mouth and gave a nervous giggle, her eyes flying to Maya, who rolled her own.

'You didn't stick to your script.'

'No, I didn't.' Beatrice looked at the stack of bullet points printed on cards that had been meant to aid her calm delivery of the facts, even factoring in a potential mind blank when it came to telling Dante.

She had not factored in a red-mist moment.

'I imagine you might get a response now,' Maya murmured as Beatrice continued to look at the phone in her hand as if it were an unexploded bomb.

'I lost my temper. What have I done now?'

It had been three in the morning before Beatrice had finally managed to drop off, so it took her a few moments to orientate herself and realise that the noise was not part of her dream, but real.

Someone—it didn't take too many guesses who—had their hand pressed to the doorbell, filling the flat with a continual tiny rendition of the 'William Tell Overture', their landlord's tasteful choice.

Maya appeared as Bea was dragging on a robe over her nightshirt.

'How did he get here this quickly?'

Beatrice shrugged.

'Shall I get it, tell him to come back later?'

'Like that's going to work…' She dragged a hand through her tousled hair and tried to dredge up some calm. 'No…no, I'll be fine.' She took another deep breath, and tightened the sash on her full-length robe as she lifted her chin to a defiant angle.

Maya looked doubtful. 'If you say so. I'll be in my bedroom if you need me.'

'Thanks.' Beatrice smiled but barely noticed her sister go; her thoughts had already moved on to the person outside the door.

She was vaguely conscious of her sister's bedroom door clicking closed as she blew out a slow calming breath, which didn't slow the speed of her pounding heart even a little, and reached for the handle.

Leaving the safety catch in place, she opened it. The action would normally have revealed the communal hallway, with a worn rug that covered the scratched parquet floor, and a noticeboard. But today all she could see through the door was Dante, who effectively blocked everything else from view.

He pushed himself off the wall and far enough away for her to see more of the dark suit he was wearing. Not his normal immaculate self—the fabric was crumpled and his white shirt was open at the neck, revealing a section of warm brown skin—but she barely noticed these details. All she saw, or rather felt, were the powerful, raw emotions that were emanating from him.

'You moved.' Dante had been keeping his emotions in check, but the sight of her standing there and he could feel them slipping through his fingers like a wet rope, taking his control with it. 'No one told me.'

The journey here—he'd been mid-Atlantic when he had received the message, a sentence that was going to literally change his life in ways he was still too shocked to imagine—had already pushed his control to the limits.

The sight of her big blue eyes looking warily at him through the gap, rimmed with red from where she had been crying, didn't make him any less furious. It just added another layer to the emotions fighting for supremacy in his chest.

'Last week—it's bigger.' Just as she would be soon. An idea that still seemed deeply strange and not quite *real*.

Dante was very real though, and *very* angry.

'The people who live there now seem… I left my security team persuading them I am not dangerous.' While he had spent several frustrating minutes finding the correct address to give his driver.

'What are you doing here?' The accusing words floated through the gap and drew a low feral disbelieving growl from his throat.

'Are you *serious*?'

'It really wasn't necessary for you to come in person. A simple acknowledgement you'd got the news would have done fine.'

'Well, I am here.'

'I'm sure everyone in the building knows that. Come back tomorrow.'

Was he meant to care what people thought?

'That isn't going to happen and we both know it. Are you going to let me in or would you like to have this discussion here?' He bestowed a scathing glance at his surroundings before fixing her with a steely bitter stare. 'Sorry, I forgot my megaphone, but I have several paparazzi on speed dial…if that is your preference? Sure, let's share the news! Oh, I forgot, you already have.' It would be interesting to know just how many people she had told before she had told him…but then he was only the father.

Her lips tightened at the sarcasm. 'Lower your voice and don't be so unreasonable.'

'I suppose I should consider myself lucky you didn't send the news by text!'

Although on second thoughts, he decided as he experienced a stomach-clenching chilled aftershock of what he had felt as he had listened to his stand-in PA tell him he was going to be a father, a text might have been preferable!

She slipped the safety chain and hastily backed away, standing there, arms folded across her chest, as he entered a hallway that had been described in the rental details as a spacious dining hall.

A slight exaggeration, but it had never felt this claustrophobically cramped before.

'I tried to contact you.'

'You didn't try very hard.'

Her lips compressed. 'I suppose it depends on your definition of hard. The number I have for you no longer exists. Though why I'm telling you this I don't know, because I assume that you're the one who arranged for my calls to be diverted to your robotic PA.'

'She's a very good PA.' And he might have sacked her, he realised, a furrow forming between his dark brows as he replayed the in-flight exchange.

The details of the incident were a little sketchy, but in his shocked state of mind he presumed he must have asked her to repeat what she had just said, because she had repeated, word for word, the message that had left him literally rigid with shock.

The second time of telling had involved the same words, but no longer a statement, more a question conveying a snide implication that he had taken exception to.

'She says *she is pregnant? Are you calling my wife a liar?'*

'She is very efficient,' he said now.

'Oh, I have no doubt that she was only saying what she was told to. I assume that it was you who told her

that any further communication would be through our
legal teams.'

'That,' he reminded her grimly, 'was your idea.'

'I should have known it would be my fault.' Without
warning the fight drained out of her, leaving her feeling
weak-kneed, shaky and fighting back tears.

'Are you all right?'

She scraped together enough defiance to throw back
a querulous, 'I'm pregnant, not ill.'

His chest lifted in a silent sigh. 'So, it's true?'

'Obviously not. I just made it up.'

'Sorry, that was a stupid thing to say.'

She squeezed her eyes closed and felt his hand on
her elbow. 'Yes, it was.' She opened her eyes and shook
her head, unable to keep a quiver of emotion out of
her voice as she tilted her head back to look him in
the face.

'You should sit down.'

'I should be in bed. I *was* in bed.' Conscious of her
shaky knees and the fact she was grateful for the support of his hand, she nodded to the door just behind him.
'The sitting room is through there,' she said, afraid that
he might take the next door, to her bedroom. Bedrooms
were where all this had started. 'Be careful. There are
boxes we haven't got around to unpacking yet.'

Skirting the packing cases, he continued to hover
protectively until she had sat down on one of the sofas.

'So, have you seen a doctor?' he asked, dropping
into a squat beside her. He scanned her pale features
and felt a gut punch of guilt. She looked as if she had
been crying for a week. Maybe she had. She looked so
fragile that he was afraid to hold her. She looked as if
she might break.

She nodded.

'So, there's no mistake.' Under the fresh wave of guilt he was conscious of something new. A possessiveness, a protectiveness.

She shook her head, feeling tears threaten again as she wondered if that was what he had been hoping. That this was all some mistake that they would laugh about. She couldn't really blame him.

'And a scan?'

'Not yet…what are you doing?'

He lifted the phone away from his ear. 'Making arrangements.'

'Dante, it's half three in the morning.'

He shook his head as though the relevance passed him by.

'I know in your world you can demand anything you want at any time of day and people will jump, but in my world we make appointments in daylight hours and get put on waiting lists.'

'*Waiting* lists?'

'If you want to do something, make me a cup of tea. Ginger. It helps the nausea. The kitchen's through that way.' She tipped her head in the direction of an arch at the end of the room that fed into the galley kitchen. 'Teas are in the bottom cupboard, first right.'

She closed her eyes, pretty much too exhausted to see if he reacted and definitely too exhausted to argue. She didn't open them until she felt a hand on her arm.

'Drink,' he said, watching her.

She did, blowing on the surface of the liquid first to cool it as he took a seat on the opposite sofa. He appeared lost in his own thoughts.

Feeling like someone sitting in the eye of a storm, knowing that any second all hell would break loose again, she drank and felt a little less wretched.

She set her mug down on a side table and waited, tensing when Dante unfolded his long, lean length and got to his feet.

'I didn't think about the time,' he admitted. 'I was—'

'In shock—I know.'

'I realise that you must feel… I know this isn't what you wanted, but it is happening, and we have to deal with it.'

'We don't need to deal with anything.' She still felt as if she had been run over by a truck, but the tea was making her slightly more coherent. 'I am already *dealing*,' she added, anxious to correct any impression to the contrary she might have given. 'I'm booked in for my first scan, just to confirm dates, I think, in a few weeks.'

'Right, I'll cancel and have them schedule one for when we get back,' he murmured half to himself.

'Back?' she said, pretending a bewilderment she wasn't feeling as a cold fist tightened in her stomach.

'I'm not going anywhere. I'm here and I'm staying here.' She drew her knees up to her chest and wrapped her arms around them. 'Relax, once the divorce comes through we can sort out the details, how things will work.'

'What the hell are you talking about?' he ground out, realising that his life had changed the moment he had met Beatrice. Nothing had been the same since that day.

'There isn't going to be a divorce now you are carrying my child.'

She looked into his eyes and saw the same steely conviction that his voice carried. She half rose and subsided, shaking as panic spilled through her body.

She looked up at him, eyes looking even bigger. The dark rings around them making him think of a trapped animal.

'You are carrying our child, the heir to the throne. That changes everything.'

'He…she won't want that,' she said, pressing a hand to her stomach, the gesture unconscious.

'Shouldn't that be their call? Are you going to try and rob that child of their heritage, their birthright?'

'It didn't make you or Carl very happy,' she slung back.

'We don't have to repeat the mistakes of my parents.'

She lifted a shaking hand to her head. 'There has to be another way. I can't go back to *that*…' She shook her head. 'I won't be manipulated and managed.'

He was looking at her with the strangest expression. 'Is that how you felt?'

His shock seemed genuine.

'It is the way it was.'

'It won't be like that when you go back. There will be changes.'

She didn't have the strength to hide her extreme scepticism even if she had wanted to. 'What changes?'

'To hell with opinion polls, I'm putting my family first. This is not about having an heir. It is about being a father.' Until this moment he had never appreciated the massive difference between the two. 'We'll make it work.'

'For the baby.'

He said nothing, the steely determination she saw shining in his eyes said it all as he took her chin between his fingers.

'You can't bring this child up alone…'

She fought the urge to turn her cheek into his palm. 'People do every day, some out of choice, some because there is no alternative.'

'But you *have* an alternative,' he cut in smoothly. 'We've had a trial separation, why not a trial marriage?'

'Another word for a sham? Been there, done that,' she said tiredly. The emotional and physical stress of the past days, and maybe the pregnancy hormones, were making their strength-sapping presence felt and her fight was being replaced by a dangerous fatalism.

Perhaps sensing her defences were failing, he leaned in towards her, bringing their faces level; she met his eyes and felt guilty for doubting his sincerity. There was nothing sham about the emotions rolling off him.

When she thought about it later, she decided it was the emotion in his face, the concern and self-recrimination that made her stop fighting the inevitable.

She lifted her chin. 'Things will *have* to change...if I come back,' she tacked on quickly.

'I promise there will be no *managing*.'

'I want to be more than a decorative accessory; I want to be treated as an equal, not patronised. Oh...' Her head dropped a little as she looked at him through the veil of her dark lashes. 'I don't want you to tell anyone, not until I'm three months along and things are...*safer*.'

'My parents?'

She gave a tiny laugh that left her blue eyes sombre. '*Especially* your parents.' She did not think she could stand any of their insincerity. They wanted a royal baby and for a while she'd be flavour of the month, but she knew that before long they'd be planning behind the scenes how to detach her from the baby.

Did the conviction make her paranoid? Well, better that than naive.

'They don't like me, they never liked me...which is fine, because I don't like them either.'

After a moment, he nodded. 'This waiting, secrecy... did the doctor indicate that anything was amiss? That there is a potential problem with this pregnancy, with you?' The tautness in him rose visibly as his sharpened glance moved across her face.

'No, it's just early, and if anything did happen like before...' She felt the tears form in her eyes and looked away, the muscles in her pale slender throat working as she fought to contain her fears. 'I don't want anyone else to know. I don't care what you tell them, just—'

Dante dropped the hand that lay curved around her cheek and, rising to his feet, stepped back. The ferocious surge of protectiveness he was experiencing as he watched her was less easy to step away from.

'Nothing will happen.'

'You can't say that,' she choked back, looking at him through glistening blue eyes. 'Because it does, for some people, over and over and—' Her voice cracked as she swallowed and felt a big fat tear trickle down her face as she felt his hand slide to the back of her head. 'I really don't think I could bear that,' she whispered, her voice muffled against his chest.

Helplessness and a fierce wave of protectiveness arched through him as he pressed a kiss to the top of her silky head and stroked her hair as she wept out her fear.

The sobs that shook her subsided but she allowed herself a few moments of lying there, taking comfort from the solidity of his chest, the strength of his arms, finally heaving a deep sigh as she pulled free.

'Thank you,' she said with a loud sniff.

Dante felt something nameless twist hard inside him as he rose from the kneeling position he had fallen to beside the sofa. 'You are welcome.'

'I must look terrible.'

'Horrific. That's better,' he approved as she gave a watery smile. 'And soon you will get fat and you won't be able to see your feet.'

Will you still love me?

The words stayed in her head because he didn't love her now.

CHAPTER SEVEN

THEY EMERGED FROM the low-lying fog that had blanketed the area around the private airport into the spirit-lifting blue above. Beatrice's spirits didn't lift; the nervous tension making her shoulders ache didn't dissipate as she undid her seat belt and leaned back in the seat that bore an imprint of the Velazquez crown on the leather headrest. It had more of a welcoming embrace than any she had received from the Velazquez family, but then they were not really a *tactile* family.

She was under no illusions that any welcome she had in the future would be because of the baby. She didn't care about that, but the equally inescapable fact was that Dante only wanted her here because of the baby. She avoided the temptation to read anything else into his determination to rekindle their marriage.

The pilot's disembodied voice spoke, adding to his words of welcome the less welcome fact that there was the possibility of some turbulence ahead. *Tell me about it*, Beatrice thought, looking around and seeing that someone had already whisked away the fur-lined parka coat she had worn for the journey to the airport. She wouldn't need it, or the layers she had on underneath, at the other end. San Macizo enjoyed an all-year-round temperate climate.

She continued to exchange her boots for the flats she had pushed into her bag as Dante translated the pilot's Italian words.

She smiled and nodded absently, even though she hadn't needed him to translate. She had continued the lessons she had begun without much optimism during her brief sojourn in San Macizo where Italian, introduced to the country by the royal family centuries before, was the official language. Though she had never encountered a native who didn't speak English and French fluently, like Dante, who was also fluent in Arabic and Spanish.

Free of her layers, she adjusted the cuffs on her white shirt and watched as Dante unfastened his own seat belt and the buttons on his dark grey suit jacket and waited, wondering if it was worth getting the paperback out of her bag. She doubted she'd be able to concentrate—her nerves were too wound up.

No massive surprise there. What she had committed to was about as sane as deliberately opening a half-healed wound, and, as it turned out, just as painful. Up to the point of being welcomed onto the private jet she had not allowed herself to think about what lay ahead. Now she couldn't *stop* thinking about it.

After a few moments, a small frown appeared between her brows. Dante hadn't got up to seek a quiet, private office space to work in; he hadn't even reached for the laptop that lay on the seat next to him, let alone buried himself in it.

She found this break in familiar routine slightly unnerving. She searched her memory and could not remember a time, at least not since he had stepped into the role his brother had walked away from, that Dante hadn't immersed himself into work at every opportunity.

She had teased him at first about his ability to totally shut out distractions until she had realised that she was one of those distractions, then it had seemed less amusing.

Dante still showed no sign of moving away, and doing so herself would seem a bit obvious, so she exhaled a resigned sigh and reached for her book. Even if she could not lose herself in the world of fiction she would have somewhere to look that wasn't directly at her husband. *Husband*... She could remember saying that word out loud and smiling—it seemed a long time ago.

These days she felt impatient with her younger self for being so naive; while she had been walking on air she doubted that, despite what was written on a piece of paper, Dante had ever felt he was her husband, not really. But he *was* the father of her child.

She desperately wanted this baby. It was that utter certainty that was getting her through; the life growing inside her was light at the end of the tunnel.

She couldn't assume that Dante would feel the same way. She had to see things the way they were and not the way she wanted them to be.

Attracted to the wrong man and refusing to see the things that she didn't want to. *Now, where have I seen that before?* An image of her mother's face floated into her mind.

Beatrice found the idea of history repeating itself through the generations deeply depressing and she intended to break that cycle. It was just a pity she hadn't displayed the insight earlier, instead of spending her short marriage living in a fantasy world of her own making.

Just thinking about it, she could taste the self-disgust

in her mouth. The irony was, of course, that when she had finally opened her eyes to the reality of her marriage it had been impossible not to be struck by the fact she had been guilty of the same weakness that she had struggled to forgive in her own mother.

But though she couldn't avoid the glaring comparison with her own mother, she had never extended it to include Dante, who was nothing like her ex-stepfather, who had been a manipulative, cruel bully with a sadistic streak.

Dante was not the man she had *wanted* him to be. She had created a fiction; that did not make him a bad person. He was absolutely straightforward, strong, complex, impatient, arrogant and had zero tolerance for incompetence, but his only real sin had only ever been not to be in love with her.

But that didn't mean she had the right to rob their child of a father's love, nor rob their child of his heritage. But she was equally determined not to allow that heritage to emotionally damage the baby.

'Are you all right?'

She jumped as the sound of Dante's voice broke into her thoughts.

'What? Yes. Why…?'

One sardonic brow hitched, he nodded towards the book on her lap. 'It's upside down.'

She felt the guilty flush climb up her neck as she turned it around and then closed it. 'I never liked flying much.'

'There are no barriers, medically speaking, for you to fly at this stage.' He caught her surprised look. 'I have been reading up a little.'

'This is staying between us for now…*right*?'

'I have made some enquiries concerning obstetricians. *Discreet* enquiries. I understand that early monitoring is important.'

She thought about that and nodded. 'So, what have you told your parents?'

'I have told them we are back together.'

'That must have gone down well!'

'They need not concern you. If it makes you feel any more relaxed about it, I stopped trying to please them a long time ago, about when I realised it was never going to happen.'

He remembered the exact moment. He had been watching the flames of an open fire lick the Christmas card he had made them. The Christmas card they hadn't even bothered to open.

By the time it had collapsed into a pile of ashes he had decided that if they considered him the wild one, the unreliable one, the one who always caused them a headache, he might as well enjoy himself and do what people expected him to.

'Ah, I almost forgot. My grandfather sends his best wishes and says he hopes you can give him a decent game.'

Still wondering about his previous comments, she allowed herself a smile. 'At least I have one friend in the palace.'

Something flicked across his face that she struggled to interpret. 'You have a husband…'

Her glance fell. 'I haven't forgotten,' she said, thinking that it was a pity he couldn't say the same about her. The moment the palace doors had closed behind them she had been delegated out, the only use he'd had for her recreational.

'That was a big sigh… It is a steep learning curve, for me too.'

Surprised by the unexpected admission, she stared at him.

'Sadly, there are no intensive courses on being a Crown Prince. I had some valuable advice. My parents advised I delegate, which, as you might have noticed, is their management style. Grandfather, whose advice was actually quite helpful, said that I should trust no one and don't believe a word you're told.'

As he had hoped, his comment drew a laugh from Beatrice. The sound made him smile too, then his smile faded as he realised how much he had missed that sound.

'And now you have found your own style?'

'I like to think I have steered a personal course somewhere in between idle disregard for anything but my own comfort and paranoia, but the jury is out.'

As their smiling glances met and clung, she was aware of the perceptible shift in the atmosphere.

She pulled in a tense breath and looked away.

'Is something wrong? You can tell me.'

The unexpected addition brought her glance sweeping upwards. 'You just seem…?'

She paused, pulling in a long steadying breath, and wondered if the day would come when she could look at him and feel only aesthetic appreciation rather than an ache of need. You'd have thought that after a while boredom would have kicked in, but she could have happily stared at him forever.

'Seem?'

'Maybe it's just that you're—'

'I'm what?' he prompted with slightly less patience.

'It's that you're still…' Her hands moved in a descriptive sweep that made the collection of silver bracelets she wore on her left wrist jangle. 'You're here.'

His dark brows knitted; he looked genuinely mystified. 'Where else would I be?'

A small laugh burst from her lips. Had Dante *really* never realised that from the moment the news had been delivered that his brother had decided to renounce his claim to the throne, Dante had tuned her out, more than distance, much more than an understandable preoccupation with the role that had been thrust upon him?

She had felt at best surplus to requirements, at worst, an embarrassment.

'Busy with more important things?' she flung out and bit her lip as her unthinking retort was laden with an inch-thick layer of bitterness.

She lifted a hank of slippery, shiny hair that was crawling down the collar of her crisp white shirt, then catching the direction of his gaze made her glance towards the folded cashmere sweater she had discarded as she gritted her teeth and fought the ludicrous impulse to fasten another button, or pull her sweater back on. Instead she smoothed the non-existent creases in the tailored pale cream trousers and fussed with the buckle on the narrow red leather belt that held them up, just to give her hands something to do.

Her lips twisted as she noticed that Dante seemed to be having a similar problem. His long fingers flexed and clenched as if he was fighting an instinct to reach for his laptop after her comment.

She vented an internal sigh. Ah, well, this looked like it was going to be a nice relaxing journey—always supposing you were the sort of person who found nail-biting tension and sitting on the edge of your seat while looking for an escape route relaxing!

She adopted a carefully neutral expression as she lifted her chin and crossed her feet neatly at the ankle. The soft leather flats she had changed into proved you could look fashionable and be comfortable. Well, at least from the ankle down—being comfortable elsewhere was hard when she remained so acutely conscious of the restrained power Dante exuded. Always a challenge to cope with, but overpowering in any enclosed space, and right now her feelings were too raw and close to the surface to make her feel confident about disguising her vulnerability.

'I'm fine, feel free to...' She made an all-encompassing motion with her hand before she gave an elaborate yawn. 'I didn't get much sleep last night.'

She and Maya had talked into the small hours, and after her sister had gone to bed she had lain fully dressed on her bed staring at the ceiling, dreading the morning. She had finally fallen asleep half an hour before her phone alarm sounded, and had felt like death warmed up.

'Nor the night before,' she continued unthinkingly, then tacked on, 'That wasn't a dig.'

'I'm sorry I disturbed your sleep.'

'It wouldn't be the first time.'

The quiver of her stomach could have been connected with the lurch as they hit a pocket of turbulence, but she knew it wasn't.

'All right?'

'Fine. I always liked roller coasters.' She breathed through a wave of nausea and missed what he said next. 'Sorry...?' she pushed out, her hand pressed to her throat.

'I said...' He paused, his heavy-lidded glance lingering on the dark smudges beneath her glorious eyes.

Dante didn't know where he stood on the nature, nurture debate, whether he'd inherited the trait from his parents or simply learnt by example didn't seem the point, but whatever the truth he had always possessed the ability to step back and observe events and people from an objective perspective.

Except with Beatrice.

'You do look tired.'

'Thanks,' she murmured drily, translating the comment that he'd framed more like an accusation as, *You do look awful*.

'Maya and I were trying to decide what to do now that I'm, well…not there.'

'Setting up a business is challenging.' And he suspected that most of the work fell on Beatrice's shoulders. He had nothing against Maya, but she didn't seem that *dynamic*, and as far as he could tell she had a habit of not finishing things. From what Beatrice had let slip he had decided Maya was one of those people who were wildly enthusiastic, then lost enthusiasm when the project needed hard work.

Not the sort of person you'd choose to enter a partnership with.

'Is your sister intending to go it alone now?'

Beatrice felt a resurgence of her guilt. She was letting Maya down once more and her sister was being so damned nice about it, but they both agreed that she couldn't put her plans on hold again. 'She says she'd be happier to go for a less ambitious format.'

'You think she's lying.'

'Of course she is.'

He looked thoughtful. 'I was actually going to suggest that… I have some contacts—would she be open, do you think, to the idea of experts coming in to offer advice? And I know someone who might be interested in investing.'

'Someone, as in…you?'

'Someone anonymous,' he said smoothly.

'That is very generous of you.'

'It is in my best interests that you not spend your pregnancy worrying.'

'Well, I'll speak to her, but she can be a bit touchy. She has come up against a lot of prejudice, a lot of people who can't see past a young pretty face.'

'I wouldn't bet against either of you once you put your mind to something.'

Bea reacted with a glowing smile to the unexpected compliment; she couldn't help it, even though she knew his good opinion shouldn't matter. 'We like a challenge.'

He watched her smile fade.

'What is it?'

'I *want* to be a good mother.' Her eyes flickered wide in dismay. Standing in front of a TV camera and confessing she was afraid she wasn't up to it would have been only *slightly* less embarrassing than revealing her insecurities this way.

'Then you will be.'

'You really think so?'

Before Dante could respond to her equally mortifying appeal for reassurance—her tongue seemed to have developed a will of its own—an attendant appeared.

Dante watched as the male attendant predictably went red and started stuttering when he spoke to Beatrice. He looked as if he was going to faint when she smiled encouragement.

Dante spoke sharply and the guy made an obvious effort to pull himself together, though his glance did keep straying to Beatrice.

While the young man waited, he turned to Beatrice. 'I ordered coffee and sandwiches, do you want some?'

Beatrice's smile held a hint of teasing triumph that he didn't understand until she turned to the young man and asked for tea and biscuits in halting but pretty good Italian.

Dante waited until the young man had vanished. 'So, when did that happen?'

She shrugged, and tried not to look complacent. 'I had a grounding. Even a not very good student can pick up quite a bit in ten months, so I carried on after I left. There are a lot of really great online courses available and some night classes at our local college. A second language is a useful skill.'

'That's a change of tune.'

'I'm doing the lessons now out of choice, not—'

His long fingers curled around his coffee cup as he raised it. 'You make it sound as though you were forced,' he said, looking at her over the rim.

'Forced? Maybe not,' she conceded. 'But I was definitely *not* consulted. Nobody asked if I wanted to have lessons.' It was only after she'd left and she'd found herself in an Italian restaurant that she had realised how much of what she had learnt had stuck. It was actually a shock to realise that she had learnt anything at all!

'And Maya has joined me, so we practise our conversational skills on each other…though Maya is much better than me. She's so much quicker than I am at picking up languages.'

He made a non-committal grunt that had her hackles rising. 'So now *you* don't believe *me*?' she challenged.

'Your sister has a gift for languages, fine, if you say so.' He put down his coffee and leaned back, planting his interlaced fingers on the tabletop.

'I *do* say so.' She fixed him with a dangerous, nar-row-eyed stare. 'Just what is your problem with my sister?'

'I don't have a problem…' he began and then stopped. 'All right, do you realise how much you sing her praises? It's constant. Maya is brilliant, Maya is beautiful, Maya says, Maya thinks,' he bit out. 'From what I understand Maya had all the same advantages as you but left school with virtually no qualifications, squeezed onto a degree course and then dropped out, worked for a charity, was it…? And yes…walked away…' He could feel his an-tagonism building. It was always *Maya's* birthday that deserved the special celebration, her crossing a road seemed to rate a hashtag, but it was Beatrice who was the powerhouse, the real talent!

'That was because…' Beatrice flared, then bit her lip. Maya was a private person and she respected that, even though she wanted to throw his assumptions in his face.

'Maya quits—*you* are the one with the exams, the degree, the successful career. Why do you defer to *her*?'

She reeled back, her hands gripping the arm-rests, shocked by the sheer vehemence of his attack. 'I don't…' She stopped, her fluttering lashes framing the realisation that dawned in her deep blue eyes as she saw how her relationship with her sister might appear to him. 'You wouldn't understand.'

'Try me.'

Her desire to defend her sister outweighed her re-luctance to confide details. 'I say those things…' She cleared the constriction in her throat. Her fists clenched, but so was everything inside too. 'I say those things, because for a long time nobody else did.'

His dark brows flattened into a line of confusion above his deep-set eyes as he shook his head. 'You're

talking as if your sister is some sort of victim.' The petite brunette he knew had a core of steel under the delicate exterior. She was quiet, yes, but no shrinking violet.
He judged it would take a very brave man to cross her
or for that matter pierce the shell under the deceptively
placid exterior.

'Not a victim, a *survivor*,' she bit back fiercely. Self-
pity was not one of her sister's traits. 'You know our father died?' Beatrice had known then that their lives had
changed, that nothing would be the same as it had been
without his big warm presence, but she hadn't known
how much it would change.

He nodded, wondering where this was going.

'And Mum made a second marriage.'

He nodded again. Rachel Monk had been divorced
for some time when he had met her; it had been hard
to tell what she would have been like under normal circumstances because the day they had met had not been
normal. How did a mother respond when her daughter
announced she had married a man the week before in
Las Vegas and—cue drum roll—here he is?

He hadn't anticipated being welcomed into the
bosom of the family, and he'd been prepared for worse
than he'd got, but his own parents had more than made
up for it. Luckily he'd been about ten when he'd last
cared about their disapproval…or maybe that was when
he'd started enjoying it.

After the initial shock, his new mother-in-law had
been polite but not warm and on the handful of subse-
quent occasions they had met she had never relaxed in
his company, continuing to view him as a threat to her
daughter's happiness. She'd been proved right.

He remembered Beatrice mentioning the second
marriage in passing, but she had not dwelt on the cir-

cumstances and he hadn't thought it warranted much curiosity in a world where very few marriages lasted long term, and those that did last, much as his parents', did not because they were happy, but because ending it would be too costly.

'They divorced years ago?'

'Yes, thank God!' There was nothing at all *in passing* about this emotional declaration.

'You didn't like him?'

'He was vile.' Beatrice aimed for statement of fact but it came out more hissing vehemence, which made it pointless to claim that time had done anything to lessen her feelings when it came to her stepfather.

Dante froze... His eyes went black; a chill slid down his spine. Suddenly it was hard to breathe. 'He *hurt* you?'

'Not me, no.'

The bunched aggression in his pumped muscles lowered fractionally, but the nerve beside his mouth continued to beat an erratic rhythm.

'He wasn't violent, he never raised a hand.' People always assumed that abuse was physical, but torture came in many forms. 'He didn't need to,' she said with quiet emphasis. 'And he never really bothered much about me. I was not his target. It turned out there are some inbuilt advantages in being too tall and gawky, which I was at that age.'

Dante's eyes swept across her face, taking in at once the soft, moulded contours of her smooth cheeks, the sensual curve of her full lips and her expressive cobalt blue eyes beneath the sweep of dark brows. It was hard to fit that face, those glorious supple curves, into an ugly duckling analogy. Impossible to imagine her anything other than jaw-droppingly beautiful.

But it might explain why she put so little store by her own beauty. Beatrice was the least vain woman he had ever met, with the most cause to be vain.

'He always liked to be the centre of attention, certainly Mum's attention, and he didn't like competition for it. He didn't consider me pretty or clever—people didn't smile when I walked into a room, unless I fell over my own feet.

'But he took against Maya from the start. She was so pretty, "like a doll" people would say—she actually hated that, she was a bit of a tomboy. And she was gifted—a precocious talent, they called it—and, you know, I think he sensed her bond with Mum... It was special.'

She paused, her blue eyes clouding with memories before she made a visible effort to compose herself.

'Mum and Dad always told her she was special because they didn't want her to feel second best when I came along. They wanted her to know that she was as much their real daughter as I was.'

'I had forgotten she was adopted.'

The description of the family dynamics brought his protective instincts to the surface. It seemed to him that it was inevitable the well-meaning parents had favoured their adopted daughter.

'What about you?'

She looked at him, startled, and shook her head.

'While Maya was being told she was special and enjoying her bond...?'

She gave a laugh and shook her head. 'No, I'm not explaining this very well.' Frustrated by her inability to describe the dynamics when they were growing up, she paused a moment before trying to explain. 'Mum and Dad wanted us to know we were *both* special, and the Maya and Mum thing…you can be loved by both parents but closer to one. I was a daddy's girl,' she admitted with sadness in her eyes. 'I was always closer to Dad than Mum.' He watched a shadow cross her face before she turned her head in a sharp negative gesture as though she was dislodging memories. 'We were just a happy family, even after Dad died. We had each other and then—'

He watched as she swallowed. She seemed unaware of her actions as she pressed a hand to the base of her throat.

'Everything changed almost overnight, but we clung together, and it was getting better. At first it was lovely to see Mum happier and getting dressed up. Maya and I would help her with her make-up before a date, and Edward was a charming man.

'Until they were married—he changed then. It was insidious, the way he cut Mum off from everything, everyone, including us. You didn't see it at the time and we were just kids. And he was careful to appear caring in front of Mum, but when she wasn't there, one of his weapons of choice against Maya was finding fault.' It sounded innocuous when she said it, but the cumulative effect had been devastating. 'He just chipped away at her on a daily basis. Nothing she did was good enough. He ridiculed her, laughed at anything she did and told her she was hopeless.'

In the end her sister had believed it.

Bea's eyes lifted from her determined contemplation of her clenched fingers in response to the harsh curses that Dante spat. They were not Italian words she was familiar with but she got the gist without a dictionary.

'He had a sadistic streak. He *wanted* to see her cry.'

Dante swore again, feeling the rage that a strong man felt for a bully. They called it coercive control; he called it being a pathetic coward. Lost in her memories, Beatrice didn't register it.

'And she tried so hard not to.' Beatrice brushed away the tears that had spilled from her eyes with an angry hand, recognising that there was an odd sense of relief that she was sharing things she had held close for years.

'She always had artistic talent. Early on, her teachers noticed it, encouraged it, and she is a brilliant artist. But Edward destroyed her confidence. He'd hold up her drawings and mock...' Her voice cracked at the painful memories that flooded her head. 'He made her feel useless. From a bright, bubbly girl she became withdrawn, but worse than all that was that Mum, when I told her, didn't believe me—not for a long time.' She sighed and looked at him, sadness behind her forced smile. 'So, you see, I do say Maya is brilliant a lot, because she is.'

'Yes, I see that.' It seemed to Dante that Maya was not the only *brilliant* Monk female.

Beatrice had been her sister's champion; there was no trace of envy in her and when he compared it with the resentment he had felt as a child, when he was pushed to the background with all the attention focused on his brother, the heir, he felt ashamed.

He felt a fresh kick of shame when he recalled how irritated he had felt about Beatrice's closeness to Maya, and his attitude when she became unreasonable, as he had seen it, at any hint of criticism of her sister.

Clearly the events of their childhood had created an unbreakable bond. If he had known, he wouldn't have wanted to break it, but he hadn't known, maybe because he had never asked. In fact, he had switched off when she'd spoken of her sister and not bothered to hide his lack of interest.

'I think the hardest part was feeling so helpless, but then I suppose I was meant to—it's all about power for creeps like Edward.'

As she stared out of the window it was almost as if she had forgotten he was there. She was saying things he wondered if she had ever said before. It was clear to Dante that Beatrice had not escaped as unscathed as she liked to think.

'Seeing what he did to Maya and then Mum, with the blasted IVF—he made her feel a failure too. Mum couldn't give him the family he wanted, his own family, and even though it was affecting her health he kept pushing her to try again and again. Telling her if she was a real wife, a proper wife, she wouldn't be sabotaging the attempts.'

His deep voice cursing jolted her free of the dark memories.

'Your mother had IVF?'

She nodded, and he swore. 'That is why you reacted to the consultation so…extremely. If I had known—'

'I don't think my reaction was extreme,' she rebutted, turning in her seat to face him. 'And, irrespective of my family history, I don't think something that personal, that intimate, should be delegated. It is something that is *discussed*.'

'I thought your reaction meant that you didn't really want children. That after the miscarriage, I assumed…'

Her hand went to her stomach, the gesture unconscious. 'I *knew* you didn't want children. You wanted an heir.'

He felt a flash of shame as he found himself thinking about the events in her life that had moulded Beatrice into the woman she was today.

He found this new experience unsettling, as he considered this woman who didn't carry resentment. Her recount had focused on how her mother's ill-fated marriage had affected her sister, but the childhood trauma had to have impacted her too.

Men who hurt those in no position to hit back were one of the things in life that made Dante see red. He'd met them; they came in all guises, and he did everything within his power to make sure they did not flourish.

What he saw, and Beatrice did not, was that she had been a victim too, watching her sister and mother suffer and feeling helpless, going to a person who was meant to protect her and being disbelieved.

'Why didn't you tell me any of this?'

'It's not really my story, it's Maya's and...' She paused, her clear blue eyes meeting his with a directness that made him think she could read his shame. 'We never reached that point, did we? We were married, but really we were still two people dating.'

He looked about to say something, but he closed his mouth when she added quietly, 'And in the end, we skipped the bit of getting to know one another and went straight to divorce. We were on fast forward, all intense and...' She shook her head, suddenly overcome by emotion. He was there, a few feet away; all she had to do was reach out. The sheer craving inside her to seek the physical comfort of his strength was, for a split second, so overwhelming that she began to move towards him.

Then at the critical moment, the pilot's voice made her snap back.

'He's inviting me to...' Dante paused. 'You already know?'

'Go join him,' she said with encouraging brightness.

He half rose and subsided. 'No, it's fine.'

'I can cope for a few minutes without you.'

'I know you can—you have been for the last six months—but now you don't have to.'

CHAPTER EIGHT

BEATRICE TOOK SOME time freshening up. She reapplied some lipstick, smudged some more soft grey shadow on her eyelids and that was it—the recent exposure to the winter Alpine sun had given her skin a deep glow that made her look deceptively healthy, even though she felt tired and washed out.

Her freshly washed hair resisted her efforts to pull it back from her forehead and into a sleek ponytail on the nape of her neck, but she persevered and got a result that made her nod faint approval at her reflection.

A quick spritz of perfume before she shrugged on a long-line oversized blazer in a swirly print. She thought she might pass muster. Her lips curved into a small, reflective smile as she remembered the first time she'd stepped off one of the royal fleet of jets onto home tarmac. Except it hadn't felt like home as she knew it.

When Dante had said *private* she had assumed that this covered both the flight and the arrival—she'd been wrong! Stepping into the sun, she had found herself faced with a military guard of honour, several dignitaries and half the royal family, complete with hats and heels. She'd stepped out wearing jeans and a tee shirt emblazoned with a cartoon of a smiling monkey, and trainers that had seen better days. Her hair, waist-length, loose and wild.

Given the way she made her living, she was used to being the focus of attention, but that was playing a part. That day she hadn't had any fake sexy persona to hide behind—she had worn less in public but she had never felt more exposed.

She had been furious with Dante for not warning her, and he had added insult to injury by suggesting that she was overreacting.

She hadn't asked about today, but she was pretty sure that, given the circumstances, this would be low-key and not a hat-and-heels-and-handshakes occasion. But even if it had been, she no longer had anything to prove.

It was quite liberating to have already flunked the exams, and actually the intervening months had made her grow in confidence. Something that hadn't really hit home until now.

With a toss of her head that set her ponytail bobbing, she pushed up the sleeves on the oversized tailored blazer and went to join Dante. She tilted a smile up at him.

'So, let's do this.'

Dante had been scrolling through his phone as he'd waited. At the sound of her voice he slid it back into his pocket and turned his head. She sounded like a sports coach giving a confidence-boosting pep talk, but she looked like a goddess. He felt the heat flash down his front and settle painfully in his groin. Beatrice could make a sack look sexy; along with a perfect supple body, she had an innate sense of style.

He remembered the first time she'd arrived; the image would stay with him forever—Beatrice dressed in jeans that showed off her incredible bottom and endless legs, carrying off the military escort reception with a queenly confidence that had filled him with pride. She'd been mad as hell, he recalled, a reminiscent smile turning the corners of his mobile mouth upwards.

Beatrice felt the heat inside her rise as his dark gaze settled on her. She stood her ground and fought not to react.

'You look good.'

She tipped her head in acknowledgement; it hid the rush of blood that warmed her cheeks.

Their arrival was indeed low-key and, like the Italian lessons, it seemed she had learnt more than she'd thought. She nodded through the handshakes and smiles in a way she would once have thought unimaginable... Maybe it was because she had not had to impress anyone.

There was something quietly liberating about it. Was this the way Dante, who never tried to impress people, felt? She slid a glance at him as she stepped through the open door of the limousine. He was conversing with someone who had a serious expression and wore a holstered gun. She gave a little shiver. That was something she could never feel nostalgia for, along with bullet-proof glass.

She had settled in her seat when the door opened, and Dante joined her. 'Sorry about that, just a message from Carl.'

She nodded but didn't ask. She was aware in the periphery of her vision that Dante was watching her.

'How is he?' she forced herself to ask.

She understood being close to a sibling, but she had never understood why Dante had never, ever displayed *any* resentment towards his older brother.

She had always been careful not to show how she

felt but his next words suggested she hadn't been entirely successful.

'Our marriage problems were not down to Carl.'

'I don't think that,' she tossed back with a small unconvincing laugh. 'I never did.'

Strong marriages survived the storms, some were even made stronger, but theirs had sunk without trace at the first squall.

Why do you think it will be any different now?

She pushed away the doubts. 'What is the hold-up?' she gritted, bouncing out of her seat as she virtually pressed her nose to the window.

His eyes went from her foot tapping on the floor to the visible tension in her slim neck.

'This is going to work, you know.'

'Are you basing that on blind faith, or have you been reading the tea leaves again?' She stopped and grimaced, instantly ashamed of her outburst. 'Sorry. I… I'm a bit nervous about this.'

He reached out and curled his hand around hers, drawing it onto his lap. His action was so unexpected that for a moment all she could do was stare at his strong fingers, dark against her pale skin.

Her emotional reaction to his action was way over the top, she knew that, but she had no control over the tears that began to spill down her cheeks.

She pulled her hand free, mumbling, 'Hormones,' as she sniffed and dashed the moisture away with the back of her hand.

He could feel the tension rolling off her in waves; he felt a stab of guilt that his first reaction was to pretend he couldn't.

'Try and relax.'

She shot him a look; did he think this was easy?

Perhaps he did, and why wouldn't he? In the past this was the point she would have nodded and hidden her nerves under a smile.

'This is me *trying*—I promise you.'

'You know what to expect this time.'

'That's the problem...' Panic closed her throat.

A wave of emotion moved through him as he watched her struggle, and he had no defence against the uncomfortable mixture of tenderness and guilt that stirred inside him as he looked into her beautiful unhappy eyes.

How many times had he made her unhappy?

Bea turned her head away, her thoughts drifting back to Dante's comments about his brother. 'I like Carl.' Although Dante was right, there was a tiny part of her that did blame Carl.

Carl doesn't want to be King.

The sentence that had changed her life, but at the time it had elicited a muted but sympathetic response from her. She remembered thinking that she could not imagine what it was like to have your life mapped out from birth.

'I am supporting his decision.'

'His decision?'

'He is renouncing his title and his claim to the throne.'

Still she hadn't got what he was telling her. 'Is that even possible? What will he do?'

'Be happy.'

She had got a horrible feeling in her stomach at that moment that his happiness might come at a cost, and she'd been proved right.

She sighed, feeling petty and mean-spirited. She did not normally struggle with empathy, but when it came to the erstwhile Crown Prince he would be linked in her head forever with losing Dante on the heels of losing their baby. But then you couldn't lose what you'd never had.

'If it helps, I will be able to be there more than—'

Her glance swivelled his way, and she arched an enquiring brow.

'More than I was. There were a lot of people waiting for me to fail.' The admission seemed drawn from him almost against his will.

Beatrice stared. He had never said anything like that to her before. He sounded almost...*vulnerable*?

'We made this baby together, and we will make decisions about this baby together. I want to make this work.'

She swallowed. 'So do I.'

He nodded and sat back in his seat just as the convoy of armoured limousines, the metallic paint catching the sun, finally drove along a wide chestnut tree–lined boulevard that dissected the capital city of San Macizo. The strict development laws meant there were no skyscrapers to compete with the old historic buildings.

There were modern buildings, the glass fronts reflecting back images, but they blended in seamlessly with the old. Traces of the historic waves of invasion and occupation were everywhere. The eclectic mix extended to culture and food—the capital featured highly on international foodies' wish lists.

As they drove past the government building, Beatrice watched Dante's face as his eyes lifted to the national flag fluttering in the breeze. She wondered what he was thinking.

As they reached the high point on the road, the panoramic vista widened and Beatrice caught a glimpse of the sea through the dense pine forest that bordered the white sand on the eastern side of the island. The western coast was where the famed colonies of seabirds nested in the protected area around the high cliffs, drawing naturalists from around the world every breeding season, and giving inspiration for countless nature documentaries.

Beatrice had read all the guidebooks about the place that Dante called home before she'd arrived, but she had quickly realised that until you experienced the place you didn't really *get* just how dramatic the contrasts they spoke about were. It wasn't just the geography of the place. San Macizo had been conquered several times over the centuries, and each successive wave of invaders had brought their own culture and genes to the mix. There was no such thing as a *typical* San Macizan, but as you walked the streets of the capital it soon became obvious there was an above average quantity of good-to-look-at people.

Great climate, pretty faces, an exceptional standard of living—small wonder the island kingdom frequently topped the list of happiest places in the world to live, and small wonder that few spoke out against the status quo of the monarchy.

Beside her, Dante was now on the phone as they left the city limits and went onto the flat plain that, though interspersed by villages and hamlets, was mostly agricultural, consisting of vineyards that produced the unique grape species that made the wine produced here famous the world over.

She didn't know if the tension she could feel in him was connected to the conversation he was having, or his recent declaration of intent. Given her tendency to hear what she wanted, she tried to retain a sense of proportion.

There was nothing proportionate about the palace that loomed into view. It was visible for miles around because of its position on a hill that rose in the middle of a flat plain. She felt *heavier* as she looked at it—not physically, more emotionally. This might be some people's happiest place to live, but it had not been hers!

A perfect defensive position, the history books she had pored over had explained, before they spoke of the family who had taken control of the island five hundred years earlier, and the generations' contributions to the towering edifice to their wealth and power.

The palace was not a home, or even a fortress, which it originally had been; it was a statement of power and in reality a small city covering many acres of ground. The main body was devoted to state apartments, but many wings and towers were private apartments housing family. Other areas, like the world-famous art gallery, were a draw for international tourists and open to the public at certain times of the year.

The closer they got, the more daunting it became.

'That's a big sigh.'

Her head turned from the window. If the expression in the blue depths was an accurate reflection of the thoughts she had been so deeply lost in, they were not happy ones. In the time it took him to push away the inconvenient slug of guilt, the shadow vanished. Beatrice really had got good at hiding her feelings…which was a good thing, he acknowledged, but also…*sad*.

His lips tightened at the intrusion of emotion, and he wondered if there was such a thing as sympathy pregnancy hormones. He'd heard of sympathy about labour pains.

'You were wishing you were somewhere else?'

The question was as much to silence the mocking

voice as anything else, but it opened the door to a question he had exerted a lot of effort to avoid. *With someone else?*

He had not forgotten her explosive reaction when he had casually dropped the subject into the conversation. His *innocent* comment had produced such an explosive response that you had to wonder if her overreaction was not about guilt.

Why guilt? asked the voice in his head. *Just because you have chosen to be celibate doesn't mean she has to follow suit...*

The golden skin stretched over the slashing angle of his cheekbones tightened, emphasising his dramatically perfect facial contours as he fought a brief internal battle to delete the images that came with the acknowledgement.

Celibacy was not a natural state, at least it wasn't for him. Sex, just plain, uncomplicated, emotion-free sex of the variety he used to enjoy, was a great stress-buster.

So, problem solved, mocked the voice in his head, *except you don't want sex, you want sex with Beatrice.*

'Wishing...?' she echoed, breaking into his thoughts.

Wishing was not going to be much practical help at this moment. Her time was better spent mentally preparing herself for what lay ahead.

As their eyes connected Beatrice pushed out a laugh that held no amusement, while Dante told himself that she would not have future relationships; he would be enough for her.

He would enjoy being enough for her.

'Wishing is for little girls who want to marry a prince. I was never one of those little girls.' One of life's little, or in this case massive, ironies. 'Actually,

I was still thinking about Carl. I wanted you to know that I think he is very brave.'

She had liked Carl on the occasions they had met. He had been about the only member of the Velazquez family other than Reynard who had made her feel welcome.

'So do I.'

'We wouldn't be here today if it wasn't for Carl's choices. I wonder sometimes where we would be, don't you?'

Dante leaned back, his head against the corner of the sumptuously upholstered limo interior as he turned his body towards her, his languid pose at odds with the tension in his jaw and the watchful stillness in his face.

Embarrassed now and wishing she'd never started this rather one-sided conversation, she dodged his stare.

'Say whatever it is you need to say. If you're going to explode there is no one here to hear.'

There was a hint of defiance in her face as she responded. 'Doesn't it ever occur to you that when we got married we never planned, we never spoke about where we would live or anything?'

He dismissed her comment with a flick of his long brown fingers, irritation at her persistence sliding into his eyes. 'I have homes.'

'Across the world, I know—the penthouse in New York, the LA beachfront villa, the Paris apartment. Yes, you own endless properties, but not *homes*.'

'I am sure you are going to tell me why my real-estate portfolio seems to bother you so much.'

'Did you plan for your life to change at all? Was I ever meant to be more than a pretty accessory?'

'Well, my life has changed now.'

'Because of Carl, and the baby,' she conceded, dashing a hand across her face. 'But not out of choice, not because you got married. People who commit plan a future. We never did. That's all I was trying to say.'

'You were never pretty. You were, you are, beautiful.'

His voice, low and driven, sent a siren shudder down her spine, and as her eyes connected with the heat in his whatever she had been about to say vanished from her head, leaving nothing but a whisper of smoke.

She squeezed her eyes closed, pushed both hands into her hair as she shook her head to shake free the sensual fog and gave vent to a low groan of frustration, before fixing him with a baleful glare that gradually faded to one suggestive of tired defeat.

'Please do not change the subject.'

'I was—'

'You haven't got a clue what I'm talking about, have you?' she said wearily.

'We—'

'No, there was never a *we*.' She forced a smile, struggling to inject some lightness into this conversation, which she wished she had never started. 'I was always a bad fit, not just here. I never would have fitted into your playboy lifestyle. I was always pretending to be something I'm not.'

'In my bed?'

She coloured. 'No, not there,' she admitted, her eyes sliding from the suggestive heat in his.

'Why do I get the feeling that all this is leading up to a declaration of hostilities?'

'Not hostilities, just a declaration of intent.'

'You are warning me.' He sounded astonished at the concept.

'I'm telling you that I'm not fitting in any more. I'm being me. I owe myself, and this baby, that much. I never want him to look at me and feel ashamed that—'

She stopped, realising a heartbeat after him where she had been going.

'You're still very angry with your mother, aren't you?'

'No...no...' she stammered out, disturbed by his perception. 'Not angry, I just... I don't want to be her.'

'You are not her and, for the record, I have no problem with you being yourself.'

She stopped and followed the direction of Dante's gaze through the tinted window. His eyes flickered to the edifice that dominated the landscape.

'Home, for me these days be it ever so humble.' He glanced her way. 'For us?'

She didn't react to the question, just nodded. 'It is beautiful. I always thought that it looked like something from a dream.'

Up close it looked real and solid, but it was not the carved stone that made her stomach tighten with nerves, it was the life inside it. A life she had never fitted into.

She had not married Dante because of his royal connections, but *despite* them. An inner voice of caution had told her she was playing out of her league, but she'd been too intoxicated by loving this incredible man and the baby they had created together to listen, and anyway he had never traded on his royalty. Dante didn't need to.

It was not his title, his blue blood or his wealth that made people listen when he spoke. She could hardly deny there was a sexual element to it; his sheer physical presence made an impact, but it was more he had an aura, a natural charisma—he was the sort of man who dominated any space he occupied.

She had turned away from him again but was no less conscious of his presence as she trained her eyes on the massive gates across the arched entrance that slid open as they approached. In profile, the purity of her golden features was quite breath-catching.

'Dream or nightmare?' he murmured sardonically.

She smiled faintly, but didn't turn her head, so he allowed himself the indulgence of allowing his gaze to drift in a slow lingering sweep over her smooth, glowing skin. The resulting tightening in his guts was as painful as it was inevitable.

She turned her head and caught a look on his face that was almost pain. 'Don't worry. I will try to make this work.'

'I never doubted it.'

CHAPTER NINE

'So, WHAT IS the cover story?'

'Cover story?'

'I mean, what is the press office going to release, or are you keeping me undercover for the time being?'

'I have a cupboard you would fit right in.'

His wilful imagination conjured a scenario where she was not alone in that space, their bodies pressed against—

He sucked in sense-sustaining air through flared nostrils and tried to halt the heat building inside him before it reached the critical point of no return.

His flippancy caused her frown to deepen. 'You know what I mean. I am assuming you want me to keep a low profile.'

'The press office will not be briefing.'

She stared. 'But that's—'

'The way it is. If asked directly the response will be the family is happy to have you back.'

'Irony, that's a change.'

'*I* am happy to have you back.'

'Oh!' She faintly willed herself not to read too much into his words, or the expression in his eyes.

'Is anyone going to believe that?'

It was clear to him that she didn't, and Dante realised

that her belief was all that mattered to him. He wanted to be the father of their child; he wanted to be half the man she deserved.

'I thought you weren't a fan of the spin doctors. Would you prefer to be in their hands or mine?'

She stared at the long brown tapering fingers extended for her scrutiny and felt her stomach muscles dissolve as she remembered how they felt on her skin, stroking…touching…

'Spin…you mean I don't like being patronised, manipulated and talked over? Yes, I am a bit odd that way.'

'Welcome to my world.'

The world she had been glad to leave. 'Nobody would dare patronise you—and as for talk over you!' She gave a hoot of laughter.

'Present company excepted?'

She fought off a smile in response to the gleam in his eyes, a gleam that held enough warmth to make her oversensitive stomach flip dangerously.

'I hate them, but they were right, weren't they?'

Despite her misgivings the supercilious suits had been right: nothing had leaked about the divorce proceedings. Certainly not to the journalists and opportunistic paparazzi who had dogged her steps for the first few weeks, along with the security detail that she had decided not to confront Dante about. They were discreet, which was a plus—there were days that she'd forgotten they were there.

The press pack had gradually lost interest when she hadn't been seen doing anything even vaguely newsworthy; she never reacted to questions and had no social media presence. A nun had a more interesting life, someone had written, and there were only so many times they could report on the length of her legs.

Beatrice had concluded being boring had its plus points.

'Did they fly back with us?'

He shook his head. 'They?'

'Seb, Roberto, Luis and the one with the really nicely trimmed beard. The security detail—my minders.' Did he really think she wouldn't notice just because she hadn't kicked up a fuss?

'You knew their names.' He swore under his breath— so much for covert surveillance. 'They stayed behind. Your sister could be a press target. You are safe with me.'

Strangely, considering how objectionable she had initially found their presence, she felt oddly comforted by this information, and felt quite guilty about the fact.

'Safe?' She slung him an ironic look and, rubbing the bridge of her nose, pushed back in her seat, digging her head into the soft leather upholstery to ease the muscles of her aching neck before she turned her head in his direction.

'You *really* think it will be that easy? I just reappear and it's all happy families? Your family must be planning your next marriage. Won't me being here throw a spanner in the works?'

'Oh, I think they were doing that before you left.'

She had been joking but, looking at his face, she wasn't sure he was. Of course it made sense. He was going to be King one day and he needed a queen and why wait? It was all about continuity.

Ignoring the sharp stab of something that could be jealousy, or loss, or hurt, she managed a flippant comeback to prove to herself as much as him that her heart was not broken.

'So, any prospective candidates standing out yet?'

'Perhaps you're better placed than most to decide what would make my perfect bride.'

'Are you flirting with me?'

Before she could react to his wicked grin, she realised that while they had been speaking they had entered the palace proper. The cars in front of them and behind had peeled away at some point, and they were now drawing up between the two elaborate stone fountains that stood outside the porticoed entrance to the private apartments she had left eight months ago.

She sat there, fighting a deep reluctance to get out of the car. Once she did it would all seem real, which up to that point it hadn't. She felt as if stepping onto the gravel would be akin to ripping a scab off a healing wound, releasing the pleasure and pain of past memories.

She took a deep breath and reminded herself this was the new, improved Beatrice. Sane Beatrice who did not lose her mind, or become malleable mush when breathing the same air as Dante.

'I am a bit tired after the journey,' she said, setting the scene for when she excused herself. A bit of aloneness was looking very tempting right now.

'*Ah...*'

She looked at him, bristling with suspicion. 'Do you mind translating that *"Ah"* into something I won't like?'

'There is a reception tonight for the French ambassador and his wife. It was arranged some time ago and it was deemed to be diplomatically unwise to cancel. We have already postponed once. Mother had a headache—actually she was hung-over.'

'Fine, don't worry, I can amuse myself.'

'*Ah...*'

She regarded him with narrowed eyes.

'The point is that should the ambassador become

aware that you are here your non-attendance could be construed as an insult.'

'You even sound like a diplomat.'

'A bit harsh, Bea.'

She fought off a grin. 'Couldn't you say I had a headache or something?' She wasn't at all sure she didn't, she decided, rubbing her temples with her fingertips before she gave a resigned sigh. 'All right, tell me the worst.'

His expression tensed. 'There is no question of you attending if you feel unwell. I will have the physician visit. In fact, this might be a good idea. You've had a long day and you shouldn't overexert yourself. Stress isn't good for the baby.'

'I'm fine,' she promised, adopting a businesslike tone. 'So, who will be at this dinner?'

As he listed the guests she gave several eye-rolls, interspersed with theatrical sighs.

'So basically, the snootiest, stuffiest—'

'I'm sure you'll cope admirably,' he cut back with an utter lack of sympathy that made her eyes narrow. 'Just be yourself.'

She opened her mouth and closed it, realising that this was almost like talking to the man she had fallen in love with, the one who didn't give a damn about protocol. They had always shared the same sense of humour, and appreciation of irony.

'Oh, I'll be fine after a bottle of champagne,' she said airily and watched the look of utter horror cross his face before adding with a sigh, '*Joke...?* You remember those?' Nine months of sobriety was not going to be a big ask for her—her normal alcohol consumption mostly involved nursing a glass for the sake of being sociable.

Not that she was making a statement. She had just never really liked the taste.

'I remember *everything*, Beatrice.'

The silence stretched as *something* in the atmosphere of the enclosed space changed. Impossible to put a name to, mainly because she didn't dare to, but it made her pulse race and her throat dry as he leaned in.

When he broke the silence all she was thinking about was his mouth and the way he tasted, the way he always tasted.

'Let's skip the dinner and go to bed!'

The feelings fizzing up inside her were making her breathless. 'You're not serious.'

He arched a brow and gave a wicked grin. 'I don't know, am I...?'

His laughter followed her out of the car as she hurried to put some safe distance between them.

She marched towards the door and past the men who stood either side, staring straight ahead. They wore bright gold-trimmed ceremonial uniforms, but the guns slung over their shoulders were not ceremonial but unfortunately very real.

It wasn't until she entered the echoing hallway with its row of glittering chandeliers suspended from a high vaulted carved ceiling that Beatrice took a deep breath, fighting against the tangle of jumbled memories that crowded her head.

For a split second panic almost took control. She had no idea if she was standing, sitting or lying, then, as she exhaled and the panicked thud in her ears of her own heartbeat receded, she was able to reel herself back to something approaching control.

The breath left her parted lips in a slow, measured,

calming hiss before she turned, masking her emotions under a slightly shaky smile.

Dante was standing a couple of feet away, his hands shoved in the pockets of his well-cut trousers. He had been watching her almost lose it. The enormity of what he was asking her to do hit him between the eyes like the proverbial blunt object.

She was distracted from this uncomfortable possibility by the fact that he was standing right in front of a larger-than-life portrait of a previous King of San Macizo, though this painting captured him when he had been Crown Prince.

She had noticed the striking similarity between the two men the first time she'd walked in, though she'd not then noted the far more modest portraits of his several wives hidden on a wall in a rarely used part of the building.

Legend had it that the first, rather plain-looking wife, who had died in childbirth, had been his one true love, but then legends rarely had substance. Still, it was a pleasingly romantic tale and she had liked to think it true.

The illusion that the figure staring down with hauteur etched on his carved features had actually stepped out of the frame lasted several blinks.

The man standing watching her had all the hauteur along with the perfect symmetry of features his ancestor had possessed. Had his ancestor possessed the same earthy sensual quality that Dante had? If he had, the artist hadn't captured it, though with those lips you had to wonder.

She pulled her shoulders back, feeling some sympathy for the long-ago wives, wondering if they too had stopped trying to figure out why their responses to their prince bypassed logic or common sense. Like her, had they just come to accept and guard against it as much as possible?

Dante watched as she made a visible effort to gather herself, but the expression on her face reminded him of a fighter who had taken too many punches, and maybe she had in the emotional sense.

He was prepared for the guilt and he accepted it. He had anticipated it. What he had not anticipated was that seeing her here, in this setting, would actually make him *more* aware of the ache that he had lived with since her departure. An ache he had refused to acknowledge, an ache that indicated weakness he couldn't own up to.

His upbringing had developed a strong streak of self-sufficiency in Dante. He had been sent to boarding school at six, where the policy was to discourage contact between siblings, the theory being part of the institute's ethos that was intended to develop a strength of character and independence.

Which in Dante's experience in practical terms translated as an ability to look after number one ahead of all others, and he had learnt the lesson. Well, the option had been enduring the misery of those who didn't, and there had been more than a few who'd never understood that showing weakness exposed you to the bullies.

Dante never had shown weakness; he had gone into the school system privileged and come out privileged and selfish as hell. The strategies developed at a tender age were coping mechanisms that had stood him in good stead. One kicked in now, stopping him acknowledging the emptiness.

'I can make your excuses?'

Her chin went up. 'I can make my own,' she began hotly and stopped, an expression of guilt spreading across her face as she saw through his offhand manner. 'There is no need to be worried about the baby. I would never do anything that put him at risk.'

'Him?'

'Or her.'

'Do you want to know?'

'I'm not sure…' Sadness settled across her features. Their first pregnancy had not lasted long enough for it to be a question she had been asked. 'Will the sex matter?' she asked, pushing the sadness away. She knew it would never go away, and she knew it was all right to feel it, but she didn't want it to overshadow the miracle that was happening to her body now.

'Matter?'

'I mean, can a female succeed to the throne?'

Her eyes widened with shock as she saw his hand move towards her; she gave a little gasp as he placed his hand on her flat belly. 'By the time it matters to this one's future, she will.'

His hand fell away, and she wanted to put it back. A dangerous shiver ran through her body as warning bells clanged in her ears.

'You intend to change things.'

'Baby steps.'

This time the words did not injure; they made her smile.

The lines around his eyes crinkled, totally disarming her fragile defences, which were jolted back into life when he angled his head towards the curving staircase with the elaborate wrought-iron balustrade that led to their private apartments that stretched along the first floor of this wing.

'I actually think tonight is a good idea. I'm going to see your parents at some point. It might as well be now.'

Meeting them in company would hopefully limit their ability to make snide digs. After all, appearances were everything in this household. 'What time...?'

'An hour?'

Dante stopped with his back to the glass-fronted lift and nodded towards the staircase. He knew that Beatrice was not keen on enclosed spaces and would walk up a heart-stopping number of steps to avoid a lift. 'After you, you know the way.'

'Which room?' she began and stopped, her eyes flying wide as his meaning hit home. 'I'm in our...*your* room?' she blurted. It was only seconds before a flush began to work its way up her neck.

Their room, but he would have long vacated it.

He was probably trying one of those suitable candidates for size in another room?

The images that accompanied the possibilities made her feel nauseous and then mad because she had been suffering and celibate and it only seemed fair that he should have been too. But then life here had never been fair or balanced; it worried her that she needed to remind herself.

'I never got around to moving my things out.'

The warning made her freeze. 'You mean you're still...!' She would have laughed outright at the suggestion that he would have been personally involved in any moving if his comment hadn't raised a number of issues. Mainly, was he assuming that they would be sharing the room? She could see how spending the night with him in the ski chalet might have led to this assumption.

'Your things are still there.'

The casual throwaway information added another layer of confusion. It could've been a housekeeping error, except such a thing did not exist inside the palace walls.

There was literally an army of people that would have made it possible for her to wake up in the morning and not have to do a single thing for herself right up to the end of the day.

There was always someone hovering, ready to relieve you of the burden of tying your own shoelace should you find that a bore, or too tiresome. It had been one of the *royal* things that she'd never got the hang of. She simply couldn't ask someone to perform a task that she was more than capable of completing herself, and she couldn't for the life of her see how it was demeaning to be seen making her own sandwich or washing out her own tights, but both had been activities that had been frowned on.

She had expected Dante to laugh with her at the sheer absurdity of people having so much time on their hands that they thought sandwich-making was a sin worth passing up the chain of command when she told him about her sugar-coated reprimand—the sugar had made it so much *less*, not *more*, acceptable—but he had just looked at her with a frown indenting his forehead.

'Can't you just go with the flow for once? Is it really worth the argument?'

It was the moment she had realised that they had stopped laughing at the same things. Actually Dante had stopped laughing altogether—that Dante had gone forever. Sometimes she wondered if he had ever really existed.

There was sadness and regret in the shaded look she angled up at his lean face.

'It's your room. I'll take one of the others.'

'It was our room,' he said without emphasis. 'You

might as well take it. I think you'll find most of your things where you left them.' Nobody had questioned his instructions to touch nothing, not even him, though now he might have to face the question that he had avoided because Beatrice was going to.

He'd kept telling himself that he'd get around to it, that he didn't like the idea of someone else touching Beatrice's things, but somehow it was a task he'd kept putting off.

He didn't sleep there any more; he slept, the little he did, on a couch in his office. Not because he was avoiding anything. It was a matter of convenience.

There was always a spare set of clothes in his office, and his running gear. He could shower there, he could shrug on a fresh shirt. It worked because he didn't keep office hours.

He wasn't avoiding anything. It wasn't in any way symbolic; it wasn't as if he were in denial. Bea had gone and it was better for her and better for him.

She was looking at him with a puzzled expression.

'But I wasn't coming back.' She had assumed her belongings would have been boxed as soon as she had gone. She had wondered more than once about asking for them to be sent on.

He shrugged, appearing exasperated by her persistence as he dragged a hand through his dark hair and sighed, managing by the flicker of an eyebrow to make her feel she was making a big deal out of nothing at all.

Maybe because you *want* it to be a big deal for him? Maybe you want it to hurt for him too? Before the horror of acknowledgement hit home, she pushed away the preposterous idea, conscious that she was guilty of overanalysing.

'But you are back.'

She couldn't argue with that, but it meant sleeping in the same bed they had shared...as if this weren't hard enough anyway. She'd stepped out of this life—stepping back in was going to present challenges regardless of where she slept.

This time, when his hand curved around her cheek, she did let her cheek fall into it.

'Look, I know this is hard for you but—' He broke off, cursing as the opening of a door to their left made Beatrice jump away from him.

Giggles entered the hallway a moment before two uniformed figures. One saw Dante and stopped so quickly that the smaller figure bumped into her.

'*Scusi*, Highness...' Eyes round with shock, her face pink with embarrassment, she dropped a curtsy and the woman behind her followed suit.

Dante addressed them, speaking Italian, and they responded in the same language. Considering she had been boastful about her language ability earlier, Beatrice didn't have a clue what was being said. Her brain wasn't functioning through the jam of conflicting emotions in her head.

She stood there with a fixed smile throughout the exchange and one thing was clear: if her arrival had not been officially announced, it had now.

He gave a sardonic smile as the women vanished through the door they had entered and closed it behind them.

'They think I don't know they use this suite as a shortcut when we're away,' he said, sounding amused. 'Don't worry, word will get around we are back.'

'My ears are already burning.'

'They'd be burning some more if we slept at opposite ends of the building,' he predicted drily.

'Was that ever an option?' she asked, with a catch in her voice.

He held her eyes and her insides tightened as he didn't say a word. The look, even without the shake of his head, was enough.

'But relax,' he added as she swung away from him. 'There's still the bed in my dressing room if that is what you want.'

Walking behind her, he watched as she almost missed the next step but after a pause carried on walking.

He caught up with her, pulling level as he added in a low voice that dragged like rough velvet across her nerve endings, *'Remember?'*

Her hand tightened on the banister as she stopped and flung him an anguished look. 'Why are you doing this, Dante?'

Remember? Of course she remembered…

She'd made her complaint after Dante had not slipped into their bed before three in the morning and had then been up before six for two weeks straight. It had been intended to ignite a discussion about his unhealthy work-life balance.

That had always been optimistic. Dante took the entire caveman-of-few-words thing to extremes, missing the point entirely and, working under the assumption she was concerned about her own disturbed beauty sleep, he'd had a bed put up in the adjoining dressing room so that he would not disturb her.

The one occasion he had used it she had lasted five minutes before she had left the massive bed they'd shared and joined him, sliding in beside him in the narrow bed. Images floated into her head, warm bodies entwined, his need to lose himself in her, her need to give. The cumulative effect had always generated heat.

She felt heat now ripple through her body and, resisting the temptation to feed it, lowered her eyes, her glance snagging on his strong brown fingers that were curled lightly around the cool metal of the banister a bare inch away from her own.

Conscious of the tingling and the tug, she pulled her own hand away and pressed it against her stomach.

'I really don't think our sleeping arrangements are anyone else's business,' she said, even though she knew this view would not be shared. The palace was filled with spies loyal to differing factions, the King's spies, the Queen's spies… Everyone took sides, at least that was how it had felt to her, or maybe she had been infected by the paranoia of the claustrophobic life inside the palace walls?

Her eyes went to Dante's face. Presumably he now had his own army of spies reporting to him. 'And now you're *making* the rules.'

She hitched her bag onto her shoulder, not anticipating that her remark would evoke much reaction, certainly not the ripple of complex emotions she saw flicker across his face.

Had she inadvertently hit a nerve?

'Well, don't you?'

'So is that how you think of me? A dictator?' He vented a wry laugh as they began to climb the sweep of stairs together. 'I sometimes think it would make life easier.'

He felt he was not just combating his own perceived inexperience but a father who, while he was reluctant to relinquish any power, was equally reluctant to leave the golf course for a long boring meeting, and senior courtiers who, accustomed to winding their King round their collective fingers, thought modernity a dirty word and equated stability with immobility.

She realised they were standing outside the open door to Dante's study. Opposite was a small salon, where her Italian tutor used to try and be polite about her progress. They were a few doors down from the bedroom suite they had shared, but he went directly to the first door and opened it.

'This is me. I've had the doors to both the adjoining suites opened up, so if you hear any noise you'll know...'

Beatrice immediately felt foolish for making such an unnecessary issue out of the room situation. 'Not very likely, the walls are about ten feet thick.'

'And there are locks on all the interconnecting doors, should you be concerned I might ravish you.'

'Maybe I'm worried that I might ravish you. It wouldn't be the first time,' she flung back recklessly.

He stood there, his eyes burning into her... Very slowly he raised his hand and, with one finger, tilted her face up to him.

'What are *you* trying to do, Beatrice?' he said, turning her own words back on her.

His hand dropped and she gave a shuddering sigh of shame, tears standing out in her eyes as she passed a shaky hand across her mouth.

'I'm sorry,' she whispered, before turning and running down the corridor to her own bedroom door. She felt his eyes burning into her back but she didn't turn around, she didn't breathe, until she was safe behind the closed door.

CHAPTER TEN

SHE STOOD THERE, back against the door, her eyes squeezed tight shut until she heard the faint sound of a door closing.

Up to this point the necessity of maintaining rigid defences had kept the exhaustion of the day, as much emotional as physical, at bay. Now as her shoulders slumped a wave of deep weariness swept over her.

Struggling against the memories being in this room evoked, images that were buzzing in her head like a swarm of wasps, she headed for the bed and sank down.

She felt her eyes fill but she was too tired for tears. How had she allowed herself to get into this position?

By saying yes to Dante—so no change there!

She was here and this was not the time for a post-mortem as to how she had put herself in this position. She just had to deal and get on with it.

This was about the baby. A soft smile curved her lips as she rested her hand on the non-existent swell of her belly.

'Your daddy loves you,' she whispered, hoping that it were true.

Dashing the hint of moisture that had seeped from the corners of her eyes, she gave a loud sniff. Puffy eyes were not a good look for a formal dinner. She pulled herself up off the bed and stood there, ignoring the heaviness in her legs and the ache in her chest. She didn't examine her immediate surroundings; instead she opened the wide interconnecting doors into the adjoining room. Outside the bedroom she was able to breathe a little easier.

Wandering through the rooms where she had lived, it was all the same, but not really.

It took her a few moments to realise that though the antique furniture was still the same, some of the heavier items that she had requested to be stowed away, like the priceless, but to her mind ugly, set of cabriole-legged chairs, had been returned. The walls were covered in the paintings that had been in situ when she had arrived; the ones that were more to her taste had presumably been put back in some vault labelled not cultured enough.

As she wandered from room to room it dawned on her that actually *all* the personal touches she had introduced had vanished from these rooms.

She had been wiped from the rooms and probably Velazquez family history.

In the west-facing sitting room where she liked to spend her morning, the light was so beautiful, she glanced wistfully at the carved stone mantle where the natural sculpted driftwood she had collected during walks on the beach was no longer evident. In its place there were pieces of delicate porcelain, which were beautiful but had none of the tactile quality she had loved.

Likewise, the church candles she had lit in the evening when it was too warm for a fire no longer filled the elaborate grate and the vases she had filled with bare branches now held rigid formal floral displays.

Without the bright splashes of colour from the cushions and throws she had scattered throughout, the rooms looked very different from how they had in her mind. Even the bookshelves had become colour-coordinated and stripped of her piles of paperbacks. There was not a single thing that could have been termed eclectic in any part of the apartment.

Leaving the places where her presence had been clinically expunged, she reopened the door to the bedroom and, with a deep sustaining breath, walked inside.

It was just a room.

No, she realised, it was the *same* room.

The same room she had walked out of eight months earlier. After the complete removal of anything that was remotely her in the other rooms, the contrast was dramatic. The room was like some sort of time capsule where her presence had been preserved.

It really was almost as though she had just walked out of the room. Stunned, she stood poised in the doorway, her wide blue eyes transmitting shock before she stepped inside.

She ran her fingers across the paperback on the bedside table, the spine still stretched open at the page she had been reading, before walking over to the dressing table where the messy pile of earrings, bracelets and make-up she had left behind still seemed to be in exactly the same place she had left them.

Every item she touched carried distracting memories, which she struggled to push away. Instead, aiming for a practical focus, she pressed the hidden button and the massive walk-in wardrobe slid silently open while the overhead recessed lights burst into life, along with those over the mirrored wall ahead, reflecting her image back at her.

She blinked, and saw her sister's face appear, her

dark eyes laughing as she walked inside the wardrobe she declared to be bigger than the entire flat they had once shared. She was laughing as she spun gracefully around, her arms spread wide as she took in the space.

The image was so real that Beatrice found the corners of her mouth lifting as she remembered Maya's reaction, then wobbling as the memory of her sister's assessment swam to the surface of the recollections.

'Oh, my God. Perfect for people who love looking at themselves.' Her husky laughter had rung out as she'd stepped inside and begun to open myriad doors to reveal racks and shelves; her laughter had turned to silent awe.

'When you said you'd stopped off in Paris to shop...' She'd rubbed her fingers across a silk catsuit that they had both last seen and admired in a high-end magazine spread. 'When will you ever wear all this?'

Beatrice had shrugged. 'I know. It's crazy.' How was she to have known that the personal shopper thought her trying something on and saying she liked it equated to *I'll take it—in several colours*?

Dante had laughed at her horror and overruled her when she'd announced her intention to send back the stacks of clothes that had come draped over hangers inside cellophane wrappers and in layers of tissue paper in ribbon-tied boxes.

'You want me to charter a plane for your clothes? Imagine the carbon footprint,' he had taunted.

Beatrice pushed away the lingering memory and replaced his voice in her head with an amused Maya saying that she might work her way through this lot in ten years or so, if she changed outfit three times a day and four on a weekend.

She never had because she hadn't stayed for ten years; she had barely stuck it out for ten months, and now she was back and all the suppressed emotions had surfaced, combining with her baby hormones to make her feel raw and vulnerable.

She dashed a hand across her eyes; she was just too tired of soul-searching. Today had gone as well as she could have expected.

Dante seemed to be making a genuine effort for the baby's sake, and that was the problem. It was for the baby. She wanted him to want her, to need her as much as she needed him.

Giving her head a tiny brisk shake, she pushed away the thoughts and turned to a section that was devoted to evening wear.

After pulling out a few dresses she finally settled on a full-length white silk gown, the style a modern take on classic Grecian. The heavy fabric swirled on the hanger as she held it up. It left one shoulder bare, the hand-embroidered sections on the skirt alleviating the stark purity of the design.

It took her half an hour from choosing suitable shoes to complement her choice—the plain court style was secondary to the fact they were made of a silver jewelled glittering fabric and the spiky heels elongated her long legs even more—to putting the finishing touches to her hair. The fact the ends were still damp made it easier to pin it into a simple topknot and at the last minute she pulled out some loose shiny strands and let the shiny wisps fall, creating a softening effect against her cheeks and long neck.

She added a light spritz of her favourite perfume, ignoring the voice in her head that said it had only become her favourite since Dante had said it was his, when there was a tap on the door that connected the adjoining suite.

She had time to suck in a hurried restorative breath,

take in the flush on her cheeks and the sparkle that was part excitement, part fear in her wide-spaced eyes, before the door opened and Dante stepped into the room, his dark head slightly bent as he adjusted the cufflinks at his right wrist.

It gave Beatrice time to close her mouth and paste in place an expression that fell disastrously short of neutral, but at least she wasn't licking her lips or drooling too obviously.

A lot of men looked good in formal evening wear, the tailoring could hide a multitude of sins, but Dante had nothing to hide and the perfect tailoring emphasised the breadth of his shoulders, the length of his legs and…well, his perfect *everything*. One day she might be able to view his earthly male beauty with objectivity, but that day was a long way off.

She felt the heat unfurl low in her belly and ignored it as she opened her mouth to offer to straighten his tie and changed her mind. Less wisdom and more self-preservation as she remembered more than one occasion when a tie-straightening offer had made them late for an official engagement.

Dante took his time over the cuff adjustment to give the heat in his blood time to cool and recover from the razor-sharp spasm of mind-numbing desire that had spiked through him in that brief moment before he'd lowered his gaze, the electricity thrumming in a steady stream through his body.

She always had been the chink in his armour, the beautiful downfall for a man who, over the years, had become smugly confident in his ability to control his carnal appetites, not have them control him.

And once again she was carrying his child. He had never expected that they would be here again, but the knowledge she was carrying his child only increased the carnal attraction.

He performed another necessary adjustment and lifted his head. He had regained some level of control, but there were limits. He didn't even attempt to prevent his eyes drifting up from her feet to the top of her shining head, knowing the effort would be useless. He recognised it was a dangerous indulgence, but things could be contained so long as he didn't touch her. Experience had taught him that the explosion would be madness.

Everywhere his eyes touched shivers zigzagged over the surface of her skin, awakening nerve pathways, making her ache. The smoky heat in his stare and the clenched tension in his jaw were some sop to her frustration. At least she wasn't the only one suffering.

'I'm ready,' she said, her voice brighter than the occasion justified. She could hear the tinge of desperation, she just hoped he couldn't.

The intensity of his hungry stare did not diminish and the longer it lasted, the harder it was for her to resist the impulse to fling herself at him. Then when he did break the silence his voice sounded so cool that she was relieved she had not reacted to it when it was quite possible that the heat she had felt pounding the air between them had been a product of her febrile imagination.

'So I see, punctual as always and, I imagine, just as impatient about being kept waiting, so you see... I didn't.' He extended a crooked arm and after a moment she moved forward to rest her hand lightly on it, aware as she did of the muscled strength of his forearm.

'You look perfect,' he said, without looking at her.

'Thank you.'

As they approached the shallow steps that led from the private apartment into the corridor that linked to what she thought of as the palace proper, Beatrice raised her gown slightly with her free hand, exposing her sparkling shoes.

The glitter caught Dante's attention; he arched a brow. 'What all the princesses are wearing these days?' he teased, not looking at her ankles any longer. His gaze had progressed to the long, lovely lines of her thighs outlined against the heavy silk fabric of her dress.

Though her heart was trying to climb its way out of her chest, she tried to replicate the blank look on the impassive faces of the two uniformed figures they were walking past.

'Do I look different?' She flashed him a worried look. She *felt* different. 'Do you think anyone will guess?'

He paused and, capturing her wrists, pulled her towards him. 'Would it matter if they did?'

'I know you think I'm being stupid about this.'

'It's your call.'

'Well, if anyone did guess,' she added on a philosophical note, 'it couldn't be any more excruciatingly awful than the last time the subject of babies came up at the dinner table.'

His blank expression made it obvious that he didn't have a clue what she was talking about.

Beatrice envied his amnesia. She would never, *could* never, forget the silence around the table that night, when she had responded to a thinly veiled hint when she had refused a glass of wine.

Suddenly everyone had been exchanging knowing glances and saying how very well she looked…positively glowing.

There had been any number of similar moments after the early loss of that first pregnancy where it had been made clear that should she prove to have good child-bearing hips all her other shortcomings might be over-looked.

Dante didn't seem to realise how agonisingly embar-rassing she'd found the entire situation. Previous to that night she had risen above the comments, had damped down her hurt over their insensitivity, but on that occa-sion something inside her had snapped. She had tried to do it Dante's way, it had been time for hers, and she had always found that the best way to deal with most situations was by being upfront, despite the fact that she'd agreed with Dante up to a point. It hadn't been anybody's business, but then no one had been staring at *his* belly waiting to see a royal bump!

Of course, there had never been any official ac-knowledgement of her miscarriage, but she'd known that her personal loss was the subject of palace gossip and speculation.

She had tried not to care, to rise above it, but as she'd looked around the table she'd known full well that there wasn't a single person present who didn't know the de-tails, a single person who hadn't discussed her fertility.

Despite her outward composure her voice had shaken a little with the effort to control the surge of emotion inside as, looking at the woman seated opposite her, she'd deliberately pitched her words to reach the entire table as she'd remarked how much she loved children and hoped to have several.

The approving smiles that had followed this group-share announcement had faded when she'd gone on to explain that she would be following her own parents' example, that she wanted to adopt as well as give birth, but that she didn't plan on doing either just yet.

By the time she'd finished speaking the entire table

had been sitting in shocked silence, broken finally by the King himself, who had announced quite simply that adoption for a member of the royal family was not an option, before proceeding to make a lot of pronouncements about bloodlines and breeding that had made her blood boil before he'd risen and left the table, indicating that the discussion was over.

So Dante hadn't leapt to her defence. She'd been prepared to cut him some slack as there hadn't been much opportunity once his father had gone into regal-pronouncement mode.

She hadn't expected to have Dante intervene on her behalf, she could defend herself, and the first lesson on royal protocol that she had learnt was that you didn't contradict the King, although she had seen Dante calmly face down his father, with an emphasis on the calm, when it had come to something he'd thought important. Dante had always emerged the victor without raising his voice, no matter how loud his father had got—but this had never happened when there were people present outside the immediate family, as there had been that night.

But she had been quite glad of his silently supportive arm around her shoulders as they'd returned to their apartments. It wasn't until the door had closed that she'd realised that the arm hadn't been supportive, more restraining, and Dante had been quite royally *unhappy* with her.

In fact he'd blamed her for reacting the way she had and making a situation where none had existed.

And now there *was* a situation.

'Are you all right?' he asked her now, scanning her face.

'A bit light-headed, that's all.'

'This is not a good idea,' he said, dragging out one of the ornately carved chairs that were set at intervals along the wall.

'No,' Beatrice said, resisting his efforts to push her into it. 'I didn't get all dressed up for nothing. I really am fine. Please stop looking at me as though I'm an unexploded time bomb. The baby is fine. I am fine.'

'You are not fine—you escaped and now you're back. The doors have closed and locked and you're wondering what the hell you were thinking of.' He smiled at her shocked expression. 'You think I have never felt that way?'

'You?'

He tipped his dark head and gave a faint twisted smile. 'I sometimes feel as if the walls are closing in on me.' His dark eyes lifted to the ornately carved ceiling high above.

'What do you do?' she asked, fascinated by the new insight. Did Dante ever think about escaping?

'I used to escape in your arms, inside you, *cara.*'

'Dante?' Her stomach clenched with helpless desire as their eyes met.

He stroked her cheek with one finger. 'Lately I remind myself that I am here to change things, that I can knock down walls, change mindsets. So long as no one guesses I don't have a clue what I'm doing I might become a man my son is not too ashamed of.'

She was moved beyond words and for several moments could not speak. 'You do know what you're doing,' she protested indignantly.

'Do I?' he said, self-mockery gleaming in his eyes. 'Frankly,' he continued in the manner of someone making a clean breast of it, 'it doesn't matter so long as people think you know what you're doing.'

She took an impetuous step towards him and almost stumbled. He caught her elbow to steady her, his own heart thudding hard in reaction to the burst of adrenalin in his bloodstream.

'Be careful!' The surge of protective concern edged his voice with gravel.

It was possibly good advice.

'Those heels are a little high, considering...'

Her smile of gratitude half formed froze in place as the warmth in his eyes hardened. 'Considering *what*?'

'Isn't that obvious?' he said, seemingly oblivious to the danger in her voice.

'Please do not try and wrap me up in cotton wool, Dante. I am a woman, not an incubator, and I'm pregnant, not ill.' Having made her point, she hoped—it was hard to tell from his expression—she didn't dwell on the subject. She took a deep breath and moved the conversation on. 'So, who is there tonight, again?'

Him going over the guest list gave her the opportunity to gather a little of her composure.

'Wow, it sounds like a fun evening.' Her mocking smile faded as she looked up at him, conscious of the gaping gap that had grown between them as they'd walked. Was there ever a time when she could have bridged it without a baby?

If so, it had gone, because without the baby she would not be here.

She damped the beads of moisture along her upper lip as she struggled to banish the questions and doubts swirling in her head.

'What am I even doing here?'

'Is that a rhetorical question?'

She shook her head. 'Sorry, just a mild panic attack, but don't worry, I'll be on my best behaviour.'

'No, don't.'

Her blue eyes fluttered wide. 'What?'

'All I want is for you to be yourself.' Infuriating, foot-in-mouth but always honest self. 'I get tired…of people…'

'Polishing your ego?'

He gave a cynical grin. 'I'm sometimes tempted to announce the world is flat just to watch them admire my amazing intellect.'

She laughed. 'I'd pay good money to see that.'

'It isn't too late to change your mind.'

'Yes, it is,' she countered as they passed into the palace proper, as she called it in her head.

The carpet underfoot now was inches deep and scarlet with a border of gold; the crystal chandeliers glittering overhead lit the long corridor that seemed to stretch into infinity, guarded by rows of portraits of more of Dante's ancestors, ancestors' wives, children and dogs and, in one case, a leopard with a jewelled collar looking almost as supercilious as its mistress.

If the intention was to impress or intimidate, it did both.

They were the last to join the guests and family in the drawing room, where the mingling involved a lot of diamond tiaras, medals on lapels and stiffly formal conversation.

'Did all conversations stop just now, or did I forget to put my clothes on?' Beatrice asked, her cheeks already starting to ache from the effort of maintaining her meaningless smile.

Her comment invited Dante to see her naked, every sleek, smooth, glorious inch of her, and his imagination obliged, which meant his smile was forced around the edges and he felt the need to loosen his tie, an action which, across the room, earned a horrified glare from his mother.

'Forget the gossips, we owe them no explanations.'

She slung an 'easy for you to say' look up at the tall, imposing figure of her husband as she gritted out through a clenched smile, 'I feel like I've stumbled into one of my nightmares. Do you think there are odds on how long I'll stay this time?' She took a deep breath and allowed her veiled blue gaze to take in all the details. 'Wow, this really is vintage Velazquez. Reminds me of everything I don't miss.'

'On the plus side, so is the champagne,' Dante said, appropriating two flutes from a passing waiter, then, realising what he'd done, slammed them back down on the tray and selected the alternative sparkling water just before the Queen, wearing a staggering amount of diamonds, bore down on them.

'How delightful you look. Good flight?' The Queen greeted her with gracious frigidity and raised a pencilled eyebrow when Beatrice drained the glass of sparkling water in her hand.

The King appeared and ignored Beatrice, so she returned the favour.

'Dante, you are escorting the countess into dinner. You can't escort your wife.'

Dante smiled at his father. 'Actually, I can.' He held out his arm to Beatrice, who, after a pause, took it, and they went to join the other guests who were pairing off to process into the state banquet hall.

'If looks could kill.' She had enjoyed the expression on her father-in-law's face, but she enjoyed even more the feeling that she and Dante were on the same team.

'They don't.'

'Don't?'

'Kill. I have conducted pretty extensive research into the subject. There have been occasional reports of minor injuries but absolutely no fatalities.'

Beatrice's gurgle of laughter drew several glances and several comments on what an attractive couple the future King and Queen made.

'Thanks for having my back.'

He looked down into her beautiful face and felt shame break loose inside him. She shouldn't be thanking him; it should have been something that she took for granted...but why would she? He had never had her back when it had counted.

He watched as she took a deep breath and straightened her shoulders, and felt the shame mingled now with pride. When had he ever acknowledged the courage she had shown?

She had wanted to blend in but she never would, he realised with a rush of pride, because she was better than them. Better than him, he decided, not immediately identifying the tightening in his chest as protective tenderness.

He didn't want her to blend in!

'I'm here if you need me.'

Under dark brows drawn into a straight line above his hawkish nose, she struggled to read his expression but made the obvious assumption he was worried she was going to fall apart. 'Don't worry. I'm not going to fall apart.'

It seemed to Beatrice that the present King had decided to deal with her presence by directing every comment he made to a point six inches above her head. For some reason Beatrice found it very funny.

Absence had not made the King any less angry than she remembered. Her glance drifted from father to son, where Dante sat with his head bent attentively to catch what the person on his left was saying.

Despite her experience of a toxic stepfather, she had known what a *proper* father should be like. How could Dante know when all he had was his own father, who was a distant, cold figure, to go by?

What sort of father would Dante make?

It was a question she had asked herself the first time around, and it had bothered her because she simply couldn't see him that way. But now? Her eyes flickered wide as she realised how surprisingly easy it was to see him in that role. Had he changed, or was it the way she saw him, thought of him, that had altered?

What did they say? Expect the worst and hope for the best? Actually, against all expectations, this evening was not so bad, as her experience of official engagements went.

A fact in large part due to the conversation she'd struck up with one of the guests of honour, who protocol decreed had been seated to her right.

The ambassador's wife, an elegant young thirty-something Frenchwoman, who Beatrice soon discovered was a new parent and self-confessedly besotted.

'Sorry, I must be boring you. We have very little conversation between night feeds, teething and the general brilliance of our son,' she admitted, glancing fondly to where her husband was holding a stilted conversation with the Queen.

'I'm not bored.' Beatrice grinned and lowered her voice. 'But if you get onto the best vintage this decade to lay down for an investment... I might doze off,' she admitted with a twinkle as she glanced to the retired general seated on her left, who was giving all his attention to his glass of red.

It was refreshing to be around someone who was so obviously happy. Maybe it would rub off, she thought wistfully. 'Did you have Alain here?' she asked. The opening of the new maternity wing of the hospital had been one of her last official duties, frustrating as usual because her expressed wish to speak to some staff and patients without the photographers had been vetoed. 'Or did you go back home?'

'Oh, I didn't give birth. I can't actually have children. We adopted.'

At the opposite end of the table Dante was conscious that several people had begun to eavesdrop on the young women's conversation, though they themselves seemed unaware of the fact. It was as if people were shocked that nobody had told the women that this event was business, not pleasure.

'Really? My parents adopted too.'

As Beatrice's voice floated across the table, he was aware of his mother looking tenser by the moment.

The ambassador leaned across; he was smiling. 'Thank you.'

Dante lifted his brows.

'These formal events are a trial for Lara—she finds them something of an ordeal… The Princess has drawn her out.'

Dante was aware of something like proprietorial pride breaking loose inside him as he nodded, and found himself wondering how differently things might have worked out if his family had decided to consider Beatrice's natural warmth and genuine interest in people a positive rather than a handicap.

And you threw that warmth away. So, what does that make you?

Maybe it was true that you didn't value what you had until it was no longer there, but now she was there, and he was determined that she would stay. She was the mother of his child; her place was with him. It was an explanation that he could live with. It meant he didn't have to delve too deeply into his tightly boxed emotions.

'Listen to them.' The ambassador's voice cut into Dante's bitter reflections.

Dante was, as were several other people who had tuned into the animated conversation between the two attractive women.

'So you're adopted?'

'No, my sister was adopted. My mum and dad had given up on getting pregnant by that point. They adopted Maya as a newborn, then a couple of months later Mum discovered that I was not a grumbling appendix.'

Lara Faure laughed and clapped her hands.

'So, you are almost twins.'

'That's what we say, except definitely not identical. Maya is dark and petite and I'm…' her brows hit her blonde hairline '…*not*! The irony is that Mum is dark and petite. I take after our dad, who was tall and blond, before he went bald, so I hope I haven't inherited that from him.' Her hand went to her head, where her frequently disobedient hair appeared to be in place, before dropping. Her fingers curled around the stem of her water glass as she swirled the contents, giving the impression she was breathing in the scent of wine as she lifted it to her lips.

'Your hair is natural!' the Frenchwoman exclaimed, her envious glance on Beatrice's glossy head.

'I had some blue streaks when I was at school.' The

admission freed a grin. 'And was a redhead for about five minutes. That's about the limit of my rebellion, but these days, yes, this is *au naturelle*.'

'How lucky. Mine costs me a fortune and far too many hours to maintain. I've forgotten what colour I actually was.' The woman patted her elegant head and gave a self-deprecating shrug. 'Your sister is the brunette, you said?'

Beatrice nodded.

'I always wanted a sister. I was an only child. We hope one day we will be able to give Alain a brother or sister...'

'Maya and I are best friends and sisters,' Beatrice said, her voice warm with affection as she thought of her sister. 'We squabble, but I know...' She paused, becoming belatedly aware that the table had grown silent and that everyone was listening to every word she said. Well, too late to stop now, even though she knew she'd strayed onto a dangerous subject area. 'I know that she is always there for me.' She put down her glass and kept her eyes steadily on the woman beside her and imagined the thought bubbles of disapproval above the collective regal heads.

'And I'm sure you have always been there for her. You know, I have a few friends coming for brunch next week, you might know some? We have started up a book club, and on the side we have some pet projects at the moment. You might know that I am...was a violinist before the arthritis...?'

She briefly extended a hand displaying swollen knuckles while in a sentence she dismissed an unfair roll of the dice that had robbed her of a short but glittering career, and the world of someone considered one of the greats in the music industry.

Her bravery was humbling, and Beatrice knew this was someone she would like to know.

'They have a great system in place here for music in schools—an innovation of your husband, according to my sources?'

Beatrice said nothing, aware that the other woman's sources were a lot better than her own.

'But the younger appreciation of music starts, the better, so we are hoping to raise some money for instruments to introduce music lessons into the nurseries in a fun way.'

'That sounds great,' Beatrice began, her smile deepening as she realised that she'd made a friend.

'Though I should warn you, you might be bored. Two others of our group are new parents too and another is pregnant, so you might get a bit tired of all the baby talk.'

Beatrice could not control the guilty colour she felt rising up her neck, even though she knew logically that nobody was about to suspect the truth. As far as anyone else was concerned they had been estranged for the last eight months and, while there might be a lot of speculation as to why she was back, a baby was not going to be on their list of possibilities.

As she continued to struggle to frame a response, aware that Lara was beginning to look puzzled by her silence, it was Dante who came to her rescue.

'Hands up.'

He held up his hands, the long tapering fingers splayed in an attitude of mea culpa that caused conversation to halt and every eye to turn his way. 'My fault.'

Beatrice's initial relief was immediately tempered with wariness. What was he going to say?

Lara Faure raised a delicate brow, her teasing eyes

flashing between the handsome Prince and his wife. 'It is in my experience that it is always the husband's fault.'

Beatrice held her breath as she waited for Dante to speak. The gleam in his dark eyes as they brushed her reminded her of the Dante she had fallen in love with, the Dante who made the outrageous sound normal, and had delighted in making her blush in public.

'I have been complaining,' he drawled, leaning back in his seat while his long, sensitive brown fingers now played an invisible tune on the white linen as they lightly drummed, 'that she spreads herself too thin— she has just so much *enthusiasm*.' His shoulders lifted in an expressive, fluid shrug. 'It makes her take on too many things. I have to book an appointment to see her.' He threw the words out, along with a heavy-lidded caressing look that sent Beatrice's core temperature up by several degrees.

Ignoring her burning blood, she focused on his ability to lie through his beautiful teeth and continued to conceal her true thoughts behind an impassive mask.

'Books and music. Two of her favourite things.' And both offering no physical danger that might harm mother or child. 'Though I have to warn you, she can't hold a tune. I can spare you, *cara*, go have fun.'

'He likes to think I actually need to ask his permission before I have fun.'

People laughed and conversations started up, but under her own smile there was hope as she allowed herself to think that this was not all pretence.

CHAPTER ELEVEN

TO BEATRICE'S RELIEF the party did not drag on long after the meal. The guests of honour excused themselves relatively early and Dante took the opportunity to extract them at the same time.

As they walked through the doors into their private drawing room, he was tugging off his tie. A moment later the top buttons of his formal shirt were unfastened, and he gave a grunt of satisfaction before he flopped onto one of the deeply upholstered sofas that were arranged around the carved fireplace.

'That could have been worse.' He threw several cushions on the floor with a grimace of irritation before angling a glance at Beatrice. 'You don't agree?'

'Your father ignored me regally all evening.'

'I'd pay to have my father ignore me.'

She failed to fight off a smile.

'So what else?'

'I wanted to tell Lara that I was pregnant.'

'Then why didn't you?'

She slung him an exasperated look. 'I may know very little about royal protocols but I'm *pretty* sure telling a dinner guest I'm pregnant before the King and Queen know they are going to have a grandchild might break a couple.'

'True…but you have made a friend?'

'I like her,' she said, ignoring the invitation when he patted the arm of the sofa beside him and choosing to sit instead opposite, with the long coffee table, with the tasteful stack of prerequisite coffee-table books that nobody was ever going to read, between them.

Her eyes went to the hand that still rested on the arm as she wondered uneasily if the gesture had been meant to remind her of another occasion when she had accepted the invitation only to find herself pulled down on top of him. She pushed away the images, but not before her core temperature had jumped several uncomfortable degrees.

'Should I have told Lara that I'd join her book club?'

'Why not? You make it sound as though you've signed your soul away. And it sounds more like a mother and baby group and you will fit right in. I have a list of the obstetricians I spoke of, if you'd like to look at them.' He scanned her face. 'We can tell my parents, if that would make you feel more comfortable.'

'But what if something goes wrong?' The words 'like the last time' hung unspoken in the airwaves between them. She shook her head, the imagined scenes of that eventuality lodged there, a nightmare mixture of their lost baby and the emotionally charged scenes that had followed her mum's unsuccessful IVF attempts.

'You cannot think that way. You need to enjoy this pregnancy and you won't if you spend the entire time anticipating a problem.' She could leave that to him, he decided as he experienced a swell of helplessness, a reminder of the way he had felt when the first pregnancy had tragically ended.

He hadn't known what to do, what to say, and anything he had said had sounded trite and inadequate. He'd felt utterly helpless to lessen the grief she'd been feeling and unwilling to examine his own grief; his conditioning had kicked in and he'd taken refuge in work.

He knew he had failed her and was determined he would not again. He could keep her safe and he would.

'And if there is a problem?'

'Then we will deal with it together.'

It sounded good but it was the part he left out that made her look away. If anything went wrong with this pregnancy there would be no reason for her to be here.

'You know what would make you feel better?'

She forced a smile and tried to ease the sadness away. 'I'm pretty sure you're going to tell me.'

'You need to brush up on your lying skills, because you really are a terrible liar.'

'You make it sound like that is a bad thing.'

'A good lie gets you out of many a sticky situation, and sincerity,' he said, 'is a very bad thing, diplomatically speaking. Of course, if you can feign it—' He reached out and caught one of her shoes before it hit him in the face.

'I wasn't aiming at you.'

'Then you have real potential. That's better,' he approved when she lost her battle to contain her mirth.

'If you wore heels you'd know they are not a subject for jokes.'

'You don't need heels, and I already struggle with door frames,' he said, watching her wriggle her toes as she stretched out her legs towards the coffee table. He registered the tiny smile playing around the corners of her mouth before, tongue between her teeth, she nudged the neatly arranged books with her outstretched foot, spoiling their geometrical precision.

With effort he prised his eyes from the long length of

her endless smooth legs. It did nothing to ease the pulsing need that had settled like a hot stone in his groin.

'Feel better now?'

'A little.'

'Sometimes saying what you want to is a luxury.'

His voice held no discernible inflection but something in his expression made her wonder if they were still talking book clubs. She somehow doubted it; the gleam she could see through the dark mesh of his lashes confirmed it.

The slow, heavy pump of her heart got louder in her ears. It was something that would be reckless to pursue, better leave it be.

Sound advice.

'What do you want to say?'

Playing with fire, Bea.

For a long moment he said nothing. 'Do you really want to know?'

She swallowed, frustrated at having the ball thrown back in her court. If she wanted this to go to the next level, he was saying she had to take the conscious step to make it happen... She'd have no one to blame but herself.

This was exactly the sort of situation she had sworn to avoid and here she was virtually running after it, running after him. She could feel that reckless *let tomorrow take care of itself* feeling creeping up on her. Even from this distance she could hear him breathing like someone who had just crossed the marathon finish line, or was that her?

Without taking his eyes off her, he levered himself into a sitting position, leaned across the table that separated them and ran a hand down the instep of one of her bare feet.

She sucked in a fractured breath, opened her mouth to say— She would never know what, because the phone that lay in the small beaded evening bag she had dumped on the table rang.

'Leave it!' he growled out as the noise shattered the moment.

Yanked back to reality and her senses and not nearly as grateful as she ought to be for the fact, Beatrice shook her head, pulled her feet back, tucking them under her as she delved into the bag. Pulling her phone out, she glanced at the screen.

'It's Maya. I have to take it.'

Dante's jaw clenched, all of him clenched as frustration pumped through his veins in a steady stream. 'Of course you do.' He doubted Beatrice heard him as she was already sweeping into the direction of the bedroom, her phone pressed to her ear.

When she returned a few minutes later Beatrice wasn't sure if Dante would still be there, then she saw him looking tall and dangerous, prowling up and down the room like a caged tiger, glass of something amber in his hand and the lamplight shading his impossibly high carved cheekbones.

'Maya says hello.'

He flashed her a look. 'I'm quite sure that's not what she said, but hello, Maya.' He raised his glass in a salute.

Beatrice's lips compressed as she glared at him. His continued pacing was really beginning to wind her up. As if she weren't already tense enough, and *guilty*.

Maya had to have picked up that she couldn't wait to get off the phone. Her concerned sister, whose only crime was to have bad or good timing, depending on how you looked at it.

She winced as she replayed the short conversation in

her head. The gratitude she ought to have felt for being saved from basically herself was absent. The problem being she wasn't sure that she'd wanted to be saved.

Who was she kidding? She definitely hadn't wanted to be saved.

He halted his relentless pacing, drained his glass and set it down. It didn't take the taint of guilt and regret from his mouth. It seemed insane now that he had ever thought he could handle the scent of her perfume, the sound of her voice. It was all part of his personal agony. Wanting her was driving him out of his mind; the lust was all-consuming—it wiped out every other consideration.

He was still the same person; his own needs always would take priority.

'I can't say I blame her.'

Beatrice felt emotion swell in her chest. He sounded tired...and while you couldn't consider someone who was six feet five of solid bone and muscle vulnerable, his defences seemed to have lowered. Whatever internal battle he was fighting might have lowered his defences, but the dangerous explosive quality that was innate to him was much closer to the surface.

'Maya has nothing against you.'

His eyes lifted and he smiled; it held no humour. 'Of course she doesn't.'

'It's true, she is...protective, that's all.'

'I get that, and I admire her for it. I admire you. You are both there for each other,' he said broodingly.

She watched as he set his glass down with a thud and reached for the brandy.

'We're sisters, that's what it's like. You know that, you have a brother.'

The moment the words left her lips she knew she'd said the wrong thing.

She could almost smell the adrenalin coming off him as he stalked towards her, stopping a foot or so away. She couldn't take her eyes off the muscle clenching and unclenching in his hollow cheek.

'I was never there for my brother!' The words came out, acrid with self-loathing.

The confusion swirling in her head deepened. She took a step towards him and laid a hand on his forearm, conscious as she did so of the quivering coiled tension in the muscle that was iron hard.

It didn't cross her mind to be afraid or even nervous; she had never been afraid of Dante.

'But you are, Dante. You are doing all this.' She gestured to the room they stood in. 'For Carl, you walked away from your life and you never blamed him once.'

'You think I am noble…that is so far from the truth, *cara*, that it is almost funny. I had no idea that he was gay, let alone that he was so unhappy.'

'Perhaps he wasn't ready to share.'

'I should have known,' Dante persisted stubbornly. 'What sort of brother doesn't know his brother is hating his life, is so unhappy?'

'Oh, Dante, I'm so sorry. But that is not your fault.'

'If I'd been any sort of brother, he would have felt able to come to me. He couldn't, he didn't. What sort of brother, man, does that make me?' He glanced down, seeming to notice for the first time the small hand on his arm.

He pushed it away and Beatrice, the hand he had rejected pressed up to her chest, stood there, absorbing his words. Her heart twisting in her chest for him, she felt helpless to ease the haunted guilt she could see shining in his dark eyes, but she knew she had to try.

'It's not your fault he was unhappy, but you could never make the decision for him, Dante. He had to find the courage in himself to do that, and he did.'

'Oh, yeah, I was a really great person to confide in,' he sneered. 'My brother was crying out for help, a silent scream, but I was too busy with my own life. I did what all certified selfish bastards do. I looked after number one.'

His anguish felt like a dull blade in her heart.

This time when she laid a hand on his arm, he didn't shrug it off.

'Have you spoken to Carl about this?' she asked, wary of putting too much pressure on him. 'Asked him how he feels? Told him how *you* feel?' Her hand slid down his forearm until it covered his hand, her fingers sliding in between his.

She already knew the answer to that. Dante was not a man who spoke about feelings, which made her sure that it would not be long before he was regretting sharing this much with her.

'We don't talk about it,' he said, thinking of the email that remained on his phone. His brother had said all he needed in that, and neither of them had referred to it since.

'Maybe you should…' She paused, her heart aching as she saw the guilt that was eating him up. 'Talk? Maybe *we* should talk too?'

'I've always lived for myself. I can't be the man… your—'

'You are my man, my husband.'

'What are you doing, Bea?' The pupils of his eyes expanded dramatically as his glance rested on his own hand, now caught between both of hers, as she raised it to her mouth and touched his fingertips with her lips.

She felt muscles bunch in rejection and let go of his hand, but only in order to reach up and grab the back of his neck, dragging his face down to enable her to slant her lips across his.

She wanted to say, *Here is my heart, Dante, let me love you*, but instead she said, 'Make love to me, Dante.'

It was a fight he was always going to lose.

He had no idea how long it lasted before a groan that reverberated through his body was wrenched from his throat as he dragged her to him.

One hand behind the back of her head, he covered her mouth with his, the heat an explosion as their lips touched, their tongues tangled. The passion released burnt everything but raw need away.

The only cool he was aware of was the feel of her hands on his skin as she pushed her hands under the fabric of his shirt, across his chest and down over his belly, causing him to suck in gasps and then groans of encouragement as she fought with the zip of his trousers.

He kissed the smooth skin of her shoulder, and both shoulders were bared as her dress slithered to the floor and lay in a silk pool at her feet.

His hands on her waist, he pushed her away, far enough for him to see the complete picture she made. Smooth golden limbs and feminine curves concealed only by a strapless bra and a minuscule pair of matching knickers.

'You look like a goddess,' he rasped with throaty awe.

'I feel like a woman. You make me feel like a woman, Dante.'

Without a word he scooped her up. She laid her head

against his bare chest as he carried her through to the bedroom they had once shared, that they would share tonight, and if this was all they had then she would take it.

She knew with total certainty that any pain down the line was worth tonight. Tonight she needed him as much as he needed her. He might not love her the way she loved him but she would take what he had to give.

Dante was *very* giving; his touch set her alight and fed the relentless hunger inside her. As he paused to fight free of his shirt, she kissed his chest, tasting the salt on his skin, and when he bent back, his body arching over her as he knelt astride her supine body, he took her face between his hands, and kissed her like a man starved.

It wasn't until he lowered himself that she realised her bra was gone, even though she hadn't felt the loss until her sensitised breasts were crushed against the hard barrier of his chest.

Her legs parted to his touch, a low moan of pleasure fighting its way through her clenched teeth as he teased the sensitive moist folds with skilful fingers.

She was mindless with the need to feel him inside her, to feel him deep, feel him touch where no other man had. The relief when her agony communicated itself to him and he settled between her parted legs made her sob, as her legs wrapped around his waist, urging him deeper; she was frustrated by the teasing strokes until finally he sank deep, wringing a feral moan from her lips as her body arched up to meet him. As her nerve endings sang all the sensations merged into one glorious whole, they merged, they were one—*almost.*

As her climax came within reach Beatrice felt she was about to shatter into a thousand pieces. It was too much, too intense, then as it hit she was not broken, but miraculously whole again. She lost herself in the feeling as wave after wave of pleasure rippled along every individual nerve ending in her body.

After it ended, and he lay breathing hard on top of her, responding to a primal need to extend this intimacy, she wrapped her arms around his waist and whispered fiercely, *'Stay,'* against the damp skin of his neck.

He kissed her and pulled her head onto his chest and they lay, still joined, until she felt him stir inside her.

Her wide eyes flicked to his face so close to her own.

'You make me hungry, *cara.*'

'You make me greedy.'

Later that night they made love again, slower and with infinite tenderness, exploring each other's bodies with an endless fascination. The lightest touch of his hand and mouth made her body vibrate with pleasure. She sobbed with the intensity of it and every touch was heightened by the shattering depth, the sheer *intensity* of emotions that accompanied each brush of her skin.

When the deep release came it took her a long time to float back to earth.

Did she say, 'I love you,' over and over as she sobbed or was that part a dream?

Beatrice was not sure.

Dante did not sleep. Beatrice lay sleeping in his arms. His heart contracted when he looked at the perfect beauty of her face. It was hard feeling what he did when he looked at her, to hold on to the lie he told himself that what they shared was just sex, but it would never be *just* anything with Beatrice. He might try and deny it but deep down he had always known that. He felt a fool that he had ever imagined he could treat Beatrice like other women. She had always been different, she had always made him feel... Jaw clenched, he blocked the thought process before it led him to a place he was not ready to go, a truth he was not ready to see.

A man could change; she had made him believe that, because against all the odds she believed in him. As he looked down at the woman lying like a sleeping angel in his arms, he vowed to deserve her faith.

CHAPTER TWELVE

It was still dark when Dante sliding away from her woke Beatrice. She stretched and stopped, the memories that explained the stiffness of her muscles flooding back. She reached out in the dark, her hand touching the smooth warm skin of his back.

Seated on the edge of the bed, he responded to her sleepy murmur of protest with a kiss that deepened as her lips softened beneath the pressure before he pulled away abruptly.

Suddenly cold even though the air was warm, she shivered.

'Who has a conference call in the middle of the night?' she complained, raising herself on one elbow and pushing the silky skein of hair from her sleepy eyes, desire ribboning through her and settling heavy and low in her abdomen as she smelt him on her skin.

'The half of the world that has been awake hours. It is what living in a global economy is all about, and it is not night...'

He heard her reach out for the lamp and covered her hand with his. 'No, leave it.' If he saw her, read the sultry invitation in her eyes and remembered feeling the aftershocks of her climax as they'd stayed joined as one, he was pretty sure that he would never get to that call.

She ignored him—of course she did.

She looked every bit as wanton and glorious as he had imagined as she sat there, her perfect breasts partially concealed by her hair.

She pouted. 'I don't want to be awake.' She didn't want the night to end; she knew it would, she just didn't want to think about it yet.

He slanted a kiss across her lips, the touch making her shiver, and flicked off the light.

'Then go back to sleep.'

It was a week later that Dante walked into the drawing room just as a young woman was walking out. This was the second time this week he had managed to arrange his day to include lunch with Beatrice.

On one level he couldn't believe he was trying to earn brownie points from his own wife, but amazingly he actually found that his new schedule made him more productive.

'Who was that?'

'My new PA.'

His eye-framing dark brows lifted. 'You are not letting the grass grow under your feet.'

'She came highly recommended.'

'By whom?'

'Jacintha.'

His brow furrowed as he loosened his tie. 'Who is Jacintha, again?'

'The maid. The one with the red hair and cool glasses.'

'You hired a PA on the say-so of a maid?'

'Should I have run it past you?' she challenged.

'Not at all.'

She smiled. 'Well, Jacintha's recommendation, and those of her previous employers.' She gave a small smug smile as she listed them, watching his eyes widen. 'I know working for me does seem like a step down, but she wants to come home because her mother has a heart condition. The best thing is she is not related even by marriage to any of *the* families.' It did not take long to figure out that most of the top positions in the palace were given to relatives or cronies of a handful of historically powerful San Macizan families.

'This will cause a storm in a champagne glass, you know that?' he mused, watching her face with a half-smile as he perched on the edge of the polished mahogany desk and began to leaf through the diary that lay open. 'Wow, you have hit the ground running,' he remarked as he skimmed through the entries written in her distinctive hand. 'Oh, leave Tuesday morning free. I've made an appointment with the obstetrician and—' He stopped and leaned in closer as he reread the most recent entry that had caught his attention before he stabbed it with his finger. 'What is this?'

'What is what?' she asked, not understanding the ice in his voice.

'"Fun run, five K, fancy dress optional",' he read out.

'Oh, that's Lara. She rang earlier. She is organising a fun run for the children's hospice. I agreed to take part.'

'That is out of the question.' The diary closed with a decisive click and he was on his feet looking tall, austere, and oozing simmering disapproval while inside his gut was churning with visceral fear.

She clung to her temper and reminded herself that this fragile peace between them required concessions on both sides. 'I don't have to wear fancy dress.'

'Running five K is a reckless risk in your condition.'

Her lips tightened as she pushed out her chin to an aggressive angle and, hands on her hips, stalked towards him, stopping a couple of feet away. 'There is nothing reckless about it. It is basically a fun jog or walk for a good cause, and I will enjoy it!'

'The risk is too great.'

Struggling to channel a calm she was not feeling, Beatrice held his stormy gaze. 'Do you really think that I would risk the life of our child on a whim?'

His eyes slid from her own, his chest lifting, before returning as he growled out reluctantly, 'No. The last time—'

The shadow of fear she glimpsed in this strong, seemingly invulnerable man's eyes drained the anger from her. She hurt for him because he couldn't own that fear, he couldn't reach out. 'I'm scared too, Dante,' she confessed, tears standing out in her eyes. 'But I can't...'

Nostrils flaring, he looked down into her face and felt the anger and frustration drain away. 'I'm your husband. Why won't you let me protect you?'

'Protect, not suffocate.' She took his silence as encouragement and added, 'And I'll make my own appointment, choose my own doctor.'

'Shall I come back later?'

Dante stepped back and gestured towards the table under the window embrasure. 'No, that's fine,' he said to the maid, without taking his eyes from Beatrice's face. 'Put it on the table.'

'Shall I fetch another cup?'

'No!' Beatrice supplied as the door closed silently behind the scared-looking young maid. 'So, I'll tell Lara, no, you won't come to cheer me on, shall I? She figured that would be worth double in sponsorship.'

He dragged a hand through his dark hair, the internal

struggle clear on the hard drawn lines on his handsome face. 'I will donate, and I'll come and support you.'

Her jaw dropped at the capitulation. 'You'll come.'

He shrugged. 'Someone has to make sure you don't decide to get competitive, but in return—'

'Return for what?' she began explosively before literally biting her tongue. 'In return what?'

'In return you go and see the doctor I made the appointment with. She is the best.'

Was it really a point worth making? She released a long hissing breath. 'All right.' She fixed him with a warning glance. 'But the next time you make a unilateral decision concerning me or the baby—don't!'

He gave a slow smile. 'I wouldn't dare.'

The walk through the private grounds calmed Beatrice after the confrontation. Gradually her pace slowed to a stroll as the healing of the quiet and solitude and nature's beauty seeped imperceptibly into her.

She remained, what? Wary, confused? Nobody in the universe made her *feel* as much as Dante did, and she couldn't get the fear she had seen in his eyes out of her head.

Instead of lunch with his wife, Dante spent a half hour pounding his body into submission in the private gym.

His mind remained another matter. Had he made the right decision? He knew that their marriage could not survive if they maintained a war of attrition. There had to be compromise even though it went against his instincts, and the idea of her running…falling… He threw himself into the next series of repetitions in the hope the pain in his muscles would drown out the torturous thought in his head.

Drenched with sweat, he was finally heading for the shower when he felt it.

Around him, weights in their cradles began to shake as the low distinctive subterranean growl of the earthquake built.

His first thought was Beatrice. He didn't pause. He grabbed his phone and got a low static buzz…and hit the ground running. Face set in grim lines, he was exiting the leisure facility when he encountered a uniformed figure who, without a word, fell into step beside him.

'We have set up a command centre in the old armoury to coordinate all rescue efforts.'

Dante nodded his approval. It made sense; the walls were ten feet thick and the building was cut into solid rock. 'Highness, we have choppers ready and waiting and the King and Queen will be evacuated as a priority. It's the communications that are the problem.'

'I'm on that…'

'My wife?'

'She left by the south-west door, heading in the direction of the sunken garden, twenty minutes ago.'

Lifting a finger in acknowledgement, Dante picked up his pace, leaving the military figure behind.

Bea dropped the flower she had just picked and froze, trying to figure out if she was having a dizzy spell or… The answer to her question came in the form of a deep primal subterranean roar that went on and on, it felt like for hours. She wasn't swaying but the ground was.

It stopped, and there was a total silence. Not even a bird sang or a bee buzzed, then, as if a switch had been flicked, individual sounds began to emerge from the silence. The noise built; there were cries from all directions mingling with the distant sound of sirens.

Beatrice hadn't moved; there'd just been an earthquake. What did she do, stay outside or go indoors? The sounds were mostly coming from the buildings.

She was still standing in frozen indecision when a familiar figure wearing running shorts and a gym vest appeared. She let out a sigh of relief. Dante was here; things would be all right. It might be illogical when you were dealing with the forces of nature, but she believed it. But he didn't know she was there.

Tears ran down her face as she tried to cry out, but nothing came, then, it was a miracle, just before he would have vanished from her eyeline, he turned.

A moment later he was racing towards her.

His name was lost in the warmth of his mouth as he grabbed her by the shoulders and dragged her into him. Crushing her as he kissed her with the hunger of a starving man.

When the kiss stopped, he lifted his head. 'Beatrice, you're safe…you're safe… Oh, God!' he groaned, dragging his hands down either side of her face, framing her delicate features, a mixture of frustration and fascination stamped on his face.

'I want…this is…' Teeth clenched, he set her away from him. 'We experienced an earthquake.' Unable to take his eyes off her, he ran his hands up and down her arms as he scanned her face. 'There may be aftershocks. You can't be here. Are you hurt?'

She shook her head. 'No, I'm fine. So that was an earthquake.'

'Yes.'

He sounded very calm and maybe it was catching

because she could breathe again without panting. 'I'm scared.'

'Yes.'

'I want to help…'

'No—no, you don't.'

Hands on her shoulders, he led her firmly back in the direction she had just come into the open green space of the gardens. He pushed her down on a stone bench and squatted down beside her.

'Listen carefully. I have to go,' he admitted, frustration etched in the strong lines of his face. 'But I won't be long. You stay here and if… There might be aftershocks and if there are, just get under this.' He patted the bench. 'You'll be safe, and I'll be back.'

She nodded. 'Be careful.'

Already feet away and jogging, he turned and grinned over his shoulder, waving a hand as though he were off for his morning run.

An hour later, Dante was relieved to see Bea sitting in the same place he had left her, but she seemed to have been joined by a dog.

The dog gave a warning growl when he approached, then licked his hand when he offered it. By the time he knelt beside Beatrice they were best friends.

'He just appeared,' she said, adding urgently, 'The earthquake, Dante?'

'So, right, first indications are it's not too bad.'

'Thank goodness!' She hadn't really been conscious of how high her tension levels were until they lowered, leaving her knees literally shaking as she reached out to stroke the fawning dog.

'What does not too bad mean?' she pressed cautiously as he pulled himself to his feet. It was weird that she loved the fluid grace of his movements, even at a time like this.

'Riota had the worse of it.'

She nodded, knowing that the only things on the un-inhabited rocky outcrop a mile off the coast were the native tough sheep who, it had been explained, were fer-ried out there each breeding season and brought back after lambing.

'The damage is concentrated on the east coast.'

She released another little gusty sigh. It was another area where the rugged terrain meant there were no set-tlements.

'There was a landslip so the coast road is blocked, which is causing some problems. As far as I can tell from reports, the damage to outlying areas is mini-mal and, though there have been a few minor injuries, nothing significant so far. Except, of course, I'm sure it feels significant for the people involved. I need to get to Mentsa. The emergency services are coping but there is some panic. The church tower there has fallen.

'We're still assessing the airport, but the helicopter that dropped Carl off has already taken my parents to the mainland, and a few essential—'

At the mention of his parents, she shook her head.

'I get it,' she said, struggling not to judge, but it was hard when you compared the powerful couple's appar-ent response to their son's. Dante's instinct was to pro-tect his people and theirs was to protect themselves.

She struggled to subdue her anger—this was not the time or the place—but she was determined to point it out the next time they criticised anything Dante did—always assuming that she would be here to say anything.

The abrupt realisation brought with it a wave of desolation as, still playing mental catch-up, she dragged her wandering thoughts back to the present.

'Carl is here?'

'He was on the mainland.' He slid his foot into his boot and looked up, meeting her eyes. 'I followed your advice and we were going to meet up and talk in person. He jumped in a chopper as soon as he heard. He's persuaded Grandfather to evacuate, along with you and some of the—'

Well, good luck with that, she thought. 'Along with me?' she interrupted.

Dante bent his head to tighten the belt on the trousers he had exchanged for his shorts. Nobody had produced a shirt; he still wore the vest that clung to the contours of his muscled chest and exposed the powerful musculature of his arms. He flashed her an impatient look.

'Don't be difficult,' he pleaded.

'I thought you said there is no danger.'

'There isn't.'

She gave an eloquent shrug and stood her ground.

'I'll just have someone gather a few essentials for you and be ready in five minutes. Someone will—'

'I've only just got back. I'm not going anywhere.' This was so frustrating; she had so much she needed to say. 'Are *you* leaving?'

He stood with his phone half raised to his ear. 'I'll be fine.'

'I have no doubt,' she countered coolly. 'That wasn't what I asked.'

'Me leave!'

He looked so offended by the mere suggestion and for a moment the surge of warmth and love she felt for this man swamped everything else she was feeling.

'That would hardly send out the right message. Panic

is the problem. My presence will hopefully help keep a lid on things. What are you doing? The helicopters are waiting. You need to get going and I need…' *You*, he thought and shooed the thought away.

She swallowed. 'You're hurt.' She walked up to him and touched the graze on his cheek that was seeping blood.

He moved back from her touch, a spasm of dismissal twisting his lips; he could not afford any distractions. 'It is nothing. You need to hurry.' He caught her wrists and looked down at her, allowing himself the indulgence for a moment of drinking in her lovely face.

'Your grandfather isn't going to go quietly.' Yet another worry for his already overburdened, though very broad, shoulders to bear.

Dante fought the reluctance to release her wrists and stepped back. 'He's a stubborn old— But don't worry,' he added, moderating his tone. 'We'll make sure he's all right.'

'Yes, I know you will,' she said, shaking back her hair and gathering it in one hand with a practised double twist of her wrist, then securing it in a haphazard ponytail on the base of her neck. 'So, what do you want me to do?'

He stared at her as though she were talking a foreign language. 'What are you talking about, Beatrice? I really don't have the time for you to— How am I supposed to focus if I'm worried about you?'

'I'm not going.'

'Beatrice…!'

'How about I trust you to take care of yourself, and you trust me? I can absolutely promise you that I have no intention of putting myself in harm's way,' she said, standing there with a protective hand pressed to her stomach.

After a moment of silence, she saw the flash of something in his eyes before he tipped his head in silent acknowledgement.

'I haven't got time for this.'

'That's what I was counting on,' she admitted and drew a grin that briefly lightened the sombre cast of his expression.

'All right. I'm staying, you're staying. But if you—'

She waved her hand in a gesture of impatience. 'Get under your feet? Faint? I get it. As always, your opinion of me is flattering,' she observed drily. 'Just go do your stuff, Dante.'

He stood there, his body clenched as duty warred with instinct. His instinct was telling him to carry her, kicking and screaming if necessary, to safety. His duty was to keep everybody safe, but how could he do that if he didn't know Beatrice was safe? His normal ability to compartmentalise deserted him in the moment as he looked down at her. Despite his terror at the thought of her and their child coming to harm, a terror that only increased when he imagined not being there for her, his eyes glowed with admiration.

The next time anyone said anything about genes he would tell the bastards that his wife knew more about the meaning of service and duty than the rest of his family put together!

Still he hesitated, unwilling, unable, to leave her, all his instincts telling him it was his job to protect her.

'Is that my protection detail?' she said, as three uniformed figures appeared on the horizon.

He nodded. 'Do as they tell you.'

'I will.'

She saw him exchange words with the approaching detail as their paths crossed, but they were too distant for her to hear what was said.

All three of the tough-looking military types, not seeming breathless even though they'd been running, paused with brief formality to bow when they reached her.

One stepped up. 'Highness, we are—' He broke off and, one hand pressed to his earpiece, turned away, listening.

'Is there a problem?' Beatrice asked anxiously.

The men exchanged glances, as though asking each other if it was appropriate to respond.

'My husband…?'

'His Highness will have received the information. It is confirmation that the palace has escaped any real structural damage, so it is safe to return. Actually the first reports suggest that there is very little structural damage at all, but there has been a partial wall collapse.'

'Inside the palace?' Beatrice asked.

He nodded. 'The nursery.'

The fine muscles around her mouth quivered. There were still wisps of panic floating through her head, but she was able to speak like a relatively calm person even if inside felt a lot less confident of her ability to cope.

'Are there casualties?' she asked, her thoughts quickly moving past her insecurities to the children she had seen on a visit earlier that week. She felt her eyes fill and blinked away the moisture as she pushed the now poignant memories away.

Tears were not going to help. Tears were for later, hopefully along with smiles. Right now she needed to focus.

'By some miracle it seems not.'

The tears she had tried to suppress spilled out, along with a laugh of sheer relief.

'Apparently they were all in the playground. There are scrapes and cuts, all minor, and a hell of a lot of hysterical parents arriving. The emergency services are having a lot of trouble. We need to keep them in one place. They need to take a headcount, but it's like—and I quote—*"herding cats"*, which makes it really hard for them to assess the situation.'

'The headmistress struck me as pretty competent. Is she still there?'

'She is concussed and has been hospitalised, so the main priority is to move the children and parents out of the immediate area without losing track of any children, so that we can secure the building against any potential aftershocks. It sounds simpler than it is. It's pandemonium.'

'But someone is helping.'

'Us, once you are safe, Highness.'

She held up a hand and wished she possessed half the calm she was channelling. 'Why waste time? Take me with you.'

The military figure shook his head. 'Our instructions are to—'

'I'm giving you new instructions. What's the harm? You said it's safe.'

CHAPTER THIRTEEN

DANTE WAS ON the way to the airport, which luckily had suffered no damage, and he was speaking to his brother via speakerphone.

'I should get there before your flight leaves. Do you have to fly straight out?'

'I've got a meeting I can't get out of tomorrow.'

'Right. I should make it before your flight if there are no hold-ups.'

'Is your heroine wife with you?'

'Heroine… Beatrice, you mean?'

'You got any other wives? They are playing the video on the big screens and there's not a dry eye in the house. She had all the kids singing and she's carrying the little guy—'

Dante could feel the pressure build in his temples as he tried to speak. He managed to get the words past his clenched lips on the third attempt. 'Beatrice is at the nursery, the one where the wall collapsed?' The news of a successful evacuation had reached him but not that his wife was involved in the process.

'Well, she was earlier, but the parents are being interviewed now and all are singing her praises. You're going to have to name a park after her, or put up a statue or something.'

Dante, who did not connect with the amusement in his brother's voice, swore loud and fluently, cutting his brother off mid-flow. He brought the car around in a vicious one-hundred-and-eighty-degree turn that sent up a dust cloud of gravel, and floored the gas pedal.

Beatrice spent a luxurious half hour in a hot shower, washing off the accumulated dirt and grime. Dressed in a blue silk robe, her long wet hair wrapped in a towel twisted into a turban, she walked back into the bedroom. She had checked her phone sixty seconds ago but she checked it again. Nothing since the missed call earlier, but the mobile mast had been down for a good part of the day and there were numerous black spots on the island.

She sighed. At times like this a fertile imagination was not a friend. She knew that she wouldn't be able to relax until she had contact from Dante again.

She walked over to the mirror, untwisted the turban and began to pat her long hair dry. She had picked up a brush to complete the task when the door burst open.

Dante stood there, his tall, lean frame filling the doorway, wearing fatigue pants that clung to his narrow hips; the vest that might once have been white was stained with dust and dirt. His dark skin seemed liberally coated with the same debris.

Relief flooded through her as her face broke into a smile of dizzy relief. 'Dante!' She was halfway across the room when she realised that something was very wrong. 'Are you hurt? Has something happ—'

'Quite a lot, it seems.'

She stopped dead. She could hear the flame pushing against the ice in his voice, and literally feel the raw emotion pulsing off him.

'I asked you to stay safe, I asked you... You promised, and what do you do?' He advanced a step towards her and paused, close enough now for her to see the muscle throbbing in his lean cheek. 'I trusted you to take care of yourself and our baby and then what do I discover? That you decided to put yourself and...and our child straight in the path of danger, quite deliberately.'

She gulped. 'The nursery, you mean? There was no danger. It was just, just...herding cats, that was all.'

'You could have died,' he rasped hoarsely.

She looked at this strange, coldly furious Dante and fell back on defiance. 'You could die crossing the road.'

A hissing sound left his white clenched lips.

'I told you to stay safe.'

Her chin lifted. 'And I made my own judgement.'

'You put our child in danger.'

'How dare you?' she cried, surging towards him, her hands clenched into fists, not sure in the moment if the anger fizzing up inside her was directed at the insulting accusation or the fact he was confirming that that was what this was about. It wasn't her safety; it was the baby. It was always about the baby, this time and last time.

Suddenly she was angry with herself as much as him for wanting to believe differently, wanting to believe she was more than a means to an end, a person, not an incubator.

He watched as, hands outstretched, she backed away from him, her chest heaving.

'How dare you even suggest that?' she began, her low, intense voice building in volume with each successive syllable. 'You are the father. Does it make you a bad father for putting yourself in danger today? No, that makes you a man doing the right thing. Well, I did the right thing today too. Women do not stay at home waiting for the heroes' return and knitting socks these days…my child was never in any danger at any point!'

Unable to stop seeing her body crushed beneath a pile of rubble, her dead eyes looking up at him, the nightmare vision playing on a loop in his head, he barely registered what she was saying.

'If it wasn't for the baby…' *for me*, the voice in his head condemned '…you wouldn't even be here today.' In danger and it was all down to him. He hadn't been there for her; he had never been there for her.

Just as he'd never been there for Carl.

She flinched as though he had struck her. 'I am aware of that,' she said, hugging the crushing hurt to herself. Did he think she needed that pointed out?

'Things need to change. Your safety is all that matters. You must come first.'

She stood there, knowing he meant the baby, but letting herself imagine for a moment how it might feel if the fierce protective emotion in his dark eyes was really for her, and when the moment passed she felt flat and empty. 'Some things you can't change.' You couldn't make someone love you and it was about time she started dealing with facts.

'I have to go.'

'Of course you do,' she said flatly.

'To the airport to say…things I need to say to my brother.'

'Well, don't expect me to be here when you get back because I'm going to keep my baby safe and I don't feel safe here, with you.' Like arrows, she aimed the words at his broad back.

Did he flinch at the impact? She didn't know, but she hoped so.

* * *

Dante got out of the car in front of the airport terminal and realised he didn't remember driving there at all. *Now that couldn't be a good thing, could it?*

As he strode in he glanced at the departure board. He had just caught his brother. He dodged some airport officials bearing down on him and tried not to notice a group sharing their experiences with a camera crew.

He almost made it.

'And here we have the Crown Prince himself, who was in the thick of it,' an enterprising journalist said, shoving a microphone in his face. 'Would you say this has been a lucky escape, sir?' He started to trot as it became obvious that Dante was not slowing down. 'The buildings here are pretty robust.'

'And the people,' Dante responded, walking on.

'The rebuilding,' the guy called after him.

Rebuilding. Dante's pace slowed for the first time as the scene with Beatrice flashed before his eyes. He had not rebuilt; he had demolished the progress they had made in a matter of minutes.

Carl, who was scanning a laptop that lay across his knees, looked up when Dante entered, closing the door on his bodyguard who stood outside. He set aside the computer and got up, walking straight across to his brother, wrapping him in a brotherly hug, which Dante returned.

Carl stepped back and, though half a head shorter than his younger brother, retained his grip on Dante's shoulders.

'Thank you for this.'

Carl looked bemused by the warm words. 'For what?'

'For coming back. And I'm sorry. I should have said it before, but I am truly.'

Carl shook his head. 'I hate to repeat myself, but for what?'

'For not being there for you. I *should* have had your back.'

Carl looked astonished. 'But you did.'

'I didn't know.'

'You were my younger brother. I couldn't burden you with my problems, with the emphasis on *"my"*. It took me a long time to get to that point. I was either going to accept the status quo or take that leap of faith, and you know me, I'm not like you. I was never one to put my head over the parapet and risk having it knocked off. I was the "toe the line for a quiet life" son.'

Though Dante looked thoughtful as he listened to this ruthless self-assessment, his expression and emotions were locked firmly in self-condemnation mode.

'I should have known how unhappy you were.'

'It wasn't about being unhappy. I was always just a wrong fit. I could never inspire the way you do. It's true!' Carl exclaimed when Dante shook his head, looking patently uncomfortable.

'This was always my decision to make and for a long time I wasn't brave enough.' His hand fell from his brother's shoulders. 'I'm happy I've met someone. And you have Beatrice back. How is the heroine?'

'I love her,' Dante said in a driven voice. He looked shocked. 'I love her,' he repeated slowly. 'Is this how it feels?' he asked, a kind of wonder in his voice. 'Oh, hell, I've been such an idiot.'

'Have you told her any of this?'

'She deserves better.'

'Than what?'

'Me! I'm a selfish bastard.'

'I have to tell you, brother, I prefer you as a bastard

than a martyr. Maybe Beatrice does too,' he added slyly, and watched the hope flare in his brother's eyes.

'What are you doing?'

Beatrice gave a start and spun around, her blonde hair almost flaring out then settling in a silky curtain to her shoulder blades as she faced Dante, who stood with his broad shoulders propped against the wall beside the door.

Once she moved past the head-spinning blood rush of adrenalin that had her poised in 'deer in the headlights' mode, she realised that, though the anger he had been nursing earlier had gone, it had been replaced by an explosive quality. He made her think of a time bomb ticking down, every taut muscle and clenched sinew stretched to the limit.

'I've just been packing.'

'So, you're running away?'

She turned away as she felt her eyes fill. 'I'm moving rooms,' she contradicted. 'I'm not sure I could be termed essential travel. It's ironic. I can cope with the petty official and your family, but, you're right, I am leaving because I can't stay with a man who doesn't trust me. You're not wrapping me in cotton wool, you're suffocating me!'

He flinched. 'I know I said some unforgivable things but when I knew that you had been... I just went like ice inside. I felt terror, real gut-freezing terror. I haven't felt that way since you lost the baby. I felt so bloody helpless.'

Her eyes fluttered wide with shock.

'I could see the pain in your eyes and I didn't know what to say. I couldn't help you. It was the worst feeling of my entire life, seeing you hurt. And being the

emotionally crippled mess-up I am, I had no words…'
He made a sound of boiling frustration between his
clenched teeth as she grabbed his head in both hands. 'I
should have been able to make you feel better. I should
have kept you safe. I failed you and this time… I cannot
bear to see you go through that again.' He swallowed
hard, and captured her eyes with his agonised gaze. 'I
swore to myself that I'd keep you safe but all I've ended
up doing is pushing you away—*again*!'

'I'm still here.'

He extended his hands towards her and after a moment she took them. 'Don't leave me, Beatrice. Stay
with me.'

'I'm frightened too,' she whispered.

'But you are no coward. You are the bravest person
I know, and now the world knows too. I am proud of
you and even if there was no baby, I would love you.'

Her lips quivered as she looked up at him, drinking
in the details of his marvellous face. 'I love you, Dante.'

He bent his head, the ferocious hunger of his kiss
leaving her limp and ludicrously happy as he trailed a
finger down the curve of her cheek. 'I adore you. I am
half a man without you but—'

She pressed a finger to his lips; she was not interested in buts. She had heard all she needed to. 'I love
you, Dante. I always have and I always will.'

He caught her hand, his eyes not leaving her face as
he pressed it to his lips. 'I love you, Beatrice. I thought
loving you meant letting you go free, but now I know
that I can't make that choice for you. It is yours to make.'

Raising herself on tiptoes, she took his face between
her hands. 'I choose love.' She kissed him. 'I choose
you.' She kissed him. 'I choose staying…say that again,'
she said fiercely.

'What part?'

'The only part that matters, idiot. Say you love me!'

'I love you, Beatrice!'

She wound her arms around his neck, her feet leaving the floor as he kissed her back.

The kisses took them to the bed where, when they finally came up for air, they lay face to face, thigh to thigh, gazing into each other's eyes.

'I love your mouth,' she husked, exploring the individual dust-engrained lines on his face slowly, as if memorising them.

'Did Carl catch his flight?'

Dante nodded, unable to take his eyes off her face.

'And you two, are you okay?'

She was relieved when he nodded again.

'I'm glad.'

'So am I.'

'So what time is your parents' flight back?'

'They've delayed until tomorrow.' A sardonic smile twisted his lips. 'So the dust will literally have settled.' He slid a hand down her thigh and pulled it up and across his waist, dragging her in closer.

'This would be much better with no clothes.'

'It will be, but there is no hurry.'

She sighed and gave a sinuous wriggle closer, loving the hard lines of his body.

'I have a message for you from them.'

'Oh, don't spoil it!'

'They have asked me to inform you that it makes them very happy that you've returned. They are talking about a renewal of our vows.'

She felt her jaw drop. 'Is that some sort of joke?'

'No joke, they tell me you are *trending...*'

Her eyes flew wide. *'What?'.*

'A photo of you has gone viral.'

He rolled far enough away to pull his phone from his pocket and scrolled to the photo that showed a golden-haired, jeans-clad Beatrice against a background of billowing dust, surrounded by a group of children who were all caught in the moment, looking up at her, while two of the smallest ones were thrown one over each shoulder. Dust particles caught by a ray of light made it seem as though she were surrounded by a shimmering golden glow.

After a slight hesitation she rolled forward, anchoring her hair from her face with her forearm. It afforded him a view of her face while she scanned the image that was the sort guaranteed to make a photographer's career.

It was no surprise to him that online fame did not seem to thrill her.

'Oh, God!'

'You don't look thrilled at the fame—*hashtag heroineprincess*.'

It took her a moment to recognise the moment someone had captured in an idealised version. The reality had involved dust and noise and a gut-wrenching sense of urgency as, afraid she would lose one of her charges, she'd tried to get them out of the exclusion zone around the unstable wall.

'It's embarrassing,' she countered, 'and I was not being brave. I was at my wits' end. It *was* like herding cats.'

'My parents are very impressed. They believe that you are an asset to the family, and, yes, that is a direct quote.'

Suddenly she was so angry she could barely breathe, let alone speak. When she finally made her vocal cords work, what her voice lacked in force it made up for in throbbing, furious sincerity. 'It really has nothing to do with them!'

'This is something I pointed out.'

She huffed out a tiny breath. 'Good!'

'They then informed me that it was my duty to save my marriage.'

'I hope you told them to stuff their duty!' she exploded.

'I did not use those words precisely, but that was the sentiment behind my response. I hate my life without you in it. It's a life with no heartbeat, no soul. I love you.' His gaze sank to the pulse pumping at the base of her throat. Her neck extended as he bent to kiss the pulse spot, his mouth moist against her hot skin.

'Because I'm an asset? Did they really say that? Should we tell them about the baby, do you think?'

The tentative question was lost on Dante. She was smiling into his eyes and he had never seen anything so beautiful in his life.

'I can't tell if I can hear your heartbeat or mine.'

'We have one, we are one. I love you, Beatrice. Being without you made me realise how much. Life without you is not a whole life. I'm not whole. I have a Beatrice-sized empty space inside me. When we married, I didn't know what love was,' he admitted. 'But you taught me how to love, and I know I will never love another woman. It isn't possible—we are two halves that make a whole.'

There were tears glimmering like diamonds in her eyes by the time he finished. 'I choose, I choose to be with you, always.'

'I love you, Beatrice. Stay with me, be my wife and

let me be *me* with you, even if I have to be royal for the world.'

She flung her arms around his neck, grinning as tears streamed down her face. 'You'll never get rid of me, Dante, not now, not ever.'

Several moments later a maid walked in; her eyes flew wide as she saw the couple locked in a passionate embrace.

Within thirty minutes the entire palace knew the Princess they loved was home for good; there was a collective sigh of relief. They knew the couple was their future.

EPILOGUE

'CAN I HOLD HER?' Rachel Monk whispered.

Standing beside the open French doors that led onto a flower-filled balcony, Beatrice smiled at her mother, who stood there looking too young to be a grandmother in her bold emerald green dress coat, a jaunty hat and heels that showed off her great legs.

Carefully she gave the sleeping baby to her mother.

'Not much point being quiet with that lot down there.' The christening party was still in full swing.

'You know I am so proud of you, don't you... Bea?'

'And I'm proud of you.' Her mum's work with the charity for women in abusive relationships had won more than her own admiration.

They had both moved on from the past.

'I wish your father was here.'

'Oh, I think he is—have you seen that chin, the dimple?' she said, looking down fondly at her daughter's face. Everything else about Sabina Elsa was pure Dante. Her daughter was going to be a beauty.

'She is a miracle.'

Beatrice turned her head. 'What are you doing, creeping up on us like that?' she asked, looking up at her tall, gorgeous husband with smiling eyes. 'She *is* a miracle,' she added softly.

They would always grieve for their lost baby, but it was balanced by the joy that his or her sister had brought into their lives. They both knew how lucky they were; they told each other so every day.

'Say cheese!'

They both turned as Maya, dressed in a bright orange minidress, appeared, camera in hand. 'Wow,' she said, looking at the results on her phone screen. 'That kid, sorry, my god-daughter, is a natural. Your mum takes a good photo too, Dante. This one of her pinching one of the waiters' bottoms is classic.'

'Oh, God, Maya, delete that right now,' Beatrice gasped.

Her sister twisted away as Beatrice went to grab her phone.

'We said no phones.'

'I'm exempt, and, anyway, Carl made me do it and he's royal.'

'You're impossible.'

Dante came up behind her and slid his arms around her waist, pulling her into him until he could rest his chin on the top of her glossy head. '*This* is my family and all that I need. A tabloid would pay good money for that snap, Maya.'

'Now he tells me.'

Grinning, Dante bent and whispered something in his wife's ear.

He laughed, loving that she could blush…loving her.

'You know, I used to think this place was a prison, but you opened the doors, let in the light that made me love you and set me free.'

'Oh, get a room!' Carl exclaimed, walking in.

It was a palace—they had a lot to choose from!

* * * * *

MILLS & BOON

Coming next month

PRIDE & THE ITALIAN'S PROPOSAL
Kate Hewitt

'I judge on what I see,' Fausto allowed as he captured her queen easily. She looked unfazed by the move, as if she'd expected it, although to Fausto's eye it had seemed a most inexpert choice. 'Doesn't everyone do the same?'

'Some people are more accepting than others.'

'Is that a criticism?'

'You seem cynical,' Liza allowed.

'I consider myself a realist,' Fausto returned, and she laughed, a crystal-clear sound that seemed to reverberate through him like the ringing of a bell.

'Isn't that what every cynic says?'

'And what are you? An optimist?' He imbued the word with the necessary scepticism.

'I'm a realist. I've learned to be.' For a second she looked bleak, and Fausto realised he was curious.

'And where did you learn that lesson?'

She gave him a pert look, although he still saw a shadow of that unsettling bleakness in her eyes. 'From people such as yourself.' She moved her knight—really, what was she thinking there? 'Your move.'

Fausto's gaze quickly swept the board and he moved a pawn. 'I don't think you know me well enough to have learned such a lesson,' he remarked.

'I've learned it before, and in any case I'm a quick study.' She looked up at him with glinting eyes, a coy smile flirting about her mouth. A mouth Fausto had a sudden, serious urge to kiss. The notion took him so forcefully and unexpectedly that he leaned forward a little over the game, and Liza's eyes widened in response, her breath hitching audibly as surprise flashed across her features.

For a second, no more, the very air between them felt tautened, vibrating with sexual tension and expectation. It would be so very easy to close the space between their mouths. So very easy to taste her sweetness, drink deep from that lovely, luscious well.

Of course he was going to do no such thing. He could never consider a serious relationship with Liza Benton; she was not at all the sort of person he was expected to marry and, in any case, he'd been burned once before, when he'd been led by something so consuming and changeable as desire.

As for a cheap affair…the idea had its tempting merits, but he knew he had neither the time nor inclination to act on it. An affair would be complicated and distracting, a reminder he needed far too much in this moment.

Fausto leaned back, thankfully breaking the tension, and Liza's smile turned cat-like, surprising him. She looked so knowing, as if she'd been party to every thought in his head, which thankfully she hadn't been, and was smugly informing him of that fact.

'Checkmate,' she said softly and, jolted, Fausto stared at her blankly before glancing down at the board.

'That's impossible,' he declared as his gaze moved over the pieces and, with another jolt, he realised it wasn't. She'd put him in checkmate and he hadn't even realised his king had been under threat. He'd indifferently moved a pawn while she'd neatly spun her web. Disbelief warred with a scorching shame as well as a reluctant admiration. All the while he'd assumed she'd been playing an amateurish, inexperienced game, she'd been neatly and slyly laying a trap.

'You snookered me.'

Her eyes widened with laughing innocence. 'I did no such thing. You just assumed I wasn't a worthy opponent.' She cocked her head, her gaze turning flirtatious—unless he was imagining that? Feeling it? 'But, of course, you judge on what you see.'

The tension twanged back again, even more electric than before. Slowly, deliberately, Fausto knocked over his king to declare his defeat. The sound of the marble clattering against the board was loud in the stillness of the room, the only other sound being their suddenly laboured breathing.

He had to kiss her. He would. Fausto leaned forward, his gaze turning sleepy and hooded as he fastened it on her lush mouth. Liza's eyes flared again and she drew an unsteady breath, as loud as a shout in the still, silent room. Then, slowly, deliberately, she leaned forward too, her dress pulling against her body so he could see quite perfectly the outline of her breasts.

There were only a few scant inches between their mouths, hardly any space at all. Fausto could already imagine the feel of her lips against his, the honeyed slide of them, her sweet, breathy surrender as she gave herself up to their kiss. Her eyes fluttered closed. He leaned forward another inch, and then another. Only centimetres between them now…

'Here you are!'

The door to the study flung open hard enough to bang against the wall, and Fausto and Liza sprang apart. Chaz gave them a beaming smile, his arm around a rather woebegone-looking Jenna. Fausto forced a courteous smile back, as both disappointment and a very necessary relief coursed through him.

That had been close. Far, far too close.

Continue reading
PRIDE & THE ITALIAN'S PROPOSAL
Kate Hewitt

Available next month
www.millsandboon.co.uk

COMING SOON!

We really hope you enjoyed reading this book.
If you're looking for more romance, be sure to
head to the shops when new books are
available on

Thursday 18th February

To see which titles are coming soon, please visit

millsandboon.co.uk/nextmonth

LET'S TALK
Romance

For exclusive extracts, competitions
and special offers, find us online:

 facebook.com/millsandboon

@MillsandBoon

@MillsandBoonUK

Get in touch on 01413 063232

For all the latest titles coming soon, visit
millsandboon.co.uk/nextmonth

JOIN US ON SOCIAL MEDIA!

Stay up to date with our latest releases, author news and gossip, special offers and discounts, and all the behind-the-scenes action from Mills & Boon...

 millsandboon

 millsandboonuk

 millsandboon

It might just be true love...

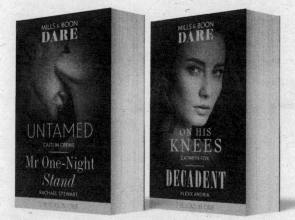